The Omega Chronicles: Book One

INVASION AT MIRATEV

BRIAN NICHOLSON

Text © 2017 by Brian Nicholson

Cover and design by Grey Gecko Press

Published by Grey Gecko Press, Katy, Texas.

www.greygeckopress.com

Printed in the United States of America

Library of Congress Cataloging-in-Publication Data
Nicholson, Brian
Invasion at miratev / Brian Nicholson
Library of Congress Control Number: 2017956670
ISBN   978-1-9388217-1-4
First Edition

To my wife Cheryl

*who has enthusiastically
supported me in this process.*

This is going to be fun.

Admiral's ready room, Sol Alliance carrier SAS Pacifica, orbiting the agricultural colony Mandis

Fleet Admiral Brandon North stared out the viewport of his ready room as the terminator slowly crept across the planet's surface, bringing the light side of the world into darkness.

Captain Mateo Drake, dressed in the platinum gray of regular Alliance Navy, and Colonel Derek Tyler, dressed in the all-black tunic of special operations, stood respectfully silent behind North, waiting for the admiral's orders. North's dark gray tunic, the uniform of an Alliance flag officer, matched the mood in the room.

"Replay the final message again," North said, and Tyler immediately keyed up the recording. The three men watched soberly as the recorded distress call appeared on the screen.

"General!" The frantic voice of Captain Reidhead, leader of the rescue mission to the Mandis agricultural colony, suddenly filled the room. "The colonists are attacking my people on all sides. Even the children and the elderly are coming at us with clubs, rocks, anything they can pick up! My troopers can't get close enough to assess their condition. It's like this all over the planet."

The man's tone became increasingly desperate, and screams and angry voices could now be heard in the background. Reidhead frantically looked around the interior of the assault shuttle in which he had sought refuge, looking for the controls that would seal the doors from inside the ship. The thunder of nearby explosions outside the ship caused the captain to pause and take cover momentarily.

He soon reappeared. "I recommend ordering a complete evacuation of our personnel, sir! There's nothing that can be done. I've lost all but two of my squad, and the other shuttles have been attacked as well!"

North's eyes squinted as a powerful explosion rocked the camera, producing more cries of anguish.

"They've breached the hull!" a voice screamed in the background, which was quickly silenced by automatic weapons fire. Reidhead turned and ducked out of view moments before a fierce explosion ended the transmission for good.

Colonel Tyler said, "That was the last report we received from any of our teams, Admiral. We've been trying for over an hour to reestablish contact with any of them, but we've had no luck. All of the remote camera units inside the shuttles show nothing but dead bodies. One of the teams reported that a member had been attacked and had his pressure suit breached. Within seconds, he was acting irrationally and firing on his own team members. They had to shoot him in order to stop him. This thing is like nothing we've ever seen."

Admiral North stood with his back toward the other two officers, staring out the window of his ready room. He watched as another suicide attacker drove his ship into the carrier's shields, immolating himself in a blaze of fire.

"That's the fifth one in the last half hour," Tyler commented.

"They aren't even trying to engage the fighters anymore," Drake said. "The rage has completely overtaken their minds. All we get on the comms are gibberish and furious, primal screams. There's no intelligence left. Brigadier Fowler said his ground teams reported their troops were attacked even before they could safely disembark from the shuttles. We've lost over twenty rescue teams, and that's not even counting the previous civilian rescue missions. In my opinion, it would be pointless to send any more down. They'd be slaughtered and become infected themselves."

The admiral gazed down at the planet, the weight of the universe and his next decision lying squarely on his shoulders.

"Do we currently have any personnel on the surface?" he asked.

"Negative, sir," Colonel Tyler said. "None survived, although that might be a good thing considering the virulent nature of the pathogen. Now that we have a full handle on the nature of this pathogen, we couldn't have allowed them to come back even if they had survived. They'd have infected the fleet."

North felt a flash of anger toward Tyler and his callous assessment but realized he was correct. He had to protect his fleet and other Alliance worlds from this pathogen. "Captain Drake," he said, looking back over his shoulder, "recover all of our fighters immediately. Advise the escorts we are going to abandon the system and set up quarantine. While the fleet is jumping, order the pickets to fire on any ship from the planet with starlane capabilities if they attempt to approach either of the two system portals. We will mine the portals to prevent anyone from jumping out. Colonel Tyler and his engineers will see to that. Is that clear?"

Drake nodded and said, "Aye, Admiral."

"Please leave me with Colonel Tyler, Captain. You're dismissed."

"Yes, sir," Drake said as he left the ready room to issue the recall order.

When Drake had left the room, the admiral turned around and faced Tyler.

"What do you think . . . as if I didn't know already?" North asked.

"You already know what I think, Admiral," Tyler replied. "They have over five hundred ships capable of starlane travel on the planet. No one wants to say it, but we cannot allow a single ship or infected person to leave this system. Even one would be disastrous . . . sufficient to infect another ship or another world. We must contain this while we can."

North turned back toward the window and whispered, "Two hundred thousand people. This is supposed to be a rescue mission. How could it have come to this?"

"I know, sir," Tyler said sympathetically, knowing the decision the admiral would soon be forced to make.

North sighed heavily and said, "Is the package in position?"

"Yes, sir," Tyler said. "Sergeant Martin is piloting."

North grimaced as he remembered he was about to order the young man to his death.

"The pilot . . . I'd almost forgotten. Do you know if he has any family?" he asked.

"None, sir," Tyler said. "He was recruited straight out of the orphanage."

"An orphan . . . that doesn't make it any easier," North said.

"Of course not, sir, but he knows what he signed up for. He's a credit to the code."

North nodded. "That much is apparent," he said as he turned to the computer station on the desk to issue his command.

"Identify," the computer interface said.

"Fleet Admiral Brandon North."

"Confirmed. Access to encrypted log granted."

North said, "On this date, I, Fleet Admiral Brandon North, do hereby order the destruction of the Mandis star via stellar disrupter, in order to contain the outbreak on the colony. This order is on my personal authority and is my full responsibility. No punitive action against any member of the military will be brought for implementing this order. Special commendation notes, Omega eyes only, for Staff Sergeant Steven Martin, who will pilot the device. Dated, September 22, 2416. End of log."

"Log terminated and encrypted. Classified eyes only, Chief of Fleet Operations, Alliance Security Council, Omega High Command," the computer intoned.

North punched up a file on the screen and transferred the contents to Tyler's handheld.

Tyler nodded as the authentication codes for the weapon appeared, and then he summarily dismissed himself. North returned his gaze to the window as the dark side of the planet came into view.

"May the Creator forgive me . . ."

CHAPTER ONE

Carrier SAS Pacifica, *Sol star system, eight years later*

Grand Commander Brandon North stood in his office adjacent to the bridge of his flagship, SAS *Pacifica*. He gazed through the huge observation portal as *Pacifica* approached Earth. He always enjoyed the view from the portal and was glad the designers had incorporated the viewport into the newer Neptune-class heavy carriers like *Pacifica*.

Despite his high rank, North had always considered himself a soldier and would have been more comfortable socializing with his men in the off-duty officers' lounge instead of having to keep the expected professional distance necessary to maintain the respect of his subordinates.

He detested the politics and bootlicking that were so common on other ships. He had been selected for the new rank of grand commander because of his accomplishments and abilities, skipping over the ranks of marshal and fleet marshal. Three years after the promotion, North felt as though he'd aged twice that much.

"Not so young anymore," North thought aloud.

North had joined the military at the minimum age of fifteen, and his aptitude scores in the top 1 percent qualified him for accelerated officer training. With forced-teaching technology available, new officers were minted in only six months, where previously, it had taken years. With combat losses mounting every day, it was critical to produce a steady supply of officer candidates.

North was fairly average height at six feet tall. He was slightly heavier than a normal civilian due to the combat and special forces training that he engaged in weekly. His dark gray tunic and jacket were standard military issue for a grand commander, as was the powerful pulse laser pistol slung on his left hip. The eight-point nova insignias on his collar were the only indication of rank or assignment. Former special forces did not advertise past missions, so there were no pips or ribbons to show.

North concentrated once again on the view of Earth. It had been too long since he'd returned home, although the prospect of coming home to an empty house made the long deployments easier to deal with. After losing his wife and son, coming home just wasn't the same. The thought of his family sent a pang of regret through him.

Shareel North and their son, James, had been killed in a traffic accident seven years before, and at times, the wound seemed as fresh as the day it happened. He pushed those thoughts out of his mind, storing them with the dark memory of what happened at Mandis. He feared they would distract him from the mission at hand.

Part of him wished the return to Earth would be permanent, but he knew better. The Alliance had too much invested in him, and the war was far from over. They would never allow his retirement, and he knew it. Not that they could stop him, technically, but they knew his sense of duty to his troops and to the worlds they defended would never allow him to quit.

President Barouq had made it next to impossible for him to retire into obscurity, personally promoting North to grand commander and giving him carte blanche to operate as he saw fit. He'd wanted North to take over as supreme commander of Alliance forces but accepted North's arguments that he could better serve as a line officer rather than from behind a desk.

The soothing, feminine voice of the shipboard computer announced, "You wished to be notified upon achieving Earth orbit, Commander."

"Please advise the flight bay to prep a Valkyrie for my trip ashore."

"Confirm you desire a fighter and not a shuttle, sir?" the computer queried.

"That's correct," North said with a slight grin. "If they're going to make me come all the way here, I may as well have some fun on the way."

"Aye, Commander," came the response from the computer.

North could have sworn it sounded amused. *Spooky*, he thought. *Those command computers are developing more complex personalities every day.*

"Secure viewport," North said.

The poly-duratanium armor shielding soon obstructed his view of the Earth.

He looked around his office, richly decorated in teal-colored simu-marble walls and flickering status panels. Lush, green wall-to-wall carpeting covered the decks. A large, well-stocked bookcase dominated one wall. Not a very efficient use of space, he realized, since the entire library could be stored on a fraction of a single virtual-memory cube. The books, he felt, lent a more personal atmosphere to the office. The other side of the room had a large, comfortable couch and a well-appointed wet bar. North didn't drink intoxicants himself, but protocol dictated that he offer refreshment to the occasional diplomat or other visitor. A small side door led to a fresher, a closet, and his personal mess. Rank did, indeed, have its privileges.

North opened a drawer in his mahogany desk and extracted a transparent box made of pure Sirian fire crystal. He carefully opened the box to verify that the contents remained undamaged. He was pleased to see that the sheed blossom inside remained intact and was currently glowing a soft amber color. Earth's Jaaleadi diplomat and liaison officer, Var Jent, had told him that the blossoms exhibited a natural luminescent quality, changing colors depending on the mood of the nearest intelligent being.

The Jaaleadi, a race of avian beings, was discovered by an Earth exploration team while exploring a remote sector of space on the fringes of the Orion Arm of the Milky Way. They were highly intelligent and technologically advanced, and—fortunately for the people of Earth—they were friendly. They had joined humanity in the fight against the T'Kharr after being attacked themselves without provocation.

Descended from bird-like ancestors, the Jaaleadi were magnificent creatures. Standing an average of 2½ meters tall, they had powerful wings which they could use to take flight. With a yellow beak featured prominently on his face, Jent was typical of his species. His close-set predator eyes and soft, gray down gave him a fearsome look but also displayed his wisdom and intelligence.

Jent had told North that the ancient Jaaleadi found the blossoms very useful. When one was walking near a patch of them, a change from silver to dark red was a sign that a predator was lying in wait. Jent had once explained that a lighter color indicated calmness, while a darker, more intense color represented more intense emotion. In this case, amber signified anticipation.

Accurate enough, North thought. He would be seeing his home on this, the seven-year anniversary of the death of his wife and son. His parents had died fifteen years earlier from a plague that ravaged one of the outer colonies, and his only brother, Jason, had been declared missing in action twenty-three years ago. All he had left was a house full of memories.

There was no time to dwell on those things now. Instead, he pondered upon the significance of an upcoming personal staff meeting between top military leaders of the Sol Alliance and the

Jaaleadi Republic. Staff meetings usually took place by conference link through a compressed-space transmitter. Apparently, Supreme Commander Terred didn't trust this one to the comm waves. To pull five battle fleets from their patrol routes, especially with the frequent raids by enemy forces, was highly unusual. It must be something big.

North pushed those thoughts to the back of his mind and tried to concentrate on what he should bring with him. He packed the small, clear data cube and the intelligence and reconnaissance reports that *Pacifica* and her fleet had amassed for the last three months, along with his portable terminal interface. Denara, the caretaker he employed to tend to his home while he was away, would have plenty of civies at the house for him, and there was nothing else he needed to bring for the meeting. He placed the crystal box into his personal secure case and snapped the lid shut. He pressed his thumb on the encoder and said, "Lock."

A metallic voice responded, "DNA scan confirmed." The case could be opened by nobody else.

The door chimed.

North called, "Come."

Rear Admiral Mateo Drake, *Pacifica*'s commanding officer and North's fleet executive officer, entered and stood in front of the desk.

"Sir," he began without preamble, "detectors report carriers *Challenger* and *Endeavor* along with their escort ships in parking orbits around Earth. Taking home fleet into account, I haven't seen this many capital ships around Earth since the '17 siege. What's going on?"

"I wish I knew, Mat," North replied. "You know about as much as I do."

North regarded Drake as he seated himself behind his desk. A few years younger than North, he was of Hispanic descent and had jet-black hair, dark eyes, and a well-proportioned, muscular body. His fitness was attested by the fact that Drake kicked

North's tail every time they played fireball together. Drake was easy to like, with a genuine enthusiasm and willing smile. His excellent command instincts made him the best executive officer that North had ever had. North had personally sponsored his promotion to admiral after *Pacifica* had been designated as one of the quadrant command ships following the reorganization of the fleet command-and-control structure and recommended him to remain in command of *Pacifica* after North was elevated to the High Command.

North sometimes suspected Drake of being psychic, due to the fact that he almost always seemed to know what North was going to order before he said it. He was also brutally honest in his evaluation of situations, which was a refreshing change for North. He wanted to know what his officers really thought, not what they thought he wanted to hear. The fact that he and Drake had become good friends helped as well.

North continued. "I do know that many of the senior staff as well as representatives from the Jaaleadi Republic military in this quadrant are all going to be there, in addition to the four sector commanders. Security must be a concern. We aren't even allowed to bring execs to the meeting. You are the exception."

Drake let out an impressed whistle.

"Boy, any T'Kharr captain would give its two right arms to take a potshot at this conference. It seems a bit risky to have all our eggs in one basket."

North grinned. "Careful about joking about eggs around Jent. You know he doesn't quite understand all of our colloquialisms. He'd probably think you were insulting his progeny."

Drake chuckled. "Yeah, I guess you're right. But it does worry me, sir, having all these ships here bunched together."

"Are the cruisers and destroyers on station at the starlane portals?" North asked.

"Ours are, Commander, but the majority of the *Challenger* and *Valor* escorts were ordered by Fleet Admiral Carlo to take up parking orbits behind the moon. He ordered our escorts to fall in behind them for some type of display. With all due respect, I think the admiral wants to try and make an impression on the Jaaleadi," Drake replied.

"Damn that arrogant ass," North fumed. "We've been allies with the Jaaleadi for over a century, and he still insists on playing intimidation games."

"That would be my guess, sir," Drake said simply.

North hit a button to activate his holographic display and ordered, "Fleet system status."

A holographic representation of the home system appeared in front of him. He saw the representation of *Pacifica* stationed above Earth's North American continent, and the remainder of his fleet positioned at points that would allow them to patrol five of the twenty starlane portals near Earth. *Challenger* and *Valor*, along with their escort fleets, were currently moving to a position behind the moon. *Valor's* escorts weren't on station as of yet and appeared to be moving toward the moon at an unusually slow pace.

North stabbed at the intercom pad. Immediately, a hazy blue holographic screen materialized in front of him, and he said, "Fleet Com."

The haze was replaced by the expectant face of the *Pacifica* communications officer, Lieutenant Annaline Vale.

"Yes, sir?" she said crisply.

"Get Admiral Price and the other fleet commanders on conference link immediately, please, including those on the incoming two fleets."

"Admirals Faulkner, Tyree, Price, and Jett are already waiting on the conference channel for you, Commander," the lieutenant replied immediately. "Engaging visual now."

North glanced sideways at Drake, who was trying his best to examine a particular carpet fiber at his feet while grinning to himself. His officers knew him all too well, and at times, it was damned irritating.

The images of the four admirals solidified onto the four holographic displays. Vice Admiral Jeffery Faulkner on *Endeavor* had been a friend for many years, as had Janice Jett of the *Valor*. Lita Tyree was fairly new to the Admiralty, and although North didn't know her very well personally, her reputation as a gutsy commander preceded her. She was scheduled to arrive within a few hours with *Victory* and her fleet. The *Challenger* and *Valor* fleets weren't normally under North's command and had been called in from the neighboring combat quadrant under the control of Grand Commander Trieste.

Price was going to be the problem. Nelson Price was the brother of a powerful senator on the Alliance Council and had achieved his rank and command through political favors. Many better-qualified admirals, with less political clout, had been passed over in favor of Price. He was also very close friends with Carlo, which by itself was a black mark in North's book. Price shared Carlo's belief that the Jaaleadi were inferior and should be totally subordinate to humankind. North thought this nonsense of displaying the fleet was probably Price's suggestion to Carlo.

Upon seeing Price's image, North adopted what Drake recognized as the "there's gonna be hell to pay" look.

North addressed the group. "Welcome, ladies . . . gentlemen. I hope the trip here was uneventful."

The four admirals nodded in acknowledgment.

North continued, "There seems to have been some misunderstanding that normal procedure was to be circumvented upon your arrival at Earth. Contrary to any orders you may have received prior to your arrival, I'm instructing you that normal intersystem security patrols at the starlane portals will be conducted as usual. Admiral Price, that includes your escorts currently taking up parking space behind the moon. I understand that Grand Commander Trieste might do things differently, but this task force is under my command, not hers."

Faulkner, Jett, and Tyree looked visibly relieved, nodding in the affirmative. North noted that Jett turned away from the screen for a moment and issued an inaudible order. *Valor's* escorts terminated their laggard approach toward the moon, accelerating instead toward the eleventh through fifteenth starlane portals. North smiled to himself. Jett had been dragging her feet until she received proper orders.

"Consider it done, Commander," Faulkner said. "We were beginning to wonder whether it was such a good idea—"

"Excuse me, Commander," Price interrupted.

Here it comes, North thought.

"But have you consulted Admiral Carlo on this matter?"

Drake was now convinced that Price must be certifiably insane. There was no other explanation. He eyed North's reaction with interest, as did the other admirals.

North answered menacingly, "Now, why would I discuss deployment of my own fleets with Admiral Carlo, Mister Price?"

Price visibly bristled at being referred to as "Mister." He responded, "Admiral Carlo thought that it would be a good idea to show our civilian leadership firsthand what their money is paying for. After all, how often does a quadrant command carrier like *Pacifica* come home? He ordered the escorts to the moon so the civilian leaders could have easier access to them. It's not often that such a large contingent of our military strength is in-system."

Pompous ass.

"I see," North said. One eyebrow arched in interest. "Since when does Admiral Carlo issue deployment orders to my fleets?"

The irritation that showed on Price's face for an instant was quickly replaced by an oily smile.

"Well, I'm sure Admiral Carlo didn't want to burden you with such trivialities, Commander," Price said, "what with the staff meeting and all. Besides, Earth is the most heavily defended planet in the Alliance."

North coldly smiled and nodded. "How thoughtful of him." Then he lowered his voice. "Since you seem to have a direct pipeline to Admiral Carlo, Mister Price, you shall inform him that I will decide what trivialities I will deal with and that the administrative wing of command does not give orders for fleet deployments. Is that understood?" Before Price could answer, North added, "And there will be no attempts at intimidating the Jaaleadi. End of discussion."

Price's face reddened at the rebuke. He was clearly angry but acknowledged tightly, "Yes, *sir.* Will that be all, Commander?"

"Yes. If there are any other . . . misunderstandings about whether standing fleet orders are to be followed, contact me directly. I'm sure Grand Commander Trieste would tell you the same thing. My orders are to be carried out immediately. *Pacifica* out."

North abruptly disconnected the link to Price, leaving just the other three admirals online.

Jett said, "I appreciate you clearing that up, sir. I certainly didn't feel comfortable leaving my fleet parked together in one place. One well-placed antimatter mine would be disastrous."

"I felt the same way," Tyree agreed. "This whole business of calling us all in at once makes me uncomfortable. But I'm sure Supreme Commander Terred knows what he's doing."

"Rest assured he does," North said. "Whatever's going on will be addressed tomorrow, so hang tight until then. The Jaaleadi won't be here for two more days, so rotate patrols so that all hands can have a taste of shore leave. We don't come home that often."

All answered in the affirmative, and North said, "Jeff, stay on the link for a moment."

"Of course," Faulkner replied.

"Janice, Lita, I'll see you at the meeting." North terminated the links to Jett and Tyree.

Faulkner noted, "You really rustled old Price's feathers, Brand. Take care, old friend. Price knows some very influential people. Doesn't Commander Trieste have some relation to Price's family?"

"He's her nephew, but privately, she's not particularly thrilled about it. I can handle Price. How far out are you, Jeff?"

"About two hours," Faulkner said. "*Victory* is about an hour behind us. We should be there with plenty of time to spare."

"Good. I'm not sure what's going on, but I want you there when we find out. Let me know when you're ready to come ashore. I'll ask Denara to make you some of her lasagna. I've brought her a present as a bribe."

"It's a deal," Faulkner said with a wink. "See you in a few." Then the comm link dissolved.

North then turned his full attention to Drake. "Mat, have Fleet Com issue the shore leave orders to Price's and our ships too."

"Of course, sir," Drake said crisply.

"And that means you too, Mat. Say hello to Maria for me." North knew Drake was dying to see his wife but wouldn't leave without North's direct order.

Drake started to object but said, "I will, sir." He knew it would do no good to argue.

"Also, issue orders to the fleets that any more 'unusual' deployment orders are to be cleared through me personally. Tell them that this is a direct order on my personal authority, just in case Carlo tries to undo what I just did."

"I'll do so immediately, Commander."

His face then took on a curious look. "Commander, do you think this meeting has something to do with Miratev Two?"

"Your guess is as good as mine, but I wouldn't doubt it," North said.

The Miratev star system had fallen to the T'Kharr two days ago. To call the Miratev Two research station a planet was a stretch. It was more of a planetoid. Rumor had it that the facility was doing more than just normal research, and Command seemed particularly frantic about its loss. It was originally thought to be too remote and unimportant to bother with, so the station had minimal defenses. The thought was that if the enemy perceived that there were few defenses, they would assume there was nothing of value there. But apparently, a T'Kharr fleet had suddenly jumped into the system and attacked the station. The station director had transmitted the information about the attack and said he was initiating invasion protocol, meaning the destruction of their work so it would not fall into enemy hands. North wondered if his XO might be right.

"Just because we got our recall orders on the same day the planet fell doesn't necessarily mean it involves Miratev. But, I'm not discounting anything at this point. I'll certainly fill you in when I know."

"Thank you, sir," Drake said. "I'm sure if it's Miratev, Captain Trent would be interested to know what's going to happen. His brother is stationed there."

"I wouldn't blame him. Please advise Command I'm about to depart. You're in command of the fleets, Admiral Drake. Take care of them while I'm gone." And with that, North picked up his case and left the room.

North strode into the expansive landing bay with rows of Valkyrie fighters tended by maintenance crews. He approached the row of fifty or so Valkyries secured in their respective slots. The massive, bustling port-side flight bay, one of three found on Neptune-class heavy carriers like the *Pacifica*, was always overwhelming to see. Fighter wings generally flew out of the port and starboard launch bays, while the dorsal bay was used primarily by the shuttles and tugs.

North strode over to the light fighter and performed a brief inspection. Not that he didn't trust the flight crews. A good pilot traditionally checked his or her own ship before launch. North preferred the tough little Valkyries to their more heavily armed brothers, the Daggers and Mustangs. It took more skill and finesse to fly a Valkyrie, whereas the heavier fighters sacrificed maneuverability and speed in exchange for heavier armor. Interceptor craft like the Valkyries were equipped with neural interfaces, virtually making the pilot and machine one entity during combat. The one-man fighters resembled an angry insect, with a sleek body that tapered down to a smooth nose.

Two powerful fusion engines were mounted just behind the cockpit. The engines were also called "Dukand Drives," after the physicist Ven Dukand who discovered compressed space. They allowed them to access the compressed space corridors—nicknamed starlanes—that existed between stars, permitting interstellar travel. Between the two engines was a Psyton generator which provided a shield to protect the occupant of the craft from the ravages wrought on living tissue by compressed space. Each of the four fins sported a sensor-guided Flechette-7 missile. Enemy shields were drained using twin pulse plasma cannons. On this trip, North was certain that he would need no armaments at all, but regulations required minimal armaments nonetheless.

North climbed into the deceptively roomy cockpit, secured his case behind the seat, and strapped in. Securing the dark gray flight helmet, he said, "Helmet interface, enable."

A small panel behind North's head glowed bright green, emitting a tight beam of light directed toward a similar panel built into the rear of the helmet. Inside the helmet, North's heads-up display and status indicators materialized before his eyes, and the cockpit panels automatically activated. The fighter's plexi-steel canopy smoothly locked into place.

The feminine computer voice queried, "Identify."

North responded, "North, Brandon F."

"Confirmed. Have a nice flight, Commander."

North felt the securing clamps release the fighter from the deck as the fusion drives hummed to life. He smoothly taxied forward to his launching position on the craft's repulsor pads. Since this wasn't a combat launch, he chose not to use the catapult. He would launch the old-fashioned way.

North spoke, "*Pacifica*, this is Victor 219. Request departure clearance."

"Clear for launch, Commander," Drake's voice responded. "Good luck."

"Thanks, Mat. I have a feeling I'll need it for this one." He punched the sturdy craft's thruster control.

North was momentarily pushed into his seat until the craft's inertial compensators adjusted. He saw the star field approaching rapidly through the atmosphere pressure field at the end of the launch bay. The fighter breached the field with a slight jolt and cleared the bay. North felt the onset of weightlessness as he escaped the effect of *Pacifica's* gravity generators. He felt the joy and freedom he always felt when he had the rare opportunity of piloting his own ship. No shuttles, no wide-eyed ensign pilot too scared to speak for fear that he might make some mistake in front of him, no civilian passengers asking how-the-war-was-really-going-because-I-don't-believe-the-media-and-if-anyone-would-know-it-would-be-you. It was just himself, the ship, and space.

He looked back at his ship with pride. *Pacifica* was the largest active fighting ship in the Alliance fleet, with a battle record that was the envy of any starship captain. First of the Neptune-class carriers to be commissioned, she'd served her three previous commanders with distinction and had served North well over the years. Over twelve hundred meters in length, she dwarfed her escort vessels. Her fighter umbrella resembled angry insects buzzing harmlessly around a behemoth. She could launch over three hundred fighter and bomber craft, and her landing bays were almost large enough to swallow an enemy destroyer.

As much as he enjoyed the view of his ship, North turned his attention to the Earth. The terminator slowly approached the North American coast, his intended destination. North wondered to himself why he didn't come home more often.

He shook himself from his thoughts as he began to descend into the atmosphere, following the flight corridor provided to him by Fleet Command that would allow him passage through the protective energy shield that surrounded and protected the planet. The Earth's atmosphere appeared to rise up to meet him as he smoothly made the transition from space to atmospheric flight. The lights of the cities began to shine.

The muffled roar of the engines grew louder as the air thickened and the Pacific Ocean sped up toward him. He approached the coast of what used to be the state of California in the ancient United States of America. What was left of Washington, DC had remained a radioactive wasteland for years after the last Great War that had nearly devastated mankind. The West Coast had hosted the new capital for hundreds of years now.

North loved the area and had a home not too far from the Supreme Command structure. As his ship homed in on the spaceport's beacon, a squadron of Valkyrie interceptors — his escort to the facility —quickly approached him from below and behind. Upon taking formation with his ship, the pilot to his right looked over and gave him a sharp salute, which North returned.

A smooth, professional voice came over the comm unit. "Approaching craft, please identify and transmit your clearance codes."

North responded, "Spaceport Control, this is Victor 219, *Pacifica*. Commencing transmission of my security code."

A moment passed. "Confirmed. Welcome home, Commander North. We were expecting you to arrive in a shuttle but were also told not to be too surprised if you showed up in a fighter. You are cleared to land on the executive field, pad C. Please follow your escorts."

"Thank you, Control. ETA is six minutes."

After he was cleared, the fighters formed a delta pattern with North in the center, standard escort pattern for an arriving flag officer. Even from ten kilometers out, he could see the outline of the sprawling spaceport covering a hundred square kilometers. His approach vector brought him in over the new capitol building, a large marble dome that housed both the Alliance Senate and Council of Worlds, the legislative arm of the government. In the approaching darkness, he had trouble making out the residence of the president of the Alliance, located a few kilometers from the capitol, even though he knew exactly where it was from his many trips there.

The Supreme Command center was located here, near what used to be Los Angeles. The temperate coastal climate was the first choice of the civilian leaders when it was decided that a new capital center was needed. The worldwide weather control net was able to control and dissipate natural threats such as earthquakes and severe weather events which used to be common to the region, making it a beautiful and ideal location.

Once North passed the outer marker, spaceport control activated a second beacon that guided North to his exact landing zone. He cut back power and slowly descended toward the now yellow-framed landing zone as his escorts pulled up and away, moving back to their patrol routes. He descended slowly to about ten feet from the ground, easing off the repulsor field power until he smoothly settled to the ground. Removing his helmet, North retrieved his case from the storage compartment.

He took in a deep breath of fresh air. The air on a planet always smelled so much better than the recycled air on a ship. He then set to the task of tugging his uniform back into proper place to make himself halfway presentable to the supreme commander.

As three maintenance crewmen converged on the fighter, North turned and walked toward the imposing oak doors that marked the VIP entrance to the facility. Each was ten feet high by ten feet wide and emblazoned with the gold seal of the Sol Alliance, a representation of the Sol solar system with the sun along with eight planets, four on each side. The Sol Alliance, formed after the Great War, had unified humanity and became the first real world government. Gone were international borders and individual nation states. Humanity was united at last, at the cost of five billion lives.

Four armed guards, their M-36B pulse rifles at port arms, stood at attention as North approached the entryway. The squad leader stepped forward in front of the others as North approached.

"Good evening, sir. Identification, please." The guard held out an identification pad. North placed his right hand on the pad, and the pad chirped, "Grand Commander Brandon North, High Command designator HQ2. Verified access."

North's case was subjected to the attention of a small hand-held scanner. The guard gave North a quick, smart salute. The tall oak doors silently slid aside, allowing him to enter. Once inside the huge building, North noted that the corridors were filled with people. Everyone was military—no civilians—and every face wore a grim expression.

The Romanesque reception area featured rich marble walls and columns. A spectacular crystal chandelier hanging from the domed roof emitted a soothing yellow glow. Three hallways lined with grayish-blue walls and thick blue carpeting went directly east, west, and south of the reception area.

Two officers approached North immediately. He recognized one of them as Captain Hansen, Supreme Commander Terred's personal aide. The other, whom he didn't recognize, was a tall, attractive, olive-skinned woman wearing a dark blue one-piece jumpsuit.

"Commander North," Hansen said as he shook North's hand. "It's good to see you again, sir."

"You too, Captain," North responded with a smile.

"This is Major Lindsay Dupree. She's with the Alliance Research section."

"Major," North said as he offered his right hand.

"A pleasure to finally meet you in person, sir," Dupree said as she firmly shook his hand.

Hansen said, "I'm sure you have a million questions, sir. Commander Terred wants to brief you privately first before the meeting tomorrow."

"I would appreciate that, Captain," North said. "I'm anxious to find out what all of this is about and why five patrol fleets had to be recalled to Earth." He realized for the first time that he was slightly irritated at being kept in the dark up to this point.

Hansen looked slightly uncomfortable. "Commander Terred will fill you in, sir. Everyone is under strict orders not to discuss the matter. Commander Terred has invoked Fleet General Order 20."

"Understood, Captain." *Fleet Order 20*, North thought. It was the highest security order given in the military. He guessed that security was going to be an issue.

The three walked down the long southern hallway to a lift. Once inside, Hansen said, "Sub level thirty."

Immediately, North felt the lift accelerate downward, and within fifteen seconds, the polished black doors slid open and revealed a reception area. Behind a desk just to the right of the lift sat a brown-haired woman in her early thirties, professionally dressed in fleet gray. North gathered that she must be Terred's office manager.

"Commander Terred's expecting you, sirs. Please go right in."

"Thanks, Kate," Hansen said as he walked up to the tall double doors that were just sliding apart to allow passage.

Hansen paused at the doorway and allowed North to enter the room first, followed by Dupree. Inside, standing with a group of other officers in the midst of a holo display representing the known galaxy, was Supreme Commander Dekker Terred, furiously chatting on a holo headset. One of only five Alliance grand commanders, and technically the same rank as North, Terred was the designated chief of operations and held the title of supreme commander of the Alliance military.

A somewhat unimposing man at just over five feet nine inches, he sported a cropped, salt-and-pepper head of hair and a thin mustache. He had a ruddy complexion obtained from his upbringing on one of the Mars colonies. Terred had a distinguished career as a battleship commander before moving up to the Admiralty. He excelled at administrative duties and was wise enough to listen to his more experienced subordinates when final battle plans were to be approved. North thought him an excellent choice as supreme commander.

Terred glanced in their direction as they entered the room, passing his headset to an officer standing next to him.

"Brandon," he said with a genuine smile as he pumped North's hand. "It's good to see you. I hope your trip here was a good one."

"The trip went well, thanks. I'm curious what was so important that my and my sector commanders' physical presence was required rather than a communication on a secured channel. With the T'Kharr trying to annex the Krieger expanse, they've kept us busy."

"I know. There have been incursions along six different fronts in just this past week," he said, indicating the map. "Sorry for all the cloak and dagger. Believe me, Brand, if I could have done it any other way, I would have. This was too important and too dangerous to leave to the comm waves. Come into my office and have a seat."

Terred led them into a room just adjacent to the situation room and indicated the plush chair in front of his desk. North seated himself. Dupree took the seat to the side of Terred's chair, and Hansen stood off to the side at parade rest.

"Did you bring the recon reports?" Terred asked.

"Right here," North said. He opened the case and extracted the data cube.

Captain Hansen took the cube to one of the wall computer access units. Terred noticed the sheed blossom and smiled.

"Gift for Denara?"

North took the crystal box out and put it on the commander's desk. "She always did appreciate unusual gifts," he said with a smile. The blossom still radiated the amber color.

Terred got down to business. "Brand, have you heard of kinetic power source technology?"

North thought for a moment, then said, "As I recall, the theory involved harnessing the kinetic energy of atoms in the surrounding environment. As long as the temperature of the environment remained above absolute zero, that energy could be harnessed. I also recall that they abandoned the research because they couldn't squeeze enough energy out of the surrounding environment to make it practical. Also, apparently, any planet or ship containing a kinetic generator would be rendered uninhabitable, and the effect would instantly kill any living being near it. Ethical considerations precluded it from being developed as a weapon, even for use against the T'Kharr. I didn't think much of it at the time because it was only a theory and was said to be unworkable."

Terred said grimly, "You're well informed. The research facility on Miratev Two was dedicated to kinetic power source research. Doctor Handel Gleen was head of the research staff on Miratev and had made a breakthrough that could be disastrous for the Alliance and Jaaleadi if it falls under T'Kharr control.

"During a routine experiment, they accidentally opened a small breach into compressed space in the lab. The accident resulted in several deaths, but they realized that by harnessing the energies within the compressed space breach, they could use the kinetic generator's harnessing matrix to tap into a virtually unlimited kinetic power source.

"They were also close to completion of a shielding alloy that would make the kinetic generator technology workable. It would allow the generator to function by focusing the kinetic-harnessing effect on the compressed space breach and preventing the field from seeking out other sources of heat, most notably any living organisms or power sources existing near it.

"If successful, it would provide a virtually unlimited source of power for an indefinite period of time. No need for physical fuel, no hydrogen collectors on ships—an inexhaustible clean source of power. A single generator could provide enough power for an entire planet. The possibilities are staggering."

"Impressive," North muttered. "No more need for consumable fuels."

Terred sighed deeply and said, "That's not the half of it, unfortunately. Apparently, this generator can produce enough power to render a planetary shield inoperable. If the T'Kharr get it, our planetary defensive shielding will be obsolete."

North's mind absorbed the implications. Planetary shielding technology was what kept a planet safe and an enemy fleet at bay until military ships could be summoned. The shields could be worn down and defeated, but only after much time and expended energy. Alliance forces could be called in long before the shield failed. If this generator could defeat the shield immediately, all Alliance worlds and colonies would be open to invasion.

"How long would it take to defeat a planetary shield with one of these generators?" North asked.

"Six solar hours," Terred said, his face grim.

North felt the blood drain from his face.

"Six hours? Is that possible?"

Terred nodded. "Major Dupree is an expert on kinetic power source technology."

North looked at Dupree and asked urgently, "How close were they to completing this alloy shielding?"

Dupree said, "They had already manufactured several thousand kilos of the shielding to be tested."

North digested this information. "And now that the T'Kharr have control of Miratev, do they have the technology?"

"No," Terred declared. "Not yet. The last transmission we received from Gleen was that he was preparing to initiate invasion protocol. He was able to destroy most of the shielding alloy they had already manufactured, but unfortunately, the T'Kharr reinforcements arrived before he was able to finish. Gleen was trying to destroy the data contained in a secret underground bunker located about fifty klicks from the facility where the data backups are stored."

"How do we know he didn't tell the interrogators the location of this bunker?" North asked.

"For security reasons, not even Gleen nor any of his staff knew the bunker's exact location," Terred said. "The only people who knew its location were two or three of the techs assigned to do maintenance there. They knew of T'Kharr interrogation methods and knew the technology was too important to risk. Once the information had been transferred there, all comm lines and transmission codes self-destructed, leaving no trail to follow. Our intelligence reports indicate that the T'Kharr haven't located the bunker yet, but they are actively looking for it. It's only a matter of time." The dread in his voice was apparent.

"Is the complex shielded?" North asked.

"The bunker is shielded from scans, but when the orbital power grid was destroyed, the bunker switched to its own internal power. The bunker's shields will power down in just under two weeks. After that, it will light up like a Christmas tree on their scanner grid. I plan on having us there long before that happens."

"What kind of T'Kharr presence is in the system?" North asked.

"The original invasion force was a full-sized battle group with one heavy carrier," Terred answered. "They've launched incursions along this entire front for weeks now. It's possible they stumbled upon it by accident. Once they found out what they had, they moved in another heavy carrier group and have three more en route from their homeworld defense fleet."

"Homeworld fleets, eh?" North said. "Pretty risky pulling some of the emperor's big boys out of their home system. Maybe we'll get lucky and there'll be another coup attempt."

"They aren't going to give this one up without a hell of a fight. There was apparently enough data left in the data banks for them to realize what type of research was going on but not enough to make it workable for them. We're assuming that Gleen and most of his staff are dead and gave up the information about the bunker when interrogated. They know it's there, just not where it is exactly."

Dupree stiffened, then looked at Terred and objected, "Sir, we have no solid proof that the T'Kharr know about the bunker. Dr. Gleen and his staff might have kept the information from them. I know most of the station staff, and they aren't coward or traitors."

North turned and regarded Dupree. "Major, how long have you been with Research?"

Dupree's expression changed from defensive to puzzled.

"Uh . . . eighteen months, Commander. Why do you ask?"

North ignored the question. "Ever had a combat posting prior to your current assignment?"

Dupree swallowed hard and said, "Umm, no, sir. I haven't. I went straight from college to Research."

North had no desire to embarrass Dupree, but he felt she needed some quick instruction on their enemy. "Let me tell you a little about our enemy and their interrogation methods. A typical T'Kharr soldier stands about six and a half feet tall. They have three rows of razor-sharp teeth and four arms ending in six taloned claws. The claws secrete a paralyzing agent that immobilizes its prey and keeps it conscious while the T'Kharr consumes it. Their exoskeleton looks like the armored skin of a dragon and is tough as leather. They have spikes protruding from the tops of their heads and spikes on the lower part of their faces that they use very effectively in close quarters combat. They view us as inferior and as prey, and their goal is to wipe us from existence.

"When I was a pilot on the *Ambrion*, my wingman and I were sent into the Aldebaran system to investigate some unusual natural transmissions. Command didn't think it important enough to send a warship. The source of the transmissions was a large asteroid in an asteroid field. Before we knew it, we found ourselves approaching a T'Kharr listening post equipped with four squadrons of their old Vondor-class medium fighters. The heavy metal content of the asteroid created a natural shield to our scanners, so we didn't know what it was until we were practically on top of it. They sent two full squadrons to deal with us, and at fifteen to one, we didn't stand much of a chance. Two minutes into the fighting, we realized they were trying to disable us rather than destroy us. We were forced to eject and self-destruct our fighters.

"The T'Kharr retrieved us and brought us back to their base to be interrogated. My wingman, Lt. Raphael Briceno, was interrogated first, and I was forced to watch. One of the guards slashed Briceno with its claws, injecting venom that would not allow him to go into shock or lose consciousness, no matter how intense the pain was. They then secured him in four-point restraints and began questioning him. Briceno did nothing but spit defiance at them for the first two questions. The interrogator motioned to one of the guards in the room, who then tore his right arm off with its razor sharp teeth. A med-bot at the side of the table cauterized Briceno's wounds and kept him from dying. He was begging them to stop, and I was helpless to do anything but watch."

Dupree began to look queasy, and her face blanched.

North continued, "The guard then walked over to where I was restrained, took Briceno's arm in its talons, and began to eat it right in front of my eyes. The whole time it was eating, it was staring at me with its cold, inhuman, red eyes. And for a second, I swore it smiled. Those razor teeth were very effective in tearing the flesh from Briceno's arm and breaking bones. I can still remember the sickening wet crunching sound the guard made while it was chewing."

Dupree's face had lost most of its color, and she said in a slightly shaky voice, "Commander, I—"

"Stand fast, Major. I'm almost finished," North interrupted. He continued, "After the guard finished Briceno's arm, the interrogator went back to Briceno and asked him another question. This time, Briceno tried to answer the question, but the interrogator wasn't satisfied. It motioned to a different guard who went over and chopped Briceno's other arm off and, as the first guard had done before, came over and consumed it in front of my face. I was forced to watch as they consumed my wingman—and my friend—down to the last piece. Mercifully, Briceno died somewhere in the middle of it all. After that, the guards put me into a cell, presumably to let me sweat for a while before my own interrogation. Before they returned, however, a rescue mission from the *Ambrion* arrived and extracted me from the station."

"The point of this story, Major, is that I watched one of the bravest, most loyal and fearless men I have ever known reduced to the point where he would have told them anything."

Dupree simply nodded and appeared to be doing her best to keep her last meal down.

North turned back to Terred and said, "I agree with you, Dek. I'm sure the T'Kharr know about the bunker and that they will eventually find it. May I assume that you've called me in to develop a plan to retake Miratev?"

Terred nodded. "That's correct. Tomorrow, we'll meet with the other fleet commanders and map out a basic strategy to retake the planet and rescue any survivors that might have escaped. We don't have much time, and I want a plan ready to present to the Jaaleadi by the time they arrive."

"Miratev is located in quadrant three. Trieste is okay with me poaching in her quadrant?"

"I've explained that your *special talents* are needed for this mission. Besides, some of your old colleagues will be joining us on this assignment."

North nodded knowingly and said, "Very good, sir."

"There's one more thing, Brand. There is some evidence that the T'Kharr may have been tipped off as to the nature of the research going on at Miratev."

North went cold inside. "A leak?"

Hansen, who had been downloading the reconnaissance information, spoke up and said, "It would appear so, Commander. The Miratev recon buoy detected a tight-beam transmission originating from inside the system just four hours prior to the invasion."

The anger was plain on North's face. "Damn."

Something then occurred to him, and he asked, "Major, what would happen if an unshielded kinetic generator was dropped onto an inhabited world, say in a torpedo casing? How much of the planet would be affected?"

Dupree, now mostly composed, answered, "Assuming that the generator is the size of a standard torpedo, the temperature of an Earth-like world would drop over two hundred degrees Celsius in just over four hours. The energy-harnessing matrix would seek out the closest heat sources, and the wave would eventually envelop the entire planet. All life would terminate long before then."

North was taken aback by this information. "By the mercy of the Creator . . ."

"Yes," Terred said, seeing the grim understanding on North's face. "Now you see why we're willing to risk calling five full fleets home. The T'Kharr don't have any ethical considerations about using this technology as a weapon. Brand, I need the best on this one."

"Thank you for the confidence, sir. I'll get right on it. One more thing, Commander. I'd like permission to brief Admiral Drake and my space group commander, Captain Trent. Also, I'd like to bring in Jeff Faulkner to help with the planning. Guy's a tactical wizard."

"Granted. But do it by courier, not by the comm channels. I don't want any leaks. The meeting's not until tomorrow, and I want you fresh and rested, so go home and settle in. Say hello to Lan and Denara for me."

North smiled and nodded but was distracted by the enormity of the information he'd just received. A creeping dread was nagging at the back of his mind as he thought of all the worlds that could be destroyed by such a weapon.

The idea that there was likely a traitor with access to the Alliance's top secrets was equally unnerving. Boiling anger was building inside him as he thought of what he'd do to the traitor if he found him. As he got up to leave, he nearly forgot the sheed blossom that he'd placed on the supreme commander's desk.

It was glowing blood red.

CHAPTER TWO

Miratev Two, Miratev Maxia star system, invasion day plus two

Jared Trent poked his head out of the cave and took a quick look around. It was difficult to see anything in this forest. He hoped that the T'Kharr would have as much difficulty seeing him. They'd been dodging T'Kharr patrols for a full day before stumbling upon this cave. His large frame nearly blocked out the sunlight coming through the mouth of the cave, leaving the interior in darkness.

He looked back at the group of six technicians and researchers huddled just inside of the cave, visible in the small sliver of light that remained. Two of them were tending to two others who were injured while the remaining two sat against the cave wall. Now and then, they would look nervously into the darkness of the cave, unsure what might be living inside; they didn't care to explore deeper and find out. The visible area of the cave went in approximately fifteen feet but stretched much deeper into the hillside. The entire group—at least those who were conscious—wore frightened, shell-shocked looks on their faces.

Jared turned toward the forest and said, "I don't see or hear anything. They may not have figured out which way we went. I think we're safe here for the time being."

"We should have stayed there," said Hugo Kloke, a lanky, light-haired man. "We should have surrendered. Maybe they just killed the others because they fired at them first." Hysteria began to creep into the man's voice. "We're going to stay out here and die because we weren't smart enough to surrender!"

"Shut up!" Jared hissed through clenched teeth. He grabbed the man by the front of his shirt and yanked him so they were face to face.

"You saw what they did to Lancaster and Forbes. They burned them slowly with their energy weapons and *ate* them! Is *that* what you want to happen to us? Is it?"

"N-no . . . no, of course not," the man whimpered. "But what are we going to do out here? We have hardly any food or water. We only have two particle pistols for seven of us. What are we going to do? Tell me!"

Jared's face took on a resigned expression, and he let go of Kloke's shirt with a sigh. He stared out of the cave into the forest.

"I don't know. For now, we stay here. After dark, we can go out and forage for food and water. Lord knows this place is lousy with water."

"Well, I'm not going to stay here and wait for them to come find us. They can't all be like the ones who killed the others. At least as prisoners, we could get food and water. M-maybe if we went back—"

"Shut up, Kloke!" snapped Julie Newman, a slender, strawberry blonde woman in her mid-twenties. "Jared is right. Our first priority is survival. We're safe for now, and we have wounded to tend to. Why don't you come help us treat them and stop whining!"

"Oh yeah?" Kloke responded with a sneer. "Who put you and Trent in charge anyway, Newman? We're all researchers and lab workers. Who elected you two to speak for us?"

The mountain that was the six-foot-six, 230-pound, burly lab tech Dram Hunter rose in the shadows. "*I* elected him. And I suggest that unless you want to join the T'Kharr troopers out there for a little lunch, you shut your mouth. Otherwise, I'll snap you in half like a twig."

The threat was clear on Dram's face and in his words, and Kloke, eyes wide with fear, decided that the best course of action to ensure his immediate welfare was to find a dark corner of the cave, sit down, and sulk.

Jared, who'd been looking on during the exchange, smiled slightly and nodded in appreciation to Dram, who returned the nod with a wink. Jared decided to double-check the bandages he had just applied to a young woman named Spinnaker.

Dram knelt back down next to Julie Newman and Jeenan Tar, one of the two Jaaleadi researchers, and helped her tend to the other wounded member of their party who was lying unconscious.

"Thanks, Dram." Julie looked sideways at him as she worked and smiled at him. "He was getting on my nerves."

"Any time, Miss Newman. I know that if anyone can get us out of this, it's you and Doctor Trent. Is it true that his brother is a fighter pilot?"

"You bet. Space Group Commander on the *Pacifica*. And Dram, we're going to be depending on each other for our lives for a while, so please call me Julie."

Dram blushed slightly and smiled. "Okay, Julie."

Jeenan chirped, and her translator converted the chirps and squeaks of her voice into standard. "Doctor Gleen sent out a distress call to Sector Command before they hit the transmitter, so I'm sure help is on the way. We just need to keep calm and keep out of sight of the T'Kharr. There's nothing more we can do for now. Glend is hurt badly but not critically. We must allow her to rest. The best medicine for a Jaaleadi in this condition is to allow the body to heal itself."

"Okay, Jeenan," Julie said as she stroked Jeenan on the cheek feathers, a Jaaleadi sign of comfort. "Let me know if you need anything else."

As a species, the Jaaleadi were magnificent to look at. Males were tall and muscular with powerful beaks and wings that could be used for flight, while the females of the species were more intellectual, and their wings and beaks were smaller and less prominent. Feathers covered their skin and varied in plumage depending on gender and age. Males typically had bright shades of blue or red, while females favored bronze or brown. Their sharp, penetrating eyes left no doubt they were hunters.

Jeenan was typical of Jaaleadi females in appearance. She had bronze plumage on her head, with just a smattering of white showing on top. Julie estimated her age to be about ten or twelve solar years, just past puberty for a Jaaleadi. Julie had learned to appreciate her quick wit, sense of humor, and ability to keep a cool head in a crisis. She would be a great help to them while they waited for rescue.

Julie looked over to where Jared was sitting, back to the wall, staring at a particle pistol in his hands.

Dram saw her looking at Jared. "He's still bothered by what he did at the lab."

Julie replied, "Yeah. It's hard to reconcile taking life when you've been trying to save it all of your professional life, even if it means your survival."

"Well, maybe you ought to explain to him that we all would've died if he hadn't killed those three T'Kharr soldiers," Dram said, giving her a knowing glance. "He might take it better coming from you than me. I think I'll stand watch at the entrance for a while." He got up and walked to the cave entrance, the other particle pistol in his hands.

Julie exhaled, got up, and walked over to where Jared was seated. She sat down quietly next to him and said, "You okay, Jared?"

Jared smiled slightly as he glanced at her.

"It's kind of ironic. I had just written my brother a long letter last month and ribbed him about how different our chosen careers were. We have this running joke, you see, about how the other has the better job. Mick always thought I had it cushy, sitting somewhere in a nice, clean lab, light years away from the enemy. I always thought of Mick as the glamorous warrior pilot and actually envied him his exciting lifestyle. He told me once about when he'd had to kill a T'Kharr pilot up close with his pistol and how strange he'd felt afterward. He said it was easier when you perceive your enemy only as a ship or an object rather than as a sentient being."

"I suppose that's true for all fighter jocks," Julie offered. "They have to be able to function and not overanalyze each action in combat."

"I'd told him that in a similar situation, I wouldn't have had any remorse over killing a T'Kharr. I've seen what they do to prisoners. He said that until I actually had to do it myself, I couldn't understand. Well, I understand now."

"I, for one, am damned glad your small bout of excitement turned out the way it did," Julie said sincerely.

"Let's just hope that, first off, they don't find the bunker; second, they don't find us; and third, that even if they don't find us, we can manage to survive long enough to be rescued. We've got a big job ahead of us."

"So, what do we do first, Chief?"

Jared started to object. "Chief? Look, Kloke has a point. I'm not . . ."

"A soldier?" Julie completed for him. "What, and we are? Look, Jared, you're a natural leader who can think on his feet. Who would you rather lead this group? Me? Kloke? We'd be dead by morning. Face it, pal. You're our man."

Jared glared at her with a stern expression, prepared to argue, but deep inside, he knew she was right. He glanced over at Dram, who was nodding his head in agreement.

"I'm not sure if the Jaaleadi—" Jared started.

Jeenan interrupted, "We agree with Julie. Males are warriors in our species, not females. You are the only acceptable choice to lead."

Jared had forgotten how keen the Jaaleadi hearing was. "Very well," he said, throwing his hands up. Then, under his breath, he added, "Don't say I didn't warn ya." He stood up and brushed off his seat. "Okay then," he said, the familiar confidence once again in his voice.

"First off, we keep watch at the entrance and wait until dark. Then we go out and locate food and water. We have enough survival rations for about two days if we eat sparingly. Julie, you and Jeenan take care of Spinnaker and Glend. This cave should provide us with adequate shelter, and there's so much life on this planet that they shouldn't be able to distinguish us from all the background images. During the night, we'll try and camouflage the entrance better. I don't think it would be wise to venture outside right now."

"Sounds good, Mister Trent," Dram said. "I'll take the first watch, and Mister Kloke will be happy to relieve me for the next watch."

Kloke rose from his seat and started to object, but a quick, deadly glare from Dram shut him up. He sullenly replied, "Yeah, sure. Whatever," and sat back down heavily where he had been.

Jared looked skyward and thought out loud, "Don't take too long, Mickey. The sooner, the better."

Captain Michael Trent, Commander-Space-Group *Pacifica*, sat alone at a dark corner table in the officers' lounge and nursed his Fomalhaut Fizz.

At six feet two inches, he barely fit into the cockpits of some of the smaller fighters. With his sandy brown hair and deep blue eyes, he was often confused with his younger brother, Jared, so similar were they in appearance. It had been three days since Miratev fell to the T'Kharr, and there had been no word on survivors or even if a plan to retake the system was in the works. He hoped this secret staff meeting was for just that purpose.

He thought about his brother and about the last time they'd corresponded. Jared was a doctor working for the research section. Jared couldn't tell him anything about what he was doing on Miratev, because it was classified top secret. Of course, some day, when the war was over, they'd have to swap stories. He would tell him of some of the more seat-of-the-pants combat missions he'd participated in, and he would have to ask him what the big secret of Miratev was. He sincerely hoped that day would still come.

He was jolted out of his mood by the familiar voice of the computer. "Captain Trent?"

"Go ahead, computer," he responded.

"Admiral Drake requires your presence in his ready room."

"On my way," Trent said. He quickly downed the remainder of his drink. Maybe now he would find out what was going on. He strode out into the hallway toward the direct bridge access lift. "Command deck."

The trip took four full minutes due to the massive size of the ship. Trent walked onto the expansive bridge of the ship, which even now was manned by over twenty people. During combat, that number tripled. Most of the stations were set down into what was known as "the pit." The center of the pit was occupied by a spherical holographic representation of the four inner planets of the system. The image could be expanded or contracted as needed and showed the locations of all ships within that area.

The admiral's ready room was set to the rear of the circular platform that skirted the perimeter of the pit. On other carriers, a captain would normally hold the post that Drake held, but the *Pacifica* was something special. She was only one of four vessels with a grand commander in charge of her fleet and was the command ship for one quarter of the Alliance military. A posting to the *Pacifica* looked very impressive on one's service record. The waiting list was very long and distinguished.

Trent reached the threshold of Drake's ready room and knocked. The door slid open, revealing Drake at the wet bar fixing a drink.

"Come in, Captain. Have a seat, please. Sorry to get you off duty. I just came off myself. Would you care for a drink?"

"Thank you, no, sir," Trent said politely as he stepped through the doors. "I just came from the officers' lounge." The doors silently closed as he seated himself in front of the Admiral's desk.

Drake got right to the point. "I just received a courier from the commander advising me that we were called here to plan the liberation of the Miratev system."

Trent's heart jumped into his throat, and he tried to keep the excitement from his face, but Drake's amused expression told Trent he wasn't hiding it well enough.

"I know your brother's on the planet, and you would have flown into the system on a garbage scow with a pocket knife if you could have. This is going to be done right. That's why the five fleets have been called in."

"Do we know the op yet?" Trent asked.

"No, that's what tomorrow's meeting is for. Just let me stress, Mick, that this is still under wraps. General Order 20. North let me tell you because of Jared, but he doesn't want anyone else knowing." Then Drake continued in a more serious tone, "If this leaks out, we're screwed."

"Understood."

"I wish I could give you more information on possible survivors, but the information Command has is sketchy. There are indications that some people may have escaped. We'll just have to go in and find out for ourselves."

"You can be assured that the flight wing will be ready, Admiral," Trent said earnestly. "If I have to check out every ship myself and push it out into space by hand, all our birds will be in space."

"Good," Drake said.

"Um, Admiral, is there any other official business to deal with right now?" Trent asked.

"No, I don't believe so," Drake replied with a curious expression.

"Well, then, if you wouldn't mind, Admiral," Trent said with a satisfied grin, "I think I'll have that drink now." ·

Drake's boisterous laugh could be heard on the entire bridge, and several heads turned toward the doors to his ready room with puzzled looks on their faces.

Upon leaving Terred's office, North was directed to an eight-man air limo. North shared the vehicle with the driver and four large, armed marines. Security demanded that while on Earth, any time the Grand Commander left a military base, he had to have a personal protection squad with him. He felt uncomfortable with all the attention, but he realized that it was a necessary evil.

"Where to, sir?" the driver asked.

"Home," he responded.

The driver headed south for the forty-five minute trip to his home just outside the city of Del Sur on the Baja coast. Lush and beautiful, Del Sur was a major commercial port of call for the North American continent. During the winter months, it attracted tourists from all over the system. His wife, Shareel, used to run a successful antique import service that specialized in the rare and exotic from all over the Alliance worlds. Jaaleadi artifacts were difficult to obtain since so many of them held cultural significance. Shareel had respected their culture enough not to try to obtain the more controversial items.

North owned a four-hundred-acre ranch only ten kilometers from the coastline, complete with horses and a lake stocked with golden and rainbow trout. Coming home was always a welcome change from the cold gray walls of his ship. There was a large landing platform in front of the house that was big enough to park five fleet shuttles on. It was one of the things Command insisted on for its flag officers. You never knew when you would need to leave suddenly. The house was a mixture of modern and traditional, and appeared more rustic on the outside. It was good to be here, even if it was just for a day.

The driver touched down silently. The corporal exited and opened the door for North. North turned to the guards and identified the sergeant.

"I'll have something brought out for you and your men, Sergeant. I know that you patrol in shifts, so there are guest quarters for you and your men."

"With respect, sir, we can all stay out here, and we brought C-rats. We'll be okay."

North smiled and said, "Sergeant, I admire your dedication, but I want your men to be rested and alert and have a decent meal while you're with me."

The Sergeant nodded and said, "Yes, sir. Thank you, Commander," and snapped off a crisp salute.

North returned the salute and turned toward the front door of the house. As he got closer, he saw Denara and her husband, Lan, half walking, half running to the pad from the house.

"We weren't expecting you until later this evening, Commander Brandon. You should have called."

Try as he might over the years, Denara refused to call him Brandon. Before, it was Admiral Brandon, now Commander Brandon.

"I finished at Command earlier than I had anticipated," North said. "You look as gorgeous as ever."

Her face flushed, and she laughed out loud. North shook Lan's hand.

"Nice to see you, Brandon," Lan said with a big grin. "Do I have to keep an eye on my wife while you're home?" he joked.

"The way she cooks, you just might," North said with a wink. "How are things here?"

"Just fine. Horses are doing great. We should do well at the next auction."

North knew little of ranches and horses, but Lan was an expert. He had carte blanche with the livestock, including buying and selling them. North rewarded him and his family with a place to live and a share of the profits. It was a perfect arrangement for someone who was gone more often than he was home. The ranch was far too big for one person. It sure seemed bigger without Shareel and James.

North indicated the men standing by the limo. "Could you see to it that those marines have access to the guest quarters and get whatever they want to eat?"

"Of course," Denara said with a smile. "I've made plenty." She loved to cook and loved to dote on anyone he brought to the house as guests, including his bodyguards.

He looked over Lan's shoulder and saw Rando, Denara and Lan's son, standing near the edge of the platform, grinning ear to ear and wearing the fresh new uniform of an ensign.

When he saw North looking at him, Rando snapped to attention and saluted.

North couldn't help but grin and said, "Listen, kid, you ran around my house in diapers for years. You're about as close to a nephew as I have."

Rando relaxed and grinned. "Good to see you, Uncle Brandon."

North regarded Rando. He was almost a carbon copy of his father, but twenty years younger. He'd graduated from the Academy almost a week earlier and was due to be assigned to a ship after a short leave. Aside from a recommendation to the Academy by North, Denara and Lan refused any offers of preferential treatment for Rando. It didn't matter. Rando was bright and talented. He sailed through command school and had a bright future ahead, all on his own merits.

"How long will you be here, Rando?" North asked.

"Unfortunately, only for a few days," he replied. "I've been assigned to *Endeavor* as a weapons section officer. We're leaving in a couple of days on some kind of mission." He could barely keep the excitement from his voice.

North's face fell almost imperceptibly, but enough for Denara to notice.

She looked concerned and said, "Is that not a good ship? We heard Admiral Faulkner is a fine commander—"

North quickly interjected, "No . . . no, don't worry. He is a very good commander. The best. You did well to post on that ship, Rando. I'm proud of you, as I'm sure your parents are as well."

Sensing that North wasn't telling them something, Lan said, "Do you know something about this mission?"

"Nothing I can discuss, I'm afraid. I'm sorry. Just be aware that Admiral Faulkner and his ship are amongst the finest in the fleet . . . after the *Pacifica* of course," North added with a wink and a grin.

Denara looked disappointed but had long ago learned to accept the realities of war. She resisted the temptation to ask what the nature of his sudden recall to Earth was about or to press about this mission; she knew better. It had been a very difficult thing to accept when her son joined the military as a career officer after his mandatory two-year tour. She'd learned, however, that soldiers don't keep information to themselves because they want to, but rather because they have to.

"Well, at least we'll have you here for a couple of days," she said. "You won't have to stay on base the whole time, will you, Commander Brandon?"

"Only as much as is absolutely necessary," he said as he smiled warmly at her. "If they want me there any more than that, they're going to have to lock me in the brig."

He then dug into his case and extracted the sheed blossom. "I almost forgot . . . I know you like this kind of stuff . . ."

Her eyes lit up, and she gently took the case. "A sheed blossom! I've heard of these, but I never thought I'd see one up close. Where did you get it?"

"Our Jaaleadi liaison. I knew you'd like it, so I finagled one."

"Oh my, thank you so much, Commander Brandon . . ." she said before a sly, knowing smile spread across her face. "All right . . . what is it that you want from me?"

North tried to feign innocence but finally said, "Is that worth some of your lasagna to take with me when I leave? Stuff's like gold on my ship."

Denara laughed out loud and said, "Of course. Enough to last you for a week." Denara was a legendary cook. More than one employer had tried to poach her from North, but she had always thought of the Norths as her own family.

Upon reaching the house, Denara walked into the kitchen area while North went to the living room and let the soft, comfortable couch envelop him. Rando and Lan also seated themselves on the couch, waiting for Denara to summon them. Lan was the patriarch of their family, without doubt, but only as much as Denara allowed him to be. He knew the drill and knew not to bother her in the kitchen while she was "creating."

The room was bright and homey, with a variety of plants and flowers from all over the Alliance worlds. The plants gave the air a fresh and pleasant quality. The sheed blossom would fit in nicely in the front room. Denara had been careful not to change too much of Shareel's décor, knowing that it was one of the few things North had to remember her by.

North recognized the aroma coming from the kitchen instantly. Denara was cooking his favorite: Maine lobster. He understood what a supreme sacrifice this was for Denara, since she hated even the smell of seafood.

"It smells great," North said eagerly. "When do we eat?"

"It will take a few more minutes," she replied. "I wasn't expecting you so soon. I haven't even started the artichokes yet."

"Well, in that case, I'm going to go upstairs and change."

North went up the stairs and into the master bedroom. He changed into a soft, worn pair of cotton jeans and a button up shirt that he left untucked. The clothes seemed to fit more loosely than before. Not enough home cooking aboard ship, he surmised.

He placed his uniform in the cleaning unit so that it would be ready for the staff meeting in the morning. He debated whether or not to put on shoes, eventually deciding against it, reveling in the feeling of the thick carpeting on his bare feet and between his toes. He never really had the opportunity to relax like this on the ship, always having to be presentable and professional for his crew.

He glanced around the room and realized that not much had changed over the years. Denara had kept the room as it was at North's request. Glancing around at the curtains, pictures, and items on the dresser, he suddenly realized that he needed to go elsewhere before he became overwhelmed with Shareel's memory, so he headed downstairs.

"I should warn you, Denara, I promised Admiral Faulkner some of your world-famous lasagna too while we were here," North said, glancing at Rando, his face filling with dread. "Rando can start sucking up to the admiral immediately. I hope you don't mind too much." North sat down on the couch again and stretched his legs out.

"Not at all. It would be good for Rando—"

"Mom!" Rando said, mortified.

North chuckled. "No worries, kid. I'll give it to him. No sucking up required."

North looked appraisingly at Rando, looking so neat and professional in his uniform. He leaned forward and rested his elbows on his knees. "You look good, kid. You've really bulked up. Those hand-to-hand instructors won't allow you to get flabby."

"Yeah," he said with a knowing smile. "They definitely keep you on your toes."

He continued, the excitement apparent in his voice, "You know, Uncle Brandon, sometimes I think I'm going to explode.

I can't wait to get out there and fight the T'Kharr first hand. To actually see one up close, not a holo simulation. In class, we've been studying the Quindari raids and the liberation of Galma Thule." His face then became more somber. "They showed us pictures of the T'Kharr doing things to the civilians . . . eating babies and torturing people in unthinkable ways. At first, I thought they were just propaganda films to get us all worked up into hating the T'Kharr, that they weren't real." Rando looked at North, questioning in his eyes.

North paused for a second, considering the right response to the boy's unspoken question, and nodded his head slowly.

"I was on Galma Thule after we took back the colony."

Rando's eyes went wide with surprise, "You were there? Actually on the planet?"

"I was a lieutenant on the *Triumph*, a Jupiter-class carrier," North said. "I wasn't too much older than you, as a matter of fact."

"We've studied those old Jupiter carriers and actually got to tour one at the museum on Calor Five. They told us they were the basic design that developed into the Saturns and Neptunes."

"That's right. She was a fine ship. Tough as nails. My C.O., Captain Varda, said that you always have a special place in your heart for your first ship."

Rando's eyes grew even wider than before. "*You* served under Fleet Marshal Varda? His tactics are legend in the Academy and required reading."

"He was everything they said. One of the finest commanders I ever served under. He led the assault on the planet, you know." North paused, thoughtful. "I still have trouble thinking about Galma Thule, even after twenty-five plus years. Seeing the survivors and watching the footage from their surveillance cameras of the T'Kharr 'interrogations.' It wasn't as bad as they teach you. It was ten times worse. Horrifying. Believe it or not, you saw the sanitized version."

"I can't imagine much worse than we saw," Rando said.

"You're still young," North said with a haunted look in his eyes. "With the Creator's grace, this blasted war will end and you'll never see worse."

Rando broke the somber mood. "Well, I still can't wait to get out there."

North smiled and cuffed the boy on the shoulder. "Don't be too anxious, junior. I need people like you to take care of me when I'm old and gray."

Rando cocked one eyebrow and deadpanned, "Well, I figure to be an admiral way before then, and I'll have subordinates to do that kind of trivial stuff for me."

"Oh, yeah?" North said with a laugh. "Well, I seem to recall seeing an opening on a tugboat for a smart-aleck newly-minted Ensign. I could always put in a good word, you know . . ."

"Okay, okay, you win," Rando said, holding his hands up in surrender.

The three men laughed heartily until Denara called from the kitchen, "All right, you three. Enough war talk for today. Come in here and help me set the table."

Dinner was delicious. North couldn't remember the last time something had tasted so good. Lobster, artichokes, fresh sourdough bread and real butter, not the synthetic spread meant to look and taste butter-like, all his favorites. It almost seemed like old times.

After attempting to help Denara clear the table and receiving a reprimand for even trying, all three of the men retired to the living room and sat down.

No sooner had they sat down than the comm unit chimed.

"Oh no!" Lan exclaimed. "You just got home. Surely they don't want you to come back already."

"I guess we'll never know until we answer it," North said with disappointment in his voice. He'd gotten too many of these calls on trips home.

North answered the unit and pushed the privacy unlock pad, enabling the view screen to transmit a two-way image. The screen flickered into life, showing a smartly dressed young woman wearing the insignia of a lieutenant commander.

North said with a resigned sigh, "Yes?"

The woman straightened her uniform and sniffed. "Please address me as 'Lieutenant Commander,' citizen." She obviously didn't recognize North in his civilian clothes. "I'm looking for Ensign Falco."

North looked amused, which seem to irritate the woman even more. "Just a moment."

Rando hadn't wanted preferential treatment during his Academy time and insisted on using his mother's maiden name. Although he wasn't related to North by blood, many knew he was connected to Lan and Denara Lareen, North's longtime friends and caretakers. Only the top Academy people who personally knew North knew any better. The young woman obviously hadn't been warned by her superiors that the number Rando had left in case they needed to contact him was classified and belonged to the North household.

"Ensign Falco, it's for you," North said as he relinquished the screen to Rando.

North sat back down on the couch and listened while Rando cleared his throat and spoke to the person on the screen. "Yes, Commander?"

She spoke in an official tone, "Ensign, your shore leave has been cut short. Admiral Faulkner has recalled all staff members back at once. You will be told why when you return."

"Yes, ma'am," Rando replied. "I'll leave right away."

"One more thing, Ensign," the woman said in a slightly irritated tone. "You might want to verse whoever that was who answered the call on proper protocol when addressing military officers."

Rando nearly choked trying to contain the laugh trying to explode from his chest.

"Are you all right, Ensign?" the woman asked.

"No. I mean yes, ma'am. I'm sorry, ma'am. I must have inhaled something the wrong way. I'll take care of it right away." Rando quickly composed himself.

"Well, fine then," the woman said. "Carry on." She cut the transmission.

"Let me guess," North offered. "Just promoted?"

"Yeah, she's quite a challenge. Wears those gold oak leaves like they were admirals' stars. I try and stay out of her way."

"Sounds like you inherited the Lareen common sense after all," North said.

"You have to leave?" Denara asked, coming from the kitchen into the living room.

"I'm sorry, Mom. I wish I could stay longer, but . . ."

Denara placed her hands on both of his cheeks and said, "I understand, mijo. You don't have to explain."

She enveloped him in a warm hug and kissed him on the cheek.

Lan stood and said, "I'll see you soon, son. Cuidate."

He admired his boy once again and said, "It just seems like last week that you were a little boy. Now you're all grown up." Lan felt the lump building in his throat and quickly hugged his son hard.

"Have a safe trip, Rando," North said warmly. Rando and James had been like brothers growing up. North thought he'd be performing this particular scene with his own son someday, but fate had had other plans.

Rando, apparently fighting his own lump down, returned his father's hug and said to North, "Bye, Uncle Brandon. You stay safe too. Don't take too many unnecessary risks."

They followed Rando outside to the land car he'd requisitioned for his trip home. He climbed in and sat behind the controls. Rando waved to his parents and drove down the driveway to the main road that would take him to the Del Sur space port. From there, he could get passage on the next orbital-bound military transport and be onboard the *Endeavor* in slightly under three hours. Denara and Lan both waved to him as he drove down the road and out of sight.

They went back into the house and sat down on the couch. Lan put his arm around Denara's shoulder and held her close, whispering comfort into her ear. He could tell she was disappointed that Rando had had to leave so abruptly.

"I can't believe how big he's gotten," North said. "I'm really proud of how he's turned out."

Denara turned to North and said, "I don't suppose you could arrange for some planet-side duty for him after this mission, could you?"

"You know better than that," Lan chided. "He'd never forgive you."

"Yes, I know. You Lareen men are so stubborn sometimes."

She let out a resigned sigh and snuggled closer to him. "At least I still have you here."

North suddenly felt uncomfortable and decided to get to work.

"Dinner was fabulous, Denara," he said. "I'm going to be in my study the rest of the night."

Realizing what North must be feeling, Denara and Lan got up and smiled at him. Suddenly, to North's surprise, Denara reached up and kissed him on the cheek.

"Thank you, Commander Brandon. For everything. I'll make sure your guards out there are well taken care of."

North was rarely rendered speechless, but this was one of those times. He simply smiled and nodded and went into his study. Once there, he sat back and pondered the day's events, activated his terminal, and began his long night's work.

CHAPTER THREE

Miratev Two

"C'mon, Dram," Jared muttered to himself as he peered into the black of the forest from the mouth of their cave. "Get back here."

Dram was over an hour overdue from his foraging mission, and Jared was getting nervous. He got up and paced. He never could stop himself from pacing when he was worried; it was a family trait.

Julie looked over at him. "Come over and sit down. It's hard enough to find your way in this forest in the daytime," she said unconvincingly. She was worried too but was able to cover it better.

Reluctantly, Jared came over and sank down next to her. He glanced at Spinnaker, who was unconscious and twitching fitfully. Julie had tied a piece of cloth around the back of Spinnaker's head and placed it in between her teeth after she'd bitten her tongue through during one particularly violent spasm.

"How is she?" Jared asked.

"Not good. She must have caught more of a blast from that neuron disrupter than we thought. She's getting worse. She'd be dead by now if we didn't keep giving her the hyperfeuron, but we only have two packs left. I hope one of us doesn't get injured, because it's only going to be splints and bandages after they're gone."

Glend had come out of her self-induced coma and was now conscious. Her left wing was obviously broken and had been set and immobilized. Other than that, she didn't appear to have any serious damage.

"I envy the Jaaleadi their recuperative powers. Glend seems a lot better."

"As I said," Jeenan piped in, "time is the best medicine for us. Hyperfeuron does help, but the old ways still work better. Jaaleadi bones are hollow and easy to break. The wing will mend."

Just then, they heard a rustling sound from outside the entrance, and Dram entered the cave.

"By the Creator, where have you been?" Jared rasped.

"Sorry I'm late. I had to play a little hide and seek with a T'Kharr patrol. Remember in training, they told us they don't hear very well, so I was quiet. But it was worth it."

Dram slid off the duffel bag he'd slung on his back and pulled out a large emergency first aid kit and a small handheld transmitter.

Julie's eyes went wide. "Where the devil did you get those?"

Jared's voice sounded simultaneously angry and delighted. "You didn't go back to the lab, did you?"

"Naw, I didn't feel that brave. I went to the shuttle pad and sorted through the debris from the shuttles that the T'Kharr blasted when they arrived. They don't have the area guarded, so I slipped in and salvaged what I could."

Jared smiled for what seemed like the first time in two days and clapped Dram on the shoulder. "Mister, I'm giving you a raise when we get back . . . assuming, of course, we do get back. These will certainly increase our chances."

"Maybe so," Dram said as he dug through the bag some more. "But I think *these* might help even more than the medicine and radio." With a grunt, he produced two of the power-ful M-36B pulse rifles and a sling of grenades.

Jared's jaw almost hit the ground. "Those were in the shut-tle?"

A sly smile spread across Dram's face. "Well, I never did much like going out on survey missions on this planet with-out being armed. Too many predators out here. Doctor Gleen wouldn't have approved if I'd asked him, so I didn't. I hid them in one of the cargo bays. Besides, my father was in the Ma-rines. He taught me to never be caught unprepared."

Jared looked Dram square in the eyes and said, "Thank the Creator for your father. Next question is, do you know how to use them?"

"I did the mandatory two years of service. These are slight-ly more advanced than the M-34s we used but basically function the same."

The M-36B pulse rifle was a handheld rail gun. The projec-tiles were accelerated to speed by an electron rail and left the gun barrel at near Mach five. At short range, they were devastating. They were also standard issue to Alliance infantry units.

Jeenan and Glend came over to join them as Dram emptied the remaining contents of the bag. In addition to the rifles, trans-mitter, and first aid kit, there were three extra magazines of am-munition for each rifle with two hundred rounds each, twenty grenades, and ten packages of emergency rations.

"You scored big, my friend," Jared said. "This gives us a fight-ing chance."

He glanced over to where Kloke was sitting in the corner sleeping and lowered his voice. "I don't know if I would trust Kloke with one of these, but we don't have much choice." He called over to Kloke, who grumbled loudly, and sleepily stum-bled over to the group.

Dram hefted one of the heavy rifles and removed the mag-azine. He showed them a switch on the side that activated the heads-up tracking and targeting holo screen and switched it on. Immediately, a hologram image of a red circle and crosshairs appeared above the rear fixed sights.

"This rifle is state of the art. Our boys and girls use these everywhere there's a military presence. See the holo image of the cross hairs? When you bring the rifle up to eye level to aim, the auto tracking sensor tracks the movement of your eyeball, and as you refocus on a more distant target, the crosshairs automatically compensate and adjust. There's no need to adjust for height or windage. If you're aiming at a target too far out of range, the cross hairs will disappear and blink that message."

Dram picked up one of the magazines and continued, "To load, you just fit the new magazine into the slot just before the trigger guard," he did so to demonstrate, "and slam it home firmly. These rifles fire an armor-piercing explosive round that's about a half inch long and about the width of a toothpick. The tip of each projectile has a particle of high explosive in it. It'll penetrate most everything and will do quite a job on living tissue, even the T'Kharr's tough skin. Notice that with a magazine loaded, there's a number at the bottom of your holo sight. That's the number of rounds remaining in the magazine. When the number reaches zero, you pull the magazine out and ram a new one home. The weapon will chamber the new round automatically."

He demonstrated the procedure to them, showing them the readouts, and let each of them try it themselves.

"There's another switch on the side that allows the rifle to fire fully automatic, three-round burst, or single shot. Since we have a limited number of rounds, I suggest we keep them on single shot or burst to conserve. You agree, Mister Trent?"

Jared nodded in full agreement. "Absolutely. How about the grenade launcher?"

Dram went through the procedure of loading the grenades into the tube attached to the launcher.

"Remember that there are two triggers on the launcher. You push forward on one and backward on the other. They installed that way to prevent accidental discharges. To throw one by hand, just push the buttons on top and bottom and throw it. I'll set the delays to maximum, ten seconds. Any questions?"

Kloke said, "But what good are these when the T'Kharr have energy weapons?"

Dram said, "Energy weapons have their good and bad points. The good points are obvious, but the handicap is that the person firing the weapon is easily pinpointed. All you need to do is follow the beam back to where it's coming from. These are better when firing from a concealed position, and they penetrate armor and T'Kharr skin better than energy weapons."

Jared looked at the others and said, "Any more questions?"

"One more thing," Dram added. "As formidable as the T'Kharr are, remember they have poor sight and hearing compared to humans. Also, if they have a weak point, it's the knees. They break easier than a human's."

Everyone nodded their heads, and Jared decided that he and Dram would carry the rifles while the Jaaleadi carried the two particle pistols. Jeenan had pointed out that the rifles were too heavy for them.

Julie had become the designated medical doctor and went back to tending to Spinnaker, who appeared to be getting worse. She inventoried the medical kit Dram had brought: one scanner, three hypos with a drug synthesizer unit, a dozen packs of hyperfeuron, several burn and pain ointments, and a variety of bandages. The synthesizer was invaluable.

"We should be able to maintain our hyperfeuron supply with this if we can find some organic matter."

"Good," Jared said. "What kind is best?"

"Preferably a small rodent or something like that. If not, then anything else that's living. It'll just take longer. The synthesizer works best with a mammal's blood. We should be able to manufacture more hyperfeuron at the rate of one standard dose every three hours."

"Okay. Jeenan, Glend, let's scout out this cave and see what we can find. Your ancestors hunted rodents. Perhaps we can use those innate hunter's instincts and skills to our benefit. I'll come with you. Kloke, it's your turn at watch. Dram, you get some sleep. You've earned it tonight, my friend."

"Thanks, Mister Trent," he said with a grin and handed his rifle to Kloke.

"I don't see what good it'll do," Kloke moaned as he took the rifle and sat down near the cave entrance, looking into the forest. "We'll probably all be dead by morning."

"Julie, why don't you grab some sleep too? You've been watching over Spinnaker all day. She appears to be resting now, and you've been up for what, seventy-two hours straight?"

"Feels that way. Maybe I will, Jared. Thanks."

Jared and the Jaaleadi went deeper into the cave, Jared with his flashlight and the Jaaleadi using their keen senses, to locate what they could for the synthesizer.

Julie went over to where Dram was lying on a blanket and said, "Would you mind terribly if I backed up to you? This blasted cave is so damp and cold at night, at least we can keep our backs warm."

Dram looked up at her, flustered for a moment, but was finally able to get out, "S-sure, Miss Newman."

He quickly scooted over and allowed her more than half of the blanket and rolled on his right side so he didn't have to meet those deep blue eyes.

She smiled to herself at Dram's obvious discomfort and shyness and said, "Thanks, but I only need half. You can scoot over a bit."

She laid down with her back to him, and he scooted just close enough that he could feel her slender back against his. She noticed with slight amusement that he was very tense. It was like sleeping up against a brick wall.

She turned around suddenly and whispered in his ear, "And I told you, it's Julie. Thanks for finding all that stuff. You may have saved all our lives." She then lightly kissed him on the cheek and rolled over, back-to-back again. "Goodnight, Dram."

"Goodnight, Miss, uh, Julie." Dram hoped she couldn't feel his heart pounding its way out of his chest. He'd always felt awkward when talking to women, especially when he was around a woman he was attracted to. Julie was definitely one of those. He'd developed a thing for her the minute he saw her, but he knew she was way out of his league.

After all, he was just a lowly lab assistant, and she was a doctor. Besides, she seemed to have something going with Dr. Trent. He'd have to learn to be content with admiring her from afar. He was suddenly overcome with a wave of fatigue and realized at that point just how tired he really was. Thoughts of Julie faded away, and he gradually slipped off into unconsciousness.

Admiral Drake stood behind Lt. Vale at her comm station on the bridge of the *Pacifica*, addressing the outraged man on the view screen. Vale looked like she'd rather be anywhere else in the universe at that moment.

"What do you mean he countermanded my orders?" Fleet Admiral Fidel Carlo seethed. "You will re-deploy forces as I originally ordered, Admiral Drake. North is on the planet now, and I am your superior officer."

Drake calmly stood behind Lt. Vale and listened as Carlo postured, but privately detested the man. Carlo, an overweight, balding man of sixty solar years, seemed to have a perpetual sneer on his face. It was generally suspected that Carlo deeply resented North for having achieved his present rank at such a young age, coupled with the fact that he now outranked him. Carlo was the textbook autocrat, unwilling to listen to the advice of subordinates and convinced that he and he alone knew what should be done and how to do it.

He'd been pulled off his old combat posting after ignoring the advice of his captains and losing more than half of his fleet during an engagement with the T'Kharr. Fleet Command, bowing to political pressure, chose not to formally discipline him but rather gave him an administrative reassignment on Earth.

"With respect, Admiral," Drake replied, "I'm under direct orders to clear any re-deployment of the fleets through Commander North. If you'd care to contact him, I'm sure this can all be cleared up."

Carlo's outraged face began to turn a dark shade of red. "Do I understand that you are refusing a direct order from me, *Rear Admiral?*"

"No, sir, but your orders are in conflict with a direct order given to me by an officer superior to you."

Drake could see the frustration building on Carlo's face. Carlo might try to bluff his way through this, but he knew Drake was right and that there was nothing he could do about it.

"Very well, Admiral Drake," Carlo said through clenched teeth. "We shall see." With a final glare at Drake, Carlo abruptly terminated the link.

"Well, that went well," Drake said with a straight face. "Carry on, Lieutenant."

Drake spun on one heel and strode back to his ready room. Lieutenant Vale put her head into her hands and began to rub her temples.

"Everything all right, Annaline?"

Vale turned to see Captain Mitchell Frost, operations officer and second-in-command of the *Pacifica* standing behind her.

Vale briefly hesitated. "Well, sir, to be quite frank, having all these admirals in one place is giving me a headache. I think I'll need a tranquilizer before my shift is over. I don't know how Admiral Drake can be so calm after being yelled at by a five-star."

Frost nodded his head, "Because, Lieutenant, one nova outranks five, or six, or even seven stars, and Drake knows that Commander North will back him up."

She smiled and said, "Yes, sir."

He patted her on the shoulder and sat back down in the command chair, concentrating on a fuel consumption report.

The following two hours were long and uneventful. Ensign Thomas Craig, alpha watch detector officer, apathetically studied his screen for any sign of . . . what? What could possibly happen to them in the best protected system in the Alliance? He thought that the brass was being just a touch paranoid. The crews deserved more than just one day of shore leave. After all, they'd been out a long time. Only one hour left until beta shift took over the watch. Maybe that nice-looking technician from the flight deck would be in the lounge. What was her name?

"Unidentified inbound detected," the computer voice reported calmly. "Projected heading, dark side of Luna."

Craig immediately became alert and examined his screen.

"Second inbound detected. Identical course and speed. Same projected heading. Configuration conforms to T'Kharr type-two fusion missiles. Five hundred megaton warhead yield. Estimated time of impact, five solar minutes . . . mark."

"Captain Frost! I'm tracking two inbound bogeys. T'Kharr fusion missiles, type-two!"

Frost covered the distance between the command seat and Craig's console in three steps. "Destination?"

As realization hit him, Craig punched the console with his fist.

"*Challenger* escort fleet. They haven't all broken formation yet. There are still eight ships parked in orbit behind the moon," said Craig.

"Warn those ships immediately, Lieutenant Vale." He punched the intercom button. "Set condition one! Launch the alert fighters. Admiral Drake to the bridge."

"Point of origin?" Frost demanded.

"Unknown, sir. No unfriendly ships within ten parsecs. It doesn't make any sense . . ."

"There! What ship is that?" Frost growled as he stared at the point where the computer first picked up the missiles. He stabbed his finger at the screen and said, "Computer, identify probable origin point of the inbounds."

"Merchant cargo vessel *Achilles*," the computer's emotionless voice said. "Schedir system registry."

"She's bugging out in a hurry," Craig reported. "Making a run for the Castor starlane portal."

"Fleet Com, order intercept!" Frost barked. "Whoever's closest, and I want you in direct contact with the gun platforms at the Castor portal. Make sure that ship does not get through!"

"Aye, sir!"

"*Endeavor* is launching her alert fighters," Craig said. "They'll get them before they hit the portal."

Drake hurried over to stand behind Frost and Craig.

"I saw it on the monitor when we went to alert. Are the *Challenger's* fleet ships moving out?"

"Sitting on their butts, Admiral," Frost replied. "Fleet Com, why haven't those ships moved out?"

Vale answered, "Sir, all eight ships only have skeleton crews. Admiral Carlo relieved the command crews for shore leave, and—"

"That idiot!" Drake yelled, the heat of his fury making the hair stand up on the back of Craig's neck.

"What about *Challenger's* combat space patrol? Maybe her fighters can intercept—"

"Sir," Frost said, "*Challenger* hasn't launched her CSP."

Drake slammed his fist on the console and said, "Do they have gunnery crews still on board?"

Vale spoke hurriedly into her headset and replied, "Negative, sir. They only have personnel essential to maintain the ships in parking orbit. Their engines are cold."

Drake ground his teeth in frustration and anger. "Direct our own CSP to intercept! Kill those bastards before they get into proximity of those ships!"

"Sir," Frost interjected, "Computer estimates 3.5 minutes until the lead missile reaches proximity. We're on the far side of Earth, opposite the moon. There's no way they'll get there in time, even at emergency speed."

"Dammit!" Drake slammed down his fist on the hand rail, then laid his head on his clenched fist for a moment, thinking. Suddenly, he had an idea.

"Fleet Com, get me Tsiolkovsky Base. Now!"

Tsiolkovsky Base was the Alliance's oldest moon base that was still in operation. Located just south of the Tsiolkovsky crater, it had been built initially as a reconnaissance platform. It now served as a surplus yard for obsolete equipment.

"Tsiolkovsky Base, this is *Pacifica*!" Vale yelled into her headset. "Do you copy?"

The holographic representation of the system was immediately replaced by a surprised face. "*Pacifica*, this is Tsiolkovsky Base, Lt. Commander Weyland. Admiral Drake, what can we do for you, sir?"

"Listen to me. We are tracking two inbound type-two fusion missiles. They will likely detonate amongst the ships currently in parking orbit above your position, but these are two of their big boys, five hundred megs each."

Weyland's face went pale. "Five hundred megatons? Even from orbit, the base will be devastated, sir. Will the ships be able to intercept them?"

"Negative. No gunnery crews. Now listen carefully. Do you still have active asteroid deflectors on the station?"

"Well, yes, sir," Weyland answered, confusion showing on his face. "But they haven't been used for over twenty years, ever since the system detection net went online." Realization dawned on him. "They should still be in working order, though, sir. Stand by."

Drake heard Weyland's voice in the background, barking orders.

"Online and powering up, Admiral. Awaiting targeting data."

"Weyland, slave your firing control to our computer," Frost ordered. "We'll fire as soon as the inbounds are in range and locked."

"You're locked in, sir," Weyland said. He added, "Please don't miss."

"We'll do our very best, Commander," Drake replied, not without sympathy. "Update."

Lt. Montgomery stared intently at his screen and, without taking his eyes off it, reported, "One minute to proximity. Targeting . . . is . . . locked!"

"Fire!" Drake commanded.

The main 2-D viewer showed an image of the moon, representations of the eight ships in orbit, and the two bogeys. Four beams lanced out from the bottom of the Tsiolkovsky crater, just south of Tsiolkovsky Base. Two of the beams touched one of the inbound missiles, and the image flared and disappeared.

The dispassionate computer voice stated, "Inbound one destroyed, 0438 hours Fleet standard. Inbound two, course deviation."

"They only winged the second one," Frost reported.

"Craig, what's its new projected course?" Drake demanded.

"Heading away from the fleet at approximately sixty degrees, but it's caught in the moon's gravity well," Craig responded crisply. "Spiraling down, Admiral."

"It'll detonate before impact," Montgomery said. "Computer is having trouble establishing a second lock. Two of the deflector emitters burned out when we fired them."

"Detonation imminent in thirty seconds . . . mark," the computer dutifully reported.

"Mister Montgomery?" Frost asked.

"Locked!"

"Fire!" Drake commanded immediately.

The screen showed two beams emerge from Tsiolkovsky, but the second missile was still there after the beams faded.

"Power overloads on both remaining emitters," Montgomery said. "They're all offline now, sir."

"Another course deviation, Admiral," Craig reported. "Inbound is now traveling away from the fleet at ninety degrees. Rotation of the moon will put Tsiolkovsky Base out of the blast radius."

"Detonation imminent . . . fifteen seconds, mark," the computer chimed.

"Advise the *Challenger* fleet to brace for a shock wave," Drake said, frustration in his voice. "Overlay damage zones and zoom in on the ships and the inbound."

Immediately, a red circle appeared on the screen with inbound two at the center. The red circle, indicating heavy damage, was inside a larger yellow circle, indicating lesser damage. Drake felt a sinking feeling as he noticed that four of the ships were still inside the red circle. Tsiolkovsky Base and the carrier were beyond both circles and appeared to be out of jeopardy.

The computer intoned, "Five seconds . . . four . . . three . . . two . . . one . . . detonation."

The *Pacifica* bridge crew stood horrified, unable to do anything but watch as the glowing fireball expanded and enveloped the closest two ships, the destroyers *Chaska* and *Trelane*. Both disintegrated on contact with the shock wave, and two others were pushed violently outward by the impact. One of those, the heavy cruiser *Jefferson*, broke apart. The fireball slowly encompassed the ship, and violent outgassing of her atmosphere was apparent as compartments became exposed to the vacuum. Several limp bodies shot away from the cloud and could be seen flying helplessly into the void.

Frost said, "Lt. Vale, order damage control and rescue teams to the launch bay, and launch when ready."

Drake stood silently from a moment, his shock turning to blind fury. In a barely audible voice he said, "Update on the pursuit of the *Achilles*, Mister Frost."

Frost looked toward Craig, "Who's intercepting that ship, Mister Craig?"

Craig, still stunned over what he'd just witnessed, took a second to compose himself, then cleared his throat. "Captain, they don't appear to have chosen their escape route very well. They will be within striking range of *Endeavor's* fighters in just under five minutes."

"Fleet Com, get me Admiral Faulkner," Drake said.

Faulkner's voice chimed in over the bridge speaker. "Faulkner here. We saw what happened. How bad did they hurt us?"

"Bad enough," Drake said bitterly. "They killed *Chaska*, *Trelane*, and probably *Jefferson*. *Santee* is reporting heavy damage and casualties. We need to capture the ship coming into your range. She's the one who launched the missiles. The commander will want them alive if possible."

"We're already on it," Faulkner said. "You take care of damage control out there. I'll keep you posted." Then he disconnected the link.

"Fleet Com, advise Command of the situation and get me Commander North."

CHAPTER FOUR

Earth, North Ranch

North sat on the edge of the chair in front of the comm unit in his upstairs study as Drake gave his report. "Three ships destroyed and one crippled," North repeated back in amazement. "I'm going to personally eviscerate that imbecile Carlo and preside at his court martial." It didn't make any sense. Carlo knew that it was a direct violation of fleet directives. Was he so arrogant as to think he could change the regs when it suited him and not have to answer for it? He was silent for a moment and then said, "This whole thing stinks. Too much coincidence. I personally don't believe in 'em. I assume you've advised Command?"

"Of course, sir."

"Good. Maybe we can shake the truth loose if the parties are unsuspecting. I'm going to Command so I can start checking some things out. Keep me posted."

"I will, sir."

"Oh, and Mat," North said before he terminated the link. "How many did we lose?"

"One hundred and fifty on the three destroyed ships," Drake reported somberly. "Casualty reports are still coming in from the

Santee. Probably around a hundred additional dead and wounded."

North stared down at the floor, jaw muscles tight. He paused for a moment and said, "Thank you, Admiral. North out."

North sat and stared at the blank screen. He angrily punched in the priority communication code for Alliance Command. The screen blinked to life, revealing a smartly dressed man bearing the insignia of a navy captain.

"Fleet Admiral Carlo's office. Captain Walker."

"I want to speak to Admiral Carlo. Now."

"I'm sorry, sir, but he's given orders not to be disturbed. Is it something I can help you with, sir?"

"Yes, Captain. Get the admiral right now. I'm giving you a direct order." North was growing irritated but resisted the temptation to take it out on Walker.

"Yes, sir. Just a moment."

Walker's face was replaced momentarily with a blinking "hold" message, and when it came back to life, it showed the bloated face of Admiral Carlo.

"North?" he said, the irritation plain on his face. "What's this all about? I have guests—"

"Admiral Carlo," North interrupted, "you will meet me in one hour at Supreme Commander Terred's office. Is that understood? We have some things to discuss."

"Can't this wait? I have—"

"I don't care if the president himself is there," North growled. "Be there in one hour." He abruptly severed the link.

Within fifteen minutes, he had showered and dressed, his uniform now clean and fresh after being in the cleaning unit. Lan surprised him in the hallway outside of his door as he exited his room.

"Everything okay, Brandon?"

"I'm sorry, Lan. I didn't mean to wake you. Something's come up. I have to go to HQ immediately."

Denara slipped out of the room into the hallway. "I planned for this. Your lasagna is in a stasis case in the back of your car. The sergeant put it in for me last night." As North walked toward the stairs, Denara couldn't resist. "Please check in on Rando once in a while, but don't tell him I said so."

North smiled and said, "You bet. Take care, you two."

The trip back to Command seemed to take forever. Drake contacted him again and said that Faulkner's fighters had captured the renegade ship. Unfortunately, the five crew members—all human—were found dead. The data banks had been wiped, but the *Endeavor's* technical staff was working on extracting anything they could from the remains of them.

Upon arriving at Supreme Commander Terred's office, North was glad to see that Terred was there, but Carlo hadn't yet arrived.

"It's inconceivable," Terred said. "Carlo a traitor? He *hates* the T'Kharr. How do you want to play it?"

North was about to respond when Terred's comm unit beeped.

"Sir, there's a Colonel Malone out here to see Commander North," his receptionist said. "He says it's urgent."

Terred looked at North. "Malone from Intel?"

North nodded his head and rose from his seat. "I called him. This won't take long, Dek. I'll be right back."

He exited Terred's office and saw Malone standing near the office manager's desk. Terred watched as North indicated one of the adjacent rooms, and they both walked inside and secured the door. At almost the precise moment the door shut, Carlo, with Captain Walker in tow, thundered past the receptionist and into Terred's office.

"What's the meaning of this?" he bellowed at Terred, who wore a carefully neutral look on his face. "I was entertaining Senator Price and his wife when North ordered me in."

Terred wanted North in here when he confronted Carlo, so he knew he'd better stall.

"Admiral, sit down."

Clearly unhappy, Carlo sat down heavily in the seat in front of Terred's desk. Terred made a pretense of studying a piece of paperwork in front of him and let Carlo sit and stew for a minute. After several minutes of uncomfortable silence, North finally entered the room, flanked by Colonel Malone.

"Well . . . Admiral Carlo," North said. "So nice to see you. And Captain . . . Walker, right?"

"What's the meaning of this, North?" Carlo began. "You interrupted a very important—"

"*Commander* North, Admiral," North ordered threateningly, silencing Carlo, his bald head turning a darker shade of red. "Be quiet." He went over to Terred's desk and activated the desktop holo-viewer. He commanded, "Playback," and the screen flickered to life with a representation of the moon, the eight ships from the *Challenger* fleet, and the *Achilles* slowly moving toward them. North paused the display.

"Do you recognize this representation, Admiral?"

"Yes. The moon with some of the *Challenger* ships in parking orbit, as I ordered. Senator Price wanted to tour some V.I.P.s through them. I felt with the number of ships in system, there would be no risk." Carlo looked puzzled.

"No risk?" North said incredulously. Suddenly, it dawned on him. "You haven't heard . . ."

"Heard what? I was ordered in here by you. I've been with the senator and his wife all evening. Then I spoke with Admiral Drake when I found out that you had ordered the ships back out on patrol. The senator was furious, by the way."

North glared at him and spoke, "Resume playback, with audio transmissions."

The *Achilles* approached the ships, discharging two smaller blips, then turned and headed away from the moon, increasing speed.

"Those are a pair of T'Kharr type two fusion missiles," North said, indicating the two blips on the screen.

"T'Kharr weapons?" Carlo said, his voice shaking slightly.

Carlo began to look ill, but he silently watched the drama unfold.

As the *Pacifica* rescue and damage control ships entered the field of view, North spoke, "End playback."

Carlo looked as if someone had kicked him in the stomach. He looked confused and frightened. "I, uh, don't know what to say."

North turned back and looked at where the screen had just been a moment before.

"Why were the command crews given leave contrary to regulations?" North asked accusingly. "Why were there only maintenance crews on board the ships and no gunners or senior officers? Why was the combat space patrol ordered to stand down? And why were the engines on those eight ships powered down and dead cold?"

"What do you mean?" Carlo yelled desperately. "I may have ordered the ships to parking orbit, but I never gave all of the command crews leave! I would never have left those ships defenseless!"

North turned toward him and said, "The Fleet Communications Monitor shows that the orders to power down and the shore leave orders for the command crew came from your office. Your personal transmission code, verified by D.N.A. scan, was used to issue the orders. How do you explain that?"

"But that's not true!" Carlo protested. "I never issued those orders!"

North said, "Then perhaps you can tell me the nature of the scrambled transmission that originated from your office to the *Achilles* fifteen minutes prior to the attack?"

"What?" Carlo was on his feet, his fists balled in frustration.

Terred looked at North, perplexed. "Brand, what transmission?"

North's eyes never left Carlo. "That was why I needed to speak with Colonel Malone. His people have been following leads on this case since it happened. He informed me a transmission was sent to the *Achilles* from Admiral Carlo's office. It also was verified with a DNA scan and with the Admiral's personal identification code. The frequency used was identical in frequency to a transmission detected from the Miratev system four days ago aimed toward T'Kharr space. The next day, the system was invaded."

"That's preposterous! Why would I be so obvious as to use my own code for sending these transmissions? I'm being set up!" Carlo slammed down his fist in frustration.

North regarded him for a moment and said, "I agree."

"W-what?" Carlo stammered.

Terred looked genuinely lost and said, "But Brand, I thought that—"

"Bear with me, sir," North said, holding his hands up. "It'll be clear in a minute."

Terred trusted North enough to know that he didn't go off half-cocked and that there was always a method to his madness. He sat back and waited.

"Admiral, do you know a young woman named Ariana Kidder?"

Carlo tensed. "She's a friend. What about her?"

"Intel has known for months about your affair with Miss Kidder. Col. Malone from Fleet Intelligence went with a security squad to visit Miss Kidder an hour ago. She claimed that a man dressed in civilian clothes approached her four months ago and offered her a large amount of money to take up with a certain admiral. She said that about a month ago, this same man approached her again and gave her a small device that she was instructed to place on the admiral's stomach—your stomach—when he fell asleep. The device was a cell collector. It collected enough cellular material from your stomach to be able to produce a clone."

"So, you're saying that someone cloned me, and that's how they verified these transmissions to make it appear that I had sent them?" Carlo asked.

Terred said, "So who is this mystery man, and where is the clone?"

"Well, sir, the colonel's men checked out the most likely leads and located the clone in a living unit. The spy's DNA was all over the place and on the cell collector found there."

North turned and looked directly into Captain Walker's eyes. "Isn't that right, Captain Walker? Only you could have gained access to the admiral's personal code. You sent the orders and the transmission to the *Achilles*."

Walker looked shocked. "Is this some kind of joke?" he sputtered. "Nonsense."

"You ever been interrogated by our intelligence unit, Captain?" North stared at him. "Let's go have a chat with you hooked up to a verifier and see what we can find out."

"Sir, I swear . . ." Walker started to rise, pausing as he felt the cold steel of a laser pistol at his temple.

"Sit down, Captain, or I'll burn you where you sit," Malone growled, tightening his grip on the nasty-looking pistol he held at Walker's head.

Walker slowly lowered himself back down into his chair, the expression on his face morphing from feigned innocence to contempt. Malone quickly relieved him of his sidearm.

"Why?" Carlo demanded. "Why would you do this?"

"Opportunity," Walker answered with a sneer. "Those ships were just too juicy a target to ignore."

"I'll see you executed for this, Walker," Carlo growled.

"I doubt it," Walker said defiantly. "The government, the military, you'll all answer for your crimes. Besides, you think I'm the only one involved in this?"

Suddenly, Walker slapped a small patch on Malone's ribs, and an explosion ripped open his chest and stomach, splattering Walker and Carlo with blood and gore. Walker grabbed for Malone's pistol as he fell and turned just in time to see the barrel of North's pistol staring him in the face.

"Don't be stupid, Walker," North said. "Don't make me kill you."

Walker quickly brought the gun up, and North felt the kick from the powerful pistol as Walker's head instantly blew apart in a splash of crimson, splattering the wall behind the chair with brain matter and hair. The headless body fell backward, propped against the wall, limp and lifeless.

"Damn," North said as he lowered his pistol.

Carlo was still sitting in his seat, shaking uncontrollably and wiping Malone's blood from his face with a handkerchief.

Terred stabbed at the comm button. "Get a medical team up here, immediately!"

North replaced his sidearm as two burly marine guards burst through the door, rifles at the ready.

"Stand down, Marines!" North barked.

As the medical personnel rushed past him and tended to Malone, one guard looked at North and Terred and said, "I'm sorry, sir, but the receptionist said there was an explosion in the room." He quickly turned to assist the corpsman who was currently placing Malone in stasis. Remarkably, Malone was still alive.

"Let's get out of their way and let them work," Terred said. "Gentlemen," he said to North and Carlo, "join me in the conference room please."

After moving to the conference room, Terred stood next to North and glanced at him, then turned and stared accusingly at Carlo. North was also staring at Carlo.

He noticed their stares and yelled, "You heard! It wasn't my fault. It was Walker!"

Terred said, "Walker didn't order those ships to orbit behind the moon. Walker didn't allow his personal command code to fall into enemy hands. You disobeyed fleet regulations to satisfy the whims of a spoiled, fat politician, the result of which cost us four ships and over 250 crewmen. Then you tried to convince Admiral Drake to disobey a direct order from *your* superior officer."

"I . . . I didn't mean for this to happen," Carlo whined.

"Your credibility and effectiveness is shot. If the circumstances surrounding this incident came to light, it would be quite embarrassing to both you and your family. A top Alliance admiral's aide, a T'Kharr spy, responsible for possibly engineering the fall of Miratev and the destruction of four ships in the heart of the Alliance."

Carlo stared at the floor, unable to think of any more defenses.

"I'll have my resignation on your desk by morning." He turned and silently walked out of the room, leaving Terred and North alone.

"You had me wondering, Brand," Terred said to North. "You had me convinced it was Carlo."

"I thought it was too. Malone and his people were moving at an incredible pace to follow the trail and provided the pieces. And despite Carlo's faults, I never thought him a traitor."

"Do you think Walker was lying about there being others?" Terred mused.

"I don't know, but you should bring Arlington in on this," North suggested.

"Agreed," Terred said. "Well, what do we do now?"

"Now we continue to plan the liberation of Miratev and find the confederate Walker had at the lab. Someone on Miratev sent that transmission to the T'Kharr, and it wasn't Walker."

Terred gravely nodded his head and exited the room, North one step behind.

Outside Terred's office, Vice Admiral Nelson Price stood, waiting. Marine guards had prevented him from entering the office, and he stood, irritated but subdued. North walked over to Price.

"Admiral Price," North said, regarding Price as something he'd blown from his nose into a handkerchief. "You left a skeleton crew onboard your ships, bunched them in orbit in violation of fleet protocols and my standing orders. Despite the fact that you issued orders to redeploy them, it happened too late. You knew better."

The irritation faded from Price's face as he realized that even his brother, the senator, couldn't help him now.

"You are relieved of your command, effective immediately. Out of respect for your family, I won't confine you to the brig. You will report to quarters on this base awaiting notification from the convening authority. And for your sake, I hope your brother knows someone at JAG. You'll need them."

"They killed Walker, found the clone, picked up Ariana, August is dead . . . it's falling apart. I'm next, I'm certain of it . . ." Kate Singer's voice hoarsely whispered into the comm unit. She kept her voice low, hoping it wouldn't echo off the walls of the lounge she'd ducked into.

"Calm yourself," said the voice of Arvil Symons from the comm unit. "We'll still be able to finish this, the two of us, and we'll both be rich beyond our wildest dreams. We'll have enough credits to buy a whole planet on the outer rim, away from everyone, including your parents. Attacking those ships was necessary in order to pacify our benefactors. I had to give them something to keep them calm after that idiot Vickers jumped the gun on Miratev."

"Remind me why we're doing this. I feel like I'm betraying Earth . . . It seems like too much—"

"You know why," Symons said, abruptly cutting her off. "Earth betrayed us a long time ago. The military killed our families in their experiment and then lied to cover it up. They deserve what's coming to them. We have too much invested in this. Too much at stake."

"I suppose," Kate said. "I . . . I just want it to be over."

"If my operative hadn't jumped the gun, had been certain the data was in the base computer, we wouldn't have to take this course of action," Symons stated grimly. "The buyers of the information are not the types you want to cross."

"I know, I know," she said, wiping her face with a cool rag. "I'd better be getting back. If I'm gone too long, they may get suspicious under the circumstances."

"Okay, but first, how did Walker die?" Symons inquired.

Singer paused for a moment, bracing herself for the reaction she knew would come.

"North shot him as he was trying to escape," she said, cringing at the howl of fury coming from the other end of the link.

"North again!?" Symons screamed, followed by sounds of items being thrown and broken.

"Why not just kill him and be done with it?" Singer hissed.

"No!" Symons shouted. "Death will come, but not until he's suffered! Suffered as much as we have!"

Silence, then, "I arrive in system in an hour." He abruptly severed the link.

Singer quickly stashed the comm unit in a pocket and checked herself in the mirror. She decided that she looked presentable and discreetly exited the lounge and returned to the office.

Later that afternoon, North sat at his desk in his office at Alliance HQ and reviewed fleet status along with several command changes that were necessary after the incident with Admiral Price's fleet.

As he reviewed the changes with Admiral Drake, his XO, a knock on his door broke his concentration, and Jeff Faulkner peeked in.

North blew out a breath and said, "About time. We have a lot of work to do. Pull up a chair. The briefing is at twelve hundred hours tomorrow."

Realizing that Drake was still on the comm, North said, "See you and Nathan tomorrow at twelve hundred, Mat. North out."

The link was cut, and North hit the intercom button, paging the yeoman who was seated outside the office North had commandeered. "Yeoman, stim drinks and something to eat. We have a long night ahead . . ."

Miratev, invasion day plus three

Jared heard them before he saw them. Pushing back the panic he felt in his chest and trying to keep as quiet as possible, he pushed back into the bush, his rifle pointed back toward the voices. He recognized the T'Kharr language, though he didn't understand it. He breathed deeply. If he panicked, the others would never know what happened to him.

Fatigue was setting in after three days of foraging missions and being cooped up in the cave. Spinnaker had finally succumbed to the effects of the neuron disrupter blast, leaving only the six of them out of a research staff of fifty. T'Kharr patrols were conducting a grid search—probably looking for the bunker—and were getting closer to their location every day. They would be forced to relocate soon.

The voices grew louder, and Jared pulled as many of the branches back into place as he could to cover his tracks. He'd remembered what Dram had said, that the T'Kharr senses of smell, hearing, and eyesight weren't as keen as a human's. He desperately hoped he was right.

"Donga chun do vand! Donga chun!"

The voice came from his left, and its owner came into view between the leaves. It was a nightmare on two legs, carrying a particularly lethal-looking rifle that needed at least two of its four arms to carry. The soldier walked past the bush, unaware of Jared's presence, followed by three more. As they went by, Jared got a close look at those rows of razor teeth he'd heard about.

This was closer than he'd ever wished to be to one of them. The last soldier was leading a large yistiden by a rope. Yistiden were large lumbering creatures with low intelligence that were indigenous to Miratev. Their meat was poisonous to humans, but Jared suspected that T'Kharr palates were not as discriminating. He guessed they were bringing the animal back to their camp for some fresh meat.

"*Vad chu vakka. Donga vand beal dorang! Gaaa, gaaaa, gaaaa!*" Whatever the soldier had said, all four of them seemed to find it amusing.

He listened to them laugh—at least the T'Kharr approximation of a laugh—and thought how odd it sounded. He'd never considered that the T'Kharr might have a sense of humor. Jared lay frozen, barely breathing, and listened as the voices went by and faded off to his right. He let out a heavy sigh and relaxed.

He lay there for a moment before clawing his way out of the bush and turned to head away from the path the soldiers had taken. He'd no sooner turned around than he found himself face-to-face with a fifth soldier who had just turned the corner, leading a second yistiden. It stopped not five feet in front of Jared and stared in surprise.

The T'Kharr soldier recovered quickly from its shock and backhanded Jared across his right cheek with one of its right arms. Jared's rifle went flying, and he flew back to the ground, momentarily stunned. Jared was fortunate that he hadn't been scratched by one of the paralyzing claws and tried to scramble backward away from the soldier. The soldier advanced on Jared, pointing its rifle menacingly at his head. Knowing that if he ran he would be cut down instantly, Jared stopped moving and lay still, staring back into the T'Kharr's wicked red eyes. A terrifying snarl spread across the soldier's face. Glancing at the animal and then at Jared, it touched a device secured tightly around its neck.

"Humans taste better than yistiden," it hissed, its translator amulet making the voice sound cold and metallic. "We'll eat well tonight."

Jared noticed that the soldier had edged closer to him. Too close. He remembered his training and that one of the T'Kharr's vulnerabilities was weak knee joints. He kicked out savagely with his right leg, catching the inside of its right knee joint. The soldier howled in pain, and Jared rolled out from under it and jumped to his feet. Throwing its rifle to the ground, the soldier howled with rage and drew a large, three-bladed knife. Jared looked around him for anything he could use as a weapon. His pulse rifle was nowhere in sight. The soldier was surprisingly agile, considering its bulk, and quickly advanced.

"You will pay for that, human," it growled through the translator. "I will make your death last." It slashed with the knife.

Jared stumbled backward, nearly tripping over a rock. He scooped it up in his hands, trying to hold it between himself and the knife. The soldier slashed twice, striking the rock and nearly severing Jared's fingers in the process. Jared realized that he wouldn't last long this way. When the soldier slashed again, he feinted as if to block, then ducked below the blade and smashed the rock into the same knee he'd kicked earlier. He heard bone snap and cartilage tear as the soldier dropped the knife and grabbed its knee with a howl of pain and fury.

Jared turned and ran, then tripped over his pulse rifle, quickly grabbing it. He pointed the muzzle in the direction of the soldier and pulled the trigger frantically, but nothing happened. The T'Kharr began to retrieve its rifle from the ground. Jared frantically threw the selector to full auto and fired. The rifle kicked violently, pulling Jared's aim low so that the rounds cut the T'Kharr's legs in half. The soldier fell hard onto its severed stumps while bringing its own rifle on target when Jared fired again.

One of the rounds from Jared's rifle pierced the T'Kharr rifle's energy cell, and the soldier was engulfed in a bright orange fireball.

Jared turned and ran as fast as he could, not looking back. The pounding in his ears obscured the soldier's screaming as he put distance between himself and the T'Kharr. Jared kept running until the sharp pain in his chest forced him to stop. He looked back, glad to see that nothing was pursuing him. Supporting himself against a tree, he gulped in deep gasps of air and became overcome with nausea. He spat out the bile taste from his mouth and wiped it with his sleeve. The other soldiers would soon realize that their companion was missing and find the body. He didn't want to be around for that.

Orienting himself, Jared realized with dismay that he was a mere half a kilometer from the cave. This patrol was a full kilometer closer to the cave than the one yesterday. They couldn't wait any longer. They had to move. Jared hustled back to the cave.

"Someone's coming," Jeenan hissed, pointing the particle pistol into the forest. She was relieved to see Jared's familiar form emerge from behind a tree and dart inside the cave.

"What happened to you?" Julie said, seeing the cuts and bruises on Jared's face and arms.

"T'Kharr patrol," Jared said, panting hard. "Not a half a klick from here. One almost had me for dinner." He touched his face and felt several long scratches. They were beginning to hurt.

"We need to leave right now," he said urgently.

Julie sensed there was something more and asked, "What's wrong? Are you okay?"

"Yeah, I'm fine," Jared replied unconvincingly. "Nothing that getting out of this hell

hole won't cure."

He fell silent as Julie cleaned and dressed his wounds with synthi-skin, and she decided not to push the issue. She peeled the adhesive from a hyperfeuron patch and stuck it behind his left ear. When the medicine was used up, it would flake away and fall off, as would the synthi-skin. Glend had located a nest of the Miratev equivalent of bats in the back of the cave. They were perfect for hyperfeuron production, so they now had a healthy supply.

Dram lumbered into view, rubbing sleep from his eyes. "When do we leave, Doctor Trent?"

"Now. As soon as we pack the gear."

"Now?" Kloke whined. "Why right this minute? This is the only shelter in the area. Where do you suggest we go?"

Jared fought back the urge to tell Kloke exactly where to go, but he had no time to trifle with him. "I think we should try for the bunker. It's got provisions and—"

"The bunker?" Kloke said incredulously. "Are you out of your mind? This is suicide! Walk fifty kilometers through the forest for some food? We have food right here and enough water for a long time."

In spite of himself, Dram questioned the wisdom of leaving the cave. Jeenan and Glend were speaking rapidly to each other in Jaaleadi.

"The T'Kharr are coming," Jared snapped, silencing them. "Here. Soon! We're dead meat, quite literally, if we stay here. The bunker has a transmitter, food, medical supplies, and it's hidden a lot better than this cave. I don't know its exact location, but Dram does."

Dram thought for a moment. "Perhaps we should travel at night. T'Kharr have lousy night vision."

Julie looked skeptical but nodded her head in assent. "You're the boss, Jared. I'm in."

Glend and Jeenan looked at each other, and Glend said, "We agree."

Kloke turned his back to the group. "Well, I'm not going anywhere. If they find me, I'll surrender. I never did buy all that propaganda about them dismembering their prisoners and eating them. Lancaster and Forbes got killed because they resisted. If they'd given up, they might still be alive."

Jared stalked toward Kloke. He spun Kloke around and belted him square in the mouth. The smaller man crumpled to the ground, blood dripping from a split lip and genuine fear in his eyes.

"If the T'Kharr find you, they'll interrogate you and find out where we're going. By the Creator, you will come with us, or I'll kill you myself right here and now!"

Kloke, eyes wide, scrambled up onto his feet. Julie looked at Jared, trying to decide if he really would've killed Kloke, and decided that it didn't matter. They had packing to do.

CHAPTER FIVE

Alliance Command, Earth

It was a beautiful, cloudless morning. The light breeze coming in from the ocean cooled the temperature down to a pleasant twenty-two degrees Celsius. An outside observer would never have guessed the tense atmosphere inside of the high command briefing room. Almost everyone was standing around the large oval table. Drake figured that if they felt like he did right now, they simply couldn't bear to sit still.

The acoustic dampening field that had been activated enhanced the buzz of voices in the room. Drake thought it sounded like they were inside of a bottle. He recognized almost everyone in the room. Newly promoted Commodore Nathan stood apart from everyone else, not yet feeling a part of the crowd. He had been given command of Admiral Price's fleets, and a single silver star now showed prominently on his collar. Marine General of the Armies Benjamin Austin, commander of the quadrant land-based forces, was seated at the far end of the table, carrying on a heated discussion with Fleet Admiral Lucille Arlington of Fleet Security and Intelligence and Brigadier General Kyle Logan, commander of *Pacifica's* marine detachment.

Several others were new faces. One female major wore the insignia of Research and Development, and two others, dressed completely in black with no insignia or rank, had to be black ops. The older of the two had a particularly nasty scar running from his right temple down to his upper lip. Most people would've had the scar repaired, but Drake figured the officer kept the scar as a memento of some past mission. On the opposite side sat Var Jent, Earth's liaison officer to the Jaaleadi, perched on a chair specially designed for Jaaleadi visitors.

Abruptly, Captain Hansen entered the room and barked, "Attention to orders!"

Terred and North strode into the room as everyone snapped to attention. The two men took their seats at the head of the table, and Terred said, "At ease. Please be seated, everyone."

Terred continued, "Thank you all for coming on such short notice. Ordinarily, I'd start out with the usual pleasantries, but this meeting is anything but ordinary.

"Brigadier Logan from *Pacifica*, which will serve as command ship in this operation, will serve as ground commander of the planetary landing force. General Austin has been given overall command of the marine landing force on this particular mission at Commander North's request."

Terred gestured toward the two figures in black and said, "This is Major General Tyler and Colonel Dunford from Omega Section, special ops."

Several raised eyebrows and looks of surprise fell upon the room's occupants. *Omega Section didn't* officially *exist*, Drake thought to himself. Their missions were above top secret. To not only acknowledge their existence but actually name two of their officers meant that things were indeed dire.

Motioning to North, Terred said, "Let's get to it."

"I'm sure by now you're all aware of the incident at the research station on Miratev Two and that the T'Kharr invaded three days ago," North said.

The majority of the people in the room slowly nodded their heads.

"What you may not know is the particular significance of this research station. The true nature of the research on Miratev was known only to a handful of people, but apparently, one of those few tipped the T'Kharr off and sent a signal to them just prior to the invasion.

"This information was considered too vital to even trust to secured channels. Whoever was responsible for sending the invasion signal was receiving intelligence from a deep cover spy at the highest level. The spy—Captain Walker, who many of you may recognize as Admiral Carlo's chief of staff—was discovered by one of our top intelligence officers but was killed before any interrogation could be held."

The room erupted into urgent, hushed whispering, and North paused for a moment, haunted by the memory of Walker's headless body.

North cleared his throat and continued, "We also believe the attacks on the *Challenger* fleet ships are somehow connected to the Miratev situation."

North turned to Dupree and said, "Major Dupree, please brief the assembled officers about the kinetic generator technology and ramifications of this attack."

Dupree stood and activated the holo simulation demonstrating, in the simplest terms, how kinetic energy technology functioned. The simulation concluded with a chilling recreation of a planetary shield being defeated by a kinetic generator torpedo being launched into a planet that resembled Earth. The time index sped up, compressing six hours into sixty seconds, as an ice wave enveloped the entire planet, leaving it a dark, frozen rock. The oceans had frozen solid, all life extinguished.

When the lights came back on, there was nothing but stunned silence.

Jett finally said, "What's the T'Kharr in-system presence?"

"They haven't moved in too many troops," North replied. "Only about four thousand or so have landed at last report. The planet isn't very large, and the research staff was small and non-military. We don't believe they're going to attempt to set up a lasting presence there. Miratev doesn't have any particular strategic significance, which is why it was chosen for this research station. They are, however, bringing in capital ships."

"Are the T'Kharr in possession of the technology?" Jett asked. "Didn't the researchers wipe the data banks per invasion protocol?"

"We believe that the T'Kharr recovered enough references in the database before the system auto-wiped to realize what they had found," North replied. "T'Kharr scientists are better at copying stolen technology than they are at creating it on their own. Doctor Gleen was also able to transmit that he had destroyed all of the shielding material they had manufactured thus far. Without having the shielding in place prior to construction of the generator, it would be impossible to build one. It'll take years for even our own scientists to reconstruct the lost data."

"Then why the urgency, Commander?" Var Jent asked. "Aside from the obvious fact that we have personnel on the planet in need of rescue, why must such a large force be risked? And why immediately?"

"This is why," North answered, activating a holo representation of the research complex on Miratev. The large main complex was easily visible on the edge of the southern continent, surrounded by heavy vegetation and forest. The image spun to a location due east of the complex, and a small building surrounded by crosshairs became visible at the base of a mountain range—so small that unless you knew where to look, you would easily miss it.

"Data backup bunker," North said matter-of-factly. "We don't know how much of the information is still there or if it's intact. If the bunker had self-destructed, we would've received a transmission from the C.S. relay buoy indicating such. None came in, so we must assume it's still intact. If they find it before we get there and retake the planet, the simulation Major Dupree just played will become a very real threat."

"Why not send in a team to destroy the bunker and the data?" Jett asked.

"The research is too valuable to the Alliance and nearly impossible to duplicate," Terred said. "To reconstruct the research already done, starting from scratch, would take years. If we are forced to destroy it rather than allow the enemy to obtain it, we will do so, but recovery is the primary goal."

Drake glanced at the Omega Section troopers sitting across the table, realizing just how significant their mere presence was, and asked, "Just how high are the stakes? Can we assume our fleets are considered expendable?"

North looked irritated at the question for a moment but then decided that it was a valid query and deserved an answer. He stood and walked toward the holo image of Miratev. He cleared his throat and paused before saying, "In the event that we are unable to secure or destroy the technology and ensure that it hasn't fallen into enemy hands . . ." He paused again, glancing sideways at Terred, who nodded gravely. "We will introduce a stellar conversion device into the Miratev star—"

"Commander," General Tyler objected and was silenced with a sharp look from North. Tyler bit his tongue, then sat back again and remained quiet. The existence of such devices was highly classified.

Bleak realization dawned on not only Drake, but all the rest of them as well. It wasn't just the fleets that were expendable. Command would actually detonate the Miratev star, sacrificing not only the fleets, but the planet itself and all life within the system. No starlane travel to the burnt-out system would be possible thereafter, and travel in adjoining systems would be affected forever.

North paused before saying, "Everyone needs to understand the gravity of the situation."

Dupree, who was listening in disbelief, leaned over and whispered to Hansen, "Is he crazy? What if there are people and troops still on the planet? Doesn't he realize—"

"Yes, Major," Hansen hissed, a sober look on his features. "He knows. He knows better than anyone."

Eight years earlier, the nerve agent that the T'Kharr had released on Mandis had driven the population hysterical with paranoia. The nerve agent was 100 percent contagious, even having the ability to breach seals on spacesuits and ships, and 100 percent fatal after exposure. Containment was of paramount concern. The images of the Mandis colonists, driven to a state beyond madness, committing unspeakable violence and mutilations, even cannibalism and sexual atrocities on themselves and anyone else near them, was too much to bear. None were spared: not the young, the old, the infirm, no one.

All attempts at providing assistance to the population were met with unspeakable, mindless violence and murder. After several failed attempts at assistance and numerous additional rescue crew casualties, it was decided that no further rescue attempts would be risked, and the planet was abandoned. The public was told that the entire population of Mandis had died and that the planet was quarantined and rendered completely uninhabitable. Travel was strictly prohibited to the system, under penalty of death. At least that's what the general population thought. Few in the room knew what had really happened to Mandis and its colonists. Drake had long suspected, after that day eight years earlier, but had never broached the subject with North.

It was the only other time that a stellar converter device had been deployed. North knew that, because he had issued the order to destroy the system himself, and Omega Section had carried it out. Trading two hundred thousand lives to preserve thirty billion was a heavy burden to bear, even when there was no alternative.

"Does the enemy know about the existence of these stellar disrupters?" Nathan asked.

"We don't believe so," North replied. "Very few people know of their existence, and we'd like it to stay that way."

North was met with sober nods. He nodded to Faulkner, then took his seat again.

Faulkner stood and expanded the holo image of Miratev to include the entire system. The starlane portals—three in all—were highlighted in yellow, while enemy units were designated in crimson. In the midst of the T'Kharr fleet were two gray blips, showing on the holo as "asset."

Drake knew what they were immediately: subs—small, fragile ships able to slip quietly in and out of systems in order to gather intelligence. They were constructed out of a material that was practically invisible to enemy scanners. While the ship was about the size of a small shuttle, containing a four-man crew, it only gave off a signature the size of a bumble bee. The ships were also practically invisible to the naked eye, the color blending in with whatever background was there. Their obvious advantages came with several disadvantages. The stealth material the ships were constructed from was very fragile by modern standards, strong enough to withstand space travel, but even a glancing strike by an energy weapon could shatter the hull as a hammer would shatter glass.

They were equipped with standard Dukand drives for insertion, but once they exited the starlane, all power output went to zero to avoid detection. In-system, the craft maneuvered using a top-secret drive that relied on momentum and gravitational forces for course corrections. They were relatively slow in stealth mode but extremely effective when in position. All scanners and detectors onboard were passive, nothing active that would give away their position.

The craft were armed with eight heavily shielded torpedoes, the extra shielding necessary so that they would give off no energy signature when approaching an enemy ship. Although they were equipped with torpedoes if called upon to use them, their primary job was not offensive; it was to listen. They were also designed to be able to piggyback intelligence data in an encrypted form that blended in with the background radiation of the sun, allowing the crew to relay information. The T'Kharr had something similar, but little was known of them or their capabilities.

"As you can see, there is a significant T'Kharr presence in the system, at least two heavy carrier groups with more on the way," Faulkner said. "Miratev has three starlane portals, all of which are most certainly mined by now. That will be the first problem to deal with.

"The Jaaleadi have committed two carrier groups to the mission and have asked us to formulate the battle plan. We will present it to them and seek their input on the details tomorrow when they arrive. We need to enter the system via the three starlane portals at the same time, hoping to not only catch them off guard but also to cut off any escape routes. A ground force of six thousand marine raiders will land and engage the T'Kharr occupation forces. We will leave the system and be underway for Miratev in two days from now."

"Commander," Drake said, "do we have any assets at all that are in a position to try and secure the bunker before we arrive? By the time we arrive, a week will have passed."

A smug grin appeared on General Tyler's face, and he said, "That's what we do best, Admiral. Things are in motion as we speak . . ."

In orbit above Miratev Two

The eight heavily armed men and women waited in silence as they perched on the hull of the T'Kharr supply tender that was entering orbit around Miratev Two. The transparent stealth bubble covering them molded to the hull of the enemy ship, allowing the soldiers to see the land masses clearly on the surface.

For a full solar day, they'd waited in this position after sneaking onto the hull of the ship from an Alliance sub. The space suits they wore processed bodily wastes and kept the wearer protected in the blazing radiation of space, in addition to scrubbing CO_2 from their air supply. Each figure wore a state-of-the-art High Altitude Low Operation (HALO) harness covering the helmeted space suits.

HALO may have described their equipment, but these were no angels. Omega Team Five always got the most difficult assignments. The team was volunteer only, and none of them wanted to be anywhere else in the entire universe.

"Sixty seconds, people," team leader Lieutenant Victor Remy whispered.

The T'Kharr ship fired braking thrusters, slowing to a speed that would allow them to enter the atmosphere. As they crossed the polar ice cap, Remy saw their objective on his heads-up display.

"Ten seconds," Remy hissed, sucking in a lungful of air.

Abruptly, the stealth covering vaporized, and all eight bodies released from the ship, pointing downward toward the surface. Remy and his team picked up speed as gravity took hold of them. Once they were far enough away from the T'Kharr ship, he activated the atmo entry shield, allowing them to cut through the thick atmosphere and accelerate. Once they reached sixty thousand feet, he spread his arms and legs, activating the HALO decelerators. Remy felt as if all of his internal organs would come through the front of his body, driven by inertia.

"Separation in three, two, one, mark."

Remy's team fanned out to the sides. Their objective appeared in crosshairs on his heads-up display. Remy spotted a small clearing and pointed toward it, the team following. The decelerators compensated, and as they touched the planet surface, they'd slowed enough that they were able to jog to a quick stop.

Once on the ground, Petty Officer First Class Reggie Keever and Sergeant Kara Sulak drew side arms and scanned the woods, looking for any sign of activity while the rest of the team wasted no time stripping off their harnesses and suits and armed their Tarantula assault rifles. Remy quickly darted toward the cover of the woods, followed by the team. His camouflage battle dress adjusted to match the hue and color of the surrounding vegetation.

"Activate your hardware," he hissed while the team stashed their extra gear under a pile of brush. "Status check."

Each member of the team closed their eyes tightly for a moment, activating their telesponder implants. Remy's team could now communicate without speaking out loud.

<Henna, check,> said a female voice, Lieutenant J.G. Amanda Henna, Remy's second-in-command.

The remaining soldiers quickly checked in.

While Remy obtained bearings to the bunker, Henna sent, <Keever, send the code.>

Keever nodded without a word and pointed a small device in the air, searching for a return carrier. When the light on the readout illuminated, Keever hit the transmit button, sending the code back to Earth advising they'd achieved planetfall and were proceeding to the objective. The message wouldn't be received for several hours.

<Dammit. We overshot our target by about thirty klicks,> Remy sent.

<Guess we're humping it,> Henna sent.

<Fan out,> Remy projected to his team. <Standard dispersal. Kill anything that looks T'Kharr. Kenyon, take point.>

Well trained, the team did as instructed, slipping into the forest and heading toward the mountain range in the distance without a sound.

CHAPTER SIX

SAS Pacifica, officers' lounge

Several of the *Pacifica's* junior officers sat around a table in the officers' lounge, mulling over the coming op. They were presently being entertained by Ensign Devin "Gambler" Truant and his last trip to the rumor mill.

"I'm telling ya, it's gotta be something big," Truant said to nobody in particular at the table. "There's no other explanation. The old man's on the planet at HQ getting another promotion. North wants to have as many people as possible here to see him get it."

"You're so full of crap, Gambler," a woman sporting lieutenant JG bars said. Adel "C Note" Franklin, who was sitting across from the man, smirked at the comment, her caramel skin glistening in the light. "Who told you that North was getting promoted?"

"I happen to have a very reliable source of information on the *Victory* who told me so," he said, taking a sip from his drink. "He said the old man is taking over Terred's job."

Ensign Devin "Gambler" Truant got his call sign not due to his gambling prowess, but the exact opposite. Truant could've been the Alliance recruitment poster boy with his short cropped brown hair, brown eyes, and pilot's physique. At the moment, his young age of eighteen years was showing, to the amusement of his squadron mates.

"Well, I think you heard wrong, or your friend did," Jake "Cooler" Randall said, shaking his head. Randall flashed a bright grin, his perfect white teeth contrasting against his dark complexion. He sported the dual bars of a full lieutenant on his collar.

"You're way off base, Gambler," Franklin said. "Chen has the flight bay prepping and checking every single fighter on the ship. This isn't for fleet day. It's an op. A big one. When's the last time you saw five heavy carrier fleets in the same system besides home-fleet?"

"Well, whatever it is, I wish someone would tell us," Truant said, taking another gulp from his drink. "The suspense is driving me crazy."

"You just want to paint that third T'Kharr symbol on your ship, kid," one of the other pilots piped in, an Amazon of a blonde, Lieutenant Valerie "Blue Eyes" Davis. "Don't be so anxious. I don't think the war will end before you can make ace. You've only been on the ship for two months."

"That's easy for you to say, Val," Truant grumbled. "You've already made ace *and* lieutenant. I'm just in a slump. When's the last time Trent let me fly recon patrol? The last five engagements were over practically before we even got to the launch bay."

"Listen, kid, you'll have plenty of uglies to shoot at soon enough," Davis chastised, her blue eyes locked to Truant's. "The waiting list for this ship is a mile long. Consider yourself lucky."

"Yeah, maybe you're right. Hey, there's Annaline." He gestured with his chin as Lt. Vale walked into the lounge and went to the dispenser for a beverage. They motioned her over to take a seat. She sat down heavily, exhaustion showing plainly on her face. Dark circles showed under her eyes.

"Geez, Annie, you look wiped," Randall observed.

"There's been so much comm traffic since we got here, I can hardly squeeze in a break," Vale said. "And too many friggin' admirals. Captain Frost brought in another communications officer to handle the escort traffic while I took care of the inter-fleet stuff. Things have just been crazy ever since the attack yesterday. I think this attack was deliberately planned for when the brass were all down on the planet at some big meeting. Someone doesn't want them to do whatever they're planning to do. I think that something big is coming down."

Randall rose from his chair. "Well, I hate to run, but I didn't realize how late it was. Me and Tuck are scheduled for a simulator run tonight. Gotta keep those skills sharp if I'm going to stay ahead of the soon-to-be ace here." He gestured toward Truant.

"I really should get going too," Vale sighed, downing her drink in one swig. "I'm beat. Gonna hit my rack. I'll see you guys later."

"I'll go with you," Davis said.

"Aw, come on, you guys," Truant complained. "The night's still young."

"Sorry, Gambler," Davis said as she stood to her full six-foot height and smoothed out her uniform. "Need my beauty sleep." She and Vale headed out of the room.

"Well, I guess it's just us then," Truant said to his glass.

Just then, the computer chirped, "Ensign Truant, report to the flight bay immediately."

"Acknowledged," he spoke, puzzlement clouding his features as he looked at his wrist chronometer.

"I wonder what's up this late," he said to himself as he jumped up and trotted out toward the hallway and the lift.

Devin Truant entered the port flight bay and went directly to Captain Trent's office. Trent noticed him and motioned him inside.

"Reporting as ordered, sir," he said a bit shakily. He wondered to himself what he'd done now.

"Lt. Syndergaard took a spill in a stairwell earlier, and the flight surgeon wants him to stay in sickbay for a shift for observation. You are assigned to cover his shift for recon duty. Your wing commander is Lt. Duncan."

He straightened up and said, "Yes, sir. Thank you, sir."

He spun on one heel and marched out the door. Once he'd rounded the corner and was sure he was out of sight, he broke into a dead run toward the flight prep area and let out an excited yell. He was too far away to hear the laughter coming from Trent's office after his yell.

He quickly suited up and met Lt. Kelly "Yo Yo" Duncan in the launch bay. At just under five foot two with jet-black hair and dark eyes that were enhanced by her pale skin, she didn't appear much of a threat. She was, however, one of the finest pilots in the fleet, with twelve confirmed kills to her credit, three of those on a single mission.

As Truant approached her, she said, "Ready for this, Gambler?"

"You bet . . .uh . . . Yo Yo?" he said.

"A bad joke from flight school. One of my ancestors made a children's toy. The name stuck." She regarded the young Ensign and said, "You ever flown starlane recon before?"

"Negative. Mostly escort duty. I managed to bag a transport and a fueler at Arcturus, but no fighter engagements."

"Well, I'd be surprised if this was anything other than a milk run. We have a large presence in-system. Stay on my wing, and listen to my instructions."

She headed toward her fighter. Truant climbed into his own ship and engaged his helmet interface. Duncan's soprano voice came over his helmet.

"Gambler, system check."

"All green, Lieutenant," he said. His hands were trembling slightly. He hadn't been this nervous since his final exam at the Academy.

Duncan's voice came over the comm. "Recon One and Recon Two ready for launch."

"Clear for launch," said the voice of the controller. "Happy hunting."

"Okay, Gambler. Let's go earn our pay." She taxied out to the marked spot in front of her and felt the catapult lock onto her forward gear. She looked to the side and saw that Gambler was also locked and ready.

She counted off, "In three, two, one, launch." She punched her thrusters and felt the inertial compensators push her forward slightly before adjusting for the acceleration. The two fighters shot out of the flight deck and into open space. Truant took position below her starboard wing.

Duncan watched as the target coordinates scrolled onto her heads-up display, and she said, "Okay, we're heading to the Castor portal."

"Isn't that where the ship that fired those missiles yesterday was heading to?" Truant asked.

"Yeah," she said. "I see the rumor mill is in full swing on the ship."

Truant cringed slightly, not knowing if that was common knowledge yet or not.

Duncan reoriented her fighter. The Castor portal was located between the system's asteroid belt and the orbit of Jupiter. "Thirty-minute ETA until we're on station."

"Copy."

The next thirty minutes went fairly quickly. Duncan told Truant to use the time to review recon protocols and procedures. When they were within a hundred thousand kilometers of the primary reconnaissance buoy, his receiver crackled to life.

"Sol CA-15 to approaching craft. You are being painted. Please transmit your identification codes."

Duncan's calm, experienced voice came over Truant's helmet. "Copy, CA-15. This is Recon One from *Pacifica* battle group on station for recon patrol. Transmission commencing."

He envied her calm demeanor, especially when they were being targeted by one of the powerful defense platforms that were protecting all the starlane portals leading into the home system. No confirmation and they would fire. He was as nervous as if he were on a first date.

"Identity confirmed. Glad to have you guys here. After yesterday, we're a bit jumpy." The controller's voice was warmer and friendlier now.

"I can imagine," Duncan replied. "If there are any bad guys out there, we'll bag em'." Then after a pause, "Hey, is that you, Hoskins?"

"Kelly? I thought I recognized your voice. What's new? I lost track of you after the Academy."

"Gambler, let me introduce you to Jimmy Hoskins. Computer nerd and all-around pain in the butt. We were in the Academy together." Her Fleet Com receiver suddenly blinked to life.

"Recon One, Recon Two, this is *Pacifica*."

"Go *Pacifica*," Duncan responded, all business again.

"Prepare to receive new orders. Coming through your navigation computers now." The data scrolled onto her screen.

"Copy, *Pacifica*. Will advise upon arrival. Recon One out. You copy the orders, Gambler?"

He'd copied them, all right. He still couldn't believe it. They were sending him and Duncan through the portal alone to check out an anomalous reading on the Castor side.

"Aye, Lieutenant, but . . ." Truant started.

Duncan cut him off abruptly, "Hold your comments until we're in the starlane. Then we can talk freely."

"Copy that," Truant replied, frustration in his voice. He should've known better. Rookie mistake, discussing ops on an unencrypted open comm.

Duncan checked her systems again to assure that her Psyton shields were charged and functioning properly.

"Sorry, Jimmy. Gotta go. We'll play catch up later. Ready, Gambler?"

"Aye, Lieutenant. Spooling up Dukand drive, now at .0012 light speed relative. Approaching the portal entrance."

"Copy. Activate your shields."

Truant touched a pad on his console. The Psyton shields hummed to life and surround his tiny craft with the protective barrier he would need to traverse the distance between Sol and Castor in the strange realm of compressed space. He glanced over at Duncan's ship and saw the light-blue haze surrounding her ship as well.

"Here we go," Duncan said over his helmet as they breached the barrier from normal to compressed space.

Truant had been through the starlanes many times on larger ships, but this was the first time he'd actually done it in a fighter. The surrounding space seemed to crackle with unbridled energy and fire. Lights streaked past him and up from behind him. It was said that if you stared into the energies long enough, the effect was euphoric, like a narcotic, robbing you of your sensibilities and will.

More than one pilot, having succumbed to this "rapture of the lanes," had inexplicably turned off his shields, destroying himself instantly. New psych screening methods were now employed so that all fighter pilots were immune to its effects. Still, looking out a viewport was quite different from seeing the effect from his cockpit, which afforded him a view from all sides. It was mesmerizing.

Duncan's concerned voice came over his helmet. "Gambler? You all right?"

Truant shook his head momentarily and concentrated on the business at hand.

"I'm okay. It's just that I've never been in a starlane in a fighter before. In sims, yeah, but not in reality. It's a bit overwhelming."

"As long as you're okay. Don't want you rapturing on me."

"No chance, ma'am. Computer estimates ETA for Castor nine hours."

"Scan for any free-floating matter in the lane. You see those particles of stellar material off to starboard?"

Truant checked the area she was referring to on his screen and said, "Yeah, I see them."

"You notice that they're traveling faster than we are?"

"Yeah. How can they do that? They're not under power."

"I'm gonna show you one of the tricks of the trade that they don't teach you in flight school. Those particles are caught in a kind of compressed space riptide. Only something as small as a fighter can use them. It's an unorthodox procedure and does have some risks, the biggest being that if you enter the riptide at too sharp of an angle, your ship can be torn apart due to the shear forces. We've been authorized to make use of the riptides to expedite our arrival at Castor. It'll cut down our travel time to about five hours."

Duncan edged her craft slightly toward the riptide, and Truant dropped in behind her.

"Inertial compensators don't work as well in compressed space, so brace yourself," she warned. "It's like diving into a fast rushing river."

Truant's fighter began to vibrate as they approached the riptide. As they eased into the current, he was pushed deep into the cushioning of his seat as his acceleration instantly doubled. Duncan's fighter blurred slightly in front of him, but after a few seconds, he could see her clearly again. Then, as suddenly as it had hit them, all was serene. He looked out to his side and saw bits of glowing matter floating motionless as if suspended in solid crystal. He realized, however, that it was only an illusion and the particles were, in fact, traveling as fast as he was. He immediately noticed his pounding headache. It quickly subsided as medication was automatically administered to compensate.

Duncan said, "Why don't you get some sleep? I'll wake you in a couple of hours."

"Yes, ma'am," he replied as he put his ship onto auto pilot. He laid his head back and thought about how he could screw up again today by opening his mouth. Oh well, at least he couldn't screw up for the next two hours. He pushed the thoughts to the back of his mind and drifted off to sleep.

CHAPTER SEVEN

Imperial planet T'Kharr Vod, Phaeda Tertiary, Imperial Palace

Alta-Tar-Vel Da'akta Te'eq hated coming to the palace. It was a stinking, festering monument to suffering, corruption, and greed. But one did not refuse a command from the shi'ia-khar, not if one wished to live. The sprawling black spires, which were constructed using slave labor at the cost of hundreds of lives, seemed to touch the sky. The surfaces of the building were black chrome and appeared damp and slimy as they glistened in the hot Phaeda sun. He walked up to the gated entry, the sun glistening off the rank insignias on his blood-red uniform, showed his identification, and strode through.

After entering the vast, dark foyer full of art and sculptures from their many conquered worlds, he had to make his way through the many individuals trying to gain access to the throne room, hoping to be granted an audience with the shi'ia-khar. Many were females, wishing to be brought out of whatever circumstance they were in, willing to be sexually debased by his highness or by his imperial guard, the Shi'ia-kree. A wall of guards blocked access to all but those approved to approach the massive throne room doors. They immediately parted for the soldier, and he approached the doors.

Two hulking, heavily armed Shi'ia-kree guards dressed in black chrome armor blocked access to the throne room itself and abruptly demanded credentials. Although they were members of the military, the Shi'ia-kree derived their authority directly from the royal family and bowed to no one else, not even the supreme head of the T'Kharr military, Alta-Tar-Vel Da'akta Te'eq.

After examining the tar-vel's identification and giving him a once-over, the guard grunted and opened the platinum-gilded doors leading to the throne room. When the doors opened, cries and pleading came from the crowd, each hoping to enter the sanctum. As he entered, prostrating and kneeling priests flogged, slashed, and otherwise mutilated themselves for the shi'ia-khar's enjoyment. The religious sect was always so dramatic. Other petitioners and politicos who had made it past the guards waited patiently to be called as the shi'ia-khar's herald announced who could approach next. A full company of Shi'ia-kree lined the walls of the room.

As Te'eq approached the throne, he noted with interest that on each side of the seat were three torture palettes, each occupied by an individual. The left three he recognized as the heads of the shi'ia-khar's internal security unit and Shi'ia-kree and the head of the Imperial Advisory Council. The ones on the right bore a military officer, the shi'ia-khar's eldest son, and his mother—one of the shi'ia-khar's many mates—sentenced to torture and death for the latest coup attempt. Although the mother had no part in the plot, the shi'ia-khar decided to punish her for producing a traitor.

Each of the prisoners had been stripped naked to add to their humiliation, their coverings having been piled at the bottom of the palettes, after which they had been splayed onto the palette and had pain enhancers driven into every available orifice. Each had had his or her vocal chords severed and had a med dispenser that administered anti-shock drugs to the victims, assuring they didn't lose consciousness from fatigue or pain.

He then directed his full attention to the throne and its occupant; Shi'ia-khar Tri'in Du'uk Va'al Vod Ke'el. He was dressed in his black-and-gold imperial robes, under which he wore a gilded harness that covered his groin area and chest. The tips of the spikes on his head and chin were covered in gold and glistened in the light of the chamber. The throne upon which he was seated was made of various precious jewels and metals found on their many worlds. The scepter he held in his left upper claw was made of platinum and a luminescent stone that had the appearance of jade. The many bladed edges of the scepter made it not only a symbol of the shi'ia-khar's authority and station but would also serve as a fierce weapon if needed.

The shi'ia-khar looked up as Te'eq approached the throne, then cleared all civilians from the immediate area and activated a privacy field, allowing the shi'ia-khar and Te'eq to converse in private. Te'eq glanced into those obsidian eyes, a trait of the ruling class, same as Te'eq, and dropped to a knee, spreading his arms wide with palms up.

"Your humble servant, Te'eq, Highness. Obedience brings honor. Glory to the Empire."

The shi'ia-khar nodded approvingly and said, "Rise, honored Da'akta Tar-Vel. What is the progress on acquiring the technology?"

Te'eq arose and stated, "The informant was correct about the nature of research on the planet. Unfortunately, as we moved in, it was learned that the information had been destroyed in the primary banks and had been transferred to a backup location somewhere on the planet."

"Prisoners?" he demanded.

"None that provided any useful information. Some may have escaped, and they are being searched for now."

The shi'ia-khar looked irritated, a dangerous mood for him. Te'eq knew that a wrong word or incomplete report could be disastrous for the bearer, even the shi'ia-khar's childhood friend.

"The humans will not sit still for this," the shi'ia-khar said. "They will move in their own reinforcements."

"It will take the humans time to gather a fleet of sufficient strength to challenge us," Te'eq answered. "By the time they arrive, we should already be in possession of the technology."

The shi'ia-khar nodded his head approvingly. "Execute the commander responsible for failing to secure the information from the primary data bank before it was destroyed," he said, the annoyance plain in his voice. "Do not allow him the honor of Terek-Va."

Terek-Va, or ritual suicide, was expected when a major mistake was made.

"Do what must be done to gain this technology," the shi'ia-khar said in a tone Te'eq recognized as a dismissal.

"It will be done, Tri'in Shi'ia-khar," Te'eq said, then spun on his heel and exited the room. The shi'ia-khar would have ordered the death of anyone else who dared refer to him in such a familiar term, but he and Te'eq had been friends for many cycles, since they were hatchlings.

As Te'eq breached the privacy field, it fell, revealing the expectant faces of the petitioners. As Te'eq walked toward the exit, the shi'ia-khar scanned the crowd and noticed a young male standing next to another male who wore councilor's robes.

The young male, feeling the shi'ia-khar's penetrating stare, averted his gaze. His heart began to race with fear, which proved justified when the shi'ia-khar said, "You," referring to him. "You will amuse me by engaging in combat with one of my Shi'ia-kree."

"Forgive me, Tre'elen," the councilor hissed, seeing the fear in his companion's eyes. "You cannot refuse."

With one last fearful glance at the councilor, he obediently walked up to the area in front of the shi'ia-khar, glancing fearfully at the torture palettes and their occupants, and accepted the large bladed weapon provided to him by one of the guards. A moment later, another guard, dwarfing the young male by a good foot, came out to face him and smiled as he drew his own blade. The young male held the blade awkwardly, his black eyes growing wide at the sight of the guard.

The shi'ia-khar regarded the councilor for a moment and said, "I will hear your petition immediately afterward, Councilor, as a reward for your loyalty to the realm, and provided your ward does not disappoint." A sick, sadistic smile graced his face as he waved his hand and shouted, "Begin!"

As soon as combat began, all the other petitioners who had companions dismissed them discreetly, hoping they wouldn't meet the same fate as the councilor's ward.

Castor starlane

"Lieutenant?" Truant said, worried. "Lt. Duncan, wake up."

Duncan stirred restlessly, still groggy from only an hour of sleep. "What's the problem?"

"I'm not getting a signal from the buoys at the exit portal. They all just went silent."

Duncan instantly awoke and checked her board. "That's not good. The odds of all three buoys going dark at once due to mechanical problems are astronomical. I want to see the last images just before they went down."

"Aye, Lieutenant. Transmitting." Truant punched buttons on his console and sent the visual and data images over to Duncan's fighter as he watched them himself.

"There!" she exclaimed. "You see it?"

"See what?" Truant replied, confused. "I don't see anything."

"Replay it again, and highlight the lower right portion of the image."

Truant did as he was told and still didn't see anything at first. Then he saw it, something that wasn't giving off any light at all. Most objects in space reflected some light, even background starlight. There was only one thing known to them that defied this universal law.

"Is that what I think it is?" Truant asked, excitement building in his chest.

"That, Gambler, my friend, is a T'Kharr sub. This is the first one I've seen. Every time someone gets close to one, the blasted thing has the bad manners to run away or self-destruct. Our science boys would give their right arms—or appendages, as it were—to take a close-up look at one of those babies. These are stealth weapons. Hit and run. And believe me, they are very hard to hit. Imagine trying to get a visual sighting on a target out here. No tracking computers."

"So, what can we do?" Truant asked, starting to feel nauseous.

"When we exit the portal, hit your thrusters and run like hell," Duncan said. "And hope your chosen vector isn't directly into the sub's flight path."

Truant could hear the tension creeping into Duncan's voice. Obviously, she didn't feel the odds were in their favor either.

Truant had been considering his options for thirty minutes when an idea popped into his head.

"Lieutenant, me and my Academy buddies used to do drills at the firing range where we'd shoot at targets using our peripheral vision only," Truant said. "We were just screwing around, but I was class champion."

"Gambler, that's nice but what—" Duncan started to say when Truant interrupted her.

"Let me finish, Lieutenant. This may sound crazy, but it just might work. What if we were to send a probe through just before we exited the starlane? They probably figure they have several seconds after we exit to target us and fire their torpedoes. I could concentrate my vision on the center of the probe's visual feed, and in that second before we exit, I might be able to pick him up out of the corner of my eye and take a shot at him. I can put my cannons on manual."

Duncan was silent for several moments. "What was your hit percentage?"

Truant smiled to himself and said, "Ninety percent. I've got the certificate in my cabin to prove it."

After several seconds, she said, "You're on, Gambler. I hope your shooting skills are better than your poker skills."

"Yes, ma'am," he said as he ran the calculations. "I'll need you to fire the probe exactly twenty seconds before we emerge into Castor."

"Copy," Duncan said as she entered the commands. "Countdown will commence at twenty seconds prior to your entry into Castor. I'll be directly behind you."

"Copy," said Truant as he concentrated on the center of his currently blank screen. He could feel his heart racing.

After thirty more minutes, the computer's voice chimed in. "Countdown commencing. Twenty seconds . . . nineteen . . . eighteen."

"Probe away," Duncan said.

"Weapons armed," the computer continued as Truant gripped the joystick tightly in front of him. "Manual control verified. Thirteen . . . twelve . . . eleven . . ."

Truant's thumb brushed the firing stud on the stick, assuring that when the time came, he wouldn't hit the wrong button.

"Six . . . five . . ." the computer continued.

Truant was barely conscious of the computer's voice, dutifully counting down the seconds.

"Three . . . two . . . one . . ."

As his brain registered the computer's voice counting down to one second, the screen he'd been concentrating on abruptly blinked to life. In his peripheral vision, he noted the small spot on the screen, a darker black area against an already black background. The object began to move.

"Zero. Normal space."

Instantly, Truant and Duncan materialized into the Castor star system. Truant quickly hit the firing stud on his stick, and two powerful bolts of raw energy leapt from his cannons. The beams swept up and across the position where he'd noticed the telltale spot, and there was a momentary flare of light as the beams made contact with something. Truant had to blink several times to get his eyes to adjust, but when they did, he saw something he'd never seen before.

It was gunmetal gray and shaped like an almond with stubby appendages sticking out all over every surface. The vessel crackled with residual energy from the laser strike and appeared to be blinking on and off. As the ship turned its tail toward Truant, the blinking ceased, and the ship was in plain view, the laser strike apparently having overloaded the shielding mechanisms.

"Bullseye, Gambler!" Duncan exclaimed as she hit her thrusters to pursue. "You nailed him. He's turning tail to run. Let's get him!"

Truant was way ahead of her, however, and hit his thrusters a split second before Duncan, already in hot pursuit.

The sub accelerated sharply and began a fast run toward the far side of the system. Truant had his throttles on full but was barely able to keep pace with the small sub. On his heads-up display, a readout near the top labeled "enemy status" blinked. The status bar showing enemy engine condition was moving higher into the danger zone.

"He must know that he's going to burn up," Truant said. "What's he doing?"

"There's a starlane portal to Beta Aurigae dead ahead," Duncan said, satisfaction in her voice. "He's trying to jump out. He'll never make it in time."

"He's slowing!" Gambler shouted. "Down to .30 light speed. Coming into range."

"He's spinning around to bring his forward tubes to bear on us. Lock him up quick, Gambler, or we're in it deep. I'm too far back to get a lock."

"Target locked," the computer intoned, and Truant immediately launched two flechette missiles.

"Break right!" Duncan yelled as she broke left and Truant peeled off to the right.

Truant switched his scanner to a rear perspective and watched as the two missiles touched their target and detonated in a spectacular flare of white-blue light and fire. Truant felt the shockwave's vibrations and saw the wave front on his scanner. He quickly turned his ship to give a minimal aspect to the wave and tightly grasped the handles built into the sides of his flight chair.

Truant shook his head and checked himself for damage. To his relief, he was uninjured, and all systems on his ship were functioning normally.

"What the hell happened?" Truant said, the surprise evident in his voice. "I've never seen a ship explode like that before."

"A nuke, that's what. My guess'd be that they knew they were had and tried to self-destruct and take us with them. Your missiles must have touched off the warhead sooner than they would've liked. Just be glad your cockpit is photo-sensitive or you'd probably be blind right now," said Duncan. She then continued, "Two missiles, Gambler? One would've been sufficient."

Truant could feel his face redden. "Yeah, well, I didn't want to take any chances."

"You bagged a sub, Rookie," Duncan said. "You do know what this means don't you?"

Figuring on a little payback, Truant replied with mock innocence, "Yeah. You're buying."

SAS Pacifica, *Sol system*

"Lt. Commander Moriarty?" said the delta watch communications officer, Ensign Beeler. "I have an incoming message from the recon patrol in Castor. Audio only."

"Audio only? That's strange. Pipe it through, Ensign."

Beeler touched several pads on his console and nodded to Moriarty.

"Recon One, this is *Pacifica*, Lt. Commander Moriarty. What's your status?"

Lt. Duncan's voice came over the speaker. "We had a little excitement when we arrived at Castor, sir. A T'Kharr sub was waiting for us when we exited the starlane. We engaged and destroyed her and got some pretty good photos."

Moriarty's brows arched in surprise at the mention of the sub. "You're sure it was a sub? All of the fighter pilots I've ever known that have engaged a sub haven't returned home to tell about it."

"I'm sure, sir. Ensign Truant pulled off a minor miracle and blasted the sucker. The sub took out the three recon buoys at the Sol starlane exit. We had to jury rig one of the buoys for Beta Aurigae to contact you. Castor Prime should be advised to send replacements with all dispatch."

"Very resourceful. Good work, Recon One. Hold your position and we'll contact Castor Prime and tell them to replace the buoys and recover the sub debris. Hold position until they arrive, then rejoin the fleet as soon as you can."

"Aye aye, sir. Duncan out."

"Computer, has Admiral Drake touched down on the surface yet?" Moriarty knew that Drake would've never gone on shore leave voluntarily. It took a direct order from North to budge him from the ship.

"Yes, sir," the computer replied. "Fifteen minutes ago."

Moriarty hit the intercom pad on the arm of the command chair. "Captain Frost to the bridge, please." Then, under his breath, "At least it'll be some reasonably good news for a change."

CHAPTER EIGHT

Miratev, invasion plus four

Jared stopped in his tracks, weapon snapping up. The others instantly caught the action and froze. Jared cocked his head to one side and turned to his left, eyes squinting in complete concentration. "Listen."

A faint whine came in on the wind from the southwest.

Glend's soft, clear voice startled them all. "I've heard that before. On Veldaron Prime. T'Kharr landing craft. Troop carriers. They're landing reinforcements."

"Damn!" Jared cursed.

They all started to move again, unconsciously moving about half a step faster. They were fortunate that this planet had numerous life forms on it. The massive life readings confused the T'Kharr detectors, allowing them to blend in to a degree.

Without warning, a large tentacle dropped from a tree and encircled Dram's legs, swiftly lifting him off the ground. A second tentacle quickly wrapped around his throat, choking off his air supply. He dropped the pulse rifle he'd been carrying and grasped futilely at the tentacle, trying to restore his airflow.

Julie shouted, "Dram!" and immediately she, Jared, and the Jaaleadi rushed to his aid, trying to prevent the creature from pulling Dram any further up into the trees.

Seeing the tentacles slithering from the dark canopy, Kloke screamed and took off at a dead run, trying to get as far away from the area as possible.

Dram had gone limp and was beginning to turning blue as white foam escaped from his mouth. Jared leveled his rifle at the tentacle surrounding Dram's windpipe and fired, instantly severing the limb. Blue fluid sprayed from the wound, and a primal screech of pain and anger erupted from the canopy overhead. He quickly fired into the other tentacle, and the creature released its hold on Dram, who fell lifelessly to the forest floor. The big man was lying on his back, unconscious.

"He's not breathing!" Julie shouted as she checked for signs of life. Jared straddled Dram and began to pump his chest while Julie breathed into his mouth. Dram suddenly began to cough, and Jared jumped off, allowing him to roll to his side and spit out the contents of his mouth.

After several deep breaths, he looked around and said, "Is it gone?"

"Yes, it's gone," Julie said, impulsively pulling Dram close, nearly choking him with a hug. "You're safe." She then abruptly let go, looking embarrassed and sheepishly said, "Sorry," with a grin.

Dram managed to conjure up a grin of his own and said, "It's okay, I promise." He tried to get up. A wave of vertigo enveloped him, and he fell on his back, squeezing his eyes shut. "Geez, I think I need to lay here for a while."

Jared said, "No problem. I think we can spare a few minutes."

Glend then looked around in alarm and said, "Kloke."

"Ran off," Jared said with disgust.

"But what if the T'Kharr find him?" Julie asked, concern in her voice.

"We can't risk looking for him," Jared said. "The best chance we have is to keep heading toward the bunker. He doesn't know the exact location of the bunker anyway. I know it sounds harsh, but he's on his own now."

Julie lowered her head and nodded, knowing in her heart he was right. She and Jared helped Dram up and watched as he steadied himself on his feet. Satisfied that he was able to walk, Julie took the rifle he'd been carrying and took the lead, with Dram at her side giving directions to the bunker while Jared brought up the rear.

He glanced back and muttered, "Good luck, Kloke. You're gonna need it."

Kloke ran faster than he'd ever run in his life. Finally, unable to go any further, he stopped and leaned against a tree, trying to catch his breath. A wave of nausea engulfed him, and he heaved up the contents of his stomach. After several more spasms, he collapsed beneath the tree. He was hopelessly lost and unarmed and had no food, water, or shelter.

This is Trent's fault, he thought. *Him and Hunter. They would get everyone killed with their stupidity.* They were a perfect product of the government-run propaganda machine, buying into the reports painting the T'Kharr as savages. He didn't buy it. No beings could be as cruel and savage as the government said.

Sheer exhaustion overtook Kloke, and he looked for someplace that he could wait, safe from any predators on the forest floor. He looked up toward the canopy and saw a tree that had what appeared to be a flat, open area at its center, surrounded by branches. It occurred to him that it would be perfect for a child's tree house. He would be safe there. Summoning all the strength he had left, he carefully climbed the tree.

The opening was more than he could have hoped for. It was perfect. The open area in the middle had a soft layer of leaves that had fallen from above, almost as if it had been made especially for someone to lie down on. A sweet, floral smell emanated from the leaf pile, and several yellow flowers similar to Terran sunflowers surrounded the area. Exhaustion finally claimed him, and he plopped down into the soft leaves. His eyes became heavy all of a sudden, and he drifted off to sleep.

Kloke awoke with a start, noting that twilight had fallen. He didn't know how many hours had passed since he fell asleep, but tried to sit up, thinking about finding some water, and realized that he was unable to move. Though he could raise his head just enough to see his body, he couldn't command his limbs to move. Panic began to spread over him, and he tried to scream for help, but he couldn't will any sound from his vocal chords. Eyes wide with fear, he could only watch as the flowers all turned in his direction and sprayed a thick mist toward him.

As the mist descended onto his paralyzed form, his nerves lit up with searing pain as if they'd been dipped in acid. He watched with horror as his clothes melted away, followed by the flesh beneath. His eyes bulged grotesquely as the pain tore into his internal organs, then shock took over and he drifted off, drawing his last breath as the flowers sprayed another cloud of mist.

After several moments, there was no trace that anyone had ever been there, only the sweet aroma of the leaf bed. The leaves drifted down and covered the spot where Kloke once lay and waited for the next victim to lie in its comforting space.

Executive field, Alliance HQ, Earth

Terred and North both stood on the tarmac, watching as the Jaaleadi corvette carrying Supreme Covey Leader Tela of the Jaaleadi Republic and his staff touched down lightly and powered down its engines. Tela descended the ramp with robes flowing, followed by five other Jaaleadi officers. Tela's feathers were all white, and his beak looked old and weathered—a striking contrast to the younger officers who accompanied him. Tela glided up to Terred, spread his powerful wings, and bowed his head out of respect for his human counterpart.

"Welcome to Earth, Supreme Covey Leader Tela," Terred said as he bowed his head in reply.

"A pleasure to see you again, Supreme Commander Terred," Tela replied, the translator converting the squeaks and squawks of the Jaaleadi language into standard. "Grand Commander North, also a pleasure. It has been a long time."

"Yes, sir, it has," North replied respectfully.

North regarded Tela for a moment. He'd served under his fleet command before at the battle of Gamoran Kald and had been impressed by his tactical instincts. Tela also had a great deal of pride in Jaaleadi accomplishments and independence. His was one of the strongest voices in the Jaaleadi government calling for less dependence on the humans. However, he was also intelligent enough to know that they would soon be overrun and conquered by the T'Kharr if they severed their alliance.

Tela fell in stride beside Terred. "Is Var Jent going to be in attendance?" he asked, glancing at North.

"Yes, sir," North replied. "He's waiting for us in the conference room, attending to last-minute details to prepare for your arrival." With a smile, he added, "You know, it's not easy finding chairs that a Jaaleadi can sit in comfortably on Earth."

Tela nodded his head and said, "I understand. That is always a problem for us when a human comes to our world. Many requirements to fulfill to ensure comfort. We are adapting."

They soon entered the conference room, dispensed with the pleasantries, and brought the Jaaleadi up to speed as to the current status and the implications it held for the allies.

"It has been a busy last few days here," Tela said. "Our condolences to the families of those who were lost. It is never easy to lose someone under your command. But now to the current situation. I understand that there is a preliminary plan?"

"Yes, Supreme Covey Leader," North said as he touched a pad on the desk in front of him, causing a holographic display of the Miratev system to appear in the air above the table in front of them.

"We propose a three-pronged attack, jumping into the Miratev system from three starlanes simultaneously. The timing will be crucial in order to achieve the surprise we'll need to overwhelm the T'Kharr forces that are in-system. What we'll need from you, Covey Leader, is a diversion."

Hansen spoke, "Computer, rundown on Kirel Dani system."

The computer's pleasant voice responded, "Kirel Dani. White Zira-class star with five primary planetary bodies. Planet four, Actucha, is the logistical headquarters for the T'Kharr fifth, ninth, and twelfth carrier fleets in this sector. Current in-system presence estimated at five Chondak C-class destroyers and various smaller patrol craft. Intelligence reports that the T'Kharr ninth fleet, whose task it is to defend this and the surrounding systems, has been redeployed and is currently out of the area. Intelligence suggests that the fleet has been sent to the Miratev Maxia system to defend against a possible counter-strike by Alliance forces. End of report."

North turned toward Tela. "We have about ten Earth days left before the scanner shields around the bunker on Miratev power down. When that happens, we might as well send up a flare, because that bunker will blink into life on every one of their detector screens. We'd like to use two Jaaleadi carrier fleets for the Kirel Dani operation to ensure that we have a numerical superiority. Can we count on your assistance, Supreme Covey Leader?"

Tela turned and consulted for a moment with one of his aides, then turned back toward the table.

"The Republic fourth and sixth wings guard this end of the frontier," Tela responded. "We will give them the glory of attacking Kirel Dani. You have our complete support."

"Thank you, sir," North continued. "We need a finalized strike plan for Kirel Dani by tomorrow. The rest is just logistics and combat prep. We want to hit Kirel Dani in two days and then hit Miratev twenty-four hours later. Can you do it, sir?"

"You can count on us, Grand Commander North," Tela replied with pride.

"Of that I never doubted, sir," North said with an appreciative nod.

"Gentlebeings, I must stress the absolute secrecy that must accompany this mission," Terred said, deadly serious. "Each fleet commander will be responsible for briefing the captains of the ships in his fleet personally on the attack plan. There will be no leaks. No one is to know of our final destination until we arrive and it's too late for the T'Kharr to call for additional reinforcements."

North then said, "Please excuse us. General Austin, General Tyler, General Logan, please accompany me."

The three officers rose and followed North out of the main conference room and into the adjacent conference room. North paused to let the others through the door before shutting it and locking it.

"The reason I wanted to speak to you privately is that I'm assigning a full company of Omega Section to land before the actual invasion begins. After scouting the lab, they'll go in and recon the landing zones and send back the clearance or abort codes. You'll need to designate several alternate landing zones in case the primaries are compromised. I'll need a list of them as soon as possible."

"I've heard rumors of Omega Section, but I've never seen any of them until yesterday's briefing," Logan said. "And there are no computer references to them at all. It's as if they don't even exist."

"You're not far off the mark, Kyle. Because you see, officially, they don't exist. For a long time, they didn't even have an official name for the unit. We call them Omega Section because we have to call them something."

Austin added, "I understand they're outfitted with state-of-the-art telesponders."

A questioning look crossed over Logan's features. "Telesponders?"

Tyler explained, "Small electronics implanted into the brain stem. They allow us to communicate telepathically to a certain degree, and if need be, they can be detonated to avoid capture."

"Remarkable," Logan breathed. "What's their range?"

"Standard implants will work anywhere on a planet," Tyler said. "The command-level upgrades can project quite a bit further. When someone with a command-level telesponder is hooked into the Cathedra in a carrier, they can broadcast throughout an entire star system. The tech continues to improve every day."

"Commander, if Omega Section is such a top secret, then why am I being briefed?"

"Because they will be traveling with us on the *Pacifica* in with your marines," North said. "They will answer only to myself or General Austin."

"It's just as well he told you about Omega Section, because the last commanding officer who asked too many questions about them disappeared and turned up a month later with a partial mind wipe," Austin added.

Logan's eyes grew wide for a moment.

"I trust you to head off any inquiries by your staff," North said. "Tell them that they're new replacements or something. Their company commander is Major Deneva."

"As a matter of fact," Tyler said as he checked his wrist chronometer, "they should be landing on the *Pacifica* right about now."

"I need to get aboard myself," North said. "We'll speak further when we're on the ship. General Tyler, good luck on your phase of the operation."

"Thank you, sir," Tyler replied. "See you at Miratev along with the surprise we spoke of earlier."

North smiled knowingly and said, "I look forward to that, General." Then the three men all left the room.

CHAPTER NINE

Earth orbit, approaching SAS Pacifica

"*Pacifica*, this is North. Request landing clearance." Drake's familiar voice cut into the transmission. "Stand by, Commander. We're going to have to put you in a holding pattern. I'm in the landing bay, and the 'package' is arriving."

The package. The Stellar Converter. He ordered up a tactical display and saw the large, bulky object being guided into the *Pacifica's* dorsal landing bay. It seemed too small to be the deadliest weapon ever devised by mankind. He thought of Bikini Atoll and the first detonation of the ancient hydrogen bomb. This monster that they were loading onto his ship by his own order made one of those bombs look like a spark at midday. He prayed they wouldn't have to use it.

"Sorry for the wait, Commander," the voice of Lieutenant Vale said. "You're clear for approach in the dorsal bay."

"Thank you, Lieutenant. North out."

North smoothly guided his fighter in through the atmosphere shield and touched down onto the deck with a slight bump. *Still haven't lost the touch*, he thought. As he exited his fighter, he saw Drake waiting for him at the edge of the landing zone, a serious look on his face.

Drake fell in stride beside him, and North said, "How much more do we have to load, Mat?"

"This is the last item," he said, taking in a deep breath. "All of the personnel and their equipment are aboard and secured. We've housed the marines in the transport quarters and the officers in the guest quarters. The escorts report they are underway and moving toward the rendezvous point at the starlane portal. This is it, Commander."

"This is it, indeed," North agreed.

They soon reached the command deck lift and were deposited on the bridge level of the huge ship.

"Grand Commander on the bridge," Frost announced.

"As you were," North responded politely and strode over to the stairs that led to his office one level above the main bridge.

Drake walked down to the command chair and addressed Frost. "I have the conn. Thank you, Captain."

He sat in his chair and looked over to the status console. Everything showed green.

"Mister Baxter, set course for the first portal."

"Aye, sir," Baxter replied crisply as he punched the buttons that would command the massive ship to move toward the Alioth starlane portal, the first of their three jumps.

Baxter came from a long line of military men and women. Sworn to do their duty and follow the orders of their superiors. In his five years in the service, Baxter had seen many engagements and had learned to trust his superiors. Yet he had no idea how much he was going to have to trust them in the upcoming days.

North entered his office and quickly removed the flight suit he was wearing. He then went to his closet, chose a fresh uniform, and slipped it on. *Much better*, he thought. He went over to the wet bar and poured himself a soft drink. No sooner had he sat down than his intercom chimed.

"Yes," he snapped a bit more sharply than he'd intended as he stabbed the intercom button.

There was a slight pause, then Drake's voice came over the speaker. "Sorry to disturb you, Commander, but Major Deneva is here and would like to speak to you. Should I have him come back later?"

North sighed inwardly. He really didn't want to do anything but relax right now, but duty called. "No, send him in, Mat," he replied as put his drink on the table next to the couch and stood, smoothing out his uniform tunic. The door chime sounded, and North said, "Come in."

The door slid open, and a smartly dressed marine officer entered. He was about twenty-five solar years old and well-muscled, with the slightest of sneers on his face. He snapped to attention and said, "Major Deneva reporting as ordered, sir."

North guessed he was a descendent of one of the old European empires, perhaps France. Classic Omega Section type. North's left eyebrow arched as he gave him a once over.

"As ordered, Major? I don't recall issuing such an order."

Deneva's face was stone.

"General Tyler *suggested* that I come and introduce myself to General Austin, sir. General Austin then suggested I come to you."

Was that a touch of disgust I heard? North thought. No, not disgust. Closer to annoyance. Deneva stood there, ramrod straight.

"I see," North said. He indicated the couch and said, "Would you like something to drink Major? I was just about to—"

"No thank you, sir," Deneva interrupted, not abrupt enough to be considered insubordinate, but definitely not polite. It was painfully clear that the man had no desire to be here. Omega Section were notorious for being independent thinkers and weren't very happy to have to take orders from the "regulars."

North regarded him for a moment, then sat down on the couch where he'd been before the interruption and snatched his drink. He took a sip, leaned back on the couch, and gave Deneva another once over.

"Was there anything else, Major, now that you've introduced yourself?" North could play the game too.

"No, sir. Now if you don't mind, I'd like to—"

"I do mind actually," North interrupted. Then in a neutral tone, he said, "Sit down."

Deneva's eyes narrowed just slightly, then he seated himself on the couch at the opposite end. He sat, back straight, hands on his lap, looking directly at North. North crossed his legs and took another sip from his drink.

He said, "Let me take a stab in the dark, Major Deneva or whatever the hell your real name is. You resent the fact that you were ordered here by me, a non-Omega-Section officer, and you don't feel I'm qualified to issue you orders since I have no idea what type of things you and your team are capable of. Am I close?"

Deneva's face was still stone.

"Permission to speak freely, sir?" he said.

"Go ahead, Major," North replied. *This ought to be good*, he thought.

"You are correct. I don't feel that you are qualified to issue my unit orders. You are correct that my team and I feel this way, because unless you have been in Omega Section, you don't know what we are truly capable of. General Tyler has told us that you are a very good commander, and I have no reason to doubt that. But you are a naval officer and not a ground trooper. Tell us the objective and give us autonomy, and we will operate effectively. We are not in need of supervision."

"Hmmm," North said, sipping his drink again. "You aren't as well informed as I thought."

Deneva's stone face cracked just slightly, then returned to normal.

"To what are you referring, sir?" he replied innocently.

North placed his drink on the table and turned toward Deneva.

<This is what I'm talking about, Major.>

Deneva's mask crumpled, and he looked as if he'd been shocked with a thousand volts. He recognized the telesponder signature as being different from those of his fellow Omega Section. Stronger and more penetrating.

North continued out loud, "Are you so presumptuous as to think that you are privy to every military secret there is?"

North then leaned forward and stared straight into the now unsure Major's eyes. "If it weren't for those people you seem to hold in contempt, you'd have probably been killed long ago. I was in Omega Section when your mother was still wiping the snot from your nose. I have a command-level telesponder implant, state-of-the-art. I can tap into yours or any other Omega team member's thoughts in this ship whenever I choose. There are only a handful of living people who know I was Omega Section. This is not something to share with your team. If you can't follow orders without question, then tell me now and I'll get someone who can. Nosy colonels aren't the only ones who have disappeared and returned mind-wiped."

"Commander, that won't be necessary," Deneva said sincerely. "I will follow your orders and those of the others to the best of my ability."

North could tell that this time, he was indeed being sincere.

"Good," North replied, his tone softer. "Then why don't you go back to General Austin and tell him we've met."

Deneva stood up and said, "Yes, sir. By your leave, Commander." Deneva bowed slightly, then exited through the door.

Austin, North thought. He was one of those few who had known North during his Omega Section days. He guessed that Austin had sent Deneva here hoping that something like what had happened would happen. Old bugger was paying him back for making him stay on the ship. North smiled to himself. *Same old Ben*, he thought, chuckling out loud as he walked over to the viewport.

The soft voice of the computer interrupted his thoughts. "Sixty seconds to starlane portal, Commander."

He watched as, one by one, the ships in front of him disappeared into the portal with a flash of brilliance. It had begun.

Earth, North Ranch

Denara Lareen was just finishing up the dinner dishes when the doorbell rang. She thought it was strange that someone would come around this late. Then she remembered that Lan had a potential buyer for the mare who said they might be coming by tonight. Must be him.

As she walked to the door, she shouted, "Lan . . . someone's at the door! I think it's your buyer!"

Lan came out of the back room, trying his best to tuck in his shirt just as Denara began to open the door. The pistol came up so fast, she didn't have time to react. The shot was so powerful, it threw her back several feet, leaving her lying flat on her back, her lifeless eyes staring straight up at the ceiling. A wisp of smoke snaked out of the scorched hole in her chest.

Lan froze where he was, unsure if he was really seeing what his eyes were showing him. He looked at Denara's lifeless form on the floor, trying to make sense of it. How could this be true? He hadn't heard a sound.

"Amor?" he said, eyes going from Denara to the black-dressed man stepping through the front door, now bringing the pistol up to point at him. He turned away, the blast hitting him on his lower back, just above the right kidney. He went down to the ground, yelling in agony as the wound lit up every nerve in his back.

The gunman brought the gun up once more and fired a second shot into the back of Lan's skull, silencing him permanently. Too bad the son had left the day before. He'd have liked to get all three of them at the same time. One more loose end he'd have to take care of later.

The assassin pulled up a file on his handheld device and looked to the right side of the room. He then quickly walked up to the wall and pushed a table out of the way, revealing a panel that almost blended in perfectly with the wall. After pulling the panel open and quickly locating the data cube, he pulled it free and stashed it in his pocket. He looked around the room once more, making sure he didn't miss anything, checked his chronometer, and sprinted out the front door, leaving it ajar. He'd made arrangements for the security cameras to malfunction, as well as the orbiting satellite that was watching the area. There was no telling how long it would take someone to find the bodies and call the authorities. No matter. He would be long gone by then.

Earth, North Ranch, several hours later

Inspector Yvonne Wilson from Del Mar PD scanned the room, looking for any obvious clues as to why the two people lying on the floor had been killed. It was very strange, she thought to herself. Nothing was taken, and neither of the two victims had criminal records or any type of shady past. It didn't make sense.

"Go pull the vids from the security system, Billy," she said.

Perkins walked over to a wall panel and looked inside. "Data cube's gone. Definitely a pro."

A team of three technician types, all holding large stainless-steel cases came through the door and placed their bags on the ground. The sniffer team.

"How long?" she asked.

"Should be done in about thirty minutes," he said. "I'll call you when we're finished."

She left the room and went outside to join Perkins. As she approached him, she heard Perkins engaged in an intense discussion with someone on the other end of the phone line.

"I heard you the first time, Sport," Perkins said to the person on the other end of the phone. "I want you to check again." He turned to lock eyes with Wilson. "All of the security feeds from yesterday, all of them, have been wiped from the system," he snapped. "Backups too."

She looked at Perkins and said, "You can't access the planetary archive from here. And to do so, you need government clearance. Our bad guy is a lot smarter than we thought."

"We found something very interesting," the sniffer tech said. "I'm flashing it to your comm unit."

She saw the information being uploaded to her unit. She looked at the phone and said, "Tell him we'll be in touch later to speak to his superior."

"Yes, ma'am," Perkins said with a smile as he unmuted the phone and relayed the message.

He positioned himself behind Wilson so he could see the sniffer data on her comm pad. The most recent entries were Wilson, Perkins, the sniffer team, and others Wilson recognized as emergency personnel or police personnel. She moved those along with the victim's profiles, the profile of their son, one Rando Falco, and the man who'd discovered the bodies to a different file and saw two anomalies remaining.

"Yesterday . . . a male with a classified DNA profile was here for approximately six hours," she muttered. "Twelve hours after he left, another male entered the room and stayed for about three minutes. Interesting . . ."

"Why is that interesting?" Perkins asked.

"Well, the first guy was here for a while," she said as she called up the most recent unidentified file. "Since there was no sign of a struggle, I'm guessing it was someone familiar to the Lareens. The son is in the military. He was here for two hours at the same time the first classified male was."

Perkins nodded his head. "Did they ID the second male?"

Wilson punched some more buttons and said, "Yeah, finally. Took long enough. Arvil Symons. Released six months ago after serving seven years of a ten-year sentence for computer fraud. Good behavior. He managed to hack into government servers and obtain classified information. Well, he's sure smart enough to pull this off. This shows he's currently on Earth, but no known address."

"Not to state the obvious, but we definitely need to talk to him," Perkins said. "Doesn't he have a parole transponder?"

"Nonviolent offense. They wouldn't have tagged him for that."

"I wonder who the military visitor was," Perkins said.

"Not sure," Wilson said. "House is owned by a B. North. I tried to look him up, but it only tells me he's off-world, and everything else comes up classified."

"North . . . that sounds familiar," Perkins said.

"Don't know," she said, "but we have some work to do back at the office. Do me a favor and let the sniffer team and the other forensic people know we'll be back at the office and to let us know what they find. I've got to call the chief."

"Will do," Perkins said.

A short time later, Wilson and Perkins headed back to the office with more questions than answers.

CHAPTER TEN

Miratev Two

Lt Remy figured they still had at least six hours of tough hiking to do before they reached the bunker. The terrain had been more treacherous than they had anticipated. If there wasn't so much blasted animal life on this world, then the T'Kharr life signs would be a lot easier to distinguish. The T'Kharr read like many of the larger animals on this stinking planet.

<Clearing ahead,> Sgt. Sulak thought, currently on point.

<Spread out,> Remy commanded.

The area would take at least an hour to skirt around. Going through to the other side would only take minutes. Remy thought for a moment, weighing the options.

<Let's do it,> he decided. <Low and slow.>

The team cautiously crept into the open.

<Three human life forms, two Jaaleadi,> Keever sent. <Ahead a hundred meters.>

The team froze. Remy glanced to the side, his team all but invisible in their camo suits.

<Eli, Kiproff. Recon.> Remy thought, and the two silently slipped out of his view.

As they drew closer to the opposite side of the clearing, they heard hushed whispers.

Jeenan tested the air with her advanced sense of smell. "Something is out there. I just don't know . . ."

A figure appeared out of nowhere and knocked Jeenan and Glend to the ground. Out of the corner of her eye she saw Julie, Jared, and Dram all hit the ground, weapons flying away from their hands. It seemed to her as if the shadows had suddenly come alive and attacked.

Jared, struggling to regain his wind, looked up, wide-eyed, at the most menacing rifle he'd ever seen. Seven more figures emerged from the brush and surrounded him and the others.

"Who are you?" the masked figure towering over him demanded.

Human, Jared thought. *Best to answer.*

"Dr. Jared Trent. Who are—"

"And the others?" the figure snapped, ignoring the pending question.

"J-Julie Newman," Julie said, her eyes wide with shock, hands held up.

Jared said, "The big man is Dram Hunter, and over there are Jeenan Tar and Glend Olk of Jaalead."

The figure glanced sideways at one of the others, who nodded and said, "They're all on the manifest, Lieutenant. Members of the research station staff."

The figure gave an almost imperceptible nod, and the eight figures all lowered their weapons. He then pulled back the mask covering his face, and Jared saw a young-looking human male of about twenty-two years. The man reached down and offered Jared his hand, which he accepted, and pulled him to his feet with surprising strength.

"Lt. Remy, Alliance special ops," he said. After that, he pointed to each member in turn and introduced them. "Lieutenant Henna, Petty Officers Eli and Keever, Chief Petty Officer Angus, Sergeants Sulak, Kenyon, and Kiproff. Now can you tell me why you're here and why you're this far from the facility?"

"We escaped into the forest after the attack," Jared replied. "We've been trying to make our way to the data backup bunker for days. We figured that was our best hope of survival until help arrived."

"Are you the rescue party?" Julie asked hopefully.

"I'm afraid not, ma'am," Remy replied. "Intel puts the bunker thirty klicks from here, north northeast. We figure six more hours at the pace we've been going."

"Wait . . . thirty klicks?" Dram asked. "It's thirty klicks if you're going for the main entrance. About ten if you use the back door."

Remy's eyebrows arched with interest. "Back door?"

"Yeah," Dram said. "The back door is situated close to a clearing so we can set a cargo shuttle down. It's also equipped with a transport rail system that'll get you to the bunker. Beats walking."

"There's no mention of an alternate entrance in the specs, sir," Henna said.

"It wouldn't be," Dram said. "I lobbied for the secondary entrance myself. We never sent the updated plans back to HQ. Off-world engineering team did the construction for us. Better that way."

<What do you think?> Remy thought.

<They read as human,> Henna replied. <No evidence of T'Kharr interrogation or mind control.>

<This mission is too important to take chances.>

<But the mission is also to obtain the objective as soon as possible.>

<If there is a second entrance, we would need to secure it anyway.>

Jared and his group watched with confusion as Lt. Remy and the other soldiers carried on what appeared to be a lively conversation but weren't speaking to each other. After many moments of uncomfortable silence, Dram chimed in. "You guys are Omega, aren't you?" The question was actually a statement.

Their silence told Dram all he needed to know.

"Omega is a myth," Remy said.

"My brother was an operative, and I was asked to join, but I declined. I know who you guys are." He turned to Jared and said, "Doctor Trent, if these guys are who I think they are, we have to get them to the bunker immediately."

Jared resisted the urge to ask what Omega was, figuring that he wouldn't get a straight answer anyway.

Dram walked over to Henna and asked to check the grid map she had on her hand pad. He indicated a point 9.6 kilometers from their current position and said, "The entrance is right here. I can get us in."

Remy nodded and then addressed the group. "You have to stay within two meters of a member of my team. Our suits have life sign dispersers. As long as they're active, our life signs will show up on the T'Kharr instruments as a life form about the same size as a fly. If you venture further away than two meters, you'll be exposed and put the whole team at risk. Understood?"

The five nodded that they understood, and Remy continued, "Take your weapons back, but don't fire unless I give you a direct order. Copy?"

They all nodded, and Jared recovered his rifle while Dram accepted the pulse rifle Julie had once held. Eli gave the recovered side arms to the Jaaleadi and motioned for them to follow. They all started off in the direction indicated by Dram, each of Jared's science team in between two of the Omega troopers in line.

Starlanes, near the Alpha Auridius Nexus

"This is great, Brand," General Austin said as he spooned another forkful of food into his mouth. "My cook never has been able to make a decent lasagna."

"It's my pleasure, Ben," North said. "Denara made a big batch and gave it to me in a stasis dish. I promised some to Faulkner, but we'll have leftovers for a few meals."

Austin chuckled and stared at his friend for a moment. They dined together every time he and North were on Earth or on the same ship, but something was different tonight. Austin probably knew North better than even his wife Shareel had, and he could see that something was bothering the commander.

North gazed into his water. Then after a long pause he said, "You know, it never gets any easier. The killing."

"It should never become easy," Austin responded, leaning back on the couch and crossing his legs. "That's just one of the realities of war. People die."

"You know," North said, "the first time I ever had to take a life was when I was an ensign on the *Triumph*. Went out on recon patrol, ran into a T'Kharr squadron, and I destroyed a T'Kharr fighter. I remember thinking to myself how easy it was, just like the sims in the academy. One second it was there, living, and the next it was gone.

"I remember when we got back to the ship, you know how it is, all giddy from cheating death after engaging the enemy, going to the officer's lounge afterward for squadron 'debriefing.' It didn't really hit me until later that night. I was lying in bed, staring at the ceiling when it dawned on me. I'd just killed something. The fact that it would have happily killed me and feasted on my corpse didn't make any difference. I wasn't raised to be a killer."

"There's no need to feel guilty about doing your job," Austin replied. "How many lives did Captain Walker cost us? How many more would've died if he'd escaped?"

North looked at the concerned look on his friend's face and said with a grin, "Don't worry, Ben. I'll deal with it. Have in the past and probably will have to again in the future. It just felt good to talk to someone about it—"

There was a sudden deceleration, and both North and Austin were thrown from their seats to the floor of the office.

Austin shook his head and said, "What the hell was that?" as he picked himself up off the floor and brushed off his uniform tunic.

North jumped up and said, "Hell if I know. Something happened that overwhelmed the inertia compensators."

North ran out into the command center. Drake was climbing back into his seat and shouted, "Damage report, all decks!"

North looked at the forward view screen and saw stars. "We aren't in the starlane anymore. We shouldn't have dropped out for another nine hours. What's our position?" He directed the question to the on-duty navigations officer, Lt. Webber.

The man looked perplexed and shook his head. "This can't be right," he said, checking the position again. "According to the nav comp, we've exited into the Alpha Auridius Nexus. I'm getting telemetry from all fifty-two starlane beacons."

"Impossible," Drake said, coming up behind the man and checking over his shoulder.

"I've checked it three times, Admiral."

The Alpha Auridius system had once been the busiest hub in the Alliance, a jumping-off point between numerous Alliance systems and allowing much shorter travel between systems throughout the Orion arm of the Milky Way. The twin stars, Alpha and Beta Auridius, interacted with the starlanes in such a way that a corridor of portals existed in the space between the two stars. The system had been cut off from the rest of the Alliance due to an unexplained shift in the stars' gravitational fields some twenty-three years earlier. Ships were unable to enter the starlane portals leading to the system, and the routes were lost. No contact had been made with the starlane beacons for those twenty-three years.

"Status of the escorts, troop carrier?" North demanded. He was particularly concerned about the troop transport *Suribachi*, holding six thousand soldiers for the ground assault on the planet.

Vale said, "I'm getting transponders from all of our escorts. It looks like everyone made it, sir."

After several moments, Drake turned to North and said, "Fleet wide damage appears to be minimal. No serious casualties. Only minor bumps and bruises. We are fully operational."

Drake hit the comm button. "Captain Trent, launch the combat space patrol. I want the entire corridor swept."

"Yes, sir," Trent replied immediately.

Almost immediately, fifteen fighters—*Pacifica's* alert squadron—catapulted out of the port and starboard flight bays.

"Admiral Drake," Lt Vale's voice said, "Captain Tanda for you."

Drake nodded, and the voice of Captain Elizabeth Tanda, captain of the electronics ship *Caloria,* came over the speaker.

"Sir, it appears that the stars' gravitational fields have returned to their original configuration as they were before the shift twenty-three years ago. We can only carry out detailed scans of the closest six portals due to the stars' background radiation, but they appear to now be functional. We won't know for sure until we launch probes, but I'm fairly certain that most, if not all, of the original portals are active again. We've even mapped two new ones that will need to eventually be explored. Looks like we won't be marooned here, Admiral."

North inwardly sighed with relief. The thought of being marooned here in a system with no planets and no way of informing the battle fleet they wouldn't be making the scheduled rendezvous wasn't pleasant.

North spoke up and said, "Captain, any indication of what sucked us out of the starlane?"

"My team speculates that the shift took place spontaneously, unfortunately at about the same time that our fleet was passing near the system in compressed space," Tanda said.

North looked at Drake and nodded. Drake said, "Thank you, Captain. Keep us informed," and he cut the link. North stared at the screen for a moment and then went over to the nav console.

"Lt Webber, bring up the starlane map with our route to Miratev, and overlay the old starlane routes for the Auridius Nexus."

Webber brought up the requested information, and North smiled. Drake had been watching and saw what North saw at the same time.

"I'll be damned . . ." he breathed. "Lt. Vale, get me Captain Tanda again."

The reply came a few moments later. "Tanda here, Admiral."

"Captain, have your science teams send a probe through the ninth starlane portal first. Advise if it still terminates in the Pol-to Nebula."

"Yes, sir," Tanda replied.

North said, "If those portals still terminate in their original locations, it will cut forty-five hours off our trip."

"Yes, sir," Drake replied with some satisfaction. "Do you want me to notify HQ of the nexus being active again?"

North said, "Not just yet. I don't want to take the chance of a leak. We don't need the T'Kharr to realize these portals are active again."

Drake nodded in understanding. Too many things could still go wrong.

Earth, Del Mar Police Department

Yvonne Wilson sat in her office in the Detective Bureau of the Del Mar Police Department. She and Perkins were reviewing what little they knew about Arvil Symons.

She also made another follow-up inquiry on the classified DNA sample. What was taking so long? A murder investigation was supposed to be able to cut through some of the normal red tape.

Suddenly, the screen on her data unit went black.

"Damned thing, I just charged it."

As she watched the screen, words began to scroll across. They read, "Plug this unit into your terminal. I want to show you something."

"What the hell?" she said. "Someone's hacked into my hand unit."

Wilson and Perkins looked at each other, and Perkins said, "You better do it."

She plugged the unit into the slot on her desktop terminal and spoke to it. "Who the hell are you?"

An unfamiliar voice issued from the unit. "Relax, Inspector. My name is Malone. FleetSec. When you ran that classified DNA for comparison, you lit up half the security boards at HQ."

Wilson said, "Well, Malone from FleetSec, you've hacked into a secure Police net—"

"I have very little time to chat, Inspector. The DNA match comes back to the owner of the ranch, Brandon North, who I am working with on another case. The Lareen family are . . . were . . . his caretakers."

Realization dawning, Perkins said, "Wait, you mean Grand Commander North?"

"We very much need to speak to Grand Commander North," Wilson said. "Can you arrange that?"

"He's unavailable."

"What about the son, Rando Falco?" she asked.

"Also unavailable."

Wilson muttered, "How convenient," a little louder than she'd intended.

"Listen, lady," Malone started, obviously irritated. "If you're thinking the commander had something to do with this, you're not a very smart cop. The Lareens were the closest thing to family he had left after his wife and son were killed seven years ago."

Wilson reconsidered her approach and cleared her throat. "I wasn't implying that he was, Mr. Malone. I need to speak with him to see if he knew another person was detected in the room."

"What's the name?" Malone growled.

"Mr. Malone, I know nothing about you except that you hacked a secure police net—"

"The *name*, Ms. Wilson. If you don't wish to tell me, I'll have it within the next fifteen minutes anyway. Time is of the essence."

Wilson considered for a moment. If FleetSec could hack a confidential police net this easily, then they probably *could* get the information.

"The name is Arvil Symons. We found—"

"As I recall, you guys quickly dismissed the traffic collision that killed Commander North's family as a simple accident," Malone said. "Both his family and the Lareens are now dead. I would recommend that you check into that 'accident' again. I'll be in touch."

The link terminated. Wilson and Perkins both stared at the blank screen.

Perkins said, "What kind of piece of crap have you gotten us into, Von?"

Alpha Auridius Nexus

"Hey, Yo-Yo, what exactly are we supposed to be looking for out here?" Devin Truant asked.

Duncan looked out her cockpit and down to her left, seeing her wingman studying his instruments intently. "Who knows? I don't think we'll have to worry about enemy ships. This system has been cut off from the rest of the galaxy for almost twenty-four standard years."

"I know, I know," Truant responded. "It's just . . . doesn't anyone else find this a little creepy?"

"Creepy?" Valerie Davis said. "Worried about ghosts, Gambler?"

"I thought you were invincible after you bagged that sub," Randall said.

The comment was greeted with a chorus of chuckles from the other pilots.

"Yeah, Gambler, you sure have the luck," said Lt. Soren Syndergaard, call sign "Stepchild." "That shoulda been me on that patrol. Lucky punk."

"Yeah, yeah," Truant replied. "I owe you, I know."

"Just set up a poker game after the mission," Syndergaard replied, again greeted with knowing laughter amongst the squadron. "That'll be payment enough. I'm a little low on funds."

"All right, knock it off," their squadron leader, Lt. Commander Thayer Jericho, said. "The twenty-six furthest starlane portals are beyond that gas cloud. COMPAC wants us to recon."

The gas cloud was nothing special. Vast amounts of ionized gas comprised the cloud, making it difficult to scan through.

After ten minutes into the sweep, Ensign Craig said, "Alert 5, Alert 5, this is *Pacifica*. We're getting a metallic reading coming from your two o'clock, vector 113. Check it out."

As they closed, the metallic reading began to take shape.

"*Pacifica*, Alert 5. It reads as an object about as big as . . . as big as a fighter . . ."

"Blue Eyes, heat up the weapons and hold position," said Jericho, who had been monitoring the exchange. "We're coming to you."

"Wilco, boss. Cooler, form on my wing and heat up the birds."

"Already there," Randall said, scrutinizing his own instruments. "I'm getting negative energy readings from the ship. Configuration is still a bit fuzzy, but I swear I've seen something like that before. It looks like one of the old Heremod-class bombers. I saw one in a museum. They were decommissioned twenty years ago."

"Alert 7, *Pacifica*," Craig said. "Archives has confirmed, it's a Heremod-class bomber."

"Damn," Randall said. "Musta been caught here when the portals went dark. No planets to land on, enough air for about a week. No way for a pilot to go."

"Alert 5, moving in," Davis said as she edged closer. As she got close enough to the bomber to verify that it was, in fact, a friendly vessel, she could see into the cockpit.

"Nobody home," she said. "Scans don't detect any bodies, living or otherwise, in the ship. Power output is zero."

Randall said, "Blue Eyes, what's that on her stern?"

Davis moved closer and saw what appeared to be a tether attached to the vessel's stern.

"It looks like a cable from a tug," she said as she moved closer still. As she passed the empty ship, following the cable, she said, "Second contact. Another bomber. Just like the first. It also appears to be tethered to something else beyond my view."

"You getting this, *Pacifica*?" Jericho asked.

"Affirm, Alert Leader."

The second bomber led to a third and fourth, all tethered together for some unknown purpose. As they edged closer to the geographical center of the cloud, the cloud appeared to thin and dissipate somewhat.

"Holy mother of the Creator . . ." was all Jericho could say.

North, Austin, and Drake, all intently watching events unfold as soon as the discovery of the first bomber was reported, watched in awe as the feed from Jericho's scanners filled the bridge view screen.

"I don't believe it," North said as he stared at a fleet of Alliance warships, all parked in a row as if in mothballs.

The bombers that Jericho's team had located led to the largest ship in the ghost fleet, a massive Saturn-class heavy carrier. She was flanked by two huge Callisto-class battleships and ten Pandora-class destroyers.

"That's a good-sized task force," Austin said. "I haven't seen a Callisto-class battleship since fleet day ten years ago. They decommissioned that class over a decade ago."

"Alert Leader, this is North. Try and get close enough to the carrier to get a name, hull registry number, anything that will identify those ships."

As Jericho steered toward the carrier, he saw that the bombers they'd originally encountered were connected in line to the carrier landing bay. In a string next to the bombers were tugs, shuttles, and even the admiral's corvette, all spaced evenly and cabled together. He caught a glimpse of a name on the side of one of the battleships. "*Pacifica*, I can see a name on the side of one of the battlewagons. It reads . . . *Teleosa* . . ."

North looked thunderstruck, his eyes growing wide at the mention the name. "It can't be . . ."

Drake noticed his reaction and said, "Are you all right, Commander?"

North kept staring at the screen and said, "If that battleship is the *Teleosa*, then the carrier should be the *Lysithea*."

"*Lysithea* . . . why do I know that name . . ." Drake said.

"Because she disappeared with all hands along with her escort fleet twenty-three years ago while in route to Tig Ferendal." North said.

"By the Creator . . . Jason's ship?" Austin asked, realization dawning on him.

"Fleet Command never knew what had happened," North said, eyes glued to the screen. "They thought the fleet had been lost in battle, but no evidence ever turned up. Their course didn't take them through the nexus, so the possibility that they were marooned here never occurred, and there was no way to verify it. How could they have ended up here?" a mixed wave of emotions swam through his mind.

Jericho's clear voice burst over the speaker. "Confirmed . . . SAS *Lysithea* . . . minimal power readings. There's something definitely operating over there. Very low levels. Engines, weapons, scanners, all cold. Indeterminate life readings . . ."

"Fleet Com, send a challenge," Drake said.

"*Lysithea, Lysithea*, this is SAS *Pacifica*, respond please," Lt. Vale said. After several moments with no response, he repeated, "*Lysithea*, this is SAS *Pacifica*. Please respond."

Suddenly, Vale perked up and held her earpiece closer to her head. "I'm getting an automated bounce back, Admiral. Their communications appear to be working, but nobody is responding."

North turned to Drake and said, "Mat, I want that ship boarded."

"Yes, Commander," he replied. He thought for a second that North might try to accompany the boarding party himself but realized that he wouldn't violate regulations, even in this situation. Sending in Logan first would keep Command happy.

North disappeared into his ready room with Drake, and captain Frost came up next to Austin.

In a low voice, he asked, "Sir, who is Jason?"

Several people at their stations paused for a second, hoping to hear the answer to that question. Austin almost reminded everyone to tend to their stations, but he knew the information would get out anyway. Better it came from an accurate source.

"Jason, as in Jason North. The Commander's twin brother. Missing in action for twenty-three years. He was a pilot on the *Lysithea*."

CHAPTER ELEVEN

Miratev Two, approaching the bunker

Dram looked to his right at Sgt. Kiproff and asked, "Clear?" The sergeant said, "No readings of anything large. I think we lucked out."

The group had finally reached the bunker loading dock, Dram's "back door," without running into any T'Kharr patrols or ravenous indigenous life.

Remy addressed Dram Hunter and said, "You're up, sir."

Dram moved over to the sheer rock wall in front of them and placed his hand over what seemed to be a random place on the rock.

When he pulled his hand away, a portion of the rock seemed to glide back, revealing a keypad. He punched in the code, and the two large doors covering the entrance slid open.

The opening was just about big enough to allow a large air-car to enter. Remy and his team entered first and saw the rail system Dram had described. There was a large, empty trailer on the rail that was attached to a hauler. The hauler could seat four people comfortably, so the others would have to ride in the trailer.

"How far from here to the main bunker?" Remy asked.

"About four klicks," Dram said. "It's a shorter distance than outside, because you go straight through the mountain."

When they reached the main receiving station in the bunker, Jared was surprised at how spartan it was. He knew of the bunker's existence but had never actually been here until now. One wall was nothing but memory cells and equipment used to monitor the shield. Remy motioned for Keever, who pulled out a small box from his pack. He located a slot on the console and inserted the box. Immediately, the lights in the room brightened and several monitors on the console turned from yellow to green.

Remy nodded in approval and said, "Chief, set charges."

"Yes, sir," Angus said. He motioned toward Sulak and Kenyon, who immediately removed charges from their packs and placed them strategically all around the data banks and console.

"Those are the dish targeting controls," Henna said, pointing to another bank of instruments.

Keever jumped into the seat next to them and punched in a set of coordinates, then typed in a text message on the keyboard. "That's it. Now we just sit and wait."

Remy nodded his head and said, "I hope someone here is a better cook than Chief Angus."

The other soldiers laughed, and Angus replied, "C-rats a la Angus is a delicacy you have to experience to appreciate, you savages."

Jared couldn't help but smile. He didn't think these guys had a sense of humor.

Dram entered the room and said, "Looks like we have food for about a month. Water is drawn from a well, so that isn't a problem."

Julie perked up at that information and said, "I have dibs on the fresher. I have about a week's worth of grime and funk to get rid of." She then trotted off into the first room and closed the door.

Remy turned to Henna and said, "Rotating guard shifts every two hours at the entrance to that back door. Send Sulak and Kiproff first. Report every fifteen."

"Yes, sir," Henna replied. She relayed the orders.

Remy then took the seat next to Keever and said, "I hope someone brought a deck of cards."

In orbit above Miratev Two

At that same moment, an occupant of one of the two Alliance subs stationed adjacent to the T'Kharr fleet above Miratev received a message from the surface.

"Bunker secured. Shield stabilized. Survivors onboard." The man silently relayed the message toward one of the starlane beacons and returned to monitoring.

Onboard the imperial destroyer *Ra'aktaka*, Subling Do'orkril saw something strange on his monitor. "Enemy transmission from the surface, Khetal."

The ship commander, Khetal Thi'is Shi'il, turned and barked, "Source?"

"One of the transmission antennae on the surface, Khetal," Do'orkril replied. "We have already secured the device, but someone tapped in from a remote location."

"Where was the transmission aimed?" Shi'il demanded.

"The vector is into deep space, Khetal," he replied, sweat beginning to trickle down his brow. "There is nothing there." He was very good at his job—better than most, including his predecessor whom Shi'il had executed several cycles past—but Khetal Shi'il was a particularly harsh and demanding taskmaster.

"Send the transmission to cryptography for decoding," Shi'il commanded. "I want to know what was said. Navigation, move us in between the source of the transmission along the destination vector."

The navigator immediately complied, and the ship moved in between the planet's surface and the sub.

Aboard the sub, the second of the four occupants said, "What's he doing?"

"I don't know," the first said. "I don't like it."

"Could he have detected us?" the second asked.

"The ship was close to the vector that the transmission came from. Even though it was a tight beam, there's a possibility he might have picked it up, determined the vector."

The second man said, "He's sending a muon neutrino beam at us. Uglies are getting smarter. Adjust position Z minus one hundred meters."

Suddenly, a blinding beam of raw energy blazed out of the destroyer's main gun port, missing the sub by mere meters.

"Whoa!" the first yelled as the second man jumped into the pilot seat.

"Time to go," the second said as he punched forward on the fusion engines and accelerated the sub away from the ship. As they streaked away, the destroyer continued firing in a random pattern, hoping to score a lucky hit.

The first said, "Arming weapons," as he activated the warheads on all eight torpedoes they carried.

Back on the destroyer, Shi'il barked orders.

"Stay on them," he said. "Do not lose them or you will pay with your life."

The subling at the scanner station reported, "We are tracking him, Khetal. As he runs at full speed, his engines are giving off much heat."

Shi'il barked, "Cease fire on main guns and arm missiles. Comm, advise the other fleet ships that this kill is ours. No interference from them."

The sub pilot juked and dodged as best he could. Several of the shots from the destroyer came far too close for comfort.

The first said, "The gunner on that ship seems frantic. He's not picking his shots. He's just firing wildly. The other ships aren't helping either . . . wait . . . he stopped firing . . ."

"Missile warning! The destroyer has fired a heat seeker at us!"

"Evasive! Try and keep ahead of him!"

The man had a thought and said, "Hey, take us closer to that other destroyer over there."

He indicated a second T'Kharr destroyer fairly close to their position. As they appeared to be preparing to fly behind the second ship, the first destroyer still in hot pursuit, the sub pilot juked to starboard, away from the second ship. He suddenly turned again to port, toward the second ship, the missile fired by the first destroyer still following closely.

The sub abruptly switched to its stealth engines, cutting their heat signature to zero momentarily. With no heat source to home in on, the missile locked onto the next hottest thing in its path—the second destroyer's engine ports.

Shi'il realized what was happening just moments too late. As the sub went dark, the missile homed in on the second destroyer's engines and scored with deadly accuracy. The port-side engine exploded with a ball of superheated plasma.

Shi'il watched in horror as secondary explosions rippled up the port side of the destroyer *Gaka'anath*. He screamed with fury and spun on the gunner, now cowering in his seat. Without thinking, Shi'il drew his sidearm and blew the gunner to pieces with several shots, spraying the gunnery and adjacent consoles with blood and gore.

Over the comm speakers, Shi'il heard the other destroyer commander screaming, "I will feast on your children's entrails, Shi'il, you voctaw lover!"

Then, "Khetal, torpedoes! Four of them heading toward the *Gaka'anath*."

Shi'il's eyes grew wide as he turned toward the view screen, and he screamed, "Fire control, intercept those torpedoes!" As realization dawned as to what he'd just done to the gunner, he turned and saw no one manning the blood-soaked gunnery station. He could do nothing but watch as the four torpedoes slammed into the port side of the *Gaka'anath*. Multiple explosions rocked the ship, and the *Gaka'anath* disappeared in a brilliant flash of fire and energy.

Shi'il slid back into his seat, speechless, watching the fireball expand. After a few moments of stunned silence, he regained his composure and screamed, "Where is that enemy ship?"

"Khetal, we have lost the enemy sub," the detector subling said. "They have gone dark."

Shi'il sat in stunned silence and knew what transmission would come in next.

The communications subling reported, "Khetal, Rinn-Tar-Vel Ka'awon demands your presence on his flagship immediately. He also commands you bring your gunnery subling and deliver yourselves for judgment."

Shi'il turned once again toward the gunnery station, his scapegoat for this debacle already dead—a much quicker and less painful death than he himself would suffer.

His executive officer, Rinn-Khetal Ri'isha, stepped up and said, "You are hereby relieved of duty, Khetal. As of this moment, I seize command. Communications, notify the flagship and note in the log."

He tore the full Khetal rankings from Shi'il's chest and motioned toward the two guards standing by the entrance to the bridge. They immediately walked up and hit Shi'il with their pain batons without warning, dropping him to his knees. The first guard slapped a restraining collar on him and hit the activator button. Shi'il screamed in agony and jumped to his feet. The guard then motioned toward the bridge entrance with their batons and led Shi'il off to the launch bay and his fate.

Alpha Auridius Nexus

Lt. Vale shouted, louder than she'd intended, "Admiral, the carrier! I'm getting the transponder beacon. It just snapped on."

"Power readings on the carrier just spiked," Ensign Craig said. "*Cyphar* and *Tibrin* report they're being scanned."

"Captain Yeager, report," Drake said.

Yeager, captain of the destroyer *Tibrin*, responded. "Standard scanner sweep, Admiral. We haven't been targeted by any weapons, but many of the key systems appear to be powering up on their own. Wait a moment . . ." He listened to a report from his bridge crew. "Something's happening in their port landing bay."

Drake said, "Zoom in on that bay."

The view changed to a view of the *Lysithea's* port landing bay. The atmosphere shield emitters surrounding the openings of the bay, which generated the energy field that kept atmosphere and life support in the massive bays and allowed ships to travel through it, started to glow a faint red color. Suddenly, the emitters turned bright blue and the bay illuminated.

"Atmosphere shield is now active," Craig reported. "The bay is pressurizing."

"Is that the welcome mat?" Drake asked.

"I don't know," North said. "No response to our challenge?"

"Not yet, sir," Vale said.

"Have you tried downloading the ship logs remotely, Lieutenant?" North asked.

"Yes, sir," she replied. "As soon as their comm gave the auto bounce back, I should have been able to access their computers, but someone has erected one hell of a firewall over there. It doesn't respond to any of our codes."

"Take us to ten thousand meters off *Lysithea's* bow and order all stop," North ordered.

Drake turned to Vale and said, "Order Fleet Condition Two." He turned to Captain Frost and said, "Spin up forward missile tubes ten through twenty and thirty through forty. Warm up the main guns. Point defenses and rail guns on manual."

"Tell Brigadier Logan to launch," North said, and Drake relayed the order to the launch bay.

On the screen, two Tyr-class assault shuttles raced away from *Pacifica* toward the now-fully-pressurized landing bay on the *Lysithea*.

"Launching probe," Logan said.

The visual scanners were linked into the main view screen of the *Pacifica*, allowing them to see what Logan was seeing. As the silver sphere launched from the assault shuttle and breached the energy shield, images from the *Lysithea's* landing bay flashed onto the screen.

North had been on a Saturn-class carrier before. Slightly larger than the more modern Neptune-class carriers like *Pacifica*, she only had two landing bays rather than three. As the probe scanned, they saw all the ship's fighter craft neatly stowed in their racks. All the support equipment and work stations were neat and tidy. As the probe penetrated deeper into the bay and came upon the spot where the tugs and bombers would've been stored, they saw something out of place.

"What are those?" Drake wondered aloud, as the probe swept an area containing what appeared to be several hundred black cylinders.

"Intense scan of one of those cylinders," Logan ordered over the speaker as the probe paused and focused its scans on the nearest tube.

Logan said, "They appear to be stasis tubes, but those are of no design that I've ever seen before."

North felt his pulse quicken at the thought that the crew might have actually survived.

"How many of them are there, General?" he asked.

"Scan shows approximately twelve hundred tubes, Commander. Most appear to still be active. No doubt they were brought down here because there are more power stations here to hook them up to. That would explain why those ships were tethered outside. They needed the room. They're heavily shielded. That's why we didn't pick up any power readings until we got closer."

Suddenly, there was a loud clanging noise to the left of the probe, and it spun quickly toward the noise.

"Probe is picking up a life sign—human—just behind that fueling station!" Logan shouted.

Logan activated the probe's speaker and said, "Show yourself! Show yourself or we will take defensive action!"

A figure dressed in filthy blue coveralls shot up from behind the console, arms raised high in the air.

"Don't shoot, don't shoot," he said as he walked out into the open, turning in a circle to show he wasn't armed. "I surrender." The man appeared to be in his fifties, with long, gray hair and a salt-and-pepper beard.

"Identify yourself," Logan ordered, and the look on the figure's face changed from surprise to curiosity.

"Who am I?" he asked as he lowered his hands to his hips. "Who are you? You come onto my ship and demand to know who I am?"

Logan looked at the screen and, despite himself, couldn't help but chuckle at the man's brashness.

He cleared his throat and said, "This is Brigadier General Kyle Logan from the Alliance carrier SAS *Pacifica*, 17th fleet marine detachment. Please identify yourself."

The man nodded and said, "Well that's a little bit better. Please and thank you will get you much further with me. Yes, they will . . ."

"Please . . . identify yourself," Logan asked again, realizing that if this man had been marooned here for the last twenty-three years, he might not have all his faculties intact.

"You don't look like a general," the man said as he walked closer to the probe and examined it more closely. "Are you a synthetic?"

Logan said, "I'm communicating through this probe. I'm in a ship outside the atmosphere shield of the landing bay."

The man looked toward the shield and said, "Outside? Well, why don't you come in? I turned on the lights for you."

Logan muted the link to the probe and said, "What do you think, Commander?"

"Your discretion, General. If you perceive no threat, proceed."

"Very well," he said. He activated the link again. "Okay, we're coming in. Be sure and stand clear."

The man jumped at the voice but broke into a wide grin. "Okay, I'll stand back."

Logan ordered the shuttles through the shield and into the bay. As they touched down, the shuttle doors opened and disgorged the marine squads inside the ships. They took up standard defensive positions as trained, and when they saw no immediate threat, the gunnery sergeant yelled, "All clear!" Logan exited the ship, followed by a colonel and a major outfitted in battle dress.

With two armed marines flanking him, Logan stood in front of the ship and waited for the man to approach. The figure then trotted up to the general and snapped to attention.

"Major Terrence Monsoor, General," he said, bringing his right hand up in a salute. "It's very good to see some human faces again."

Logan returned the salute. "At ease, soldier. Major, are you the only crew member awake? We noticed the stasis tubes."

Monsoor looked toward the back of the bay and said, "Yes, sir. I'm the only survivor of the science team. We all volunteered to remain awake and tend to the stasis pods."

Logan nodded and said, "And the rest of the crew?"

"All in stasis, including the admiral . . ." Monsoor appeared to suddenly become overwhelmed with emotion, and his legs unexpectedly gave way and he fell to his knees. Logan grabbed his right arm for support and nodded to two marines standing nearby.

"It'll be all right, Major," Logan said sympathetically. He'd obviously been alone a long time.

"I'm sorry, sir. It's been so long . . . so long . . ."

"We'll finish this on *Pacifica*."

"Aye, sir," the marines responded as they gently carried Monsoor into the shuttle.

Logan activated the link to the *Pacifica*. "Commander North, the major says the entire crew is here in stasis. He's the only one awake. I'm coming back to *Pacifica* with him, and I'm placing Colonel Shaddra in charge of the recon."

"Acknowledged, General," North said. "Bring him to sickbay. We'll meet you there."

North spun toward the lift and looked at Austin. "You coming?"

Austin, who'd been standing back, taking everything in, said, "Are you kidding?" and ran into the lift behind North.

North stopped in the lift and said, "Mat, order the fleet to Condition Three. If the marine sweep turns up what we expect, go to Condition Four. I'll be in sickbay."

"Aye aye, sir," Drake said, a bit envious of Austin. He was dying to find out what this Major Monsoor had to say.

Monsoor, now more coherent after a hyperfeuron and vitamin injection from one of the medics, looked out the viewport. His eyes grew wide, "What ship is that? I'm not familiar with that configuration."

"She's the *Pacifica*, Neptune-class, flagship of the Alliance 17th fleet," Logan said.

Monsoor whistled. "Neptune . . . three landing bays. Nice upgrade." Monsoor regarded the carrier for a moment and asked, "The missile tubes, did they change the bore? Are they the same size as the Saturn-class?"

Logan thought for a moment, nodded, and said, "They are the same as the Saturn-class tubes. No change."

Monsoor took in the information and nodded, muttering, "Interesting. They should fit."

"Come again?" Logan said.

Monsoor shook his head and said, "Nothing, sir. Just thinking out loud."

Logan said, "One more thing. We're having trouble linking up the Inter-Fleet Tactical Net because of some firewall. Your doing, I'm guessing?"

"Yes, sir," Monsoor replied. "Can you hook me into the comm net?"

Logan motioned to one of the soldiers who brought a remote terminal to Monsoor. He punched in a complex code and hit the transmit button, then handed the terminal back to the soldier.

Back on *Pacifica*, Lt. Vale said, "I now have access to the Inter-Fleet Tactical Net, Admiral. We now have access to the command and control codes of the other fleet."

Drake nodded. "Very good. Download logs and tactical data. Continue to power up systems on the *Lysithea*, starting with the starboard landing bay. Hold off on her escorts until we have the carrier up and running." Lights began to come on all over the ship.

The remainder of Monsoor's ride to the *Pacifica* was relatively silent. When they arrived, a medical team greeted them and took charge of the major. In short order, they wheeled him to sickbay where a very anxious looking Commander North was waiting.

The large, well-appointed sickbay on Neptune-class ships could easily treat a hundred casualties in their multiple wards. Monitors, medical scanners, and other equipment lined the walls behind the beds, and several doctors and nurses attended to the few people in the room who'd come in with minor ailments.

As they wheeled him by, Monsoor gave North a once-over while sitting in the hoverchair and squinted as he looked at the rank insignia on his collar. Not recognizing the significance of the nova emblem, his eyes then went to the six stars on Austin's collar, a pentagon of five stars and one in the center. He stood and offered a weak salute.

Austin glanced sideways at North and said to Monsoor, "Major, protocol demands you salute the senior officer in the room."

North looked at Monsoor and held up his hand, then said, "It's all right under the circumstances. The Grand Commander rank didn't exist twenty years ago. I'm Grand Commander North." He returned Monsoor's salute and said, "Please sit down, Major. We have a lot of questions after the doctors look you over."

Monsoor nodded and sat down and asked, "Grand Commander?"

North said, "Equivalent to eight stars. Command thought the emblem might be a bit cumbersome, so they created an eight-point nova."

Monsoor nodded and said, "Forgive me, sir. I have a bit of catching up to do."

Two med techs directed him from the chair to a bed, and several doctors began scanning him. Logan came up to North and asked to speak to him privately.

"Damage control and recon teams report that the ship interior is in good shape. We brought over a few portable fusion generators to bring the systems up more quickly. The hull is another matter. Lots of degradation from the years of exposure to the radiation. No battle damage though. Looks as if the ship was squared away and put into storage."

North took in the information and said, "Crew?"

Logan replied, "Teams searched the second bay after it pressurized and found another twelve hundred or so stasis tubes. They haven't reached the cargo deck yet. Of the ones they found, around 95 percent of the stasis tubes are still functioning. They said the design is something they've never seen before, so they haven't tried to revive anyone just yet."

Austin said, "Stasis tubes aren't supposed to be used for long-term storage. The longest I've ever heard of them being used was two years or so. Amazing that more of them didn't malfunction."

"That was our primary job, to maintain the tubes," Monsoor said from the bed.

North, Austin, and Logan turned toward the man, who was being hooked up to an IV cuff by a med-tech. After his comment, he noticed just how attractive she was.

"Boy," he breathed. "I forgot what a good-looking woman looks like."

The med-tech smiled and blushed and continued hooking up the IV.

North cleared his throat, and Monsoor shifted his attention back to the matter at hand.

"Sorry, sir. I guess I'm still a little overwhelmed. Haven't had any live humans to speak to in a long time."

North smiled and said, "Understandable under the circumstances, but we need you to focus. How did the crew wind up in stasis?"

"After about six months with no hope of using the starlanes, Admiral Thorne asked me and my science team to come up with a design that would extend the effectiveness of the stasis tubes. He knew that unless we could leave, everyone would slowly die. At maximum rationing, our provisions would only last about two and a half to three years, even if we grew our own food and recycled everything we could."

North said, "So what happened?"

Monsoor replied, "We found a way to connect the tubes in series, allowing the fields to overlap and enhance one another. Several other tweaks to the circuitry allowed us to reasonably extend the effectiveness of the tubes to approximately thirty-five years, or so we thought."

"What do you mean?" Austin asked.

"Well, the problem was, nobody had ever tried what we were trying before. We lost several dozen people in the first year before we were able to stabilize the tubes."

At the comment that several dozen had perished, Austin glanced over at North, who seemed especially disturbed by this. He knew his friend was dying to learn the fate of his brother, but he also knew there were more pressing matters that needed to be addressed first.

"Keep going, Major," North said.

"The plan was that after putting the crew to sleep, we would put ourselves under and await rescue. If rescue didn't come for thirty-five years, we would have all died without even knowing what had happened. We realized after that first year that adjustments had to be made to the system. We tried to make the tubes self-maintaining, but it was impossible. Someone had to remain awake to tend to the tubes, make minor adjustments and such. As a result, myself and a dozen others volunteered to stay awake for as long as it would take. Over time, the others died due to accidents. I am the last survivor. I spent my time maintaining the tubes, going from ship to ship in the fleet, and waiting for someone to show up. That was sixteen years ago."

Austin said, "You've been on your own for sixteen years?"

Monsoor nodded and said, "Yes, sir. I considered waking someone else up, but the tubes are rigged in such a way that you'd have to awaken an entire group of tubes. You can't revive just one person. They need to be revived in a specific order and in groups of thirty. If one is awakened individually, it could kill the rest in that grouping." He suddenly looked alarmed and said, "I should have said something before now . . ."

Logan said, "Don't worry, Major. My teams have been instructed to assess damage and the general condition of the ship. They've been specifically ordered not to try and revive anyone."

Monsoor lay back on his pillow, a look of relief on his face.

Logan's data pad chimed, and he stepped away to read the message. He then said, "Commander, I have an update."

North and Austin stepped away again and Logan said, "Damage control and recon teams have searched the ship and located a total of 4,929 tubes. Ninety-four percent of those are still functioning."

North said, "Crew complement of five thousand, that's almost everyone." He thought a moment and said, "Order damage control and recon teams to the other ships. Tell Lt. Vale to power up the other ships remotely before our people board them."

"Yes, sir. And Commander, there's something else. In one of the smaller of the eight cargo bays, they found something interesting. Scientific equipment, schematics, and racks and racks of missiles."

"Maybe they moved them from the magazine for some reason," North said.

Logan said, "I thought about that, sir, so I instructed them to check the magazines. They were full of the standard Mark 105 missiles common to ships of that time. These in the cargo hold have been modified. Some type of device has been attached to the warhead. About fifty were in racks, and four appeared to be under modification. That's not all. He has a whole bunch of things over there that he's either modified or simply created. Our guys can't figure out the function of half of the devices in there."

North turned back to Monsoor and asked, "Those missiles in the cargo bay, what are the modifications for?"

Monsoor seemed to concentrate for a moment and then said, "Oh, those . . . multi-phasic warheads. Able to pass through an enemy bulkhead or shield and slip back into phase inside of the enemy vessel." He took a drink from a cup next to his bed and asked the med-tech, "Do you think I could get something to eat?"

Monsoor had said it so casually that North thought he might have heard him wrong. "What did you say?"

Monsoor shrugged his shoulders and said, "I had lots of time on my hands, sir. The cargo bay was my workshop."

North and Austin looked at each other in stunned silence, and North turned back to him and said, "Are you telling me you've developed a missile that will travel through solid matter and enemy shields?"

Monsoor nodded. "Yes, sir. I've finished about fifty of them."

North said, "Have you tested them?"

"Sure," Monsoor replied. "I fired a dummy missile from one of the shuttles and watched it pass through an asteroid and come out the other side completely intact. I have the video footage of the test if you'd like to see it. They work perfectly, although you have to be within a hundred kilometers of the target for the matrix to remain active. Why wouldn't they work?" Monsoor seemed genuinely perplexed by their questions. Of course they worked.

"Unreal," Austin said.

Monsoor said, "I made a lot of stuff . . . combat auto-med dispenser, handheld Voron rifle, but the really cool stuff is in the data banks. I have a great design for a starlane inhibitor. Closes off one end of the starlane unless the arriving ship has the proper code. Only on the drawing board though. Six months or so, I should have a prototype ready."

North and Austin stood in awe, taking in what Monsoor was saying.

Finally, Logan asked, "You modified Mark 105 missiles?"

"Of course, sir," he replied. "They pack the biggest punch in the arsenal."

Logan asked, "Is your design specific to the 105, or can it be used on another type of missile?"

"What did you have in mind, sir?" Monsoor asked.

"Our current state-of-the-art ship-to-ship missile is the Mark 112," he said. "Twice the explosive yield of the 105 and twice as fast."

Monsoor nodded and said, "The explosive component is independent of the multi-phasic matrix. It can be used for any type of the larger missiles, I imagine."

North smiled and said, "Major, I know that if anyone deserves a rest, it's you, but I need you to go back to the *Lysithea* and wake the crew. Then I need you to speak to my science and weapons teams. You may have just given us the advantage we'll need in the coming days. Also, back up that database on *Pacifica's* computers. I don't want any of that data lost."

Monsoor look puzzled and said, "Advantage for what?"

Earth, Del Mar Police Department

Yvonne Wilson sat in her cubicle, trying her best to piece together the crash that had killed Shareel and James North seven years ago. The squad building was fairly new—only a few years old—but lean on space. Data pads and hard copies of reports littered her desk, along with a cup of a stim drink that had long ago gone cold alongside a half-eaten bagel. She had to concentrate hard to filter out the buzz of the voices of the other detectives in the room.

The more she read about the North family, the more astonished she became. The accident was a hit and run, but the traffic cams in the area were conveniently out of service at the time of the accident. All the alleged eye witnesses apparently saw nothing and couldn't identify the other car or driver. The vehicle monitoring net showed all the vehicles in the area at the time, but the suspect vehicle wasn't broadcasting a transponder. She decided to examine the crime scene photos to see if there was anything that had been overlooked at the time.

"Hey, Billy, beam me a copy of the accident scene photos," she said to Perkins, who was scanning the photos on a terminal across the room.

Perkins entered a command into the computer, and the photos were loaded into Wilson's personal hand device. She scanned the photos for anything that seemed unusual but found nothing obvious.

Perkins walked up behind Wilson and said, "What do you expect to find in those pictures?"

Wilson blew out an exasperated breath and said, "I don't know. Smoking gun, someone pointing to the bad guy, saying, 'Right here,' something . . ."

Abruptly, the screen on her unit went black again, and Perkins said, "I think our friend is back."

"Relax, Inspector. This is Malone. We chatted earlier. I thought this might interest you."

A picture of the accident scene flashed onto the screen and zoomed in on a man in the crowd with his back to the camera, his arms covered with tattoos.

"Watch this," the words scrolled as the view zoomed in on the man's left arm. Once the man's arm filled the screen, the computer moved through several bandwidths of color before stopping on a certain band. There, as if drawn on by a fluorescent marker, were the letters "V.O.M."

"A genetic tattoo," Perkins said.

Genetic tattoos were popular with a number of groups whose members only wished to be identified by other members of the group. Only those who knew the exact light frequency of the group's tattoo would be able to identify its members. The groups used the tattoos to prevent infiltrators from penetrating their ranks.

"What's the significance of this?" she asked.

"We found a similar genetic tattoo on a traitor who caused a lot of damage a couple of days ago. I can't go into more specifics, because we're conducting our own investigation into that incident, but I noticed some connections in our cases. I can tell you this . . . this man and others caused hundreds of deaths and may be responsible for many other acts."

"Why don't you ask this traitor what it means?" Perkins asked.

"Because we discovered the tattoo during the guy's autopsy."

"Oh, I see," Perkins said.

Wilson asked, "Do you have any idea what V.O.M. might stand for?"

"Unfortunately, yes," Malone said, then a stellarnet site popped up on the screen.

"Voices of Mandis," Perkins read.

"Mandis," Wilson said. "I know that name from somewhere. Yeah . . . that was the agro colony where the T'Kharr wiped out the population with some kind of nerve agent."

"The same," Malone said.

"I still don't see the connection," Wilson said.

"I think I might," Perkins said, who had been reading the website over Wilson's shoulder. "This group blames the government—specifically the military—for the deaths of the colonists. They say the government didn't do enough to save them and decided to exterminate them instead."

"Keep reading," Malone said.

Perkins read, "We, the mothers and fathers, brothers and sisters, sons and daughters of the victims of Mandis scream in outrage, since they cannot. We accuse the government and military of the murder and subsequent cover-up of the 201,498 souls who were colonists of the planet. We accuse the Alliance Council of fabricating the video footage, blaming the enemy for their own government experiment gone wrong and accuse them of using weapons of mass destruction to wipe out the evidence. We have tried to travel to Mandis to see for ourselves the evidence of the military atrocities, but the starlanes are dead. This means the Mandis star is dead, destroyed by the military. The blood of those innocent victims stains their hands. If the Alliance populace won't hold those responsible accountable, we will avenge their deaths ourselves using whatever means at our disposal."

"Strong stuff," Wilson said. "Borders on sedition."

"The group staged a few rallies and screamed bloody murder to whoever would listen, but nobody bought into it," Malone said. "We thought they'd faded into obscurity until now."

"How is Commander North connected with this?" Wilson asked.

"I don't know. Then-Fleet-Admiral North was involved in the Mandis operation, but only the highest levels know how far he was involved, and they aren't talking. They might blame him for something. Remember, Arvil Symons was jailed because he hacked into the military mainframe. They never revealed any of the classified data he obtained."

"What do you suggest?" Wilson asked.

"I suggest you try and contact the scumbag reporter who tried to sensationalize the incident and fan the flames," Malone typed. "Chuck Ryther. He had contacts in the group and made a name for himself with the story."

"He got spanked a few years ago for running stories with unconfirmed sources," Perkins said. "I remember when he got fired from the network. Works for some gossip rag out of the Valley now."

"We'll follow up on this, Malone," Wilson said. "You try and piece things together on your end. How do we contact you?"

"I'll contact you when I'm ready," Malone said. "I'm not exactly supposed to be sharing with you guys, but this is too important, and you can go places I'm unable to at the moment. I'll be in touch." Then the connection went dead.

"I hate friggin reporters," Perkins said.

"Me too, Billy, but it's all we got," Wilson said as she grabbed her coat and trotted out of the room, Perkins in tow. "Let's go."

Chuck Ryther sat in his office at the headquarters of *The Real Truth*, a gossip web magazine that made a name for itself, not because of its hard-hitting news stories, but rather because of the record number of lawsuits filed against it for slander and libel. Ryther had been the perfect choice as editor after his unceremonious departure from the Alliance Broadcast Network for airing a story slandering President Barouq. He was fired the next day and escorted from the building by security.

Despite his title, being editor of a gossip rag was far from glamorous. His office in the run-down building the owner leased wasn't fit for human habitation. Papers and old articles covered the walls, the carpet was stained and worn-out, and the air was infused with smells they just couldn't seem to get rid of. The rest of the building was no better. Vermin and bad plumbing were the order of the day, and everyone working there wore unhappy scowls on their faces.

As Ryther reviewed the coming issue, he pondered how he'd arrived at his current state. He'd been the top-rated news anchor at ABN, the largest of the twelve major Alliance networks. He was the king, without question. Whatever he said, the people of the Alliance believed. When he'd aired the story of President Barouq and the child he supposedly fathered out of wedlock, they should've believed him. Unfortunately, the paternity test turned out to be fabricated, and Ryther hadn't checked his facts. After that, no legitimate news organization would touch him.

He sighed and pulled out the bottle of Centauran whiskey he kept in his desk, noting that he was down to only half a bottle. Again. He made a mental note to stop by the liquor dispensary on his way home that night, and then he heard a knock on his door.

"Come in," he said.

A man and woman entered the room. The woman said, "Mister Ryther? I'm Inspector Wilson, and this is Detective Perkins from Del Mar PD. I was wondering if we could ask you a couple of questions."

"Do I need an advocate?" Ryther asked.

Wilson replied, "No, sir. You aren't suspected in anything."

"Then with all due respect, leave my office," he said, taking a shot of whiskey. "I don't like cops."

Perkins chuckled and said, "What a coincidence. I don't like reporters. Especially disgraced news reporters."

Ryther stiffened at the comment but was smart enough to maintain his cool. He knew better than to provoke the police, but he also knew his rights.

"Under the First Guarantee of the Alliance Charter, the press has the right—"

Wilson cut him off and said, "We know what the First Guarantee says. We aren't here about anything you've printed. We wanted to ask you about a group you had dealings with about eight years ago. Voices of Mandis."

The mention of the group caught Ryther's attention.

"What about them?" he asked, too curious to renew his demand that they leave his office.

Wilson adopted a softer tone and took a seat in front of Ryther's desk. "They appear to be active again. We also think they may have moved from vocal protests to assassination."

"Assassination?" he said, 100 percent interested now. "Does this have something to do with the murders at Grand Commander North's house yesterday?"

Wilson looked genuinely surprised and asked, "How do you know about that? What makes you think that incident was an assassination?"

"I'll assume by your reaction that it was indeed an assassination and not an accident," Ryther said with a smirk.

Wilson silently cursed herself, falling into Ryther's verbal trap so easily. Whatever he might be, he was obviously smart. Best not to underestimate him again.

"You're awfully well informed, Mr. Ryther," Perkins said.

Ryther said, "Just because I'm out of the big game doesn't mean I don't still have sources out and about, even in the police department and military."

Wilson nodded and thought for a moment before saying, "Your sources are correct. We believe it was an assassination."

Ryther looked stunned for a moment. Wilson noticed his surprise and realized that he had been expecting the old game of accusation and denial that was typical for this type of exchange. She had to choose her next words carefully.

"Voices of Mandis . . . what can you tell me about them?"

"You think I know who they all are because I did a story on them years ago?" he asked.

"Something like that," she replied.

Ryther rose from his chair and went to the window. "Well, you can't compel me to tell you anything, and you can't hook me up to a verifier without a warrant, so what do I get in return for telling you what I know?" he asked, now staring her in the face.

Wilson glanced sideways at Perkins, who shrugged his shoulders. She said, "What do you want?"

"My dignity back," he replied.

"I'm afraid that's beyond my power, Mr. Ryther," Wilson said with a shake of her head.

"N-no, I know that," he stammered, not wanting to blow this opportunity at some legitimacy, but not wanting to show he was too anxious either. They both possessed something the other wanted, and he needed to make sure he got his due.

He continued, "What I meant was, you can give me some semblance of legitimacy."

"How so?" Wilson asked.

"I've had it with this rag . . . it's all I can do to not jump out this window," he said, losing his voice for a moment.

For the first time since they'd arrived, Wilson couldn't help but pity the man. "So, what did you have in mind?"

"An exclusive. If this lead with this group pans out, I want an exclusive story. I can shop it to the networks or papers as an op-ed piece or sell it to *Systemweek Magazine*."

Wilson thought for a moment. "Agreed. I'll give you the best damned interview ever if this pans out. Now please tell us what you know about the group."

"Voices of Mandis, as you probably know, was a group of family members of the victims of the nerve weapon attacks on the Mandis agro colonies. They never bought the government line that it was the T'Kharr and that everyone had died after everything possible had been done to save them. They believed that the government used the colony as a testing ground for a new weapon and then fabricated the vids to cover up their experiments. It didn't help when they tried to go to the system and found the starlanes weren't active. I know because I was on the ship when they tried. The group employed a starlane physicist to research the problem, and he determined that the starlanes didn't work anymore because the Mandis star had been destroyed."

"Okay," Perkins said. "So far, you've told us everything from their website."

Ryther nodded and said, "Yes, but what the website didn't say is that there were radical elements in the group that blamed the military, particularly Grand Commander North, for what happened."

Wilson said, "Why blame North?"

"North commanded the mission. Understand, most of the group were just everyday, law-abiding citizens who wanted answers as to why their loved ones were gone. There was, however, a radical arm of the group that had no problem resorting to violence. They blamed the government and the people of the Alliance. Eventually, people didn't seem to care anymore. They forgot about Mandis. But that radical arm, they didn't let it go.

"One of them, a computer genius named Symons, got caught hacking into the military mainframe looking for information on Mandis. He learned that North led the fleet that was the last to leave the Mandis system. He also managed to catch references to something called Omega but wasn't able to decrypt it before the cops arrested him and threw him in jail. He was fanatical about North, called him a war criminal. He thought that this Omega reference might be the code name of the weapon they used on the colony."

Wilson said, "Are you sure the name was Symons? S-Y-M-O-N-S?"

"Yeah, I'm sure. Arvil was his first name. He was a scary guy. Most of the group stopped coming to the rallies after he started going off on North. I think they were scared of him. But there were a few who bought into his story."

"Do you know the names of the people who believed him, might have helped him get back at North?" Wilson asked.

Ryther shook his head and said, "No, I don't think most of them even knew who the others were. One of Symons's inner circle was supposedly in the military."

"This Symons, do you think he's capable of killing someone?" Wilson asked.

Ryther took another sip from his whiskey glass and looked her square in the eye. "Absolutely."

Wilson then pulled up the photo of the tattooed man at Shareel North's accident scene and asked, "Do you recognize this man?"

Ryther looked at the photo and said, "That looks like August Kidder. I recognize the tattoos. He piloted the ship we used to try and get to Mandis. He had a sister named Ariana that came on that trip. Quite a looker. They lost their parents and a brother on Mandis. He was pretty tight with Symons, now that I think about it."

Wilson pulled back her hand unit and turned the photo off. She then said, "Anything else you can tell us?"

Ryther thought for a second and said, "That was a photo of an accident scene . . . what accident was that?" He then got up and started to think out loud. "Accident scene, about seven or eight years ago, judging by the tags on the cars passing by . . . North's family. Was that a picture of the accident that killed his wife and son?"

Wilson nodded and said, "Yes."

"And you think Voices of Mandis was responsible for that too." It was a statement rather than a question. "Interesting," Ryther said, the gears starting to turn in his head. Maybe this was a bigger story than he thought and even these cops didn't realize it.

Wilson got up and said, "Well, thanks, Mr. Ryther. If you think of anything else, please give us a call."

"No problem," he said. "And don't forget our deal."

As soon as they were gone, Ryther sat behind his desk and pulled up his encrypted notes on Voices of Mandis. He thought that maybe they'd be worth reviewing again, especially the names of everyone in the group. He could've given them the names, but why make their jobs any easier? Besides, he hated cops.

"I hate reporters," Perkins said on their way out of the building.

"I know," Wilson said. "I feel like taking a shower every time I have to deal with one, but they're a necessary evil, I suppose."

Her hand unit buzzed.

"Wilson," she said.

Malone answered in a gravelly voice, "Good work. As soon as you two left his office, the lying bastard opened an encrypted file on his computer with a roster of names for Voices of Mandis. We grabbed a copy of it."

"That dirty son of a . . . and to think I almost felt sorry for him," Wilson said.

"You already know August Kidder is dead. He hijacked a ship and caused quite a bit of damage a few days ago. Killed the crew and then himself when he realized he couldn't escape. I can't tell you more than that. Classified."

"And his sister, Ariana?" Wilson asked.

"Already in our custody," Malone replied. "She's involved in another matter I'm investigating. She has some inexplicable resistance to our verifier, so we've called in a specialist."

"I don't want to know what that means . . . I don't suppose you could forward us that list of names from Ryther's computer," Wilson requested.

"You realize that you can't use it in court," he said. "Fruit of the poisonous tree and all."

"Yeah, I know, but anonymous tips come in all the time," Wilson said.

"I like how you think," Malone said.

The list arrived in a file on Wilson's hand unit.

"Thanks, Malone," she said. "We'll run down the local names."

"Sounds good," Malone said. "I'll be in touch." Then he hung up.

Exasperated, Wilson said, "That guy is going to drive me to drink."

"But you got the list," Perkins said with a smile.

"Yep," she said. "We've got a lot of work to do."

CHAPTER TWELVE

Imperial Command Carrier Ka'athiol, *fleet commander's chambers*

Rinn-Tar-Vel Ve'erdren Ka'awon sat in his damp chambers as he studied the reports from the new khetal of the destroyer *Ra'aktaka*. The high heat and humidity, set to simulate conditions of the homeworld, soothed him and helped keep his anger in check as he studied the communiqués. The destroyer *Gaka'anath* was lost due to the incompetence of its former captain, Khetal Shi'il.

To make matters worse, they'd allowed the enemy sub to go dark. The only good news was the arrival of the three reinforcement fleets from the homeworld. Only two fleets had been expected. The third was a blessing from the Under-Deity itself. That brought the total to five fleets in the system, more than sufficient to hold the planet and fend off any human attack. A knock on his chamber door broke his train of thought.

"I ordered no disturbances!" he snapped.

The door opened, and Alta-Tar-Vel Da'akta Te'eq entered the room.

Ka'awon jumped to his feet and bowed his head, all four arms spread in submission. "Forgive me, Alta-Tar-Vel. I was not informed that you were arriving. I will punish my communications subling immediately."

Te'eq silenced him with a wave of his upper right arm. "I instructed your bridge crew not to announce my arrival. No punishment is required."

"As you command, of course, Alta-Tar-Vel," he said, rising to stand respectfully in front of his superior.

"I am here to observe. The shi'ia-khar is very interested in this human technology, and intelligence reports that five human carrier fleets left their home system two cycles past, destination unknown. It is the opinion of intelligence that they are on their way here to attempt to remove us from the system and prevent our capture of the technology."

Te'eq then walked over to Ka'awon's chair and seated himself, making no offer to his subordinate to sit. Ka'awon knew this small lack of courtesy between flag officers was significant.

"Tell me of the debacle with the *Ra'aktaka*," Te'eq said, danger in his voice.

Ka'awon recounted the events, ending with the execution by vivisection of former Khetal Shi'il. "I have sent word to the homeworld that Shi'il's mate and offspring be exiled to a prison world as punishment for his incompetence."

"Fortunately for you, Rinn-Tar-Vel, flag officers are much more difficult to replace than a khetal on a destroyer," Te'eq rumbled.

"You are most wise, Alta-Tar-Vel."

Te'eq then motioned for Ka'awon to sit.

"While I am angered by the destruction of the *Gaka'anath*, I believe the blame lies squarely on Khetal Shi'il and his bridge gunner," Te'eq said. "I can only hold you responsible to a point."

Ka'awon nearly fell out of his chair. Mercy from a superior? This was a new tactic. Ka'awon immediately became suspicious.

Te'eq saw the conflict in the eyes of his subordinate. "You are surprised?"

Ka'awon knew better than to lie. "Honestly, a little, Alta-Tar-Vel," he said cautiously.

"Answer this, Ka'awon. Why did you not order the exile of the gunner's family? Most commanders would have punished the families of all involved."

Ka'awon thought for a moment and said, "I felt it unnecessary, Alta-Tar-Vel. It would accomplish nothing. He was acting under orders from Shi'il."

"You are learning wisdom, Ka'awon," Te'eq said, a disturbing smile crossing his face. "I will have to watch you. What progress in the search for this bunker complex?"

"Ground forces are looking, but there is nothing to indicate where it might be. It is not a big planet, Alta-Tar-Vel, but the forest impedes our search efforts. We will find it eventually. I am certain."

The comm chimed, and the voice of Ka'awon's executive officer came over the loudspeaker. "Forgive the intrusion, Rinn-Tar-Vel. Two Jaaleadi carrier fleets have just jumped into the Kirel Dani system. They have launched fighters and are forming to attack the supply base. In-system presence is only five destroyers, as we were called here. What are your orders, Rinn-Tar-Vel?"

"Stand by, Zha'ar," Ka'awon said as he rose and paced the floor.

Te'eq spat, "Cursed Jaaleadi! They make a better meal than adversary. What do you plan to do? Kirel Dani is the logistical center for this entire sector."

Ka'awon thought carefully before saying, "Alta-Tar-Vel, I believe this is a ruse to attempt to draw our forces away from this system. If we draw forces off to defend Kirel Dani, two fleets would be required, and if those five human fleets show up unexpectedly, they will outnumber us five to three. Reinforcements must be called in from other sectors."

Te'eq's first instinct was to reprimand his subordinate for his line of thinking, but as he pondered the situation, he was impressed by the cogent argument made by Ka'awon. The humans may very well have expected them to draw off forces to defend the supply base. Miratev was far more important. The humans knew that and were likely hoping the T'Kharr didn't realize that until it was too late. He was forced to concur with Ka'awon's assessment.

"Your fleets will remain here, Ka'awon," Te'eq said, rising and walking toward the door. "I will deal with the incursion at Kirel Dani." He stopped short of the door and said, "You have impressed me today, Rinn-Tar-Vel. Continue to do so."

Alpha Auridius Nexus

North was back in his office, as much as he wished to board the *Lysithea* and look for Jason himself. After speaking to Monsoor, he left sickbay to board a shuttle to the other ship, but Austin had talked him out of it. He conceded that his presence there would only hinder, not help.

Major Monsoor was now back on the ship helping his damage control teams revive the crew and briefing the science teams on the specifications for his multi-phasic warheads. If they performed as Monsoor promised, they'd be a huge leap forward in weapons technology and a great advantage in the coming battle. He checked the chronometer and saw they had only thirty-seven more hours until they had to make the jump to the Polto Nebula, their jumping-off point into Miratev.

Caloria's teams determined that the ninth starlane portal still terminated in the nebula. As he stared out the viewport of his ready room, he wondered if the enemy commanders did the same thing. The waiting was the worst. Logan promised him an update when all the *Lysithea's* crew was awake. It had now been over an hour and a half.

Logan's initial report was disappointing at best. Although the stasis units on the carrier had a fairly high survival rate, the rest of *Lysithea's* fleet didn't fare as well. All in all, they suffered a 60 percent failure rate in the stasis tubes, despite Monsoor's efforts. There were simply too many of them for one man to tend, and the power requirements had overwhelmed the resources of the smaller ships.

Also, with no operating navigation shielding, twenty-plus years of exposure to the radiation and cosmic dust, micro meteorite impacts, and other factors had degraded the hulls on all the ships. Several had small breaches in their outer hulls and in the worst cases were in such a state of disrepair, they would have to be scuttled. North had initially hoped they could integrate the new fleet into the coming fight, but the reality was such that they would do well to make the necessary repairs to make it back home safely, let alone engage in combat.

North went over to his desk and pulled out a small holo unit. He touched the activation stud on the side, and a photo of himself, Jason, and their parents appeared in the air above the device. Both he and Jason wore their Academy blues, both newly-minted ensigns. They had their arms around each other's shoulders and were all smiles. North remembered that day like it was yesterday. He then switched the photo to one of himself and Shareel and James.

As he looked at the photo, he thought that he'd never foreseen a future devoid of family. They'd always been important to him, but he never realized just how important until they were all gone. He'd never anticipated the emptiness, the void in his life. Even the slightest of chances that Jason was alive would be the biggest miracle he could imagine.

A knock on his door brought him out of his brooding. He turned the unit off, stowed it back in his drawer and said, "Enter."

Drake came into the room, followed by an officer North didn't recognize, dressed in an old-style uniform. When he saw the two silver stars on the man's collar, he knew who he was. The man walked up to North's desk and snapped to attention.

"Rear Admiral Steven Thorne of the *Lysithea*, Grand Commander Brandon North," Drake said.

"At ease, Admiral," North said before coming around his desk and offering his hand. Thorne took his hand and shook it warmly.

"A pleasure, sir."

"Sit down, Admiral," North said, indicating the chair in front of his desk.

"Thank you, sir," he replied and took a seat.

Drake ducked out and closed the door behind him.

Thorne smiled, looked down at his out-of-date uniform, and said, "I appear to be out of uniform, Commander. Please excuse my appearance."

North smiled and said, "I'm certainly not worried about that, Admiral, but if you'd like, I can have ships stores provide you with a new one and transfer the current specs to your ship."

Thorne nodded and said, "That would be appreciated, sir." Then, after several moments, "I think I know how Rip Van Winkle felt. Twenty-three years. It's difficult to grasp. I lost a lot of people . . ."

North nodded sympathetically. "I can only imagine. It's a miracle any of you survived. I was about to have a drink. Would you like one?"

Thorne nodded and said, "Actually, I'd love one. Thank you, sir."

North went to the bar and retrieved a clear stasis bottle from down below. The liquid in the container was also clear but seemed to catch every color in the spectrum. He looked on in interest as North poured two glasses of the liquid and gave one to him.

Thorne sniffed the liquid and took in the sweet scent. He looked at the drink again through the glass and asked, "What is this?"

North smiled and said, "That's right. You wouldn't know about this. Short version, about fifteen years ago, a fruit was discovered on a moon in the Aleen system. It was determined that the fruit contained microorganisms that had a psychotropic effect on whoever consumed it. In short, whatever beverage you desire, that's what your brain perceives as the taste of the liquid."

Thorne looked confused, and North said, "Okay . . . think of whatever kind of drink you would like to have right now. Something you've had before."

Thorne thought for a moment and said, "All right."

"Now take a sip," North said as he took a drink from his own glass.

Thorne took a small sip from the glass, and his eyes went wide. "I'll be damned. I'd swear that this was Macallan thirty-year-old single-malt scotch. The best I've ever had."

North nodded and said, "You have expensive tastes. Your brain stores every experience you've ever had, and these microorganisms are able to tap into that memory and make the experience as real as if you were actually drinking scotch or whatever else you might like at that moment. The upside is, it has no intoxicants but still gives the drinker a feeling of well-being. All of the enjoyment of the beverage without the negative side effects."

Thorne took a second sip and said, "Amazing."

North said, "It's called Tendrog. It's quite the rage back home. Quite a bit cheaper than your Macallans to boot. I'll arrange to ship a few crates of it over for your mess."

Thorne nodded and said, "Thank you, sir."

"Now," North said as he took a seat behind his desk. "How are things going on the *Lysithea*? How are you progressing in reviving the crew?"

Thorne placed his drink on the desk and said, "We're still in the process of reviving all that are still viable. Monsoor says we have to be careful and not rush the process or we could have more failures. So far, I've lost about two hundred of the crew between stasis failures and the science team, including my exec. He'll be difficult to replace. The rest of the fleet didn't appear to fare as well."

"I understand. It's never easy to lose people under your command, no matter how they're lost. Take the time you need. There's no rush."

Thorne nodded, and North cleared his throat and said, "Admiral, I know there are lots of other important things going on, but I wonder if you were acquainted with one of your pilots, Lt. Jason North."

"Lt. North? Of course. He's a fine officer. One of my best pilots," Thorne replied, realization dawning on him. "Relative?"

"My brother," North replied.

"Brother . . . I see the resemblance now that you mention it," Thorne said.

"Your entire fleet had been listed as missing in action for the last twenty-three years. I was just wondering—"

"Commander, I wish I could give you more definitive news, but I don't know as of yet. He's not among those that have been revived, but that doesn't mean anything. I'll try and find out and will notify you straight away when I do know."

North rose from his seat and walked to the viewport, not wanting Thorne to see him struggle with his emotions and wondering what to say next.

As he gazed out of the portal, he said, "We're twins, you know. He posted to the *Lysithea*, and I had just transferred to the *Ambrion* when they decommissioned the *Triumph*. He disappeared six months later."

"*Ambrion*. She's a Saturn-class, same as *Lysithea*. I knew her skipper. What became of her?"

"We lost her at Aldebaran . . . along with a lot of good friends," he said, still staring out the portal.

Thorne nodded soberly and said, "I'm sorry to hear that. I had a lot of respect for Admiral Farrell."

"Me too," North said. He then turned to Thorne and asked, "I was wondering . . . how did you end up in the nexus? Tig Ferendal is an extra starlane jump if you use the nexus."

Thorne said, "We received intelligence that there was a T'Kharr fleet at one of our through points. We went through the nexus hoping to get there as soon as we could without being detected. When we got here, something happened to the twin stars, and we discovered we were trapped."

North nodded and said, "I see. Fleet Command never knew what had happened. It's a miracle you survived."

Thorne said, "By the way, sir, what happened at Tig Ferendal? I haven't had time to look at the archives from *Pacifica*."

North paused a moment. "Our forces were defeated and driven from the system," he said matter-of-factly. "The T'Kharr then destroyed the colony completely by orbital bombardment. Only a handful of survivors were able to be evacuated before we were forced to leave. We lost a first-line carrier, the *Telioth*, and several escorts in the battle."

Thorne's eyes went to the floor, and North realized he could've been more diplomatic. "I apologize if that came out as a recrimination, Admiral. There was nothing you could have done."

Thorne nodded and said, "Thank you, sir. I know that, but it still feels personal. If we had made it, we could've made a difference."

"That was twenty-three years ago, Admiral. A lot has happened since then." North decided it was time to get down to business. "How fast can you have your fleet ready to travel?"

"I'm not sure, sir. Seventy-two hours if we go by the book. If your science and engineering teams can assist in helping us do some upgrades and repairs, we can be combat ready—"

North looked soberly at the man and said, "Wait a minute, Admiral. As much as I'd love to make use of more ships for the coming operation, your fleet is in no shape to accompany us. No, I want to know how soon you can leave for *Earth*. You are to take your fleet home to the hero's welcome you all very much deserve."

Thorne protested, "With respect, we missed the fight at Tig Ferendal, Commander. I have no intention of running out on another fight where we might tip the balance."

"Let me show you what we're up against," North said as he laid out the plans for the Miratev invasion and explained the stakes.

When Thorne found his voice, he said, "Sounds like a dicey one."

"Even with the Cathedra, it will be a lot to coordinate."

Thorne looked confused. "Cathedra?"

"A new way to command and coordinate ships. The Cathedra allows simultaneous control of a large number of ships. The reason you haven't heard of it is because it's relatively new technology and rather expensive to build. There are standard Cathedras in all Alliance carriers but only four enhanced Cathedras in operation in the entire fleet at this moment, one on each quadrant-command ship. The plan is to eventually equip each carrier in a fleet with an enhanced system. I can't get into the enhancement specifics at this time, but it'll become common knowledge soon."

"Sounds interesting," he said. "I can't wait to try it out."

"You'll be amazed at the difference in the Cathedra and the old holographic tech standard to Saturn-class ships," North said. "Night and day."

"So, what do you need me to do, sir?" Thorne asked.

"I need you to take your people home, Admiral. This is our fight. You and your crew have sacrificed more than anyone could imagine. I won't have you risk their lives on what may very well be a suicide mission. They've earned the right to go home."

"But, sir, the T'Kharr don't know about us. They'll be taken completely by surprise."

"But your ships are outdated, over twenty years old," North stated. "They'll be no match for state of the art enemy ships."

"Not necessarily," Thorne said, eyebrows raising. "My science and engineering teams tell me that our fighter complement lacks some of the electronic upgrades that the modern versions have but can take just as much of a pounding and are just as fast as your fighters. They tell me that we can refit our ships with your Flechette-7 missiles with no further modification to fire control than a software update.

"Those two battleships we have out there, I'm told their class of ship was retired not because they were ineffective but because they were less cost efficient than smaller frigates and cruisers. In fact, they pack more of a punch with their main batteries than your frigates. They just burn twice as much fuel and are slower. Once the T'Kharr commander identifies us and our ships, they'll underestimate us. That'll be a great advantage for you."

North looked unconvinced.

Thorne continued, "The biggest advantage, however, are those jewels Major Monsoor came up with. The multi-phasic missile warheads. There isn't enough time to construct more of them, unfortunately, but my science and weapons teams say they can refit about one-third of them to your Mark 112s. The remainder can remain on *Lysithea*, so those will be your aces in the hole. The T'Kharr commanders won't know what hit them."

North paused, not wanting to cut the man off. He felt Thorne's frustration and anguish about missing the battle at Tig Ferendal, his belief that the battle might have been won had they shown up as planned, and his desire for redemption for that perceived failure. But he couldn't risk it. He wouldn't condemn the crews of those ships that had already given more than anyone could have expected from them.

"Actually, you just hit on another reason we need you to leave," North said. "Major Monsoor and his inventions need to be kept safe at all costs. Your top priority is his safety and the safety of your crews."

"Please reconsider, sir. I can send Monsoor ahead on one of my other ships, but—"

"No, Admiral. I'm sorry, but it's out of the question. With the hull degradation and personnel losses you've suffered, I'll be happy for you to make it back to Earth in one piece. Make repairs and take any ships that are able to be made space worthy and set course for Earth as soon as possible. That is a direct order."

Thorne stood and said, "Commander, please, we may have missed Tig Ferendal, but we can't miss this party, sir. You can count on us."

North nodded and said, "I know I can, Admiral. But my mind is made up. I've sent my section chief, Lt. Commander Chen, and her flight maintenance crews to assist you and your crews. She'll do as much as she can to get your fleet ready for your trip home and make sure if you do run into trouble, heaven forbid, you can defend yourselves. Use her well and any other support personnel from my fleet that you need."

Thorne saw that any further argument would be fruitless and replied in a resigned tone, "Yes, sir."

As they left *Pacifica's* dorsal bay, Thorne saw the *Lysithea* fleet bustling with activity. Some of the ships were now illuminated, a constant stream of shuttles and tugs flying between the fleets.

The shuttle pilot smoothly touched down in the *Lysithea's* port bay, which was now alive with technicians and other workers trying to help the crew bring the carrier back on line. By this time, over half of the stasis tubes were gone from the rear of the bay, and the bombers and other ships that had been tethered outside were being brought back inside and berthed. *Pacifica's* damage control teams had brought recyclers aboard, and the technicians operating them had converted the materials from the stasis tubes back into raw metallic material, which could be used for any type of repair.

He saw Lieutenant Commander Chen and her crews from *Pacifica*. Chen was in full swing, barking orders and jumping into the thick of it when something wasn't being done fast enough. Dozens of portable computer terminals littered the deck, all being used to update the avionic software of the fighters and other ships.

As the ramp lowered, Thorne stepped onto the deck and saw a row of men and women he knew to be the captains or surviving senior officers of his escort ships waiting to greet their admiral and be briefed.

The marine guard announced, "Admiral on deck."

The captains immediately snapped to attention, and then Thorne said, "At ease. We need to discuss what comes next. I've received my orders from our fleet commander. Conference room, ladies and gentlemen."

CHAPTER THIRTEEN

Miratev Two, the bunker

Petty Officer Eli sent an urgent thought to Sgt Kenyon. <Life signs outside the door.>

Kenyon activated the surveillance cameras they'd placed around the entrance to the bunker's back door. What he saw made him curse out loud. He transmitted to Remy, <Berserkers outside the door. Two of them.>

Remy jumped to his feet immediately, startling everyone else in the room. <Only two? No handlers?>

<None in scanner range. Collars read as neutral, so they may have cut them loose to recon.> Kenyon replied.

<Have they alerted to the entrance?> Remy asked.

<Not yet,> Kenyon sent. <They look like they're tracking on scent.>

<No others on the scanners,> Eli sent. <Just the two.>

Remy looked concerned and sent, <If they find the entrance and try to breach, bug out and detonate the mines as you retreat. Keep me posted.>

Remy sat down and looked at Henna. "Berserkers."

"What is a berserker?" Jared asked.

Remy nodded to Angus and said, "The T'Kharr call them 'inchitaz' in their language. The closest translation into standard is 'berserker,' because that's how they act. They're T'Kharr line troopers that have been genetically mutated to kill and nothing else. They don't speak, breed, or have any other higher functions. They have had their pain receptors neutralized and are pumped full of stims and metabolic accelerators. They act on predatory animal instinct and nothing else."

"Sounds like they don't have a very long lifespan," Julie said.

"They don't," Remy said. "They last about one standard year before the modifications kill them, but in that time, their strength and endurance is quadrupled. They have bladed weapons surgically implanted into their limbs so they can slash and maim at will. Their handlers are able to control them with a collar that pacifies them until they're to be used. Once the collar is removed or deactivated, they track like a bloodhound and slaughter anything in their path."

"Why would anyone volunteer for something like that?" she asked.

Angus looked surprised and said, "Volunteer? T'Kharr military commanders don't ask for volunteers, Miss Newman."

"Oh," she replied with a shudder.

"So, what happens if they find the door?" Dram asked.

"We implode the tunnel and bury ourselves in here and hope that rescue comes before the bad guys can dig us out," Remy said. "If it looks like they'll get here first, we blow up the bunker and all the data."

Julie looked queasy and said, "I think I need to lie down for a while." She then walked over to one of the bedrooms and closed the door.

Jared got up and said, "Lt. Remy, could I speak to you in private for a moment?"

Remy got up and followed Jared into one of the rooms and shut the door.

"Lieutenant, tell me what is the contingency plan if, for some reason, we were to be captured. I've heard of T'Kharr interrogation techniques and seen some of it firsthand."

Remy regarded Jared thoughtfully for a moment and said, "If it comes to that, just stay close to any member of my team and we'll take care of it." Seeing the look of understanding dawn on Jared's face, he continued, "Don't worry, Doctor. Our boys are on the way. It won't come to that." Remy turned and left the room.

Jared stood there for a moment and said to himself, "Where do they find people like this?" He looked skyward and said, "Mickey, I hope you're on the way. These guys are all nuts."

Meanwhile, Dram went up to the door to the room that Julie had gone to, and after knocking quietly, he heard, "Come in."

He saw Julie lying on her back on one of the beds, arm draped over her eyes.

"Is there anything I can get for you? I know all this military stuff can get overwhelming."

"I don't suppose you have anything stronger than water in here, do you?"

Dram looked apologetic and said, "I wish I did, but sorry. Best I can do is a fresh pot of coffee."

She looked over at him and smiled, tears streaming down her face.

His first instinct was to go over and comfort her, but the attraction he felt for her stopped him. He didn't want to be inappropriate. She seemed to sense what he was thinking and got up from the bed. She walked over to him and unexpectedly pulled him into the room, shutting the door and locking it. Dram stood looking down at her, unsure what he should do, when she reached up and pulled him in, kissing him warmly on the lips. Dram's initial shocked reaction gave way to his attraction to her, and he enveloped her with his arms and returned the kiss.

She wrapped her arms around his chest and held him tightly. All he could do was stand there and return the hug, not saying a word.

She then looked into his eyes and said, "Stay with me."

He nodded and said, "I'll stay with you as long as you want . . . but what about . . ."

"Jared?" she said for him. "Everyone seems to think he and I had something going on, but it wasn't true. I don't want to be with Jared. I want to be with you."

She took his hand and led him toward the bed, and he said, under his breath, "I swear I'll kill anyone who knocks on the door."

Earth, parking garage of The Real Truth offices

Chuck Ryther exited the elevator that led into the parking garage of his office building, feeling just a bit happier than usual.

He'd placed some discreet inquiries regarding Voices of Mandis and offered a bounty on any information regarding the killings at Grand Commander North's house and his current mission and rumors about some incident several days ago where ships had been lost close to the moon.

His instincts told him there was a big story there and that all these seemingly unrelated events were pieces to the same puzzle. He would put that puzzle together, sell the story, and regain his reputation. Things were definitely looking up.

As he walked to his hovercar, he felt a sharp pain at the base of his neck. His legs immediately went dead, his spinal cord severed by a vibro-blade, and he crumpled to the ground. Ryther had no control of his lungs. All he could do was listen.

Arvil Symons knelt down and calmly wiped the blood from his blade onto Ryther's shirt. "You've been talking to the cops. That lady cop and her partner have been talking to everyone on that list they got from you since yesterday, asking questions about me! Did you tell them about Kate?"

Ryther's eyes went wide with fear, and he tried to shake his head.

With that, Symons drove the blade into the base of Ryther's skull, into his medulla oblongata. He died instantly without even a twitch, and Symons dropped his head to the ground. He then stood and spat on Ryther's forehead, the look of shock still frozen on the reporter's face.

As he turned and left, he muttered, "I hate reporters."

At that same moment, Wilson and Perkins exited her hovercar and looked at the address she was parked in front of once again.

"You sure this is right?" Perkins asked.

"That's what it says on the list," Wilson said, checking the address again. The house they stood in front of had a gate and a guard shack and was fenced all around.

"The note on the list said that this person is affiliated with the group somehow but not an official member," Wilson said as they walked up to the guard shack, currently occupied by a military-looking type with a shaved head and a permanent sneer on his face. "Let's see if anyone's at home."

As they approached the shack, the guard pushed a button and said in an irritated tone, "Yes?"

"Inspector Wilson and Detective Perkins with Del Mar PD," she said as the two held up their badges and credentials. "We'd like to speak to Mr. or Mrs. Singer."

"Do you have an appointment?" he asked with a sniff.

"No," Wilson said. "We were hoping for a moment of their time."

"What's this regarding?" the guard asked.

"It's an official police matter," Wilson said.

The guard said, "Well, if you don't tell me what it is, you ain't getting in."

Wilson looked closely at the guard's security badge and read "Praetor Security." She turned to Perkins and said, "You know, Chief Heller plays poker with the guy who owns Praetor Security. . . Dimitry Vostok, right?"

At the mention of his boss's name, the guard began to look concerned, the cocky smile fading from his face.

"Why don't we call him and let him know what's going on and explain how you're interfering with a police investigation?" Wilson said.

The guard glared at them and then said, "Wait right here." He picked up a phone and spoke to someone. After a few moments, he turned back to them. "Go ahead." He buzzed them through the gate.

As they drove up the driveway toward the front door of the house, Perkins said, "I didn't know that Heller played poker with Vostok."

Wilson smiled sweetly and said, "He doesn't, as far as I know."

As they approached the circular driveway, they noticed two other vehicles parked in front of the house. Wilson pulled up behind the first—a red Rolls Royce Quantum VX1 sedan—and turned off the ignition. The car in front of it was a black Lexus Nebula 800SLC. As she exited her vehicle, she looked at the Rolls with admiration.

"Man, I'm in the wrong business," Wilson said.

Perkins smiled. "That car costs more than my house."

Perkins ran the vehicle tags on each on his hand held and said, "The Rolls is registered to William & Victoria Singer, this address. The other is registered to a Kate Singer-Linder, address in the city."

They both noticed shouting coming from the front door and turned toward the noise.

"I can't believe you told them to come up here!" a female voice shouted.

"Keep your voice down," a male voice said in harsh tones. "They'll be at the door any second. Besides, why wouldn't we talk to the police? It's not like she's done anything wrong, has she?"

"Thanks a lot, Dad," a different female voice said, dripping with sarcasm. "I know I can always count on you."

"Are you stupid, Bill?" the first female said. "Get rid of them!"

After several more moments of silence, Wilson decided to ring the bell.

A tall, thin, austere-looking man answered the door and said, "Yes?"

"Inspector Wilson, Detective Perkins. We're with the Police Department. I was hoping to speak to Mr. or Mrs. Singer, please."

"I'm afraid they've changed their minds, Inspector. They have asked me to tell you, with respect, that they don't wish to speak to any law enforcement officials without an advocate present."

"I see," Wilson said, looking at Perkins, then back at the man. "Well, then, please give them my card and have them call me when they do have representation. Thank you."

The man took the card, then shut the door without another word.

As they walked toward their car, Wilson whispered, "Billy," and pointed her chin toward the two vehicles.

Perkins reached into his front right pocket and retrieved two small metal balls, which he casually dropped between the two parked cars as they walked between them, partially obscuring them from the video cameras watching the property. As they continued toward their own vehicle, the two small balls split off, one rolling under the Rolls and the other under the Lexus. The balls shot up and attached themselves to the undercarriage of each. The tracking tags would now send a signal that could be traced anywhere on the planet.

Wilson looked toward the front door and said, "Let's get out of here. I'm sure their video system is watching us."

She gunned the car and exited through the front gate. As they passed by the guard shack, the guard smirked and flipped them off as they left.

"Mental note," Perkins said. "When this is over, I think I'd like to hang a few parking tags on that guy's car."

"Shake it off, Billy," Wilson said. "He's small potatoes. I'm more interested in what we heard at the door. If I were to guess, I'd bet that this Kate Singer-Linder is daddy's little girl and Momma thinks she shouldn't talk to us for some reason."

Once they were out of sight of the house, Wilson pulled over and set her handheld to track the two vehicles. When she entered in the commands, the two signals showed up clearly on the screen, still parked in front of the residence.

"Did you have your recorder on while we were at the door, get a copy of the voices?" asked Wilson.

"Of course," he replied. "SOP."

"Run the voice prints through AVRS. See if the voices were clear enough."

Perkins held up his handheld and said, "Link to AVRS. Check voice prints from following recording excerpt." He then linked to the audio file he'd recorded while they were standing at the door. The Audio Voice Recognition System came up with an answer almost immediately.

"First voice we heard was Victoria Singer, second was William Singer, third was Katherine Singer," he said. "Ninety-two percent certainty."

Wilson then ran Katherine on her screen and said, "Here she is. Katherine Singer, thirty-five years old, daughter of William and Victoria Singer. She shows up in the database as single. Why the hyphenated last name?"

Perkins thought for a moment and said, "Linder . . . that rings a bell."

Wilson nodded and said, "Now that you mention it, it does. Try cross referencing the name Linder and Singer with the member roster and victims of Mandis. Maybe there's a connection."

Perkins punched up the information and said, "Here we go. There were a number of Linders on Mandis. Hey, this is interesting."

Wilson said, "Go on."

"The global search turned up a wedding registry entry from nine years ago. Wayne Linder and . . . well, what do you know? Katherine Singer. They were apparently engaged. Linder was killed on Mandis along with the rest of the population."

"Maybe she took his name to honor his memory or something," Wilson said.

Perkins shook his head and said, "Don't know, but that's got to be the connection between the Singers and V.O.M. Her mother seemed to think she shouldn't talk to us. Maybe they know the connection but are trying to protect her."

"It says here that her parents tried to buy her way out of the mandatory two-years military service, but she joined anyway against their wishes," Wilson said. "That must've pissed off her mom. This says she still works with the military as a civilian. Get this, she's Supreme Commander Terred's civilian office manager."

Wilson was about to answer when her handheld chimed.

"Wilson," she answered.

"This is Malone. Stay where you are. We have troops on the way to your location to pick up Kate Singer for questioning. You guys are better than I thought."

Wilson frowned and said, "You've been monitoring our computer searches, I take it?"

"Your investigation was what I needed to convince my superiors that we needed to chat with Kate. I suspected there was someone in the military besides our dead traitor with a connection to Mandis. You guys stirred up a hornet's nest. Her father is prominent in the defense industry, and he's been tearing up the phone lines since you guys left the house, demanding to know why the police wanted to speak to his family."

"How are you going to bring her in?" Wilson asked. "You got a warrant that quickly?"

"You forget, my dear, that military rules of evidence and questioning of suspects—particularly involving possible incidents of espionage—are quite different from the rules binding you," Malone said.

"But she's a civilian," Perkins said.

"Employed by the military. She has to submit, no matter who her parents are."

"Malone, Kate Singer's car is on the move. We put a tracker on it. She's leaving the house—"

"I have the tracker frequency. We'll be there as soon as possible." He terminated the link, and Wilson shifted her concentration to the screen.

Wilson watched the blip on her screen and pulled out onto the road, following the car. As they came around the corner, they could see the Lexus in the distance, driving away from her parents' house in a big hurry.

Kate Singer nervously activated the personal transmitter she'd retrieved from her purse.

"Why are you calling me, Katie?" Symons asked in an irritated voice from the other end. "What's wrong?"

"Everything's wrong, Arvil!" she shouted. "The police were at my house not fifteen minutes ago wanting to talk to my mother and father."

"Did they talk to them?" he asked, concerned.

"No, they told them they wouldn't speak to anyone without an advocate," she replied.

There was a long pause at the other end of the line, then Symons said, "Whatever you do, don't go back to work or your house. They'll be waiting for you."

Kate felt the panic rising in her chest, and her mouth went dry.

"Where should I go, Arvil? I want to come to you. Tell me where to go."

In a smooth, soothing voice, Symons responded, "Easy, Katie, easy. Come to the safe house, the one where we met that first night. Do you still have the necklace I gave you? It'll open the electronic lock to the door there."

His calming tone started to put her at ease, and she pulled out the silver-and-gold pendant he'd given her on that first night. "Yes, I have it right here."

"Now just put it on and think of me while you drive there," he said reassuringly. "It'll all be over soon, and we'll be together. Don't worry."

She pulled the chain over her head and looked at the necklace once again, the thought of being with him starting to calm her down.

"Do you have it on?" he asked.

"Yes," she said, tears streaming down her face. "Yes, I do. I'll get there as fast as I can."

Another long pause from the other end, then Kate said, "Arvil, are you still there?"

"Yes, my love . . . still here . . ."

Kate Singer's car disappeared in a blinding white light and a huge white-and-yellow fireball. Wilson's vehicle was blown off the road and into a ditch on the side of the road by the shockwave. Wilson and Perkins's restraining harnesses stopped them from being ejected as the car impacted the ground and rolled over, coming to rest right side up.

The next thing Wilson knew, she was being lifted from her vehicle and placed on a military stretcher. Her vision was blurry, and her mouth had a bloody, metallic taste. She tried to look at the soldier standing over her, realizing he was saying something to her, but she couldn't bring her eyes into focus and couldn't make out the words. The last thing she remembered was a stinging sensation in her arm, then blackness.

CHAPTER FOURTEEN

Alpha Auridius Nexus

North sat at his desk in his office adjacent to the bridge, reviewing status reports from both fleets. His holographic display showed his ships as green, indicating they were combat ready, but the *Lysithea* and her escorts display yellow and red icons.

So far, 38 percent of the twenty-three thousand crew members in the *Lysithea* fleet hadn't survived the extended stasis. It was a miracle that any of them had survived at all, but North knew that Thorne was taking the loss of almost 8,800 people pretty hard. Many of the casualties were people he'd personally known and fought with.

There was still no word on whether Jason was among the survivors. Thorne had promised an hourly update, but time was running out. He might not learn his brother's fate until after they'd returned home, assuming they did return home.

North's comm beeped.

"Yes?" he said.

"*Teleosa* is ready for the test, Commander," Drake said. "You said you wanted to be informed."

"On my way," North said as he arose from his desk and went to the bridge.

The screen displayed a dual image with one half showing a large asteroid just outside of the gas cloud and the other showing the captain of the battleship *Teleosa*, Captain Aaron Jackson. Next to him was Major Monsoor, furiously typing on a hand-held interface unit. They watched as the modified Mark 105 missile accelerated toward the center of the asteroid, seconds from impacting the surface.

Monsoor counted, "Five seconds to impact . . . four . . . three . . . two . . . one . . . impact."

The missile disappeared into the asteroid without even raising a speck of dust.

"Plus one . . . plus two . . . plus three . . . detonation," Monsoor said as the asteroid fractured in half, blown apart from the explosion at its core.

Austin whistled and said in a low voice, "If this is what he came up with on his own, imagine what he could do with a science facility and a team of engineers."

"I'm way ahead of you," North said. He then turned his attention to Monsoor and said, "Well done, Major. You certainly deliver what you promise."

"Thank you, sir," he replied with a smile.

North turned and walked back into his office, followed by Austin.

"Do you have everything you need?"

"We're good to go," Austin responded. "My commanders have been briefed, including the Omega guys. Once we're in-system, they'll be cut loose. Recon, infiltration, kill as many of the unholy bastards as they can—usual Omega stuff," he added with a smirk.

"We jump in six hours." North rubbed his eyes.

"With respect, you look like hell," Austin said, genuinely concerned that his friend was pushing himself too hard. "Let Drake take care of the admin crap. He *is* your XO, you know."

North thought of responding with a rebuke but then realized that Austin was correct. The fact that he'd nearly shouted back at the man indicated that maybe he did need some rest.

"All right . . . a few hours of down time does sound kind of good. You think—"

"I'll tell Drake not to disturb you," Austin said.

"Thanks, Ben," North said with a grateful nod.

With that, Austin stood and left the office. Once the doors closed, North went over to the couch in the room and stretched out, trying to clear his mind. Before he knew it, he'd drifted off into a dreamless sleep. It seemed like only a few moments when he heard a familiar chime.

He was instantly awake and said, "Yes?"

Drakes voice came over the comm and said, "General Austin said to wake you now, sir."

North rubbed his eyes and said, "Thanks, Mat. Any word?"

"Not yet, sir. I'm sorry."

"All right. Give me thirty."

"Yes, sir," Drake said, terminating the comm.

North checked the chronometer and saw they were one hour away from jumping. He'd slept nearly five hours and felt better than he had in days. After a quick shower and fresh uniform, he felt as good as new. He emerged from his office onto the bridge, just as the alpha watch was coming on duty.

"Status," North said.

Drake responded, "All ships report Psyton shields at full power, moving toward the Polto Nebula starlane. ETA is ten minutes."

"Very well," North said as he took a seat in the command area of the bridge next to Drake, Captain Frost on the other side.

North didn't usually sit on the bridge for entry into the starlanes but felt compelled to watch this particular entry firsthand. These portals had been dormant for almost a quarter of a century. As they approached the starlane, all stations reported in and reported systems were nominal.

Lt. Vale said, "Message from *Lysithea* for Commander North."

"Put it through, Lieutenant," North said.

The face of Admiral Thorne filled the screen.

"Commander, no word on Lt. North yet. I'm sorry, sir. We'll need another twenty-four hours or so before we have everyone revived. Things were crazy during that time going into stasis. Also, I just wanted to wish you good hunting on the op. I wish we were going with you."

"So do I, Admiral, but you've earned your trip home," North replied, secretly glad they weren't coming. "Godspeed. Get your people home safely." If Jason did end up surviving, he didn't want him on what could turn out to be a one-way mission.

"I will, sir," Thorne said. "*Lysithea* out." His image faded from the screen.

North watched the screen fade out with a pang of sadness. He knew there was nothing more he could do or say. Time had run out.

Frost ordered, "Slave escorts to *Pacifica* and slow to .0012 light speed relative, Mister Webber."

"Point zero-zero-one-two, aye, sir," the nav officer responded.

"Lt. Vale, advise all commands. Stand by to enter the lane."

Vale relayed the order and Webber counted down, "Three . . . two . . . one . . . entry."

One by one, the ships flashed out of normal space and into the starlane.

Once in the starlane, Webber reported, "We are in the lane. All ships accounted for. Five point six hours until entry into the Polto Nebula."

North let out a sigh of relief and looked to his right at Drake, who looked similarly relieved.

Drake shook his head and said, "I half thought—"

"I know," North said. "I wanted to see for myself that we weren't going to disappear into oblivion."

The Polto Nebula

"Stand by for entry into the nebula . . . three . . . two . . . one . . ." Lt. Webber said as the swirling tides of compressed space changed into the brilliant colors of the Polto Nebula, the *Pacifica's* jumping-off point into the Miratev system.

Upon entry into the system, computer banks that had been idle while in the starlane suddenly hummed to life, taking readings from particle concentrations to radiation levels in the area.

"All escorts report normal entry into the system, Admiral," Lt. Vale said.

"Four hours to the Miratev starlane portal, sir," Webber said.

"Very good," Drake said. "Launch a four-man recon patrol. I want to make sure nobody else is here while we make our way to the Miratev starlane."

Captain Frost, *Pacifica's* second-in-command, turned to his communications console on the right arm of his chair and issued the order to the launch bay. Within seconds, four of the fast Valkyrie fighters screamed out of the starboard launch bay and assumed a diamond formation to allow maximum gain on their detector arrays.

Lt. Vale turned toward Drake and said, "Admiral, I'm receiving flash traffic from the starlane comm buoys. Grand Commander's eyes only."

Drake nodded and said, "Advise the Commander, Lieutenant."

Vale complied.

North sat at his desk, going over every possible detail of the plan, trying to see anything that might've been overlooked. His comm unit chimed and he said, "Yes?"

"Flash traffic for you, Commander," Vale said. "Eyes only."

"Put it through, Lieutenant," he said as he activated his terminal and entered in his personal security code. As he read through the transmissions, he felt cold dread in the pit of his stomach. "Damn," he said out loud before punching the comm button.

"Lt. Vale, have Generals Austin and Logan come to my ready room. When they arrive, ask Admiral Drake to join us."

"Yes, sir," Vale replied.

Within ten minutes, the three flag officers entered North's office.

Without preamble, North said, "I just received flash traffic from the buoys. It had good news and bad news. The good news is that the other four fleets are all on station and ready to jump on our order. The bad news came from the two stealth assets in-system at Miratev. Apparently, the feint in Kirel Dani didn't work. The T'Kharr allowed the depot to be destroyed and kept their fleets in the Miratev system. Their commander is savvier than I'd hoped."

"Unfortunate," Austin said, looking concerned.

North replied, "We're evenly matched in ships, five fleets to five. I was hoping for a more lopsided fight. Another bit of hope, the dreadnought rendezvoused with the *Valor*. She's going to be in the fight. Between her and the multi-phasic missiles, or 'specials' as Monsoor calls them, we need to inflict as much damage in the initial stages of the battle as possible before they can realize what's going on and can regroup."

Drake and Logan looked confused for a moment. Drake said, "Dreadnought?"

"A little surprise from our Omega friends," North said, not offering any more information than that. He then turned to Austin and asked, "Ben, how are the troops?"

"Edgy," Austin replied. "They're cooped up in those ships and ready to fight. There's only so much poker you can play without going buggy. And remember, there's six thousand of 'em."

"Well, they may get to fight sooner than they thought. Look at this. I received this image in the flash from the stealth assets in the Miratev system monitoring the T'Kharr fleets."

North punched up an image of a ship moving into formation amongst the T'Kharr ships. It was rectangular in shape and seemed to be a framework housing stacks of cylindrical pods. The ship appeared to contain about a hundred of the pods.

Logan cursed under his breath. He'd seen T'Kharr breaching pods before. Each pod contained a squad of T'Kharr shock troops. They would attach magnetically and burn their way through the hull of a ship. Once inside, their primary mission was to create as much damage and havoc as possible. Of the hundred pods that would be launched from the pod ship, maybe one or two would make it past the point defenses of a ship, but those one or two pods could be a serious problem to the crews.

"Is it only the one pod ship?" Logan asked.

"So far," North replied. "And it appears to be heavily shielded. With any luck, they won't send any more. Intelligence reports that they've never seen breaching ships with this many pods. This one may even be a prototype. The ships usually don't get deployed in time, because the battles are usually over before they can reach the battle theater. The fact that they've brought one in tells us they're going for broke."

"I'm familiar with these ships, but this one's the biggest I've ever seen," Austin replied. "The pod ships I've seen have only about twenty-five pods."

"This causes us to modify our initial strategy. I originally wanted to concentrate the specials on the nearest carriers, hopefully make them panic and break formation, but now I think that this pod ship deserves attention. As fortune would have it, the ship is currently closest to our exit point into the system, allowing us a chance to shoot at it first. The downside is—"

"That if we don't get them all, *Pacifica* will undoubtedly be their primary target," Drake finished for him.

North switched to another view that showed several floating objects orbiting near the starlane portals. He said, "And as we thought, they've mined the portals with antimatter proximity mines. We anticipated this and brought some of the new third-generation sweepers."

Austin let out a loud breath and said, "Boy, you're just full of good news, aren't you?"

North turned his attention to Drake and asked, "Recon patrol?"

"Clear from here to the lane," he replied. "We seem to have slipped in unnoticed."

"Good," North said. "Mat, send flash traffic to Admirals Faulkner and Jett. Tell them to enter the lane with their task forces as scheduled. Also, make sure they deploy their sweepers before entry. I don't want to lose any ships to mines."

"Aye aye, sir," he replied, then turned and left the room.

"I should get down to my boys and girls and make sure they're ready, Commander," Austin said as Logan nodded in agreement.

"Of course," North said with a half-smile. "Dismissed, gentlemen." Then he returned to his battle plans.

He'd initially wanted to hit the nearest carrier with their specials. Now, with this new threat, they'd have to target the pod ship's shield generator and then target the carrier. After the pod ship is disabled, *Pacifica's* fighter squadrons would be tasked with destroying every single pod. Even a single surviving pod would be a threat.

North just hoped that there were no more bad surprises.

CHAPTER FIFTEEN

Earth, hospital in Del Mar

The first thing Wilson noticed were the lights. They were entirely too bright. They bored into her brain like tiny needles and exploded inside of her head. She blinked her eyes several times. As her vision cleared, she looked down and saw that she was in a bed covered in white sheets. She became aware of the antiseptic smell lingering in the air and realized she was in a hospital room.

She tried to sit up and was rewarded with pain that sliced through her head like a hot knife. Falling back on her pillow, she tried her best to push back the wave of nausea that enveloped her. A medic came into the room.

"You're awake," she said cheerfully as she pulled up the electronic pad at the end of the bed that had Wilson's chart on it. "That's good."

Wilson willed her voice to speak. "Billy . . . Perkins, my partner . . . how . . ."

The medic said, "He's banged up, concussion, but he'll be okay. In the next room. You can see him in a little while. For now, you need to rest and let the anti-rad drugs do their thing."

Wilson looked down to her left arm and realized the pressure she'd felt there was an IV.

The medic touched several buttons on the cuff, and she felt the nausea subside.

"Better?"

Wilson let out a breath and said, "Yes, thank you."

The medic then went to the door and spoke to someone outside. "Sir, she's awake."

She turned back to Wilson and said, "Buzz if you need something," then left the room.

A man using a cane came into the room.

She tried to focus on him and said, "Do I know you?"

"You look like crap," he said with a grin.

"Malone? What happened to you?" Wilson almost smiled, but it hurt too much.

"Long story. I've been communicating with you from a hospital room until recently."

"Did I hear the medic say 'anti-rad' drugs?" she asked.

Malone nodded. "Micro-nuke. While you guys were following her, she used a scrambled communications device to contact Symons. We heard the whole conversation. He probably thought that she wouldn't hold up under interrogation."

Wilson said, "So Symons was responsible . . ." Then she had to lay back again as another wave of nausea overcame her.

"You rest," Malone said as he left the room. "We'll talk later." He'd thought about mentioning that Ryther was dead, but he figured he could do that later. Besides, he had an appointment that he just couldn't miss.

Alliance Fleet Security Headquarters

The special interrogator, Gaspar, walked down the long hallway toward the guard post, the clicking of his boots reverberating against the walls. His black uniform showed no indication of rank or station. His short-cropped hair showed wisps of gray throughout, and his thin lips were locked in a permanent frown. He carried a large attaché case in his right hand.

He approached the guard station, manned by three heavily armed marines, and the sergeant said, "I.D."

Gaspar leaned forward and allowed the retinal scanner to take a print of his eye. He placed his left thumb on the hand scanner, allowing the computer to confirm his DNA.

Upon seeing the results on the screen, the guards snapped to attention, the Sergeant said, "Go right in, sir."

Gaspar nodded and walked through the checkpoint without a word, then entered the door at the end of the hallway which led to the underground bunker that served as the headquarters of Alliance Fleet Security and Intelligence. As he passed through the doorway, his stoic face softened a bit as he recognized his old friend waiting for him in the lobby.

"Gaspar," Malone said with a small grin as he came up and offered his hand.

Gaspar took his hand and said, "Garrett. Good to see you again, old friend. How long has it been?"

"Three years, I think," he replied. "Just after the Teldar incident."

"Ahh, yes," he said. "That was a particularly interesting case. It sounds like this'll be just as much of a challenge. I apologize for the delay. The governor of Anzatar Prime was having an issue with the head of his private security team and required my services. To his credit, he avoided an assassination attempt."

Malone nodded and said, "Your talents are unsurpassed. Come with me, and we can get started."

He led Gaspar down a secondary hallway that led to an observation room. The occupant, a woman seemingly in her mid-twenties wearing a standard prison-issue gray jumpsuit, paced the floor of the small cell like a caged animal. Two guards armed with stun batons stood in front of the doorway leading out of the cell, eyeing her warily.

"We did have a single guard in the cell at first, but she managed to break his nose and knock out three of his teeth before she could be subdued," Malone said. "It took three of them."

Gaspar's eyebrows raised in surprise. "Impressive for such a small girl."

"She's been well conditioned. She withstood a level five scan on the verifier without even giving up her name—Ariana Kidder—which we already knew. We've gone as far as we can, which is why we called you."

Gaspar looked at Malone and said, "The admiral?"

"Admiral Arlington is aware you've been summoned but for obvious reasons isn't here," Malone said, turning to look back into the cell. "She needs some kind of deniability in this."

"Of course," Gaspar responded with a satisfied nod. "How far am I authorized to go?"

Malone turned back to him and looked him square in the eye. "As far as necessary. She already knows her brother is dead, so I doubt you can use that information for anything useful."

"Very good," he said without emotion. He then left the room and walked to the doorway leading to the cell. As he came through the door, the two guards stepped aside to allow him to enter. The woman immediately stopped her pacing and stood against the wall opposite of the door, glaring defiantly at the new arrival.

Gaspar placed his attaché case on the table in the room, then turned to the guards and said, "You can leave us now."

The two guards looked at each other, and the larger of the two said, "Sir, are you sure?"

"Yes," he said calmly as he removed a pair of black gloves from the pocket of his jacket and pulled them onto his hands.

The guards left the room without a word, and Ariana looked toward the open door, thinking for a moment that she might make it to the door before it slammed shut. The last guard out eyed her and pulled the door shut firmly, and she turned toward Gaspar, who was now standing with his hands clasped behind his back, staring at her dispassionately.

She looked him up and down, assessing his apparent strengths and weaknesses and finally said, "So who are you, the comic relief? Not very smart, letting those goons leave. The last guy who was in here alone with me left spitting teeth."

Gaspar regarded her for another moment and said, "Miss Kidder, you have information relevant to an ongoing investigation. I have been summoned to obtain that information."

Ariana Kidder laughed out loud and said, "They already tried a verifier and truth drugs. Those didn't work. You won't torture me, because any information you gain may not be reliable, and by the looks of you, I'm pretty sure you won't charm anything out of me."

He nodded and said, "Don't be so sure. I might be extremely charming. Nonetheless, please take a seat in the chair." He indicated the chair in the center of the room, which was bolted to the floor.

"Not a chance," she spat.

In a flash, she launched herself at Gaspar, aiming a strike toward his throat that she thought would likely incapacitate him. With surprising speed, he effortlessly dodged the blow, then knocked her legs out from under her with a sweep of his right leg. She crashed messily to the floor and slid up against the far wall. She looked up at him and saw that he was calmly standing where he'd been before, hands behind his back.

Rage overtook her, and she launched herself at him again with a feral scream, this time feinting with another blow to the face and at the last moment aiming for a vicious scissor kick to his genitals. He easily sidestepped the attack and allowed her momentum to throw her off balance. For an instant, her back was turned toward him, and he struck a nerve plexus near the center of her back with the tips of his middle two fingers.

She screamed in pain as the blow connected, her back arching in an uncontrollable spasm. He then grabbed her jumpsuit by the collar and dumped her painfully into the chair. Before she could react, he'd secured her arms and feet to the chair, completely immobilizing her. Once secured, he jammed his thumb into a spot by her neck, and the back spasm ceased.

Once the pain had ceased and her wits returned, she struggled against the arm restraints and screamed, "Let go of me, you bastard! I demand an advocate!"

Meanwhile, Gaspar had turned toward the table containing his attaché case and opened it, revealing a dull, silver skull cap with a control panel on the side.

He turned to her once again and said, "Do you know what this is, Miss Kidder?"

She screamed, "I said I demand an advocate!"

He shook his head slowly and said, "Miss Kidder, you are an enemy of the state. Under the Articles of War Act, traitors are allowed advocates only after interrogation. So stop wasting your breath and answer my question. Do you know what this is?"

She looked at the device and said, "It's another one of those verifiers. Your flunkies already tried that, and it didn't work."

His eyebrows raised and he said, "Ah, true. It is, indeed, a verifier, but a very special model. The police and civilian authorities use those . . . basic models. This one has a particularly interesting upgrade package that I'm sure will be of interest to you."

He'd now captured Kidder's attention, and she said, "Upgrades, huh? It doesn't matter how many levels it has. I still won't cooperate."

"Oh, you won't have to, Miss Kidder. You see, I possess a particular skill set that makes me perfectly suited to this job. Interrogations of suspects, especially particularly difficult ones such as yourself, are my specialty. As such, the Alliance has seen fit to provide me with state-of-the-art equipment such as this. Allow me to demonstrate."

He then picked up the cap—by all outward appearances a standard verifier—and touched a stud on the side, activating the computer interface.

"Demonstration mode," he said, and four small, blunt studs slid out from the edges of the cap. They were positioned so that one each would touch front to back and side to side on her head.

"Level six," he said, and a plasma shock arched between the four studs.

"You see, Miss Kidder, this particular model has four upgrade settings beyond the basic five levels. Level six delivers a shock when the verifier determines you are being untruthful or refuse to answer a question in a timely manner. Primitive, but effective in most cases."

"You're wasting your time," she snarled. "I've been shocked before."

He nodded and said, "I'm sure you're right, which is why we will begin with level seven."

He touched a pad on the side of the unit, and the studs suddenly shot outward, doubling in length. Despite herself, Kidder jumped when the studs extended, and she began to eye the device warily.

"Level seven taps directly into your pleasure and pain receptors. I can direct it to stimulate any portion of your physiology in a positive or negative way. The pain compared to the shock received at level six is twenty times more powerful. This is where operation of the device becomes more of an art form and requires a professional hand."

Kidder glared at him and the device, not saying anything.

"No sarcastic remark?" he prodded. When she said nothing and continued to glare at him, he said, "Good. Let's move on, shall we?"

He touched another pad on the device, and the ends of the studs opened up. Thin fibers snaked out, waving in the air like the tentacles of a jellyfish.

"Now, level eight is a bit more . . . invasive, shall we say? The tendrils are able to seek out the memories that you're trying to suppress and force you to vocalize them. It also allows us to deaden certain parts of your memory, effectively wiping entire blocks of your memory out. Particularly effective if we don't feel like having you talk about the existence of this kind of device."

"You'll have to kill me, because I won't tell you anything no matter how many levels you have in that thing," she spat, still defiant.

"Be patient. I'm almost done. Now, level nine is the final level and a last resort, I'm afraid. However unlikely, if you are able to resist level eight in any fashion, level nine directs the tendrils to probe into your long-term memory centers and allows us to literally download the entire contents of your brain. The problem is that the process is akin to wiping the virtual memory drive on a computer.

"Once we download the information, you will be a blank slate, unable to perform even the most basic bodily functions. Subjects who have been 'downloaded' generally live out their days hooked to a respirator and an intravenous feeding tube. The makers of this device disagree as to whether the subject is conscious and aware during this time, as they cannot speak or communicate at all. I suppose we should do a study on that someday . . ."

Kidder's eyes went wide, and she said, "You aren't using that on me. You can't. It's a violation of my rights!"

"Miss Kidder, you forfeited your rights when you compromised Admiral Carlo and contributed to the deaths of over two hundred sailors. You can avoid the use of this device by answering my questions. It's up to you."

"Go to hell," she spat.

Gaspar reset the device and placed the cap on Kidder's head. "As you wish."

He activated the recording device clipped to his shirt pocket and said, "Now . . . where shall we begin . . ."

Two hours later, Gaspar pushed the comm button on the door and asked to be let out. When the door opened, he carried his attaché case and coat in one hand and gently led Kidder out of the room with his other arm. She had four oozing puncture wounds around her skull but otherwise appeared to be unharmed.

As Malone and the two security guards approached, Gaspar said, "Please tend to this young woman. I explained that she'd been in an accident and was brought here for help. Sadly, she can't remember her name or anything about who she is or what happened to her."

The guards looked wary and had their stun batons at the ready.

Malone stepped between the guards and Kidder and said, "Those won't be necessary, Sergeant. Please take this young lady up to the medical ward. I'll be up shortly. She is to be treated as our guest until she feels better."

Kidder looked at the guards, then turned back to Gaspar and said, "Thank you so much for helping me and for your kindness. I wish I could remember what happened to me."

Gaspar patted her arm gently and said, "Don't worry, Miss. These guards will keep you safe and take you to where the doctors can examine you."

She turned toward the guards, now sporting looks of disbelief. She smiled weakly and said, "Ready when you guys are."

The guards regained their poker faces and each took an arm and gently escorted her to the lift leading to the medical ward.

As Gaspar collected his things, he turned to Malone and said, "What'll become of her now? It would be a shame to waste a woman with such obvious talents. I left her combat training intact. Perhaps you could train her as a field operative."

Malone pondered this and said, "That's not a bad idea. All of her family is dead, so no one will miss her. I'll speak to the admiral about it."

"Very well," Gaspar said. "Well, I'm off to my next assignment. We should have a drink soon, old friend."

"I would like that," Malone said. "Safe travels, Gaspar."

"You too, my friend," he replied as he turned and headed for the exit.

An hour later, Malone found himself in a conference room with Supreme Commander Terred and Fleet Admiral Arlington.

Malone began by saying, "I'm sorry for the late hour, Commander, but this couldn't wait. I've given Admiral Arlington a basic briefing on our way here, and now I need to fill you in on the latest developments."

"Okay," Terred said. "First off, tell me how Kate Singer got involved in this. Two traitors in the High Command offices and one of them my own office manager . . . I don't know who to trust anymore."

Arlington said, "Fortunately, Singer didn't have access to any classified information. We think she was keeping this Arvil Symons apprised of Commander North's whereabouts when she was able to. However, she did know about Walker and Ariana Kidder. She was also romantically involved with Symons."

"What? Romantically involved with this traitor?" Terred said, genuinely surprised. "Maybe you should start from the beginning." He rubbed his eyes, already feeling the beginnings of a headache.

Arlington nodded to Malone, and he began. "Well, Commander, it started with the Mandis incident. I know that Commander North's involvement in that operation is classified above my pay grade. The families of the victims of Mandis created an organization several years ago and blamed the government for the loss of their loved ones. Most were nonviolent people trying to cope with their grief, but a small group of them were very militant and, for whatever reason, targeted Commander North as being responsible for the deaths of the colonists."

Terred said nothing but knew that North did play his part, however unwillingly and necessarily.

Malone continued, "The most militant of them, Arvil Symons, took out his anger on North's family and arranged the 'accident' that killed his wife and son. He was also responsible for the deaths of his caretakers, the Lareens, two days ago."

Terred leaned forward and said, "He murdered them? To get at North?"

"It appears so, sir," Arlington said.

"North still thinks that the death of his family was an accident, and he doesn't even know about Lan and Denara yet," Terred said. "I haven't told him. He has enough to deal with at the moment."

"This core militant group consisted of Captain Walker, Ariana Kidder and her brother August, Arvil Symons, and later on, Kate Singer. All had lost family or loved ones on Mandis. August Kidder was responsible for the attack on the *Challenger* fleet and took his own life rather than be captured. Symons obtained T'Kharr weapons with assistance from Walker. Walker made sure the fleet was vulnerable and set Carlo up to take the fall."

Terred nodded, and Malone continued, "Unfortunately, Walker was killed. We just extracted information from Ariana Kidder, however, that Symons has compromised a member of an Alliance research team that was working on some new power source, something that could also be used as a devastating weapon."

Terred and Arlington exchanged glances, which didn't go unnoticed to Malone.

"I'm guessing you already know this part," Malone said.

"Proceed, Colonel," Terred said.

"Yes, sir. Symons's operative apparently didn't deliver as promised, and the T'Kharr invaded the system prematurely. Kidder told us that Symons had been instructed by the T'Kharr to remain on Earth until they've obtained the technology. We also believe that he'll attempt to kill Commander North when he returns from his current mission."

"Sold out his entire race for a blood feud and a few credits," Terred said. "I still can't believe Kate was involved with this. I've known her for over five years."

"No one knew of her connection to Mandis or Symons. We were monitoring a communication between him and Kate when he killed her with an explosive."

Terred regarded Malone for a moment. He turned to Arlington and said, "Admiral, under the circumstances, I'm authorizing you to brief Colonel Malone on the Miratev operation. See to it that he understands the stakes."

"I'll do so immediately, Commander."

"Well done, Colonel. I'll expect a full report on my desk as soon as possible." Terred stood up and left the room.

Arlington said, "It's not easy to impress a grand commander, you know. Yet I understand you've impressed two of them in as many days. You did good work today, Malone. I should be chewing you out for ignoring me and working on this from your hospital room."

"Thank you, Admiral," he said, taking his seat again. "Now tell me about Miratev."

CHAPTER SIXTEEN

Miratev Two

"Here they come!" Kiproff shouted as the wall covering the back entrance to the bunker blew inward, showering him and Sulak with rocks and debris. Four T'Kharr berserkers burst into the tunnel.

Kiproff's aim was deadly. His first grenade round blasted off both of the left arms of the nearest berserker but didn't even slow it down. He switched to automatic fire and sprayed explosive-tipped rounds toward the creature as he retreated toward the hauler. Sulak had already made it to the vehicle and was laying down covering fire.

<Blow the first mine,> Kiproff sent, and Sulak immediately detonated the first of the thirty vicious mines they had laid.

The explosion imploded several metric tons of rock from the ceiling and crushed two of the berserkers, leaving two remaining and sealing off the entrance. Sulak resumed her cover fire until Kiproff reached the vehicle and jumped into the driver's seat. Sulak scored a hit on the second berserker's leg just as the first caught up to the hauler. It used its two remaining arms and pulled itself up onto the cargo trailer.

"Go, go, go!" she screamed as Kiproff pushed the accelerator to maximum.

Sulak ducked the first slash as the beast advanced on her and parried a second with her weapon. The third slash sent her weapon skittering to the back of the cargo trailer and out of reach. She sent a vicious kick to its right knee and was rewarded with the sound of breaking bones and tearing cartilage. As it raised its blades for a killing blow, its head exploded from a round from Kiproff's weapon, and it fell from the trailer onto the floor of the cave.

"Thanks," she said, blowing out a relieved breath, then retrieved the detonator from the floor of the vehicle.

<We're coming in hot,> Kiproff sent to Remy. <Blowing the mines now.>

Remy and his team abruptly retrieved their weapons and ran to the bunker passage leading to the tunnel. Jared looked on in bewilderment as the soldiers left the room without a word. He'd learned in the last two days not to be surprised at such behavior from this strange group. Remy and his team took up firing positions along the end of the tunnel.

"Fire in the hole!" Sulak shouted from the cargo trailer as she began detonating the explosives in series.

Each explosion produced mountains of rock and debris as the tunnel caved in on itself. As they approached the end of the rail, Sulak set off the last charge and watched the last part of the tunnel collapse. Somewhere back near the entrance, the four berserkers were entombed under the tons of rock.

"Let's hope the fleet arrives before they dig us out," Remy said.

Upon seeing their exit blocked, Jared began to utter a protest. Turning toward the research team, Remy added, "As I told you before, we're all expendable if it means denying the T'Kharr that data—all of us, including you and your mates. If Kiproff and Sulak had allowed those berserkers to get in here, we'd all be overrun by T'Kharr troopers by now. I doubt you'd want to be interrogated by them." Remy nodded to the others, and they went back into the bunker.

Dram looked after the soldiers, then turned back to Jared and said, "Mister Trent, if you knew who these guys really were, you wouldn't be surprised. They won't talk about their unit and will claim to civilians that it doesn't exist, but as I said to them before, my brother was in Omega Section. I was offered a spot to join them but declined. Research was more appealing to me. My brother was killed somewhere on a mission, and the military told my parents it was a training accident, special-forces-speak for being killed while on a classified mission."

"What exactly is Omega anyway?" Jared asked. "You obviously know. I've never heard of them."

"And you won't hear anyone acknowledge their existence. You won't find any reference to them anywhere, except on the conspiracy theory websites. These soldiers are handpicked for any number of attributes, put through specialized neuro training and conditioning. They get assignments that would most certainly be suicide missions for normal troopers, but these guys complete them and come back for more."

"But why?" Jared asked. "Why would anyone volunteer for such a thing?"

Dram nodded and said, "Well, some of them are simply adrenaline junkies. Some like to blow stuff up . . . some just want the chance to kill as many of the T'Kharr as possible with the most advanced weapons available. You see those rifles they carry? The line troopers won't see anything like that for another five or six years."

"They're all so young. That Lieutenant Remy can't be more than twenty-one or twenty-two."

"And did you notice? He's already a full lieutenant. If he survives to his thirtieth birthday, he'll be a captain, maybe even an admiral before his other classmates in the regular military make lieutenant commander. That's another advantage . . . provided you survive."

Jared shook his head and said, "Crazy. I thought I'd seen it all."

Dram then clapped him on the shoulder and said, "We should get back in there. Hopefully, help will arrive soon. They communicated with somebody when we first arrived."

The men turned toward the bunker. As they entered, Jared muttered, "If anyone's alive when they get here . . ."

ICC Ka'athiol

Rinn-Tar-Vel Ka'awon activated the view screen in his chambers and demanded an update from his ground forces commander, Vett-Tar-Von Gra'akk.

"The location of this bunker continues to elude us, Rinn-Tar-Vel. These cursed humans have covered their trail well. Their uplink antennae have no hard-wired connections to trace back anywhere and have extremely high encryption levels to prevent us from tracing the signals back to the origin. We have found a few stray civilians, but none of them gave any useful information under interrogation. I'm not sure there are any live humans left on this stinking world."

Ka'awon said, "Someone is down there, Gra'akk. *Ra'aktaka* intercepted an encrypted message from a ground station. We have been unable to decode a single word from the transmission. Someone has to be at this bunker alive."

Gra'akk asked, "Is there any indication of where the transmission originated?"

"From every one of their two dozen uplink stations," Ka'awon growled, clearly frustrated. "They appear to have transmitted from all locations at once in order to mask their whereabouts. My cryptography and communications sections can't even figure out how they did that without leaving some type of trail."

"My assessment would be some type of special enemy military unit, Rinn-Tar-Vel. Judging by the humans we have captured, none possess more than a basic knowledge of military operations or encryption."

"I concur," Ka'awon said.

A subordinate approached Gra'akk and urgently whispered something in his ear. He then turned to Ka'awon and said, "Excuse me for a moment, sir," before turning back to the subordinate, who appeared to relay some piece of urgent information, based on his demeanor and excitement.

Gra'akk turned back to the screen and said, "Rinn-Tar-Vel, I just received a report of an inchitaz unit that encountered two humans in a cave last cycle. The humans imploded the cave they were hiding in rather than face capture. A cowardly act for certain, but perhaps they were there for a reason other than to hide."

"I have read many reports of humans located in caves near the main complex," Ka'awon said wearily.

"This cave was twelve grenta from the main complex, a long distance for a few scared humans to traverse without a specific destination in mind. They had to travel day and night to reach this location, passing up more easily accessible hiding spots."

"And you think that they might have been heading for someplace specific, like this bunker complex?" Ka'awon suggested, his interest now piqued.

"Possibly, Rinn-Tar-Vel," Gra'akk said. "The manner in which they imploded the cave at first seemed an act of desperation, but if they were a military unit, they may have placed the explosives in order to cover their retreat deeper into the mountain."

"Move more units into the area and begin to excavate this cave," Ka'awon said. "I want to see the human bodies for myself."

"As you command, Rinn-Tar-Vel," Gra'akk said, and he cut the link.

Ka'awon knew that this lead might turn up nothing, but it was more tangible than anything else they had at the moment. His instincts told him that there was more to this incident, and he would determine what it was. His reflection was broken by a chime on his comm unit from his subordinate.

"Speak," he ordered.

"Alta-Tar-Vel Te'eq commands you to communicate with him, sir," Dath-Tar-Vel Zha'ar said.

"Put it through," Ka'awon ordered, and Te'eq's features appeared on his communications screen.

Without preamble, Te'eq said, "We have learned from our contacts on the human homeworld that the five human fleets that left there have disappeared, dropped off the detection grid. At first, it seemed they were there to discuss something at a high level, then left for different locations at different times. The problem is none of them resumed their normal patrol routes. Our analysts now believe they are going to coordinate an attack on your location at any time. You must prepare."

Ka'awon nodded and said, "I believed as much, Alta-Tar-Vel. We have mined the starlane portals and are prepared if they arrive. We will be equally matched in ships, thanks to the reinforcements."

"I also wanted to inform you that the human carrier *Pacifica* was one of the five fleets that left their home system. You are familiar with this ship?"

Ka'awon was genuinely surprised. "They are sending one of their grand commanders to deal with us? Surprisingly foolish and arrogant. I've fought against their Grand Commander North before. He is a savvy warrior. If we can destroy that ship, it would be a great victory."

"Agreed," Te'eq said. "I have sent you a breaching ship, one of our newest containing one hundred breaching pods and one thousand shock troops. You will use it to attempt to board the *Pacifica* and capture their grand commander. We may never have this good of an opportunity again."

"Capture . . . Alta-Tar-Vel?" Ka'awon began. "Are you certain—"

"Do not make me rethink my assessment of you, Ka'awon," Te'eq snapped.

Ka'awon immediately said, "I meant no disrespect, Alta-Tar-Vel. It will be done."

"Good," Te'eq said. "See to it that it is. I will also be sending a surprise with the breaching ship that should help if those fleets show up. Use them well." Then he cut the link.

Ka'awon sat back and thought privately that his superiors were insane. To try to board the enemy flagship, of all ships, would be difficult enough, even if their mission was to simply disrupt ship operations, but to try to locate and capture their fleet commander? It was suicide. But suicide or not, he had committed to it. On the other hand, to return home with one of the human grand commanders as a prize would be an amazing feat. He might even be able to challenge Te'eq's position.

He hit the comm button and said, "Zha'ar, double the number of ships patrolling the starlane portals and raise the fleetwide alert level to 'imminent.'"

"Sir, if we double the patrol, it will further disperse the fleets. Are you certain—"

"Carry out my orders, Zha'ar!" Ka'awon snapped before cutting the link.

On one of the two Alliance subs monitoring the T'Kharr fleet, the communications operator listened intently to his headset. "You're not going to believe this," he said. "The T'Kharr fleet admiral just received orders to capture Grand Commander North . . . not just kill him, capture him."

"Are you sure that's what they said?" the sub pilot asked.

"The transmission was from their homeworld from the big T'Kharr chief himself. They used one of their standard codes, one we decrypted a long time ago."

"We can't risk sending another transmission. It was risky enough sending the last one and nearly got us destroyed. We'll have to wait until they jump into the system to tell them."

CHAPTER SEVENTEEN

SAS Pacifica, *Polto-Miratev starlane*

North entered the Cathedra and sat in the control chair in the center of the room. Although the room wasn't especially large, once the chair was activated, the operator seemed to be able to view the entire universe from this vantage point.

As he took his place in the Cathedra control chair and the program activated, he felt the connection initiate between his mind and the chair. He noted *Pacifica* heading toward a blinking point that represented their exit from the starlane into the Miratev system.

North pulled the view back and saw the two subs, still on station at Miratev, and the information they relayed about the current position of the T'Kharr task force.

Thirty mine sweeper units sped ahead of the fleets, trailed by four starlane reconnaissance buoys. North pulled the view out so he could see all three starlane portals and watched the countdown to when the sweepers entered the system.

On one of the cramped subs monitoring the Miratev system, the man monitoring the ship's multiple passive detector arrays suddenly sat bolt upright in his chair.

"Multiple entries through the starlanes . . . all three of them. Simultaneous flashes from all three locations."

The other three officers went over to the man's screen and looked over his shoulder as he zoomed in on the objects exiting the starlane portals. He zoomed in on one in particular and saw the object in detail, a silver cylinder, five meters in length, covered with what appeared to be gray spikes.

"Sweepers."

One of the men sat at the communications station and said, "I'm sending the coordinates of the pod ship and the information about their plan to abduct the commander through the telesponder node to the Cathedra."

They watched as the first sweeper detonated at its core, sending the spikes out in all directions toward the floating antimatter mines. The mines detected the metallic objects and began to move toward them per their programming. As the spikes spread out, the chemical engines in their tails accelerated them toward the mines until they impacted.

The men in the sub had to shield their eyes from the blinding flash as the first mine exploded. More sweepers emerged from the starlane and propelled their own spikes outward, and soon, the entire area looked like an elaborate fireworks display, with multiple explosions inside the ever-expanding radiation cloud.

Dath-Tar-Vel Zha'ar, sitting at his post on the bridge of the *Ka'a-thiol*, reported, "Detonations at the starlane portals, Rinn-Tar-Vel!"

"Which one?" he demanded.

"All three of them!" Zha'ar said with a smug nod of his head. "The humans appear to have fallen into the trap." He looked toward his superior and saw not joy but apprehension as he stared into the view screen.

"Their commander would not foolishly jump blindly into a mine field. They have intelligence assets in-system, like that accursed sub that destroyed the *Gaka'anath*. They are using sweepers! I was assured that our new mines had shielding that made them impervious to their sweepers!" Ka'awon snarled as he walked down the stairs to stand next to Zha'ar's command chair.

"Enemy ships at the first and second portals!" the excited subling at the detector station shouted.

Ka'awon focused on the display and saw dozens of enemy ships emerge from the radiation clouds left over by the mines' detonations and take up a formation around one large ship at the center.

"Enemy ships at the third portal also, Rinn-Tar-Vel," the detector subling reported.

Zha'ar wondered no more why Ka'awon hadn't sent reinforcements to Kirel Dani. He smelled a trap.

Ka'awon watched as the ship names and classes popped up onto the holographic tactical display. He saw the first group consisted of the carriers *Challenger* and *Valor*, the second group included the *Victory* and *Endeavor*, and the third group . . .

"Move the *Ba'akteer* and *Ke'efex* toward the *Pacifica*, Zha'ar!" Ka'awon yelled. "She and her commander will be my prize from this battle! Have the pod ship form on *Ke'efex* and stay within the protection of their energy shields. I want them in as close as possible before deploying."

"As you order, Tar-Vel," Zha'ar said.

North watched all of his fleets emerge unscathed from the minefields. None of the enemy mines had survived. Two T'Kharr fleets and the pod ship moved toward his position. He issued the coordinates of the pod ship to *Pacifica*'s missile batteries. The other three T'Kharr fleets were forming up into a single unit and were converging on the other fleets. He ordered his heavy cruisers to ignore the T'Kharr escort ships and move in close to the ship protecting the pod ship.

North ordered the escorts to flank the enemy fleets and engage the *Ba'akteer* and *Ke'efex* escort fleets. *Ba'akteer* came into range, and *Pacifica* opened up with their main Voron batteries, pummeling *Ba'akteer*'s starboard shields. North noted a small decrease in *Ba'akteer*'s shields, but nothing that would cause serious damage. Only a sustained barrage from multiple ships would bring down the shields sufficiently to make it vulnerable to fighters or missiles.

On the bridge of the *Ba'akteer*, Dath-Tar-Vel Va'adja held onto his chair as the impact of the onslaught of the human carrier rocked his ship.

"Minimal damage, Tar-Vel," the ship's khetal, Kehe'el, reported. "Shields are regenerating."

North watched as two heavy cruisers, *Miria* and *Kegar*, were moved into position to flank the *Ke'efex*, pouring millions of terawatts of energy into her shields. The T'Kharr carriers returned fire, giving just as much as they were receiving. He felt a shake as he sat in his chair and knew from the interface that *Pacifica* was taking heavy fire as well.

A blinking red warning message took his attention as the frigate *Adam Carling* registered dangerously low shields. North ordered *Adam Carling* to fall back and switch places with the frigate *Kariva*. As large and powerful as his cruisers were, they were still outgunned by the larger T'Kharr ships and their more powerful weapons. The T'Kharr ship's shield status was beginning to dip into the yellow range. He knew they had to speed things up and ordered his ships to close the gap to one hundred kilometers.

After several moments, *Adam Carling's* shield indicator turned red. The two T'Kharr destroyers ignored *Kariva* and sent a tremendous volley into the tail of *Adam Carling*. It was over in seconds. North saw the ship spin out of control, her engines destroyed beyond repair, and saw systems fall into the red throughout the crippled ship. He sent the order to abandon ship just moments before her reactor went critical.

The *Adam Carling* disappeared in a brilliant flare of light along with all two thousand of her crew.

"Graaaaaaaa!" Va'adja screamed as he witnessed the destruction of the *Adam Carling* on his display. "Tell the destroyer khetals we will feast on our enemy's corpses together! The first kill is ours!"

The entire bridge crew of the *Ba'akteer* shouted in unison, cheering the ship's destruction and building up their bloodlust.

Although being connected to the Cathedra dulled certain senses in the operator, North felt the anger rising inside of him. He commandeered missile fire control from the *Pacifica* and cruisers.

The last of the two capital ships had slipped into range. He simultaneously fired two of the specials from each ship and ordered *Pacifica* to launch fighters.

"Missiles, Tar-Vel! Both cruisers and the *Pacifica* have fired . . . this is strange . . . they have fired only two missiles each . . . two at us, two at the *Ke'efex* and two at the breaching ship," the puzzled subling manning the detector station reported.

"Shield status?" Va'adja snapped.

"Energy shields are holding on all ships, Tar-Vel. The missiles have no chance of penetrating."

"A desperate act of frustration," he growled with satisfaction. "Foolishness. Point defenses on automatic. Destroy them before they reach us."

"Enemy carrier is launching fighters, Tar-Vel," the subling reported, the confusion clear in his voice.

Now Va'adja was really confused. Fighters didn't have the firepower to penetrate operational shields on capital ships. To launch them against ships whose shields weren't drained to 50 percent or lower was futile, and he wouldn't launch his own fighters just to waste them in ship-to-ship combat with the enemy fighters. As long as their shields were up, they were protected.

"Tar-Vel! Our weapons are having no effect on the incoming missiles! The beams appear to be passing through the objects!"

"What?" Va'ajda said, eyes locked on the screen. "It makes no sense . . ."

The weapons subling said, "If they can pass through the beams, they could pass through our shields. . ."

"Evasive maneuvers!" Va'adja screamed, eyes wide with the realization of what was happening. "Launch all fighter wings!"

The ship suddenly turned away violently from the incoming missiles, but it was too late. The missiles impacted the *Ba'akteer's* shields simultaneously and passed through unscathed as if the shields had been made of tissue paper.

As they breached the shield perimeter, the missiles accelerated and homed in on the main shielding control centers located just below the shield generator rings. As on human carriers, T'Kharr carriers were protected by energy shields generated by two large rings that circled the ship, one fore and one aft. Both missiles passed through the outer bulkheads of the ship and snapped back into phase just as they reached the control centers.

Captain Michael Trent watched his screen with satisfaction as the shield-generating rings on the ship went dark, plumes of fire erupting from the control centers directly beneath them.

"Shields are down!" Trent shouted as he dove his own fighter toward the *Ba'akteer's* forward launch bay, now beginning to spew out waves of enemy fighters. "Shields are down! Attack!"

While human Neptune-class carriers like *Pacifica* had three landing bays, T'Kharr ships had only two—one located in front of the ship, one to the rear. He watched the waves of Valkyries move in and pick off fighters coming out of the landing bays and the Daggers go after the ship's defensive batteries.

He toggled the targeting stud on his control grip and moved the crosshair over the gaping maw of the forward landing bay, sending the commands through his neural interface. He sent two powerful Javelin ship-to-ship missiles toward the bay. His wingman fired two of his own, and both of them pulled up and away.

Engaging his rear view, he was rewarded with a blinding explosion as the four missiles impacted on the exposed opening of the bay. Several enemy fighters were blown out of the bay from the impact, and the fireball enveloped two others as they were leaving the ship.

"Nice shooting, Skipper," his wingman said. "That's going to take a while to sweep up."

Ba'akteer's point defense batteries raked across the port shields, causing Trent's ship to shudder violently.

"Let's get some distance. They aren't too happy about that one."

The two ships pulled away to regroup for a second run.

North watched with satisfaction as all six missiles found their targets and destroyed the shielding generator control centers on all three ships. As he watched *Pacifica's* forces move in on the *Ba'akteer* on bombing runs, he saw an unexpected opening and quickly changed orders for the *Kegar* to switch its attention from the *Ke'efex* to the pod ship.

Aboard *Miria*, they watched the impact of their missiles on the *Ke'efex* and saw her shields fail. *Ke'efex* abruptly spun away to starboard. *Miria's* captain saw the opening and was about to issue a fire order when twenty of his port side missile launchers, in perfect broadside configuration in respect to *Ke'efex*, fired in unison by direct command from the Cathedra.

The missiles streaked toward the enemy carrier and impacted on her unshielded port side. Multiple internal explosions could be seen rippling through the *Ke'efex*. The *Ke'efex's* port engines were reduced to a molten pile of slag. The lights inside the stricken carrier suddenly went dark, and *Ke'efex's* power readings went dead, her guns falling silent. The only light visible in the ship came from the fires and multiple explosions still rocking the vessel.

Miria and *Kegar* then received targeting coordinates at *Ke'efex's* center and were commanded to fire. Both ships cut loose with their Voron batteries, and the enemy carrier split into two pieces, both halves spinning wildly out of control, disgorging atmosphere, bodies, and debris into the void. North saw fire belching out of both forward and aft landing bays of the carrier, and he noted that not a single fighter craft had been successfully launched.

A chorus of cheers rose up on the *Miria* and *Kegar* bridges as they watched the assault break the enemy carrier's back.

"For *Adam Carling*, you unholy bastards," North muttered before turning his attention to the pod ship.

"Destroyed?" an incredulous Ka'awon demanded. "Completely?"

"Some new type of weapon that penetrated their shields, Rinn-Tar-Vel," Zha'ar replied, still reeling from the images coming in of the wreckage of the *Ke'efex*. "*Ba'akteer* has suffered moderate-to-heavy damage on her defensive batteries and lost about one-fourth of her fighters. Va'adja reports they are rerouting systems to bring up her shields once again."

"Order *Ba'akteer* to withdraw to the designated rally coordinates, and order our forces to break off," Ka'awon ordered as he turned toward his ready room. "We will move between the enemy fleets and the planet and attack in a unified wave."

"Yes, Rinn-Tar-Vel."

Ka'awon spun around and snapped, "And order the breaching ship to deploy. Maybe the alta-tar-vel's surprise will even the playing field a bit."

"At once, Tar-Vel," Zha'ar replied.

Once the pod ship's shields went down, automatic systems immediately launched all the pods simultaneously. Each of the pods, containing a full squad of T'Kharr shock troops set to board an enemy ship, burst away from the frame of the ship.

On the far side of the pod ship, away from enemy detectors, ten dark objects detached from the ship and remained stationary, allowing the battling ships to move away from the immediate area. Once clear of the ship, two subs and eight pods, constructed of the same stealth material as the T'Kharr subs, engaged their stealth drives and moved in behind the nearest ship, *Kegar*, to quietly wait.

North saw the breaching pods break away and ordered the fighters to attack.

"There they are, boys and girls," Trent said. "Get 'em all and be quick about it."

Devin Truant instructed his targeting computer to lock on to the five closest pods.

"You with me, Gambler?" Truant's wingman, Colby "Cheeseball" Gates, asked.

"I'm on your three o'clock, Cheesy," Truant replied, dropping down to the right of his partner.

As they closed on the targets, Truant saw that the rest of his buddies were quickly dispatching the remaining breaching pods. They were relatively slow compared to the fighters and had no place to go since the carrier's shields were still in place.

"I'm locked up," Truant said as he fired a short pulse from his cannons, vaporizing the first pod. Another shot, and it was two down, three to go.

As they approached the third pod, Truant saw that two of his fellow pilots had dispensed with the fourth and fifth pods, leaving only one left for him and his wingman.

"Next one is mine," Gates said as they closed on the last target. As Gates focused on the target hashes on his display, he failed to notice the rear hatch of the pod slide open. Two four-armed nightmares in space suits emerged, one carrying a very large missile launcher and the other a rifle.

"Cheesy, break off!" Truant yelled. "Break off!"

The T'Kharr shock trooper aimed his weapon at Gates's ship and fired. The missile impacted on his gun ports, the most vulnerable part of his fighter, where shield protection was at a minimum. Sparks exploded in the cockpit, and smoke from the ruined electronics obscured his vision, but he was able to pull away before a round of shots from the second trooper struck his ship.

Truant saw the second trooper look toward him and swing his rifle his way, so he instinctively fired a snap shot, scoring a glancing hit on the side of the pod. The strike was enough to wrench loose the first trooper's grip, and the trooper spun away from the pod, helplessly headed out into deep space.

As the second trooper brought his rifle to bear, Truant increased his speed and tapped his thrusters to spin ninety degrees. As his momentum carried him past the pod, he fired his cannons and raked the side of the pod. He was rewarded with a satisfying implosion.

He turned back and approached his friend's ship, which was trailing smoke and venting atmosphere. The canopy of the craft was badly cracked, but he saw that Gates had been able to lock down his atmo helmet.

"Gates?" he called. "Colby! Are you okay?"

But there was no response from his friend. As he edged closer, he saw that the pilot appeared to be unconscious and was bleeding from his nose.

"*Pacifica*, this is Alert 4, request S&R to my location. Alert 2 is disabled and in need of assistance. I will remain in the area until their arrival and provide cover."

The reply came from *Pacifica*. "S&R is busy right now and will be dispatched at the earliest convenience. We are moving toward the planet and will soon be out of range."

"But he'll die if you . . ." Truant began.

A new voice came over the air and interrupted him. "Alert 4, this is PAC-CSG. Devin, S&R won't make it in time. Do what you can to bring him in."

He replied, "Acknowledged, Captain. I won't leave him behind. Alert 4 out."

As soon as he terminated the link, he unsnapped his harness, checked his atmo suit and helmet, and depressurized his cockpit. As his canopy slid back, he engaged his autopilot, tethered himself, and climbed out onto the nose. He could see the handhold just behind the cockpit on his friend's ship. Taking a deep breath,

Truant kicked off his own ship. As he approached the other ship, he realized that he'd kicked off too hard and slammed into the side of the other ship, knocking the wind out of himself. He managed to snag the handhold and dangled there for several seconds, trying to will his lungs to draw in breath.

After what seemed an eternity, he drew a deep breath full of air into his lungs and quickly attached a tether to his own ship so it didn't drift away from Gates's ship. He located the exterior controls and hit the canopy release to Gates's ship. He could feel the vibrations of the motors trying to open the damaged cockpit canopy, but the canopy wouldn't budge.

Realizing he was running out of time, he opened the access panel to the cockpit diagnostic controls and located the emergency ejection system. He carefully disabled the seat jets, then stabbed at the button. The explosive bolts blew, and the shattered canopy spun away from the ship. Truant attached the tether to Gates's suit, unbuckled his seat harness, and pulled him gently up and out of the cockpit.

Wrapping his arm around Gates's waist, Truant gently tugged on the tether. The two pilots slowly drifted toward Truant's fighter and touched down, much softer this time, on the nose of the ship. He pulled himself and Gates inside of the now very cramped cockpit and slid the canopy closed.

After pressurizing the cockpit, he quickly pulled off his helmet and disengaged the automatic pilot, plotting the most direct course back to *Pacifica*. He hoped that he could still catch up in time before running out of fuel.

"*Pacifica*, this is Alert 4 with Alert 2 onboard. Request emergency landing clearance and a medical team standing by in the landing bay."

There was a pause, then, "Alert 4, you are cleared for immediate landing in the port bay. The pattern is clearing for you now."

Truant saw that several of the ships ahead of him in the approach pattern peeled off, allowing him to jump to the front of the line. He touched down and opened his canopy as a medical team ran up to the ship and gently lifted the limp form of Lt. Gates out.

Truant jumped down and watched as they put Gates on a hover stretcher. As he watched them go, the stretcher slid past a stern figure standing with his hands clasped behind his back. Captain Trent stopped the last man and muttered something to him, to which the medic nodded his head and then motioned toward the doorway where the other medics were headed.

Trent turned toward Truant and nodded to him respectfully. He then flashed him a grin and turned and walked toward his office.

Truant smiled to himself, glad that both he and Gates had made it back in one piece.

CHAPTER EIGHTEEN

North saw that *Ba'akteer* and her escorts were turning to run. She was retreating quickly. *Pacifica's* pilots reported that only ninety of the pods had been destroyed and there was no sign of the others. He issued recall orders to *Pacifica's* fighters. It was time to regroup and move toward the planet to cover the marine landing.

His other four carriers appeared to be holding their own against the T'Kharr flagship and two other enemy heavy carriers. *Challenger* and two destroyers had suffered moderate damage. North ordered *Challenger* to drop back to effect repairs while *Endeavor* covered her. Both Alliance and T'Kharr fleets still had operational shields, so fighters hadn't yet been deployed by either side.

At that moment, their escorts were engaged in a furious exchange in the space between the carriers, both shielding them from any direct attack and attempting to destroy each other's escort fleet. Only a combined attack by multiple ships would bring down the shields of one of the larger ships. One-on-one was a stalemate. The multi-phasic missiles had been an even better advantage than he'd hoped.

They'd come into the fight evenly matched but had taken out one of their top-of-the-line carriers and the breaching ship. He noted that the enemy fleet was disengaging and appeared as if they were preparing to retreat. He figured they were moving to regroup with the *Ba'akteer* and defend the planet. Fortunately, *Pacifica* would arrive first.

North felt a familiar tingling in his telesponder implant.

<This is Tyler. We are ready.>

<Proceed,> North answered.

Ka'awon seethed with anger. He watched the playback of the broadside attack on the *Ke'efex* and cringed as the missiles from the human cruiser struck home and destroyed the ship. He'd recalled the *Ba'akteer* to join up with him. Perhaps they could tip the scales in their favor by combining their forces. He hoped the humans didn't have any more surprises. He was wrong.

"Dath-Tar-Vel, new enemy contact emerging from the radiation cloud," the detector subling reported. "Whatever it is, it's big and heading toward the planet at a high rate of speed."

Zha'ar sat up straight in his chair and said, "Identify . . . class of ship."

"Unknown configuration. Despite its size, it appears to be twice as fast as a destroyer."

"Magnify," Zha'ar growled, and the view zoomed in on a large ship nearly as big as the carriers, bristling with gun ports and a huge, gaping maw that ran down its axis, big enough to swallow one of their destroyers whole. It moved quickly toward the planet and approached the orbiting squadron of destroyers.

"The ship appears to be attacking solo, Dath-Tar-Vel. The other enemy ships are not breaking off to cover it."

Ka'awon stepped away from his office where he'd been monitoring the battle and looked at the screen.

"What is that?" he demanded.

"Unidentified enemy ship, Tar-Vel," Zha'ar answered. "It is moving toward the squadron defending the planet. The ship will be outgunned eight ships to one. Should I send reinforcements?"

Ka'awon squinted at the rapidly retreating ship and felt uneasy. These humans didn't make suicide runs.

"No," he said. "Eight ships should be able to handle it. Keep the fleet together and in formation. Inform me when the new ship is destroyed." He stepped back in his office without waiting for a reply.

On the bridge of the AX-2107 dreadnought prototype, Colonel Nicole Lauren turned to General Tyler and said, "All systems are ready, General. We have enough antimatter to fire ten full-power shots with the main battery. After that, I would suggest a hasty retreat."

"Commander North will be happy if we can give them a nice bloody nose and put the fear of the Creator in them. They've never seen the likes of this weapon before."

"Yes, sir," she replied as they approached the enemy squadron, now moving to flank them.

Two of the T'Kharr destroyers moved around the ship, hoping to attack it from both sides. Both ships opened fire simultaneously and shook the dreadnought with hits to its port and starboard shield arrays.

Tyler held onto the handrail next to where he was standing to steady himself as the ship rocked from the strikes.

"Unfortunate that the multi-layered shields aren't online yet. Another layer would help us tremendously. How soon until we're in firing position, Colonel? I don't want us to get vaporized before we've even had a chance to fire a shot."

"Almost in position, General," Lauren said. "Two of the destroyers have us in between them . . . now watch this." She ordered the ship to turn ninety degrees, bringing one destroyer directly in front of them and one directly astern.

She turned to fire control and said, "Fire when ready."

Deep in the core of the ship, a small amount of antimatter dropped into the magnetic reaction chamber and began to react with the vapor in the chamber, building up a massive amount of energy. The energy generated by the weapon was so vast that it needed two openings—fore and aft—in order for the ship to avoid being torn to pieces by the recoil.

From the front and rear of the ship, it appeared that a swirling hurricane was forming in the open space running down the center axis of the dreadnought. Bolts of lightning shot from the center of the vortex, striking the interior sides of the discharge corridor.

"Energy build up reaching maximum," the officer at fire control reported. "Firing . . . now."

Suddenly, two waves of energy flashed out of the front and rear discharge corridors of the dreadnought, enveloping both ships in a blistering shockwave and throwing them violently off course, as if they'd been swept aside by a giant's hand.

"Enemy shields are down to 29 percent, Colonel," the detector officer reported. "Structural damage to both ships. Both ships are adrift."

"Reset the chamber and prepare to fire again," she commanded. She turned to the general and said, "It takes several minutes to prepare the weapon for another shot. That's something they need to work on to make this practical."

"Noted, Colonel, but impressive nonetheless," Tyler said with a satisfied grin. Lauren returned the grin and turned her attention to the rapidly approaching attack wave in front of her.

The ship's navigator kept both of the drifting destroyers aligned with the front and rear discharge corridors of the dreadnought while Lauren willed the weapon to recharge quickly before the other ships reached them.

"Detectors show that the ships have regenerated their shields to 38 percent," the detector officer reported.

"Battery is ready to fire," fire control advised.

"Fire!" Lauren yelled. Once again, twin waves of destruction lanced out of the ship, overwhelming the two drifting ships. As the wave swept over both ships, enemy shield strength dropped quickly to zero, and both ships blew apart, fire belching out of the fractures in their hulls.

"Yes!" Lauren said with a thrust of her fist.

"Enemy ships have halted their approach and are maintaining their distance . . . probably arguing over who gets to attack next," the detector officer advised.

"Move us closer to one of those light carriers," Lauren ordered.

The navigator steered the ship toward the nearest of the two smaller carriers, boasting a complement of fifty fighter craft and assault landers. As the dreadnought shifted position, the enemy ships kept a wary distance until they could formulate a strategy. The weapons officer informed Lauren that the weapon was once again ready to fire.

Lauren then noticed that one of the destroyers had moved close to the light carrier and seemed to be using the ship as cover to shield itself. She would've liked to tap in on the comm waves and hear what the carrier captain had to say about that.

"That will undoubtedly be the squadron commander's ship," she said to Tyler. "Well, this shot will have to be aimed at only one of them this time. I think they'll be wary of approaching our stern after that last shot."

"Moving to bear on the carrier," the weapons officer reported.

"Wait until that destroyer is directly behind the carrier," Lauren said as the ship slipped into position.

"In range."

"Commence firing sequence," Lauren commanded, and she watched the power build up once again on the monitors.

As the weapon was about to fire, she ordered a sharp turn to bring the carrier to bear for a shot on her port shields. The weapon blasted into the side of the carrier, pushing it into the shields of the destroyer behind it. Lauren watched with glee as the two shield grids from the two ships overloaded each other and blinked out.

Momentum from the blast pushed the carrier toward the now unprotected destroyer, and both ships collided violently. Pieces of the two ships' hulls and plumes of gas could be seen flying away from the ships, both bearing massive scars from the impact with each other.

"That collision depressurized the forward three decks of the destroyer and the main landing bay of the carrier."

"Heat 'er up again, Lieutenant," Lauren said.

The weapons officer prepared the gun for a fourth volley.

"Colonel, all of the remaining enemy ships are moving to flank us. They're taking care to stay clear of our bow and stern. They'll have us surrounded before the weapon is ready to fire again."

Lauren took in the information and said, "We're close enough for torpedoes. Lock onto the destroyer."

The dreadnought carried the same huge ship-to-ship torpedoes that the subs carried. They were larger and carried a much heavier payload than the missiles commonly used on other ships but were much slower. They would only have a brief window of opportunity, so she decided to act.

"Target acquired."

"Fire torpedoes, full spread."

Torpedo tubes on either side of the forward discharge corridor spat out three of the big torpedoes each, all streaking toward the crippled destroyer. The other ships that had been moving to surround the dreadnought turned and opened fire, trying to pick off the torpedoes before they could hit their targets.

Beams of energy crisscrossed the void between the dreadnought and the targeted destroyer, hoping for a lucky hit that would intercept the torpedoes. Lauren and Tyler watched as the T'Kharr destroyers shot down one, then a second and third torpedo, but as they streaked on toward the target, it was apparent that the last three of them would get through.

"Impact in three . . . two . . . one," the weapons officer said as the three remaining torpedoes slammed into the side of the destroyer, blowing it apart in a fiery, gaseous explosion. The explosion enveloped the front part of the carrier, still too close from the collision, jarring it violently and causing secondary explosions on that ship as well. She wouldn't be launching ships any time in the near future.

"Colonel . . . malfunction in the main battery," the weapons officer reported. "It's offline."

"Time to repair?"

"Unknown. It's one of the bugs we've been dealing with."

Tyler then turned to Lauren and said, "Retreat. We did what we came to do, and I don't want to lose this ship."

Lauren looked disappointed, but she knew what she had to do.

"Nav, head for the second starlane . . . maximum speed."

The destroyers, still caught off guard by the torpedo attack, couldn't react in time to pursue the dreadnought, which quickly accelerated toward the starlane portal.

As they approached the starlane, the radiation cloud had mostly dissipated, and no enemy ships were in a position to stop them. Lauren ordered the ship to slow to .0012 light speed and, just prior to entering the starlane, launched four starlane buoys to surround the gateway. She hoped the radiation in the cloud would mask the buoys long enough to do some good.

<I hate to run away, Commander,> Tyler sent.

<Three ships destroyed, one crippled,> replied North. <Not bad.>

<Still.>

<If this goes badly, we'll need that ship more than ever,> North sent.

<Good hunting, sir.>

<Same.>

With that, the dreadnought blinked out and entered the star-lane.

Zha'ar nervously glanced toward Ka'awon's office. Screams and howls of fury came as he heard objects being thrown against the wall. As abruptly as the tirade had commenced, the office grew ominously silent. Zha'ar preferred the tirade, finding the silence unsettling.

Ka'awon burst out of his office and stopped several steps outside of the door, obviously struggling to maintain his composure.

"Who is the leader of the destroyer squadron that engaged the unknown enemy ship?" Ka'awon asked through gritted teeth.

Zha'ar had anticipated this question and said, "Alta-Khet-al Ha'arun, Tar-Vel. He was killed when the *Ne'elval* was destroyed."

Ka'awon looked even angrier and hissed through gritted teeth, "That coward should thank the Under-Deity he is not alive to face me after that despicable display. Send word to the homeworld. Execute his mates and their spawn. Their cowardly bloodline will not plague our species ever again."

"As you order, Rinn-Tar-Vel," Zha'ar replied.

A subordinate approached Zha'ar with a readout. "You asked to be kept informed of enemy comm traffic, Tar-Vel."

Zha'ar read the dispatch and sprang out of his chair. Ka'awon was just turning to go back into his office.

"Rinn-Tar-Vel, this is what we have been waiting for!"

Ka'awon stopped in his tracks and read the message. "Send a coded message to these coordinates . . . tight beam transmission. Send the following . . ."

Alliance cruiser Miria

Aboard the *Miria*, Captain Jacob Armstrong sat in his command chair reviewing damage control reports and noticed a disturbing entry.

"Get me the admiral," Armstrong said, and the communications station connected him promptly.

"Drake."

"Admiral, we're having trouble with some of our shield components. We're currently only able to generate 70 percent shields. We need replacements from *Pacifica*."

Drake turned to Lt. Vale. "Advise ship stores to send *Miria* everything on this list as soon as possible. Tell them to be sure to coordinate the transfer since we'll have to drop our rear shields momentarily to launch the shuttle."

At that moment, the ten stealth ships separated into two groups, the eight breaching pods heading toward *Pacifica* and the two subs heading toward the *Miria*. The pods hovered just outside the shield perimeter. They waited patiently as the shuttle approached and saw their opening. A small section of the rear shields dropped, allowing the shuttle to slip through, and at the same time, the eight pods slipped inside and headed toward the carrier.

Meanwhile, the two subs hovered just aft of *Miria*. As the shuttle approached, *Miria* dropped the rear shields, and the subs slipped inside. They knew that this was a suicide mission. The enemy ships flanking the cruiser would surely detect the torpedo launches and fire on them, but it didn't matter. One sub dropped in behind the *Miria's* main engines, and the second took position near the front of the ship. When the first ship was ready, it sent a coded message to the second, and they armed their torpedoes.

The communications officer spun toward Armstrong and said, "Captain, enemy transmission from *inside* our shield perimeter!"

"What?" Armstrong said before ordering point defenses to sweep the area around the ship.

Both T'Kharr subs simultaneously launched all eight of their torpedoes from point-blank range, tearing into the *Miria's* hull and breaching her power distribution hub. Explosions rippled down the length of the ship through the network of power conduits. The explosion blew the cruiser apart, instantly destroying the subs, their hulls shattering like glass as they touched the expanding wave. *Pacifica's* shields were pummeled with fire and smoking debris.

Drake watched in horror as the cruiser and her twenty-five hundred crewmen disintegrated into smoking debris and dust. He quickly turned to the detector station and yelled, "Full sweep of our inner shield perimeter, both active and visual scans! Activate all point defenses! Fire on anything that doesn't look right!"

For the next few moments, gunners on the point-defense stations frantically searched the area for anything out of place, hoping that more enemy subs weren't in the area.

"Hull strike, Admiral!" the detector officer yelled. "Something impacted the hull in Gamma section!"

"Exterior view on the monitor!" Drake shouted. Eight pitch-black tubes appeared on the monitor and were attaching themselves to the hull.

Drake immediately slammed the alert button on his chair, activating klaxons throughout the ship. "All security teams, breaching pods in starboard midship sections Gamma through Juliet! All personnel prepare to repel boarders!"

On that order, automated systems immediately engaged and slammed all bulkheads to adjoining sections shut.

"All bulkheads are secured in those sections, Admiral, including the access ways to the point defense batteries," the detector officer reported. "Brigadier Logan advises his marines are geared up and on their way."

"Point defenses . . . open—" Drake started when he was interrupted by Ensign Craig, the detector officer.

"Admiral, outer hull has been breached in eight areas! Shock troops are boarding!"

"Belay that fire order!" he shouted. "I don't want to decompress the whole deck. Get me Logan." He brought up the areas on the holo display.

On the comm, he said, "Logan."

"They've already breached in areas Gamma through Juliet, so I can't destroy the pods yet. It'll vent the whole deck, and we still have people in there. One team appears to be moving forward, the other aft. We received intel that they'll try and capture the commander. That cannot happen, General."

"It won't, Admiral," Logan said. "We're moving up on the forward group now with Colonel Shaddra. Colonel Fargo is moving up on the rear team. I'll keep you posted." Then he closed the link.

Specialist Kevin McNabb jogged down the corridor back toward his post after grabbing a sandwich for himself and his crewmates in the third starboard railgun battery. He'd drawn the short straw and ran down to the food dispenser just down the corridor. He heard Admiral Drake's voice give the order to repel boarders in sections Gamma through Juliet. McNabb's mouth went dry as he heard bulkhead doors slam shut at both ends of his section. He abruptly ditched the food he'd been carrying and fumbled for his sidearm, struggling to unsnap the latch.

He jumped as something slammed against the hull on the exterior of the ship. Two circular patterns of red hot metal formed on the wall in front of him, then exploded inward, slamming his lifeless body against the far wall. Fate had done him a favor, sparing him the nightmare that stepped through the opening.

Twenty T'Kharr shock troops, all dressed in blood-red space suits and carrying large rifles that could only be wielded by a being with four arms, poured into the corridor. One trooper aimed his rifle at the man's body and blew a large hole in his chest. Once satisfied that the human was really dead, he moved aft with the others.

The shock troops ran to bulkhead leading to section Juliet and placed shaped explosive charges around the perimeter of the doorway. Another did the same on the forward bulkhead leading into section Hotel. The T'Kharr platoon leader activated his comm unit and contacted the other squads, ordering all doors blown simultaneously.

The shaped charges directed the entire force of the blast inward, shattering the metal bulkheads at both ends of the section. The four groups of troopers split up, pouring into the newly opened spaces. Rifle fire and human screams could be heard as the troopers moved forward and aft toward their objectives.

"First wave, move forward . . . second wave, on me," the lead trooper said, motioning for his twenty troopers to follow. "We are moving aft toward the engineering section."

"Shock Leader, I cannot contact the flagship," one of the troopers reported. "The humans are jamming communications."

"Keep trying," the leader growled as he turned to move aft with his group.

Brigadier Logan's group was just approaching the bulkhead leading into section Foxtrot when his comm buzzed.

He grabbed the comm, the irritation plain in his voice, and hissed, "What is it?"

"This is Major Deneva, General. My team and I are in position to engage the group heading toward engineering. Please ask Colonel Fargo to hold position."

Logan stopped for a moment. "How many of you are there, Major?"

"Eight of us in my team, General."

"Only eight? There are forty shock troops heading in your direction. That's suicide."

"General, please . . . I don't have time to explain."

Was this Omega trooper's pride speaking? Hopefully, they were as effective as they thought they were. Logan considered for a moment, then turned and barked an order. "I'm ordering Fargo to hold position in Papa section. Advise status when you can. Godspeed, Major."

"Copy," Deneva replied.

Colonel Fargo and his group were just passing through midship section Papa. Fargo acknowledged the order and had his troops form a defensive line between the midship sections and the passageway leading into the engineering section. Soldiers quickly took up positions along each wall and pocket, bringing their rifles to bear on the opening. The platoon sergeant closest to the bulkhead ordered the placement of claymore-10 anti-personnel mines.

Someone yelled, "Make a path!" and eight obsidian-clad figures sprinted past Fargo and the other troops, leaping through the doorway and toward the direction of the oncoming T'Kharr shock troops.

"What the hell?" was all Fargo could say as he watched the Omega team disappear through the doorway, convinced they'd lost their minds. Logan told him that a strike team was on its way, but he didn't know what to expect.

Deneva and his team stopped just short of midship section Oscar and scanned the section ahead. There were twenty shock troopers advancing through section November, heading toward their position and killing everything in their path. The troopers were firing into any room with an open door. Deneva heard an occasional scream and the staccato sound of rifle fire as the troopers approached.

<Deploy,> he sent, and the other men nodded.

Shock Leader Re'ekk cautiously moved down the hallway up to the bulkhead leading into section Oscar just five sections away from Engineering. Their job was to disable the engines if possible and otherwise occupy the carrier's security forces while the main group tried to make their way to the command deck and capture the human grand commander. He could sense the blood lust from his troopers. So far, the humans had been easily dealt with. He knew, however, that as they penetrated deeper into the ship, they would soon encounter combat troops.

Re'ekk checked his scanner and saw they were approaching the junction between section November and section Oscar. The bulkhead hadn't been secured. Sensing a trap, he ordered grenades deployed through the open doorway. Three sonic flash grenades produced a satisfying blinding white light and concussion wave, and twelve shock troopers burst through the doorway, ready to dispatch the stunned human soldiers.

Once through the doorway, however, they saw . . . nothing. This section was different from the others they'd passed through. There were no side doors or passageways leading to gunnery stations. The outer walls were smooth, and the inner walls midway through the section were covered with conduits, computer terminals, and data ports but no personnel.

One of the forward scouts advised that the door on the aft end was sealed like the others. Re'ekk ordered the team to set up defensive lines around the computer terminals, hoping his techs could hack into the ship systems from there and possibly override the lockdown. The amount of explosives required to open one of the bulkheads was substantial, and they were going to quickly run short if they couldn't find another way to breach them. When they ran out of explosives, they would have to burn through, and that would take time . . . too much time.

As Re'ekk stood behind the tech attempting to hack into the computer terminal, Deneva and his team watched and waited, their heads-up displays switching to life sign mode at his command. As the T'Kharr tech entered a command he hoped would override the lockdown, the open door slammed shut, and smoke began to pour out of a vent in the wall, quickly obscuring their vision.

"Secure helmets!" Re'ekk snarled, guessing that the mist was some type of airborne agent.

Deneva and his team deactivated their camouflage fields and dropped from the ceiling right in the midst of the troopers.

Re'ekk spun around as he heard screams in front of him and behind him. "Report!"

The only answers he received were screams and frantic weapons fire. The tech that had been trying to hack the computer terminal stiffened abruptly, blood splashing across the inside of his visor. He fell to the ground, a smoking hole in the back of his helmet. Re'ekk spun around, firing blindly into the mist. He howled in pain as a vicious slash across his two right arms dislodged his rifle, and he heard it skitter across the deck into the mist.

Re'ekk drew a blade from its sheath, then backed himself against the wall, trying desperately to see into the mist when he heard air recyclers activate. The mist quickly dissipated, and he found that he was standing alone amongst the twisted bodies of his team. Thick pools of T'Kharr blood and severed limbs littered the area, and eight silent figures, dressed all in black with dark visors hiding their features, stood on either side of him.

"Surrender," one of the figures said. The human was speaking in perfect T'Kharr, not through a translator.

"What are you?" he snarled.

The soldier who had spoken blasted his right kneecap off, and he crumpled to the ground, howling in agony. When he hit the ground, the knife fell to the floor and was kicked away by one of the figures.

"I said surrender, you ugly bastard," he repeated.

Re'ekk tried to grab a rifle lying on the deck in front of him. A second trooper fired a shot that shorted out the electrical systems in Re'ekk's suit, making his other limbs go numb. The last thing he remembered was a rifle butt approaching the side of his face.

CHAPTER NINETEEN

SAS Pacifica

On the command deck, Drake let out a deep breath as he heard the report, and a cheer rose from the bridge crew. Deneva had reported the team heading aft had been stopped, and Logan's marines had stopped those heading forward. The bad news was that the general himself had been injured and was currently being taken to sickbay. His marines had suffered numerous casualties before they were able to put down the boarders a mere fifty meters from the ventilation access port to the Cathedra.

He activated the comm. "Damage control teams, report status to the XO."

Turning to Frost, he asked, "What's the status of those pods?"

"Fargo said his EOD teams disabled the internal systems and assured me there are no explosives inside. He wants to detach the pods once the hull breaches are sealed and bring them into one of the launch bays."

Drake nodded and said, "Tell him to do it quickly and use whatever resources he needs. We still have a landing to cover. Use the dorsal bay."

"Yes, sir," Frost replied and then turned away to receive the damage reports.

Drake had received the report earlier that Logan was seriously injured but out of danger. The ship surgeon said the general would be fit for duty in a few hours. Drake knew Logan would have to be near death before he'd give up his command.

Drake turned to Lt. Vale and said, "Please ask General Austin to come to the bridge."

"Yes, sir. And Admiral, there's a Major Deneva on the comm who says he urgently needs to speak to you."

"Put him through."

"Admiral, this is Major Deneva. I think we may have been given an opportunity here."

Drake replied, "Explain."

Deneva explained what he had in mind, and Drake said, "Interesting. What do you need?"

"Let us interrogate the prisoners first, and I'll get back to you," Deneva replied.

The three captured T'Kharr troopers paced angrily in their cells, knowing that death would've been preferable to being captured. The three had been placed in individual cells that allowed them to see and speak to each other but stopped them from interacting physically. Too many T'Kharr prisoners in the past had killed each other to avoid capture and interrogation, usually culminating with the last one killing himself.

None spoke, assuming that there were listening devices in the cell, but they eyed the door contemptuously. Three very large marines stood outside of the door. Lt. Frederick Aubrey, the officer in charge of brig security, walked into the control room and asked for a report.

"No change, Lieutenant," the largest of the three marines replied. "Every now and then, the first one will pound on the door and scream something in T'Kharr that the translators have trouble with."

Major Deneva and two other members of Omega, Lieutenant Gabriel and Lieutenant Lewis, followed Aubrey into the room. All three were dressed in black, and Gabriel carried a dark case.

"He was inferring that your maternal grandmother mates with multiple partners outside of her species," Deneva said.

Aubrey looked at him skeptically and said, "You understand him, sir?"

Deneva looked past Aubrey and said, "We need to speak to the prisoners, Lieutenant. Alone."

"I'm under standing orders to hold any enemy prisoners for fleet intelligence, Major."

"New orders from the Admiral," Deneva said. "Why don't you and your guards check the security of the outer door to the brig?"

Aubrey looked skeptical but said, "Yes, sir." Then he and the others left the room.

When the others had left, Deneva said, "Gabriel, find the leader. And Lewis, deactivate the external feeds to the cells."

Gabriel entered the corridor in front of the cells and regarded the three prisoners. Two of the three remained against the far walls of their cells and snarled at the man. The third, sporting a thick bandage around his knee, lunged toward the door of the cell. Gabriel didn't flinch and smiled back at the creature. This seemed to infuriate the trooper even more.

Addressing Deneva, he said, "This one's the leader."

Deneva entered the corridor with Lewis, stood in front of the cell door, and said in the T'Kharr dialect, "I don't suppose you are going to talk, are you?"

The T'Kharr leader, Re'ekk, lunged again toward the door. "When we escape from this cell, I will take great pleasure in dismembering you and your friends." He then focused on Lewis and growled, "I have never defiled one of your females, but there is always a first time."

Lewis stood stone-faced and said, "You things smell worse when you are alive than you do when you are dead. We are going to have to disinfect these cells when we are through."

During this exchange, Gabriel opened the case and carefully attached leads to two places near the base of the door. He signaled Deneva.

"There is no need for any further violence. Tell me what I want to know, and we will release you on a world where your people can retrieve you. Otherwise, we will have to extract the information forcibly."

Re'ekk snarled, "We will all die before allowing you to interrogate any of us."

Deneva turned toward Re'ekk and said, "Are you referring to the suicide pill implanted in your second bicuspid? We removed those while you were unconscious."

Re'ekk and the other troopers looked surprised and felt around their mouths with their tongues. Upon realization that the pill was gone, Re'ekk pounded on the door once again, baring his teeth and claws.

"You have denied us Terek-Va! Vile abomination! You and your entire race will feed our people for a thousand years—"

Deneva nodded, and Gabriel touched a switch inside of the case. Bolts of lightning sprang from the floor of the cell and crisscrossed in the air. Several of the bolts entered Re'ekk, who screamed in agony. The screams weren't just screams of pain—they were primal, animalistic. Deneva signaled for Gabriel to stop, and the shock knocked Re'ekk to the floor, where he lay silent and panting.

Deneva looked at the other prisoners and said, "The plasma energy used in the shocks is specifically tuned for T'Kharr physiology. It is the precise frequency of your pain centers and delivers an exquisite amount of discomfort. The shock can be of any duration. My personal record is thirty minutes before the prisoner gave up the information I required. Unfortunately, the last jolt was lethal."

From the floor, Re'ekk looked up at Deneva with raw contempt. When he spoke, it was barely audible, his vocal chords still stunned by the jolt. "You will not kill us. You humans have laws regarding the treatment of prisoners—"

Deneva interrupted, "You should all know that we are not like the other troops you have encountered. They might beat you or shoot you, but we will make you suffer. Eventually, you will tell us everything anyway. Save yourselves the pain. If you cooperate, I may even be persuaded to allow you Terek-Va."

The other two looked at their leader and stayed silent, not wishing to disgrace themselves with any signs of fear.

"As you wish," said Deneva. He nodded to Gabriel once again, drawing his hand across his throat. The man hit the button once more, and this time, Re'ekk spasmed and screamed in agony, and his eyes bulged out. Smoke began to waft from his open, gaping mouth. Sparks jumped between his rows of teeth, and his tongue swelled and began to bleed. As the jolt moved into the ten second mark, Re'ekk's red eyes burst, and he collapsed onto the cell floor, twitching. An acrid smell of ozone and burnt flesh filled the room.

The other two prisoners looked on as their leader died, and Deneva saw what he was hoping for: fear. He knew that only the T'Kharr shock troop leaders were the true believers. The military leaders used mostly conscripts for their shock troops due to their high mortality rate. They were cannon fodder. Most breaching pods were destroyed before being able to attach to a ship; hence, most shock troops perished. He knew he wouldn't get anything out of the leader.

Deneva then moved over to the second cell and said, "You're next."

The trooper inside watched with intense interest as Gabriel detached the wires from the leader's cell floor and began attaching them to his. Deneva studied the faces of the two troopers intently and picked up on something he'd missed before. The younger trooper looked extremely concerned, not so much for himself, but for the other soldier. As Gabriel finished attaching the wires, he turned toward Deneva and signaled he was ready.

Deneva squinted his eyes as he studied the two soldiers, who now looked genuinely concerned. The only question was which one would break first.

"You are of the same brood," Deneva declared, not as a question but a statement of fact.

The two troopers looked at each other, and the younger one finally spoke.

"We share the same mother."

"Silence!" the other hissed.

"Te'elaa, if we are to die, let it be by our own hand," he said as the other glared at him.

"They are lying, Se'elakk. They will get the information they require, then kill us with that machine anyway."

"Not true," Deneva said. "We know you and your hatchling brother are conscripts. Our intelligence tells us that not all in the T'Kharr military are bent on conquest. That is your shi'ia-khar's desire. Those like you two were forced into service under penalty of death or the deaths of your families."

Te'elaa mulled over what Deneva was saying. He wanted to believe what the human was saying, but he was conflicted. The T'Kharr indoctrinated their soldiers to hate and despise humans. They were to be viewed as prey, not as an equal sentient species. Yet this human knew their language. He'd even deduced that he and Se'elakk were hatchling brothers. He still wasn't completely convinced.

"You killed the leader."

"Only to prove my resolve. You don't have to suffer. We are used to interrogating regular military troops. Shock troops generally do not survive the attempt to breach the ship long enough to be interrogated."

He thought further and looked toward his brother in the cell next to him. He looked back at the charred corpse of the leader and back again to Deneva.

"We cannot go home."

"That is your choice. We can either release you on a planet where you can live in peace, away from the military, or I can give you back your suicide pills."

Silence hung in the air for a long moment.

"Where would we go?" he asked, a glimmer of hope in his voice.

"The Alliance has a prison colony on one of our fringe worlds," Deneva said. "Your government doesn't know about it, but there are about five hundred other T'Kharr prisoners who chose to cooperate rather than die like your leader just did."

He watched as Te'elaa regarded the younger one once again.

"What are the conditions on this world?"

"You are provided food and shelter and the ability to govern yourselves. Game is plentiful. Our people didn't colonize it because the gravity is outside our comfort zone but within yours. The system is quarantined, and certain technology is not permitted, but it is livable. And as you said, you can't return home. You would be executed on sight."

"Females?" he asked.

"Over two-thirds of the population is female," Deneva answered.

"Two to one?" Se'elakk said, doing the math in his head.

Te'elaa thought hard for a moment before saying, "Se'elakk is young. He does not deserve to die senselessly for the shi'ia-khar's dreams of conquest. This is not our war."

"No one will know you are still alive. All of your fellow shock troops were killed. You can live out your lives in peace."

"How do I know you won't kill my brother?" Se'elakk asked.

Deneva nodded to Gabriel, and he detached the leads to the second cell.

Both T'Kharr troopers visibly relaxed, and Te'elaa said, "What information do you require?"

After approximately thirty minutes, Deneva and the others exited the room and walked past Aubrey and the three marines.

"Hey, wait a minute," Aubrey said. "What happened in there?"

Deneva and Gabriel kept walking, and Lewis stopped to speak to Aubrey.

"They're cooperating with us. We need you to feed them, but otherwise leave them alone."

One of the marines said, "Cooperating? Uglies don't cooperate. The only thing they're good for is target practice."

"Please see to it that they are well treated, Lieutenant. Admiral's orders."

Aubrey looked irritated and walked past her into the control room. Lewis started to leave, but her exit was blocked by the three marines. The largest one stepped in close and said, "What are you, some kind of black ops bitch? I can't believe they let split-tails into combat units."

She smiled and stepped forward, grabbing the big man's hand and twisting it in such a way that it drove him face-first into the ground. The other two were so shocked that she was able to take the man down, they backed away, not wanting to get involved with her. Their friend was easily twice her size.

"This split-tail is perfectly capable of kicking your ass, Jarhead," she said sweetly.

"What the hell?" Aubrey shouted from the control room. "Who authorized this? I have a crispy critter in one of these cells!"

Lewis looked toward the open door, then down to the grimacing marine on the floor.

"You guys might want to get a mop," she said just before releasing him and dumping him onto the floor. She then turned to leave, and the other two marines stepped aside, allowing her passage.

The marines watched her walk down the corridor, and one said, "I think I'm in love."

Lt. Remy woke with a start, pushing the panic back down as he remembered where he was. Damned nightmares. He rarely slept more than four hours at a stretch, and when he did lately, it seemed that nightmares were the only dreams he had. It had been almost a full day since the T'Kharr berserkers forced them to implode the tunnel, sealing the back door of the bunker. Fortunately, they had plenty of food and water.

Everyone seemed to be okay, considering their situation. The two Jaaleadi turned out to be more entertaining than anyone had suspected. Once Glend had come out of her recuperative hibernation, she was a veritable chatterbox. The two researchers even taught them some Jaaleadi games and mind teasers that helped pass the time.

Waiting was the worst. Even though he was prepared to destroy the bunker and die with everyone else, the obvious first choice was survival. Remy and his team understood the stakes far too well. He knew the scientists did too, but they weren't as prepared for death as he and his Omega teammates were.

He decided to try to get a couple more hours of sleep and had just closed his eyes again when Sulak popped her head in the room.

"Activity, Boss. You'd better come out here."

Remy popped up and walked out of the room, buttoning his shirt at the same time. Everyone stood around the main console. Keever listened to an earpiece while viewing lines of code scrolling across the screen. After several moments, he spun around to face the others.

"What is it?" Remy asked.

"One of the subs made a low orbital pass and flashed a packet at the planet surface. I guess the T'Kharr haven't destroyed the uplink network just yet, because it came to us through one of the ground antennas."

Eli said, "Probably kept it active after our initial transmission, hoping they could trace a second transmission to the source."

Heads bobbed in agreement, and Keever said, "The message is part voice, part visual. It'll take me a minute to decrypt it."

"Get started," Remy said, and he turned away and rubbed his eyes.

Jared was behind him and said, "You get any sleep?"

"Not enough. Too much happening."

"I have it," Keever said.

Remy and Jared went back over to the console and looked at the screen, currently showing four Alliance carriers and their escorts trading fire with three T'Kharr carrier groups.

The screen switched to the face of a man sitting at a console.

"Hey, you guys. Just thought you'd like to know that the cavalry has arrived and is on the way to the planet surface. You guys just need to hold tight. The other bit of news isn't as pleasant. We've detected earth movers on their way toward your position. It looks like they're going to try and dig you out. One of the enemy ground commanders was speaking to the T'Kharr admiral and reported you guys destroying the tunnel and that squad of berserkers.

"The admiral wants to make sure that you're only a couple of the researchers who escaped and killed yourselves to avoid capture. That's what their guy on the ground thinks. Anyway, stay sharp. We'll try and communicate again if we can. For the code. Out."

The atmosphere went from joyous to somber in a second.

"For the code?" Jared asked.

Dram whispered, "It's an Omega thing. It's like the marines saying 'semper fi.'"

Out of the corner of his eye, Dram caught Julie glancing at him knowingly and grinned at her. He knew she'd needed comfort before, and he didn't regret it a bit. They'd decided that discretion was better and didn't want to broadcast what they'd shared. She returned the grin and then turned her attention to the screen once more.

Dram turned to Remy and said, "Lieutenant, why not transmit the kinetic generator data to the ships in orbit and leave this place? Why stay here and await rescue?"

Jared jumped in and said, "Because there is simply too much data. It would take days of steady transmission to send all of the data. By that time, the enemy would've traced the signal back here and taken us out. We need to bring the actual computer core module with us, along with the prototype."

Remy and the other troopers turned to look at Jared, surprise written on their faces.

"Prototype?" Remy said. "We weren't informed that there was a prototype."

Jared glanced at Julie and said, "We have a working kinetic generator here, but it's unshielded."

Remy let that information sink in, and Henna said, "How big is it?"

"It's a small one, only about two meters square," Jared said, motioning for them to follow.

Remy and the others followed him into a room further back from the living quarters and storage rooms. To the side of one of the storage rooms, hidden from anyone who didn't know it was there, was a doorway. Jared punched in an access code into the keypad on the wall, and the door slid open. Inside of the room, sitting on an anti-grav pallet, was a cube made of dull gray metal. A computer interface was built into the side and indicated that the unit was currently idle. Even though the generator was in standby mode, the inside of the room was as cold as a meat locker.

Remy looked at Jared and sent a command through his telesponder. Sulak and Eli immediately walked up to the unit and began attaching implosion mines on the surfaces of the device. Jared thought about objecting but decided to keep his mouth shut.

"Anything else you should tell us, Doctor?" Remy asked, his breath visible in the air.

Jared said, "No . . . I think that's all the surprises we have left."

"Why didn't you tell us this thing was here?"

"I thought you knew. You seem to know as much about this facility and the nature of our research as we do. I just assumed—"

"No, we had no idea. If the enemy got ahold of this, could they reverse engineer it?"

Jared nodded his head and said, "Probably, but they don't have any of the shielding necessary to make it practical."

Remy digested this information, and after a moment's thought, he said, "Can you activate it if you needed to?"

Jared looked surprised and said, "Well, of course. But the compressed space breach would kill all of us instantly, and the kinetic power matrix component would shortly kill anything on the planet after that. Like I said, it's unshielded."

Jared picked up on the implication and added, "I'll rig a remote trigger. If need be, I can activate it."

Remy nodded in agreement.

"How long will it take to dig in from the caved-in entrance to the bunker with those machines?" Julie asked.

Remy looked to Angus, who said, "No more than a day. Problem is, we're blind in here. Our monitoring equipment outside of the entrance was destroyed when we imploded the tunnel."

"Well let's hope our troops get here first," Jared said.

Remy turned to Kenyon and said, "Check the claymores we set leading out into the collapsed tunnel and make sure they're still good to go. Kiproff, check the ones at the entrance. We may need them if we have to bug out."

The two soldiers moved off without a word.

Remy turned to Keever. "Check the explosive on the computer core. Just in case."

Keever nodded and went back into the control room.

"Doc, you and your people should try and get some sleep," Remy said. "We may have to move fast. I want you rested."

Jared nodded in agreement.

As soon as Jared and the others left the room, Keever sent a message with his telesponder.

<Lieutenant, there's a problem.>

Remy sent, <What is it?>

<Someone has deactivated the explosive on the computer core.>

<What?>

<I checked the detonator and someone has tampered with it. It would've misfired if we'd tried to set it off.>

<Any idea who?>

<No way to tell. Everyone's been in and out of here in the last few days.>

Remy thought for a moment and sent, <Fix it and keep this to yourself.>

<Copy.>

<From this point on, one of our team stays in here at all times, no exceptions,> he said. Then he left the room, wondering if things could get much worse.

The man on the sub knew that it was dangerous to transmit the information to Remy and his soldiers, but he felt they needed to know what they were facing. The next problem was going to be how to transmit the same information to the *Pacifica* without being detected.

"Enemy contact to starboard. That destroyer is moving a little too close to our position. I don't believe he picked up our transmission. Looks like he's on normal patrol duty."

"Ease us out of here into open space as quickly as you dare. We don't want to leave an atmospheric wake that they can see."

The pilot moved the sub away from the planet at as sharp of an angle as he could to gain as much distance from the destroyer as quickly as possible. He was about to make another course correction when a loud noise echoed through the ship and sparks burst out of the neighboring console. Warning lights lit up the pilot's console, indicating they were venting atmosphere.

"Hull strike! I'm not sure if it was a micro meteor or debris from the destroyed satellite network, but we're losing air!"

The first man leapt out of his chair and quickly retrieved the hull patch kit under the opposite console. Suddenly, warning klaxons rang throughout the ship.

The pilot yelled, "Our cloak is failing! We need to—"

The beam that shot out of the T'Kharr destroyer was ten times the circumference of the sub. After the earlier failure, there would be no pursuit and attempts to disable the sub. As the beam contacted the sub's brittle hull, it shattered into thousands of glass-like shards, then imploded upon itself. The subs power source breached immediately, and the craft, along with its four crewmen, disappeared in a flash of brilliant white light.

CHAPTER TWENTY

SAS Pacifica

North was remotely aware of the battle that had taken place inside of his ship but could do nothing about it at the moment. He'd noted the destruction of one of the two alliance subs and watched the four purple telesponder signatures blink out suddenly. Four more brave souls lost. Right now, he concentrated on landing troops before the enemy fleet re-formed.

The rest of the Alliance fleets were keeping the bulk of the enemy fleet occupied while they made their run toward the planet. Tyler's ship had worked as he'd hoped, despite the malfunction in the main gun. *Pacifica* had been trailing the *Ba'akteer* and her surviving escorts until she'd altered course toward the bulk of the T'Kharr fleet, leaving an open corridor to the planet.

North had moved the troop ship *Suribachi* into position between the *Pacifica* and *Kegar*, meshing their shields. The troop ship was not aesthetically pleasing to look at. Long and rectangular, that class of ship was built for one purpose only, to deliver combat troops and materiel to the battle theater and pick them up when they were done.

The ship contained up to one hundred landing craft capable of dropping seventy-five soldiers each into a combat zone. They had twenty special containers that held ground vehicles, hover tanks, and armored personnel carriers with heavy weapons.

North read the ship's systems and determined that *Pacifica* was battle ready, despite the boarders and the damage they'd caused. The intruders had inflicted over seventy casualties, including Logan. More than fifty had succumbed to their wounds. Logan wasn't among the dead, and if North knew the general, he would have to be comatose before he would miss the landing.

"General, please!" one of the doctors in the *Pacifica's* sickbay pleaded.

"Get this crap off me!" Logan yelled, pointing to the two IV cuffs he had, one on each arm. "I have a landing to coordinate!"

Taking advantage of a lull while *Pacifica* travelled toward the planet, General Austin was walking by sickbay on his way back to the bridge when he heard the commotion from inside.

"What's going on?" Austin asked as he strode into the sickbay. "I heard they had a very uncooperative patient in here. Figures it would be you."

Logan stared daggers at the doctor and med techs standing near him. He knew that the doctor could keep him in sickbay as long as he deemed necessary, despite the general's threats and attempts at intimidation. Regulations shielded the doctor from any punitive action, regardless of the patient's rank.

"The general has about a dozen shrapnel wounds that have been repaired, but they still need some time to heal," the doctor stated. "The hyperfeuron IVs will facilitate the healing and prevent infection, but they have to be left on."

"Is he ambulatory?" Austin asked.

"W-well, yes, but—"

"Can't he walk around with those IV cuffs, or does he have to stay in sickbay?" Austin asked.

The doctor thought hard for a moment. Austin was a six-star general. He could make life very difficult for him in the future.

The doctor let out a resigned sigh. "Tell your med tech to check the hyperfeuron levels every hour and to keep those wounds clean."

Austin smiled and said, "Thank you, Doctor." He then looked at Logan and said, "Come on, you pain in the ass."

Logan climbed out of the bed and gave the doctor one last lingering glare as he limped out of sickbay. Once outside, he turned to Austin and said, "Thank you, sir. That doctor—"

"Probably saved your life, General," Austin finished for him.

Logan nodded grudgingly. "Yeah, I suppose so."

The two men turned to walk toward the lift, and Austin noticed the limp.

"You all right? Why don't you have your med tech dial up some pain killer for those wounds?"

Logan said, "The pain keeps my head clear. Where are we on the landing?"

"We should be in orbit of the planet in about an hour. Faulkner and the others are still engaging the bulk of the enemy fleet near the first starlane portal. As soon as you're ready, *Pacifica* will launch her fighters and cover the drop ships. Drake wants the bombers to pound the landing zone first to thin out any enemy ground troops hiding in the bush and any triple A. The fighters should keep the enemy pilots from jumping your ships from above and keep them off your backs."

"Good. I need to shuttle over to the troop ship and oversee the drop. Apparently, I've been ordered to descend in an assault shuttle and not with the drop ships. Your doing?"

Austin looked thoughtful and said, "Some suggestions were made, and I agreed. I don't need you blown up by a lucky shot from a ground battery."

"I'd rather go down with the troops," Logan protested, but he knew it was in vain, and Austin ignored the comment.

When they reached the bank of lifts, Austin turned to Logan and said, "You know, North warned me you were a good officer but you could be surly when you were injured."

Logan looked chastened and said, "Sorry, sir."

"Give 'em hell, General. I'll see you when you get back." The lift door closed.

The ride to the bridge took several minutes, and Austin exited the lift and walked toward Drake.

"Logan is on his way to the launch bay to shuttle over to the *Suribachi*," Austin said.

"That's good. I had your staff shuttle over from the troop ship. You'll find them waiting for you in the commander's office."

Austin looked at Drake quizzically. "Do you do that to North? Read his mind?"

"As much as I can, sir."

"Thank you, Admiral," he said with a smile. "I'll try and leave the office like I found it."

He turned and went to North's office. Once inside, he saw his five Marine staff officers and one Navy officer standing around a floating holographic display of the planet.

"General on deck." They snapped to attention.

"At ease," he said and went up to the Navy officer. "Aren't you the CSG? Captain Trent, right?"

Trent said, "Yes, sir. I'm going to act as liaison between the space wing and ground forces. I thought I could be better utilized here than down in my office."

Austin noticed that Trent had a bandage inside of his left ear and had an adhesive hyperfeuron patch stuck just below the ear.

"Are you injured, Captain?" he asked.

"Ruptured my ear drum when we were attacking the T'Kharr carrier. Screwed up my equilibrium. Flight surgeon has grounded me until it heals. Otherwise, I'd be in my ship flying this mission."

"You have a brother on the ground, right?"

"Yes, sir. He's one of the research scientists."

"We'll do our best to find him, son," Austin said. "Glad you're here."

Trent nodded and said, "Thank you, sir."

Austin walked to the display and said, "Okay, catch me up."

ICC Ka'athiol

Ka'awon paced back and forth behind Zha'ar, and it made him uneasy. Ka'awon had been on edge ever since they signaled to the pods and subs to move in. They watched with joy as one of the human heavy cruisers was destroyed by the subs, but that was only one victory offset by many losses. In all, they had lost fifteen ships, including the carrier *Ke'efex*, to the humans' six ships. Too many things had not gone as planned.

First, the appearance of missiles that penetrated their shields, then the appearance and disappearance of the new unidentified ship that had destroyed three of his destroyers and crippled the *Za'adjeer*. If they could capture the human grand commander, they could salvage this campaign.

"A coded transponder, Tar-Vel," one of the sublings reported. "It is coming from an area near the *Pacifica*."

Ka'awon ceased his pacing and walked over to the communication station. "Position."

"It is still inside of the carriers' shield perimeter, Tar-Vel."

Ka'awon could barely believe their good fortune. He'd all but given up when they lost contact. He knew that only eight of the pods had survived and assumed they'd all perished like the subs.

"Signal has changed. I'm getting a coded message now. They have acquired the target and have detached from the ship. They are going to reattach near the engine core to try to mask their location until they have an opportunity to breach the shields. They say they are the only surviving pod and are currently undetected by the humans."

Ka'awon could barely contain himself. "Bring up a diagram of the *Pacifica*!" he bellowed.

An image of the human carrier materialized. Zha'ar studied the image and pointed to a plasma vent near the engine core. "That would make sense. This spot is shielded from their point defense batteries and is close enough to that vent that the background radiation would mask their location. It is a perfect hiding spot."

"Instruct our escorts and fighters that this area of the carrier is not to be fired upon unless by direct order from me," Ka'awon said, the delight plain in his voice. "Is that clear?"

"Clear, Rinn-Tar-Vel," Zha'ar said. "Communications, issue the order."

"Zha'ar, they have captured the human grand commander. Imagine the look on the shi'ia-khar's face when we present this Grand Commander North to him. Transmit that information back to the homeworld through the buoys." Ka'awon returned to his office.

Several seconds after the door shut . . .

"Coded transmission between the *Pacifica* and the other enemy carriers, Tar-Vel. Most recent code to be compromised by cryptography, designated Bravo Six Alpha."

"What does it say?"

The subling smiled and replied, "Transmission reports that their grand commander has been abducted by our shock troops and that they are attempting to locate the stealth ship they left in."

Zha'ar closed his eyes, thanked the Under-Deity for his blessing upon them, and said, "Relay that message to the rinn-tar-vel."

SAS Pacifica

Aboard the *Pacifica*, Deneva chuckled to himself as he monitored the T'Kharr transmissions.

"We've achieved orbit, Admiral," Lt. Webber reported. "The escorts are moving to engage what's left of the enemy destroyer squadron."

Drake turned to Trent, who was standing just outside of North's office, currently occupied by Austin and his aides. Omega operatives were already on the ground and had identified the T'Kharr landing zones and ground batteries.

"Launch fighters and bombers. I want the T'Kharr landing zones pulverized before we land our troops. Initiate jamming."

Valkyrie and Dagger fighters streaked out of the port and starboard launch bays, quickly forming into fighter groups. Thirty Thor-class bombers slipped out of the dorsal bay and formed up into waves headed for bombing runs around the area of the research facility. One squadron of fifteen Daggers entered the atmosphere and headed toward the area where the bunker was located.

Detectors currently showed that the bulk of the T'Kharr landing force was still concentrated in that area. Planetary bombardment by the capital ships would normally be sufficient to take out the landing areas, but they needed pinpoint accuracy this time— a scalpel rather than a sledge hammer.

One of the special version bombers descended to a lower altitude, and a small door on the bottom of the craft opened, revealing a silver, dome-like apparatus. The device emitted hundreds of individual laser beams directed at the enemy ground positions around the research facility.

Miratev Two, near the research complex

On the ground, Sub-Lek Fre'elk watched his detector screen, bored out of his mind. He'd been assigned to an anti-aircraft battery to await the rumored ground assault. They'd been told that the humans had suffered heavy losses and were demoralized. The T'Kharr fleet was invincible. He would be shocked if they landed a single troop on the ground.

He wouldn't mind if they did. He'd had but a taste of the human prisoners. The officers had taken the biggest share, but what he tasted, he liked. That was a meal he'd like to indulge in more often. Perhaps he'd have the chance soon.

As he pondered his situation, he became subtly aware of the low hum surrounding him. His targeting screen suddenly filled with static.

"Fraan telak!" he cursed and smacked the side of the console. That did no good, so he called over to his squad mate in the adjacent turret.

"What?" his squad mate replied, clearly irritated by the interruption.

"My scope is malfunctioning. What should I do?"

"Check the manual, idiot," he said before returning to his game of Chel-tuval with the others in their squad. He was so involved with the game that he failed to notice that his own screen was also full of static.

Fre'elk grabbed the data pad next to the console and scrolled through the operating specs for this particular unit. He'd just located the troubleshooting section when the low hum changed into a higher-pitched sound.

He turned back to the squadmate and said, "Do you hear that?"

"Hear what?" he shouted just prior to several deafening explosions from across the landing field.

Fre'elk heard screams and saw several soldiers running from the area of the explosions, many engulfed in flames. When the light from the fireball dimmed, Fre'elk saw the contrails from dozens of objects streaking toward their positions.

"Incoming!" he screamed as he jumped into the control seat of his turret. He swung the gun skyward, trying to visually locate the source of the attack, and three more loud concussions rocked the area of the landing field.

Two transports took direct hits and exploded violently, taking many of the troops that had been using the ship as cover with it. He instinctively came to bear on the incoming objects and fired wildly, hoping to score a lucky hit on some of the incoming weapons. His squadmates had abandoned their game and were frantically scrambling to man their own guns. Five precision-guided concussion bombs screamed in at Mach two and struck home on his squad's turrets, consuming them in a mass of fire and smoke.

North zoomed in on the area of the bombardment and watched in satisfaction as yellow and orange plumes of fire lit up the sky around the research facility. The bombers had smashed a clear zone that circled the facility for a thousand yards on every side. There were no life signs at all in the target area.

There were still multiple life signs within the facility, though their detectors were unable to clearly distinguish which signs were T'Kharr and which were not. North sent an order to the *Suriba-chi's* captain to launch the landing craft.

The target zone was still in flames, and the enemy troops still scattered as two minelayers screamed over the facility and launched their payloads, consisting of hundreds of small discs referred to by the marines as "creepers." The creepers flew into the designated area, avoiding the structures and forest and scattered over the entire target area, settling onto the ground surrounding the facility just short of the forest foliage.

Once planted, appendages like spider legs sprung from the units, and the tops opened up, revealing a rotating green scanner. The creepers were keyed to fire at any image or object resembling a T'Kharr soldier and ignore both human and Jaaleadi figures.

"Creepers have been deployed and are covering the landing area," the pilot in the minelayer reported as he pulled up and headed back to the *Suribachi*. "Returning to base."

"Acknowledged," the marine manning communications on Logan's assault shuttle said.

Logan nodded and said, "Order the landers to put down and dig in. Instruct the creepers to open fire."

The T'Kharr troops that had fled the bombardment and were lucky enough not to have encountered Omega were just beginning to regroup and move cautiously back into the area when the creeper onslaught began. Those not struck by the initial barrage dove for cover and remained on the ground to avoid the deadly bolts of energy sizzling overhead.

The troop landers struck the ground first, and large doors in the rear of the ships fell open, disgorging hundreds of armed marines who quickly set up defensive fields of fire around the landing area. The next to land were the materiel pods containing the heavy weapons and ground vehicles. As they touched down, several marines ran inside of the pods and retrieved tripod-mounted heavy guns that required two-man crews to operate.

Logan turned toward the pilot and said, "Put us down in the middle of the landers and activate defenses."

Colonel Fargo's men activated the defensive shield that surrounded the landing zone in a circle on all sides. Once the shield went up, the creepers fell silent but continued to scan the forest area.

As Logan exited his ship, he saw Colonel Fargo barking orders to his aides. He was momentarily distracted as a squadron of Valkyries from the *Pacifica* screamed overhead, circling the area. The sight gave him some small sense of security.

Logan limped up to Fargo and said, "Report."

Fargo pointed to a spot in the forest area. "As soon as the creepers stopped firing, the enemy began to regroup. They appear to be massing for a counter attack. I'm guessing they're staying dark until they can regroup and attack in force."

Logan nodded and said, "How many enemy troops inside of the facility?"

"There are approximately two hundred enemy troops inside of the structure itself. So far, only T'Kharr life signs have been detected. We killed about three hundred in the bombing runs. The rest either fled into the forest or into the facility."

He turned and said, "Colonel Shaddra, clean those *things* out of our research station. If possible, get me prisoners."

Shaddra smiled and replied, "Yes, sir," then turned and walked toward a large group of soldiers forming up into squads.

Logan turned back to Fargo and said, "How many of their landing craft did we destroy in the bombardment?"

"There were about fifty landing craft left on the ground when the flyboys bombed them," Fargo said. "I'm more concerned about those things." He pointed to a burnt-out hulk of a cargo ship.

"There were several of those in the area, and whatever was in there was big. We're not sure what kind of armor they landed."

"Keep me informed," Logan said as he turned and walked back toward his shuttle, now set up as a command post.

Shaddra entered one of the landers that was closer to the facility and looked over the shoulder of the specialist manning a particularly intricate bank of sensors and readouts.

"Send in the creepers. Full safety protocols on. I don't want them to kill any friendlies in there. Also, activate the rank-recognition database in their programming. The general would like some prisoners. Officers, preferably."

The creepers moved in on the entrances of the facility like a swarm of spiders. As they got within range, enemy weapons fire erupted from the doorways and windows and tore several of them to shreds, but there were simply too many of them.

As the first creeper entered through the main doors to the facility's administrative offices, it immediately targeted two T'Kharr troopers using a desk as cover and opened fire, blasting a hole through the desk and instantly killing the soldiers. The creeper moved in closer and scanned the two crumpled bodies on the ground as more creepers entered the building, followed by several fire teams of marines.

Shaddra directed the specialist to have the creepers clear the command centers and computer core rooms as soon as possible. He watched as the mass of blinking dots on the screen swarmed into the facility and pushed deeper toward the control center. As a group of creepers rounded the corner to the main corridor leading to the control room, they encountered three enemy gun emplacements with crew-served cannons.

The T'Kharr troops immediately opened fire as the creepers moved into the corridor, and the creepers immediately returned fire on the positions. The energy bolts poured into the enemy targets had no effect. The T'Kharr troops, however, were quickly thinning out the wave of creepers.

"Colonel, they've erected a portable energy barrier," the specialist said. "Unless we can take out the shield emitters, our troops will be caught in a bottleneck."

Shaddra knew that although the creepers' particle weapons were highly effective on flesh-and blood-targets, their effectiveness was nullified by energy barriers. "Order the remaining creepers in that corridor to switch to recon mode and target for the fire teams."

The marine lieutenant barked an order to the gunnery sergeant in charge on the platoon, who motioned for two of his grenadiers to move up and interface with one of the creepers waiting at their feet. The men programmed their warheads appropriately and interfaced their scanners with the targeting sensors in the creeper.

The grenadiers armed their missiles, and their heads-up displays flashed to life, the readout reflecting the image currently coming through the sensors of the creeper. The first man turned to the sergeant and nodded, and the two toggled the buttons on their weapons that would send the creeper back out into the line of fire.

The creeper instantly sprang to life and darted into the corridor, immediately identifying the two portable shield generator units on the lower right and left sides of the hallway in front of the gun emplacements. The grenadiers received targeting confirmation on their weapons and fired just as the creeper blew apart from a barrage from the T'Kharr gun emplacements.

Both missiles erupted out of their launchers and executed ninety-degree turns around the corner, screaming down the corridor to impact the shield just in front of the two generators. The tiny breaches produced in the shield were enough to shut them down.

A second pair of grenadiers moved up while the first pair quickly reloaded their launchers. The second pair had programmed their warheads for maximum yield and linked with a second creeper that waited patiently at their feet. As soon as the shield went down, the second creeper slid into the corridor and sent the targeting information. The men heard frantic T'Kharr shouting as the second pair of missiles screamed down the corridor and bore into the guns, the concussion nearly knocking the grenadiers off their feet.

The remaining creepers sprang to life and swarmed around the corner, followed by the marine riflemen. Although powerful, the second missiles were only able to disable two of the emplacements, and the soldiers manning the remaining one opened up on the first squad of marines to come around the corner.

Seeing four of his men go down in quick succession, the lieutenant ordered the remaining marines to hold back until the creepers could cover their advance. Under fire from the creepers, the T'Kharr soldiers were forced to abandon their positions and withdraw into the control room, securing the door behind them.

"Corpsman, we have wounded!" the sergeant barked as several men sprinted out into the fire zone to drag their stricken comrades back behind cover.

PFC Mark Bradley and his squad cautiously moved down the hallway, taking advantage of the lull in gunfire, and took up positions in the doorways on either side of the hall.

"Alpha team, clear those rooms!" the lieutenant shouted. "Bravo team, secure the entrance to the control room and make sure nothing leaves! Tango company is assaulting from the opposite entrance!"

Bradley and his teammates took the closest set of doors while other teams spread out along the other side. Bradley hit the door activator and stayed around the corner in the corridor while the others covered the corridor and remaining doorways. When the door slid open, staccato weapons fire erupted from inside of the room, striking the wall opposite the doorway in the corridor. Bradley and the man opposite him, PFC Owen Norwood, dove into the room, rolled, and quickly identified the lone T'Kharr trooper in the room.

The T'Kharr soldier fired a burst that nearly struck Norwood, and Bradley reacted with a snap shot that blew the trooper's chest apart in a spray of thick blood. The men immediately scanned the room for more targets and spotted two other T'Kharr, both dressed in blood-stained coveralls, hands held high in an obvious sign of surrender.

"Get on the ground! Get on the ground!" both men screamed, motioning with their weapons.

The two beings quickly complied, dropping to their knees. Both began babbling in a tone that sounded like pleading, but neither Bradley nor Norwood could understand them.

As Bradley's tunnel vision subsided, he became acutely aware of the nature of their surroundings. Both men fell silent, and their jaws dropped open as they struggled to cope with the scene that lay in front of them.

"Sergeant Dawkins!" Bradley shouted as he stared in disgust. "We need you in here immediately!"

Gunnery Sergeant Dawkins and two other marines sprinted into the room, and the sergeant said, "What's the problem? I've got—"

Dawkins never finished his statement as he surveyed the scene. It was apparent that they were in the research facility mess, but the tables that were used to hold the food that was served on the buffet line now held body parts, barely recognizable as human. Thick pools of brownish-red blood dripped from the tables and snaked into the drains on the floor under them.

The tables held heads, arms, legs, torsos, and piles of entrails. A few of the heads and body parts were obviously Jaaleadi, judging by the hollow bones and feathers. Several of the torsos and legs were on spits and were roasting over the heating elements usually used to keep food warm during meal service.

A bloody pile of white lab coats was piled in one of the corners, and the mostly intact body of a twenty-something male lay on one of the carving stations, his arm severed at the shoulder, his dead eyes wide with shock. Judging by the arterial spray on the exposed surfaces, the victims had apparently been very much alive prior to being dismembered. A quick count of the heads showed that nearly all the research staff had been brought here and killed.

Dawkins looked at the two pleading aliens and swallowed hard before shouting, "Translator!"

A marine corporal ran up and gave the sergeant a small device just as Norwood turned away from the scene and vomited violently. The alien gibberish transformed into broken English, and the men heard, "We were under orders . . . not our fault . . . we didn't eat any of them . . . the officers demanded . . ."

Dawkins snarled, "Are you telling me that you two . . . are cooks?"

Both aliens fell silent and looked at each other, trying to decide what the best answer would be.

Dawkins, insane with outrage, leveled his rifle at the two aliens and flipped the switch on the side that changed from conventional to incendiary rounds. He then fired a burst into both beings, and their bodies ignited into flames from the inside out. Both aliens screamed as the flames engulfed their bodies, and the soldiers stepped back as the two rolled on the ground, writhing in agony. After several seconds, both figures ceased moving and lay on the floor, sizzling.

The corporal received a call on his comm and said, "Tango company has secured the control room. They want us to come in and assist in data retrieval. Foxtrot company has secured the computer core. The lieutenant—"

Just then, the company commander, Lieutenant Herr, burst into the room.

"What the hell is going on in here?" he demanded just before catching sight of the smoldering corpses on the floor. He looked up at Dawkins and then others, about to demand answers until he caught the scene behind them in the mess. He looked back at the T'Kharr corpses and then back to Dawkins, who stood respectfully silent.

Herr cleared his throat and said, in a more subdued tone, "Gunny, police these bodies and then you and your computer tech come with me. Captain Tassano needs our help in the control center. Figure out how many victims are in here. The colonel will want a full accounting of the base personnel."

Herr then turned and left the room, headed for the control room.

Dawkins, having prepared himself for some severe discipline from Herr, started to breathe again, then looked back at the carnage on the mess tables and said, "Bradley, get a count. Norwood, you, Phillips, and McCaffrey police up these uglies. Corporal, come with me."

He and the corporal followed Herr out of the room, leaving Bradley and the others to their own grisly tasks.

"We captured five live T'Kharr officers, Colonel, but they aren't talking," Captain Tassano said. "All are middle-ranking officers, but the T'Kharr brigadier isn't here. His name is Vett-Tar-Von Gra'akk. Sierra company said they received intelligence from one of their captured prisoners that this Gra'akk went off with half of their troops and some earth-moving equipment."

"Get me the general."

At that moment, Logan was monitoring Fargo's progress with the counter attack from the other T'Kharr forces that had fled into the forest.

"We routed them good, sir. There were only about eight hundred troopers out in the forest. They were no match for our boys, especially when we outnumbered them more than two to one. They didn't use any of their artillery, though. We haven't located any, either. They must've moved it somewhere else. Between those we killed in the bombardment and those in the facility, that accounts for about twelve hundred troops. I thought intelligence reported over two thousand in the invasion force."

Logan replied, "That's what the reports said. Where did the rest of them go?"

Fargo said, "Good question, General."

An aide sought Logan's attention, and he said, "Keep me informed, Colonel. I want casualty reports on both sides. Also, have your teams sweep the area for any other ugly surprises."

"Of course, sir. Fargo out."

Logan turned his attention to Shaddra's report on the radio.

"Report, Colonel."

"Facility is secured, sir. Data banks were still on lockdown, not that the T'Kharr techies didn't try. When we unlocked them, the data banks had been wiped. Codes indicate this was done as the invasion force was landing. My specialists don't believe the T'Kharr retrieved any useful data."

"But they aren't 100 percent certain?"

Shaddra paused and said, "No, sir. There is no way to know for sure, but the fact that they're still on the planet might indicate they haven't found what they're looking for yet."

Logan nodded in agreement. "What about prisoners, other survivors?"

"None of the human or Jaaleadi research staff was located alive. Not all are accounted for, however. We captured several T'Kharr officers, but they aren't providing any information. Initial intelligence reports from some of the enlisted prisoners indicate that your T'Kharr counterpart left with a large force of troops to look for a second facility."

Logan digested that information. "How could they know where it is? I thought that even the research staff didn't know."

"Not sure, sir. We're trying to decrypt the T'Kharr transmissions in the transmitter buffer. Maybe that'll help us figure it out. In the meantime, I'd suggest an aerial recon of the bunker location."

"It's already underway, Colonel. Inform me if you gain any more intelligence. Logan out."

CHAPTER TWENTY-ONE

Miratev Two, the bunker

Jared Trent was just coming from the fresher when he felt a concussion inside of the bunker that nearly knocked him to the ground. He heard shouting and cursing coming from the open doorway and ran to the control room. He could hear gunfire coming from the area of the tunnel the soldiers had collapsed.

"What was that?" he shouted to Remy, who was looking over Keever's shoulder at the console.

"Claymores. The uglies are better at digging than we thought. They've cleared a path through the tunnel and are bringing in troops. Angus, Kiproff, and Sulak are trying to hold them off until we can retreat. Kenyon and Henna are retrieving the prototype, and we're about to blow this computer core. I sent the Jaaleadi and Hunter up to the primary entrance with Eli. We have to leave through the front door."

"Wait!" Jared protested. "Can't we take the core with us?" Jared was desperate not to lose all of their research.

"No time. Get to the main entrance. I couldn't find your friend Julie. Get her and get up there!"

<We can't hold them off much longer!> Angus sent. <Kiproff is dead, and Sulak took a hit in the leg. How much longer, Lieutenant?>

<Get out now,> Remy replied. <We're ready to blow the core.>

<Yes, sir,> Angus replied. He then looked over to Sulak, who was firing with one hand and trying to stem the flow of blood from the wound in her left leg with the other.

<Time to go,> he sent to her.

<What about Kiproff?>

Angus looked over at Kiproff's still form crumpled on the ground between them and the enemy troops.

<Leave him. He would want us to get out alive.>

As much as Sulak hated to leave her comrade, trying to recover his body would be suicide. She turned to make her way to the entrance to the bunker complex when a round struck Angus at the base of his back, throwing him against the wall.

Sulak tried to move toward him, only to be driven back by enemy fire.

"Angus?" she shouted, too startled to send the message via telesponder. "Chief! How bad?"

For several moments, he didn't move.

She assumed the worst.

Angus sent, <Took a round through the base of my spine. Legs don't work. Get out of here, Kara.>

<I can't leave you. Give me a chance to get to you.>

<Negative,> he sent. <I can still shoot. I'll lay down cover fire until you get out the door. That's an order. I'm invoking special directive five.> He opened fire once again on the advancing troops.

Sulak looked back at him, and he shot her a desperate look.

<Go! Secure the door behind you. For the code.>

Sulak gave him one last look before limping up to the doorway and diving through, slamming the door shut behind her. She cycled the heavy locking mechanisms in the door, sealing it from the tunnel. Nothing short of high explosives would open it now.

She lay there panting. Part of her was angry with herself that she and her fellow Omega troops had been conditioned to comply with Omega special "directives" without thinking. It was part of their conditioning. When Angus had invoked special directive five, she was conditioned to immediately comply without argument. Angus knew that, the bastard. He knew she wouldn't leave without him unless he gave the command. She sat there, waiting for what she knew would come next and felt a tear roll down her cheek.

<For the code, Chief.>

As soon as the door slammed shut, Angus raised his weapon above his head and yelled, "Cease fire! I surrender!" in T'Kharr.

"Throw out your weapons!"

Angus tossed the rifle out into the open and held both of his hands high over his head. Moments later, three T'Kharr troopers ran up and trained their weapons at his head, snarling and growling at him.

"I need to speak to your commanding officer," he said.

One of the troopers responded by striking him in the face with the butt of his rifle. Angus reeled from the blow and tasted blood in his mouth but was able to remain conscious. One of the troopers roughly grabbed him and dragged him out into the open, where he dumped him messily on the ground next to Kiproff's body.

"Do not move, human," one of the troopers who covered him with his rifle snarled while the other two stripped him of his equipment and cut away his outer garments. Blood and spinal fluid drained from the wound in his back, and he could feel coldness moving up to his midsection.

"Clear!" one of the troopers shouted, and Angus looked up and saw the circle of troopers part, allowing a T'Kharr soldier dressed in combat armor to walk up to him. The soldier had a nasty scar running down the middle of his face, and the look on his face was pure contempt.

The T'Kharr soldier regarded him coldly with his blood red eyes.

"He has been stripped of all of his weapons and equipment, Kheton," the nearest trooper said. "It is safe."

"Are you the commanding officer?" Angus asked, looking up into the officer's face.

"How do you know our language?" he asked, glaring at Angus.

"I am only authorized to speak with the commanding officer," Angus replied.

The armored soldier balled up his upper right fist and back-handed Angus across his already shattered lip. Angus took the blow and turned back to face the soldier, staring defiantly. He spat a glob of spittle and blood at the feet of the soldier.

One of the other troopers moved forward to strike him again when the soldier in charge stopped him.

He said, "I am Kheton Ve'ellda, second-in-command to Vett-Tar-Von Gra'akk. You will tell me what you have to say or we will obtain the information through interrogation."

He placed particular emphasis on the word "interrogation," hoping the threat alone would suffice.

"Kheton, eh?" Angus said. "Close enough." He looked over at Kiproff's body next to him and placed his hand on the man's shoulder. Angus then closed his eyes, linked with Kiproff's still-active telesponder and sent the final command to both of their implants.

Sulak felt the explosion through the door and knew at that moment that Angus was gone along with any enemy soldiers within five meters of him. Directive five. What a bitch.

Jared searched the living quarters without finding Julie, then decided to check back in the storage room.

"Julie?" he shouted into the dimly lit room. "Julie, are you in here?"

As his eyes struggled to adjust to the low light, he tripped over something on the floor and went down to the ground. When he looked up, he was face-to-face with the dead eyes of Lt. Henna, eyes wide with shock, pupils fixed and dilated. He jumped back with a start and pushed away and entangled his legs with the object that had tripped him.

He turned and saw Sgt. Kenyon, lying unmoving on the floor, bleeding from his mouth. By appearances, he'd been shot in the head from behind. A glimpse of movement caught his eye, and he looked up at the doorway leading to the storage room containing the prototype. There, standing in the doorway, was Julie Newman, holding a pistol in her hand, pointing it at Jared's head.

"Julie? What happened? What the hell are you doing?"

"I'm giving you the chance to leave, Jared," she said, eyes cold and emotionless. "Those two would've never left, so I had to take care of them."

"Julie? What—"

"I don't have the time to explain to you. Throw me the remote activator."

"What?"

I'm giving you to the count of five to throw me the activator and get out before I shoot you. If you don't, I'll shoot you and take the activator from your corpse."

"You can't possibly—"

Julie fired a round at Jared's feet, missing him by mere millimeters.

"One . . . two . . . three . . ."

Jared scrambled to his feet just as Julie began to tighten her grip on the pistol and take careful aim at his head. He pulled the activator from his pocket and tossed it to her.

"Jared, there's one more thing," she said, her eyes tearing up. "Tell Dram . . . that it wasn't an act. Whatever I might have said or done, that part was real. He'll know what I'm talking about."

"But, I don't understand—"

"Now get out!" she snapped, firing another warning shot at his feet.

Jared regarded her for a moment, then dashed out the door back toward the control room. He heard the door to the storage room slam and lock behind him.

"We have a problem," he said as he burst into the control room, catching sight of Remy and Keever, each putting one of Sulak's arms over their shoulders.

"You have a gift for understatement, Doc," Keever replied as they started toward the passageway leading up to the front entrance.

Just then, a powerful explosion ripped through the passageway leading to the tunnel where Sulak had just come from, covering them with dust and debris.

"We gotta get outta here right now!" Remy yelled as the four of them stumbled through the door to the passageway leading to the main entrance and slammed the door shut behind them. Weapons fire could be heard bouncing off the door as Keever pulled open the panel and disabled the door controls, sealing it shut.

"Henna and Kenyon are dead!" Jared said, panting. "Julie killed them and sealed herself in the room with the prototype!"

Remy turned to him and said, "What?"

He then sent, <Henna? Henna, do you read? Kenyon, do you copy?>

He turned to Keever. "Blow the core and the prototype! Do it quickly before they get to them!"

Keever let Jared take Sulak's arm and he said, "Get up the passageway. I'm not sure if this door will take the full force of the explosion or not."

Remy, Sulak, and Jared struggled toward the ascending passageway as Keever armed the explosives and moved away from the door. He then turned his back to the door and flipped the switch. The explosion rocked the passageway, littering them with dust and pebbles from the ceiling. The door held fast, and the weapons fire on the other side ceased momentarily.

Keever looked around the area he was presently in and linked his detonator with the explosive charges they'd placed on the ceiling and walls. He ran up to Remy and the others and waited until they were around a corner, then triggered the charges behind them. The explosions ripped through the rock walls and ceiling, collapsing several metric tons of rock against the control room door, effectively sealing it permanently.

The four moved up the passageway as quickly as they could and soon made it to the lift at the end of the passageway that would take them to the top of the mountain and the entrance of the bunker complex.

<Eli?> Remy sent.

<Go,> he replied.

<We're boarding the lift right now. Get clear. We're blowing the shaft as soon as we reach the top.>

<Copy.>

Jared, Sulak, and Keever all entered the lift, followed by Remy, who stepped in last and pushed the button.

The lift came to life and began the two-kilometer ascent. As they approached the midpoint, Remy looked up and saw the descending car coming toward them, then stopped the car as it came up alongside them.

<Mini-nuke,> Remy sent.

Keever nodded and removed a small obsidian sphere from his satchel. He placed it in the cart that was traveling downward. He programmed several commands into his detonator pad, then gave Remy a thumbs-up. They resumed their long trip to the top.

In the tunnel, Gra'akk walked up to the crumpled form of his second-in-command, Ve'ellda, and felt a brief pang of regret.

Ve'ellda had served him well over the years and deserved a better death than this, but he'd been careless and overconfident.

A soldier ran up to Gra'akk and said, "Tar-Von, detectors indicate one human survivor inside of the complex."

Gra'akk followed the soldier with urgency, hoping that the survivor would be of use to them. He followed the soldier into the rear of the complex, past the destroyed main control room and into a rear area that appeared to be for storage. He followed the soldier to a door that several engineers were attempting to breach with torches.

Suddenly, the intercom next to the door blinked to life, and a human voice came through.

"Aku laki san! Aku laki san!"

Gra'akk recognized the code words and yelled, "Cease!"

The engineers extinguished their torches and stepped away from the door, and Gra'akk went to the intercom and keyed the pad.

"Who is this?" he demanded.

He heard rustling from the other end of the speaker and then a metallic voice responded, "I am the contact. I possess the prototype. Stand back and I will open the door."

Gra'akk withdrew and motioned for several soldiers to cover the door with their weapons. Moments later, the door slid open, and Julie Newman walked out of the room, arms held high over her head. She turned in a complete circle, showing the soldiers that she was unarmed and then waited, the translator device slung around her neck.

"Aku laki san," she repeated.

Gra'akk walked up to her. "Lower your arms," he said.

She slowly lowered her arms and said, "Our mutual friend activated me after your premature invasion triggered the invasion protocol. Sloppy."

Gra'akk bristled at the impudence of this small female and glowered menacingly at her. His harsh tone translated through the device, the threat plain.

"Who do you think you are speaking to, human?"

"Save it, General," she said, voice firm and cold. "I'm not as weak as that idiot Vickers. The pain the implant causes me is far worse than anything you can threaten me with."

Gra'akk pondered this for a moment, then said, "Where is the data?"

"Destroyed," she answered bluntly. "The soldiers that brought us here blew up the data core when your people breached the tunnel."

Gra'akk felt the anger building inside of him, and he snarled, "Then what is the point of keeping you alive?"

Julie looked him square in his red eyes and motioned behind her. "This is why."

She stepped into the rear of the room and pointed to the prototype sitting on an anti-grav pallet. The explosives that had been placed on the device by Remy's troops lay on the floor next to the pallet, inactive.

Gra'akk walked up to the object and turned to her.

"This is a working prototype of the generator," she said. "With it, your scientists can reverse engineer as many as you want."

Gra'akk ran his hand over the device and smiled.

"Activate it," he said.

"Not a good idea unless you have a death wish," she stated. "This prototype is unshielded. It would kill us all."

Gra'akk turned toward her and said, "Of what use is it if there is no shielding?"

Clearly tiring of the exchange, Julie stepped closer to Gra'akk and said, "I possess enough of the alloy to shield this generator, but no more than that. The pieces have been synthesized, but the casing has not been assembled and calibrated. It is unlikely that your scientists could synthesize the shielding alloy without my assistance. The matrix is much too complex and requires specific expertise to create. I was one of the project leaders and can manufacture more, but it will cost you. Ten times what I was supposed to be paid. Also, I want this implant removed."

Gra'akk kept his anger in check, pondering what she'd said. Any other time, such impudence would be rewarded with torture and a trip to the mess hall, but this technology was far too valuable.

"What assurance do we have that you will live up to your end of the bargain?" he finally asked.

Julie paused before saying, "I was compelled to comply because of this implant. Since then, I have killed my own kind and committed acts of treason against my race. I cannot go back home, regardless of what happens. Symons, that festering, pus-filled boil of a traitor, will likely activate my implant the moment you tell him you have the technology the same way he killed Vickers. Treason still carries the death penalty on my world. Whether you kill me, my people kill me, or Symons kills me, I'm still dead. I have nothing to lose. Besides, you need me to make this generator work. If I die, the shielding alloy formula dies with me."

Gra'akk turned his back to her and considered what she'd said. He then turned to Ve'ellda's successor and said, "Take her and the device to the ship. She is not to be harmed. Any breach of this order, no matter how slight, will be dealt with most severely. The shi'ia-khar is very interested in this technology. I'm sure he and Rinn-Tar-Vel Ka'awon would be extremely displeased if it slipped from their grasp because of someone's stupidity. Is that understood?"

"Of course, Vett-Tar-Von," he replied.

Gra'akk turned to Julie and said, "This is my second-in-command, Dath-Kheton Pla'agg. He will escort you to the ship. He has been instructed not to allow harm to come to you. Once on the ship, you will plead your case to Rinn-Tar-Vel Ka'awon. If he agrees, we will remove the implant."

Julie nodded and said, "Good enough." She followed Pla'agg out through the corridor and into the tunnel, followed by two soldiers pushing the anti-grav pallet with the generator and shielding alloy pieces behind her. As she walked past the lines of soldiers, several glared at her uncomfortably and were rewarded with a harsh reprimand by Pla'agg. Once in the tunnel, they boarded a troop carrier that took them out toward the bunker's rear entrance, now cleared of debris.

As they accelerated toward the tunnel entrance, Julie pondered the events that led to her current predicament. If she could take her own life, she would in an instant, but the implant AI prevented that. Whether she liked it or not, they owned her. She saw no way out.

The Omega soldiers would've never understood, never allowed her to simply give the tech to the T'Kharr in order to keep the balance of power. They claimed they fought for survival, just as the humans do. After the day's events, however, she wished she could kill them all, every last one of them from their Emperor down to the youngest hatchling. She just didn't know how to do it.

Inside the storage room, Gra'akk kicked at the body of Lt. Henna sprawled at his feet.

"This is one of the soldiers like the one that caused Ve'ellda's death?"

The soldier standing near him replied, "Yes, Tar-Von. Their coverings are the same."

Gra'akk then looked over to Kenyon's body and said, "Take these bodies back to the ship for dissection. I want to know—"

Suddenly, a soldier burst into the room. "Tar-Von, the scanning team just detected a nuclear signature that just went active!"

Gra'akks eyes went wide.

"Where is it?" he demanded.

"The signature appears to be descending from someplace east of here into the mountain. We cannot access the chamber near it. The walls and ceiling have collapsed."

Gra'akk turned and screamed, "Evacuate right now!" He turned and ran full-speed back out toward the tunnel. As he ran out, he heard the command to retreat being passed down the line and watched his troops turn and run toward the entrance to the tunnel. Gra'akk saw an armored trooper starting up a small, two-man, four-wheeled attack buggy to retreat, and Gra'akk knocked him off of it and climbed aboard himself. He started the vehicle and sped off toward the entrance to the tunnel, speeding by the retreating troopers. He caught up with Pla'agg and Julie's vehicle and shouted for them to get into the ship immediately.

Pla'agg knew better than to ask why and grabbed Julie by the arm, dragging her urgently into the shuttle. He placed Julie into a seat and secured the restraints, then watched as the soldiers that had been with them loaded the pallet with the generator.

As soon as they were inside of the cargo bay, Gra'akk yelled, "Launch, now!"

The shuttle pilot complied immediately and lifted off the ground as T'Kharr troops continued pouring out of the tunnel entrance. They'd just lifted from the ground when the ship rocked violently from an explosion so intense, it felt as if their shuttle would split in half. Gra'akk watched the tunnel entrance belch out debris and troopers who didn't get out in time.

As they ascended away from the landing site, the entire mountain seemed to shrink in size, permanently burying any more secrets that might have been in the bunker along with the dead human soldiers' bodies. Pity they couldn't be recovered and studied. That was secondary, however, because he possessed the grandest prize of all, a working generator and the human scientist who could make it practical. His future looked bright. Bright indeed.

Remy, Sulak, Keever, and Jared sprinted from the lift doors to the front entrance of the bunker, which was hidden from both scanners and the naked eye by camouflage devices. They met Eli, Dram, and the Jaaleadi who were waiting for them just outside of the doors.

"Everything set?" Eli asked as he traded places with Remy under Sulak's arm.

Dram looked behind them and said, "Where's Julie?"

"She's gone to the other side," Remy said. "I'll explain later, but we need to get to cover now."

Dram took one last look toward the entrance, then turned and ran toward a clump of trees just as the explosion rocked the mountain. The underground explosion knocked all of them to the ground, and they seemed to be falling for several seconds as parts of the mountain caved in on itself. All of them fell heavily onto the hard ground, their ears ringing from the thunderclap.

Once the rumbling stopped, Remy did a quick assessment, concluding that none were the worse for the wear. He retrieved his field binoculars and ran to the edge of the nearest slope, which looked out over the forest. He took several moments to focus but eventually found what he was looking for—the landing field outside of the bunker's back door. He spotted the earthmoving equipment next to the tunnel entrance, then saw troops running around frantically, trying to get to their shuttles. Several shuttles had left the ground and were rapidly ascending into the sky.

He trained his sight down to the tunnel entrance that the earthmovers had excavated and saw, with satisfaction, that the entire tunnel area had caved in. The explosion had collapsed thousands of times more rock and debris into the tunnel than they'd managed to collapse with their mines. There would be no digging it out this time.

Remy still saw hundreds of troopers milling about in the area, trying to get their bearings. Without warning, anti-aircraft fire erupted from numerous places in the forest and clearing, aimed toward the sky. It was then that he noticed the low rumbling approaching from beyond the forest, growing louder by the second. Seconds later, a squadron of Dagger fighters screamed over the troops, strafing them with their Gatling guns and firing air-to-ground missiles at the transports still loading troops. As they completed their first pass, they over flew Remy and the others, nearly deafening them with the scream of their engines.

"*Pacifica*, this is Hunter Leader. Numerous hostiles on the ground. We are moving to engage."

"Commander Haynes, half of the mountain just collapsed in on itself, and my rad detector just lit up," the radar intercept officer said. "I think someone sparked off a nuke inside the mountain."

Lt. Commander Marco "Hunter Leader" Haynes keyed his transmitter. "Scan for human life signs, ladies. I doubt the uglies nuked themselves."

"Hunter Nine, they're on you!" one of the other pilots yelled just before Hunter Nine exploded in a bright fireball.

"Hunter Six, watch that triple A to the north!" one of the other pilots said on the open frequency. "They got Taggs."

Haynes asked his RIO, "Any friendlies on the valley floor?"

"Negative."

Haynes switched to the squadron frequency. "There are no friendlies on the valley floor. Set your Demon warheads to full power."

"What about those transports lifting off, Commander?" the RIO asked.

"Let the Valkyries take care of them. We've got enough to worry about on the ground. Relay their position to *Pacifica*."

"Hunter Leader, Hunter Four. I've got friendlies on the mountain top. Six humans and two Jaaleadi."

"Try and make contact with them. I'll try and arrange a ride for them."

On the mountain, Remy and Keever watched intently as the Daggers strafed the T'Kharr soldiers. Remy watched a pair of missiles snake out and away from one ship, then arc down into the forest to obliterate a location that had been pouring out anti-aircraft fire. Another fighter spat a barrage of rounds from its Gatling gun at a cluster of enemy troops, strafing across a transport ship that was slowly lifting off the ground. The transport erupted in a huge fireball, throwing burning debris and bodies in every direction.

Dram Hunter stared dejectedly at the ground. He knelt by Petty Officer Eli as he dressed Sulak's leg wound, placing a tight field dressing on it and administering a dose of morphine and hyperfeuron.

Jared turned his attention from the battle and walked over to Dram.

Dram looked up at him. "I just can't believe it. Julie a traitor? What possible reason could she have?"

Jared shook his head. "I don't know what to tell you. She fooled us all. If I hadn't seen it with my own eyes, I wouldn't have believed it myself."

"I . . . I just didn't see it . . ."

Jared said, "She gave me a message for you. She said you would know what she was talking about. She said that whatever she had said or done, the part with you was real. It wasn't an act. What did she mean?"

Dram pondered the information for a moment and said, "Nothing. It doesn't matter now . . . but I appreciate you telling me. Thanks."

He turned his attention back to Sulak and Eli.

Keever ran up to them. "We've made contact with one of the Dagger pilots. A shuttle is on the way to pick us up. Get ready to move."

Eli repacked his medical items while Dram helped Sulak to her feet.

Two more loud explosions rocked the valley floor, and Jared saw two more anti-aircraft batteries fall silent. The Daggers had done their job. Only smoking hulks of destroyed transport shuttles remained, and dead bodies littered the ground. Jared looked up and saw the contrails from three enemy transports that had escaped the barrage. He had no way of knowing if Julie made it out with her new friends.

As they began to escape the planet's gravitational pull, Gra'akk noticed the wave of enemy fighters coming up on them from the rear.

"What is the closest ship?" he barked.

"The destroyer *Thi'ispa*, Tar-Von," the pilot responded. "They are moving toward the *Ba'akteer* on the far side of the planet."

"Head for that ship immediately," he said just as he saw a group of T'Kharr fighters moving to intercept the enemy fighters.

Gra'akk turned to Julie and said, "It would seem that you will survive to serve the T'Kharr Empire after all, human."

Julie looked at him with undisguised contempt. "I would have been just as happy to have been destroyed along with you and this generator. Make no mistake, General, I'm doing this for myself. Not for you or your emperor."

Frustration boiled up inside of her. Had it not been for the implant, she would have put a gun to her head long ago. The implant's artificial intelligence prevented her from doing anything to harm herself intentionally, ensuring her no easy out.

Gra'akk chose to ignore the impudent comment and instead concentrated on the shape of the *Thi'ispa*, now growing larger on the screen. Every kilometer closer they came, the more triumphant he felt. He then noticed the main force of T'Kharr carriers coming into range, moving toward the far side of the planet. The four enemy carriers had broken off their pursuit and were now moving toward the enemy carrier that was already in orbit above the research facility. He guessed they were going to form their fleets together while the planet was between them and the enemy ships and attack in a unified wave. Brute force against brute force. He hoped they would survive long enough to bring his prize home.

Logan examined his data pad, following the progress of the battles raging both on the planet surface and in space above. He saw what he'd been waiting for. "Colonel Fargo, the bunker complex has been destroyed, and we've picked up survivors. General Austin has issued the recall orders. Order your troops to their shuttles. We're bugging out."

"Yes, sir," Fargo said. "What about them?" He gestured toward a large group of T'Kharr prisoners inside of an electronic containment field.

"We'll take the officers with us for interrogation and leave the rest. Make sure all of their weapons are destroyed. Program the electronic fences to drop once all of our troops have left the surface. Let the planet's wildlife have at them."

Fargo nodded and turned to relay the orders.

Colonel Shaddra walked up to Logan and said, "Charges are set, General."

"Very good," Logan replied as he watched troops file into their transports and begin to lift off the surface.

The wounded had already been evacuated, and the T'Kharr officers were presently being led into an armored lander, all wearing shock collars, hand binders, and scowls on their faces.

Logan shielded his eyes as the first wave of the troop landers lifted off, stirring up dust and debris in their wake. Soon, dozens of landers lifted off and headed back to their mother ship.

A beefy marine captain trotted up and said, "Your ship is ready, sir."

Without looking at him, Logan said, "We'll be the last to leave, Captain. I want to make sure everyone gets away safely."

"But sir, General Austin specifically instructed me to . . . well . . . to drag you into the shuttle if you didn't come willingly, sir."

Logan turned to look at the marine and said, "I may be older than you, son, but I'd like to see you try that."

The captain looked uncomfortable, then said, "No disrespect intended, sir. You know how insistent the general can be."

Logan paused, then begrudgingly turned to Fargo, who'd just come from relaying instructions to the guards around the electric containment fence.

"I've been ordered to leave immediately. How many troops are left?"

"About a third, sir. They should be off the surface in about fifteen minutes."

"Very well. See to it, Colonel. I'll see you on the *Suribachi*."

"Aye, sir," he replied, then turned and walked off.

Logan turned toward the captain and said, "All right, Captain. You're getting your wish."

The captain looked relieved and motioned toward a nearby shuttle, then fell in behind Logan as he walked toward it. Logan paused for a moment when he heard, "Fire in the hole!" He watched with satisfaction as the research facility imploded in a mass of twisted metal and duracrete. Satisfied, Logan turned and boarded his shuttle.

CHAPTER TWENTY-TWO

SAS Pacifica

Michael Trent stood off to the side of the landing area and watched as the shuttle pierced the atmosphere shield. It gently settled onto the deck. The hatch opened, and two med techs ran inside, then returned moments later with a young female soldier between them, helping her down to a gurney waiting at the bottom of the ramp.

She was covered with dirt and grime and had a bloody bandage on her left thigh. Three similarly dressed soldiers and two civilians followed her. One of the civilians made eye contact with Trent, the weary, grim look on his face suddenly replaced with a broad smile.

"Mickey!"

Michael returned the smile and stepped up to Jared, each grasping the other's right forearm in a brotherly handshake.

Jared let out a weary sigh and said, "Took you long enough."

"Sorry pal. I'm not the driver of this beast. I'm glad you made it out all right. Mom would have given me no end of grief."

The smile faded from Jared's face. "I need to speak to your commander right away. We have a big problem."

"Aside from the obvious, what do you mean?" Michael asked just before the klaxons sounded. He reached for his hand unit just as it buzzed.

"Trent."

"We've recovered all of our fighters, Captain. The enemy carriers have linked up and are moving into range. I need you up here."

"Yes, sir. On my way."

Michael glanced at Jared and said, "Follow me."

Jared was nearly thrown off his feet by a jolt that shook the entire ship. "I'm afraid to ask what they're firing that would rock a ship of this size."

Michael increased his pace to a trot and said, "That was probably a nuke. Don't sweat it. They can't penetrate our shields with those."

"Easy for you to say. I've had enough nuclear explosions for one day."

"What was that?" Michael said as he stabbed the panel that would take them to the command center in a matter of moments.

Jared looked at him and said, "Never mind. I just want this whole thing to be over."

"What do you need to speak to the admiral about?" Michael asked.

"Can you pull up the data on the T'Kharr ships that made it off the surface?"

Michael was growing frustrated and said, "Yeah, but—"

"Then I need you to do that as soon as we get to the bridge. It's vital."

Michael looked perplexed but knew his brother well enough not to argue. Jared was his junior by three years but was a very capable scientist. If he needed the data, he'd get it for him.

"I'll put in a request for it, and it'll be waiting by the time we get there."

The remaining few minutes sped by quickly, interrupted by several jarring shocks that shook the ship. When the lift doors finally opened, Michael motioned for Jared to follow him to one of the detector stations.

He scanned it briefly, then turned to Jared and said, "Only three shuttles made it off the surface. What do you need?"

Jared moved closer to the screen and said, "Energy readings, life signs, strange fluctuations, that kind of stuff."

Michael pulled up the display for each of the three ships, and Jared's blood ran cold when he saw the readings on the second ship.

"You'd better get your admiral over here," Jared said.

Michael looked at him like he'd lost his mind.

"You didn't happen to notice the space battle going on right now, did you?"

"Believe it or not, this is more important."

"You'd better give me some indication . . ." Michael started just before Drake walked up behind him.

"What's going on, Captain? I'm guessing it must be urgent to keep you away from the bridge during a battle."

Michael turned to Drake and motioned toward Jared. "I apologize, sir. This is my brother, Jared Trent."

Jared nodded and said, "Admiral, you need to see this." He then pointed at the screen. "This human life sign is Julie Newman. She's a research scientist from our facility now working with the T'Kharr."

That bit of news caught Drake off guard. "What? Are you serious?"

Jared looked pained and continued, "It gets worse. We had a working prototype in the bunker. The special forces team did all they could, including detonating a nuclear weapon in the bunker to try and make sure that the T'Kharr didn't get to it. Problem is, Julie surprised us all with her betrayal. She killed two of the soldiers and locked herself in a room with the device just as the enemy troops breached the interior."

Jared pointed to a complex wave frequency pattern on the screen. "This pattern is what the device puts out when it's idle. They have both her and the generator, Admiral. And if she's working with them, we have a big problem."

Drake digested the information and went back down to his chair. He activated the priority vocal interface that would allow him to speak to North in the Cathedra.

"Commander, we've received credible data that indicates the T'Kharr recovered a working prototype of the generator along with one of the research staff who was working with them. I suggest we move to blockade the starlane portals to prevent them from leaving the system."

Jared spoke up. "Admiral, there is one other thing . . ."

North immediately issued orders to the fleets to deploy between the T'Kharr fleet and the three starlane portals. He watched as the enemy fleets combined and formed a picket line of destroyers, with their carriers and support ships behind the wall.

Fortunately, Faulkner and the others had arrived and were forming ranks of their own. With the loss of the *Miria*, only *Pacifica* and *Kegar* were still equipped with Monsoor's "specials." Between the two ships, they had twenty-six of the new missiles left. They would have to be used judiciously.

North received the detector readings that Doctor Trent had isolated and determined that the generator was now on the *Ka'athiol*. Their current position placed them between the T'Kharr fleet and the Miratev star. He inwardly shuddered at the order he was about to give but knew it had to be done. He'd ordered men and women to their deaths before. It never got easier.

<Major Deneva, this is North. I'm invoking Command Priority Order One. Authentication codes will follow. Launch the package and await my instructions for final detonation.>

Deneva, who'd been debriefing Remy and the other survivors, acknowledged and checked his data pad.

<Authentication received and confirmed. Heading to the launch bay now.>

<I understand you will pilot the package. I'm sorry, Major.>

<Don't be, Commander. We all knew this was a possibility.>

<For the code.>

<For the code, sir.>

Remy noticed the signs of someone sending and receiving commands on their telesponder and studied Major Deneva's face. He noticed just the slightest trace of regret. Deneva turned toward his second-in-command and sent an order over his telesponder before stepping up to the man and shaking his hand. Deneva headed to the door and left the room.

Remy looked at the other soldier and said, "Captain, may I ask where the major has gone?"

The captain looked back at him and said, "We've been ordered to deploy the package. It seems that the T'Kharr made it off the surface with a working prototype. Commander North has ordered the package launched as a last line of defense in case we're unable to destroy the T'Kharr flagship."

The words stung. Even though they weren't meant as a recrimination, Remy felt as if he'd been punched in the gut. It was his responsibility, and he'd failed. He knew where Deneva was going. The package had to be piloted manually and flown into the star.

Remy looked over at Eli and Keever, who were resting in chairs with hyperfeuron IVs attached to their arms. Sulak had been transferred to the medical bay due to the severity of her injuries. He wasn't sure where the civilians had been taken. He thought about the mission and their failure—his failure. He reached over and removed the IV cuff from his own arm and ran out the door after Deneva.

"Lieutenant!" the captain called as Remy ran out the door.

"Major, hold up," he said as he jogged up to Deneva, who was now heading toward the lift that would take him to the dorsal bay.

Deneva stopped in front of the lift doors and said, "Lieutenant, you need rest. Go back and finish your hyperfeuron treatment."

"Sir, I want to volunteer to pilot the package."

Deneva turned to meet his gaze and said soberly, "You've performed your part of this mission, Lieutenant. This part is mine. Go back to the room and await debriefing."

"Sir," Remy said a little louder than he'd intended. He switched to a quieter tone and said, "Sir, my mission was to secure the bunker and deny the enemy possession of the technology. My mission isn't completed yet. Please let me do this. I owe it to Henna and the others who didn't make it."

Deneva considered Remy's words carefully. Remy knew what he was volunteering for, and Deneva understood the shame he was feeling at what he'd perceived as his failure on the planet. He knew that if the roles were reversed, he might be making the same request.

He turned to face Remy head on and said, "Under any other circumstance I'd argue with you, but there isn't time. I'll allow you to take my place."

Remy nodded and said, "Thank you, sir. I won't let you down again."

Deneva's stone façade relaxed just slightly, and he said, "You and your team haven't let anyone down." He handed Remy the data pad containing the authentication codes he would need to power up the weapon, then saluted him. "For the code."

Remy returned the salute. "For the code, sir."

The lift arrived and Remy stepped inside. When the doors closed, Deneva sent a message to North, advising him of the change, then turned and headed back to the room.

ICC Ka'athiol

Gra'akk strode triumphantly onto the *Ka'athiol* bridge, trailed by Julie Newman and two security guards. Dath-Tar-Vel Zha'ar was busy deploying the fleets to counter the human fleet movements and was of no concern to him. Gra'akk never particularly liked Zha'ar, and the feeling was mutual. Gra'akk couldn't wait to show Ka'awon his prize and perhaps get a chance to rub it in Zha'ar's face. When this whole affair was over, perhaps Zha'ar would be the one saluting him rather than the reverse. He approached Ka'awon's office.

"Enter," Ka'awon barked.

Ka'awon stood and walked from behind his desk, where he'd been monitoring the battle that was forming. Walking up to Julie, he looked down at her imposingly. Ka'awon was tall by T'Kharr standards and stood a full two and a half feet taller than Julie.

He regarded her for several moments before commenting, "You are not what I expected."

Julie looked up at him defiantly. "Sorry to disappoint you."

"I doubt that," he said. "Tar-Von Gra'akk has informed me of your request to have the implant deactivated in return for your cooperation. Why should I acquiesce to such a demand? You might change your mind afterward and leave us with unworkable technology."

"I have nothing to lose, and you have everything to gain," she said. "If I fail to deliver, you can always replace the implant."

"But it would require us to deactivate the artificial intelligence that prohibits you from harming yourself. You could take your own life, and we would be left with one single working generator and no practical way to replicate it."

"That is true, but the prospect of living out my life in relative comfort is more attractive than death. You could kill me whenever you pleased."

"There are many ways to die, Miss Newman," Ka'awon growled. "We have gleaned much knowledge of human physiology during our . . . experiments."

Despite her hard veneer, Julie shuddered involuntarily. She glanced at Gra'akk, then turned back to Ka'awon and said, "Admiral, as I have explained to your flunky here, I cannot go back. I have committed treason, which carries the death penalty on my world. I would rather not see my work destroyed."

Gra'akk bristled at the "flunky" comment, mainly because the translation came through more as "excrement," but he held his tongue.

"What if that use is the destruction of your race?" Ka'awon asked.

"I doubt you would do that. If you used the device, my people would respond in kind. I believe they called it 'mutually assured destruction' in the old days. I am just interested in maintaining the balance of power." Julie had used this argument to convince herself that what she was doing was for the greater good. The fact that Symons had threatened to torture and kill her family was truly the primary driving force behind her actions in addition to the pain inflicted by the device he'd implanted.

She'd realized early in the conversation that Ka'awon was not a being to be trifled with. He was unlike the others she'd encountered. He was calm and thoughtful, but Julie could sense the tremendous aura of potential violence and lethal cunning just below the surface. Also, it was obvious that he was highly intelligent, something that seemed to be a rarity among the T'Kharr she'd met. His pitch-black eyes oozed intelligent malevolence.

Ka'awon considered what she'd said for several moments. "I will order the device removed, but only *after* you have assembled and tested the device you brought with you. If the device works, you will have demonstrated your trustworthiness. If it doesn't work . . ."

"Admiral, if it doesn't work and something goes wrong, everyone in close proximity will be killed by the field. As you have pointed out, my implant prevents me from committing suicide."

"Very well. I will order the intensity of the lingering pain to be diminished to assist you in your work. The quicker you get it to work, the quicker you will have the device removed."

"Thank you, Admiral," she said as she rose from her seat.

Ka'awon then turned to Gra'akk and said, "Take her to the medical bay and have them adjust the implant. Give her whatever resources she needs to make the generator operational. I want the device assembled and tested as soon as possible."

"As you command, Rinn-Tar-Vel," Gra'akk said. He then left the room with Julie.

Ka'awon hit the comm button and said, "Update!"

Zha'ar answered, "The human fleets have placed themselves between us and the starlane portals. We will have to blast our way through."

"Listen to me, Zha'ar. This ship must survive. Even if we have to sacrifice all of the others, this technology must be brought back to the homeworld."

"Yes, Rinn-Tar-Vel. One more thing, sir. A ship launched from the *Pacifica* a few minutes ago, headed toward the Miratev star."

Ka'awon was concerned. "What kind of ship?"

"It appeared to be a series of linked probes, sir. We detected no weapons on board and only one human life sign. It is significantly larger than a standard probe. It is also extremely fast. Much too fast to pursue."

"Show me," he demanded, and an image came onto the screen of a multi-segmented ship that resembled five large probes connected end-to-end. It was obviously not constructed to fly in an atmosphere and lacked the lines of a fighter or bomber.

"They are launching an unarmed probe toward the star? Monitor it and keep me informed. Also, pull two destroyers from each of the remaining fleets to enhance the protective bubble around the *Ka'athiol*."

Ka'awon severed the link and brought up a view of the *Pacifica*. From their current angle, he couldn't see the location where their stealth pod was attached, and he hoped it was still there. They'd already scored one huge victory. If they could make it out of here with both the generator and Grand Commander North, this day would go down in history.

His biggest problem right now was that they were currently outnumbered five carriers to four, and the humans might have more of the weapons that destroyed the *Ke'efex*.

The insistent chiming of his comm broke him from his thoughts.

He stabbed the toggle and said, "What is it now?" the irritation plain in his voice.

"Sir," Zha'ar said excitedly. "The Under-Deity has blessed us!"

"What are you babbling about, Zha'ar?"

Ka'awon saw the data appear on his console and nearly exploded with joy.

The open comm channel burst to life. "Alliance ships, this is Alta-Tar-Vel Da'akta Te'eq of the imperial flagship *Thola'aris*. I wish to speak to your commander immediately."

SAS Pacifica

In the Cathedra, North received the same information as Ka'awon but had a distinctly different reaction. As flashes started to appear on his tactical map near the primary starlane portal, North felt his blood run cold. When the flashes subsided, North counted *four* new T'Kharr heavy carriers and their escorts—eighty ships in all—now moving up to surround them and reinforce the *Ka'a-thiol.*

Their five-to-four advantage had just dissolved to an eight-to-five disadvantage. He also recognized the name of their commander, Fleet Marshal Te'eq. Not only was he a personal friend to the Emperor and the highest ranking military officer of their empire, he had arrived in the *Thola'aris,* the emperor's personal flagship.

Vigorous comm traffic was now flying between his carriers. North issued the order to stand by and brace for the impending onslaught. He checked the position of the package. It would take another forty minutes to be in a position to launch. The T'Kharr, as hoped, had no idea what the true nature of the ship was and had apparently assumed it was a harmless probe. One small victory. Even if they did realize what it was, it was now too late for them to do anything about it.

The Alliance forces only needed to hold them off long enough to prevent their escape into the starlanes. This was the ultimate last resort for North. Not only would he have to sacrifice his five fleets with thousands of people, but he would once again have to order the destruction of a star system. At least they would take eight top-of-the-line carriers with them and hopefully deal a crippling blow to the T'Kharr defenses. They must've stripped their defenses bare in order to muster another task force of that strength.

"Repeat . . . Alliance ships, this is Alta-Tar-Vel Da'akta Te'eq of the imperial flagship *Thola'aris.* I have ordered my ships to hold position for the moment. Cease your advance or you will be fired upon. I require communication with your current commander."

Current commander? North noticed that Te'eq didn't ask for him by name, meaning the T'Kharr commanders were still under the impression that he was a prisoner of the T'Kharr boarding party. He quickly opened the encrypted command conference and ordered Faulkner to answer for the fleet.

"This is Vice Admiral Jeffery Faulkner of the SAS *Endeavor*. I am the current fleet commander. What do you want, Fleet Marshal?"

The translation took several moments before Te'eq replied.

"You are outnumbered and outgunned. By now, you know that we have the generator, and there's nothing you can do about it. I am willing to consider a peaceful resolution to this situation rather than have to resort to blasting your ships out of space."

Faulkner paused for the translation before saying, "You might want to check with the captains of your carriers *Ba'akteer* and *Ke'efex* before jumping to that conclusion. However, the *Ke'efex* captain might be difficult to communicate with unless you have a direct comm line to the afterlife."

Te'eq had to check his temper before continuing.

"While it is true that you apparently have new weaponry that appears to be able to penetrate our shields, our analysis has determined that you must be in close proximity in order to activate the weapon's special abilities. I assure you we won't allow you to get that close to another of our capital ships."

Faulkner felt he'd made his point and replied, "What is it you propose?"

Te'eq said, "I am somewhat a student of human psychology and tactics. I am certain that if I were to attempt to board or capture your ships, you would simply blow them up, and I would lose many soldiers."

"You are correct."

"We only want the generator in order to maintain the balance of power. Were the roles reversed, you would want the same thing."

Faulkner didn't believe for one minute that their pursuit of the technology was for noble purposes but decided to play along.

"Go on."

"Therefore, this is my proposal. Withdraw from this system. Allow any of my troops still alive on the *Pacifica* to return to our fleet, and we will allow you safe passage."

North sent Faulkner a message.

"And what about Grand Commander North?"

"He will return with us to T'Kharr-Vod as our guest. I give you my personal guarantee he will not be harmed."

Faulkner paused for effect before saying, "You know I cannot allow that, Fleet Marshal, any more than your people would allow us to leave with you as our 'guest.'"

"I'm sure that is true, Admiral, but would the commander agree with you? I have studied him for many years, even before he came to his current rank, and I do not believe he would approve of sacrificing thousands of crew members in battle just to save him. The technology is lost. The one thing you *can* change is the fate of your ships and crews. One life for tens of thousands and all of your ships. Do not be foolish. It is a fair trade."

"Why not take me instead? Release the commander, and I will take his place."

"A grand commander of the Alliance fleet is worth much more to us than a mere vice admiral. It will be North."

North sent another urgent message to Faulkner, then sent a telesponder message to Deneva.

"Stand by, Fleet Marshal," Faulkner said. "I need to discuss this with my commanders."

"I will give you thirty of your standard minutes to consult with your commanders."

"I will contact you then," he said. Faulkner out." Then he severed the link.

"Well done, Jeff," North said. "Are you there, Mat?"

"Yes, sir," Drake replied, now on the secured frequency.

"Is Major Deneva on the bridge yet?"

"Yes, Commander," Deneva answered, now standing next to Drake.

North said, "All right . . . they still think that their shock troops have me on that stealth pod. This is what I need you to do . . ."

CHAPTER TWENTY-THREE

ICC Ka'athiol

"**A**lta-Tar-Vel Te'eq wishes to speak to you, Tar-Vel," the communications subling said.

"Put him through," Ka'awon said, activating the link.

"Alta-Tar-Vel, may the Under-Deity bless you and your brood. Your timing could not have been better."

Te'eq nodded and said, "The Under-Deity has indeed blessed us today. You have done well, Ka'awon. I would have apprised you of our arrival, but I could not risk alerting the humans. We have stripped our frontier severely to assemble this task force. We are taking a great risk, but the reward should outweigh those risks."

"Agreed, Alta-Tar-Vel."

"What is the status of the generator?"

"The human prisoner has agreed to assemble and activate the generator we acquired in exchange for certain concessions," Ka'awon said. "Nothing of note. She will serve us for a very long time, whether she's aware of that or not."

"Good. I do not want to leave this system without knowing for certain the technology works. If it does not, we will destroy the human ships."

Ka'awon nodded in agreement. "What of their grand commander?"

"They do not give any indication that they know where he is. I have studied human tactics for many cycles. If I am correct, the human commanders are discussing whether to fight us or abandon their commander. They will demand a voice communication with Grand Commander North, and he will tell them to withdraw and sacrifice himself in order to save his ships and crews."

"Well thought out, Tar-Vel. But to allow so many ships to leave . . . we have them at our mercy."

"Perhaps, but as confident as I am of our ability to prevail, we still do not know how many of those ships are equipped with the new weapons. They may also have more of their subs in the system equipped with the new missiles. I cannot risk the destruction of the *Ka'athiol* or the technology, even if it means letting them go. Besides, do not underestimate their resolve; they are formidable adversaries."

Ka'awon pondered Te'eq's words. He didn't have the same confidence that Te'eq had of what North would do. If it were him, he would order his ships to attack, regardless of their losses. If North surrendered without a fight, it would be an extreme act of cowardice.

Not worthy of a commander of North's repute. Every instinct in him told him something about this whole situation was wrong. However, he couldn't challenge his superior. Not without solid proof.

"As you order, Tar-Vel. What do you command?"

"How long until the generator is ready to test?" Te'eq asked.

"My subordinate Gra'akk is supervising. He says it will be ready to test in three cycles."

"A little over one human standard hour," Te'eq said. "Very well. Advise me when the test is to be conducted. Until then, I will stall the humans." Then he abruptly severed the link.

Ka'awon leaned back in his chair feeling . . . uneasy. Something wasn't right. He was sure of it.

SAS Endeavor

At the thirty-minute mark, Faulkner ordered the channel opened.

"T'Kharr commander, this is Faulkner."

A few moments passed, and Te'eq responded, "This is Te'eq."

"We demand verification that Commander North is alive and wish to speak to him directly. I will not withdraw without his direct order."

"Voice transmission will not be possible," Te'eq responded. "It would reveal the location of my troops who have North in their custody."

Faulkner played along. "We will not comply without verification. What do you suggest?"

"Send a recognition code to us that we can encrypt and send to our troops. Ask the commander to respond using something that only you would recognize as authentic. Then ask him your questions."

"Stand by," Faulkner said as he composed his message.

"Transmitting now," he said.

Te'eq watched the message come in and read, "Did Denara like the gift you gave her? What was it again?"

Te'eq addressed Faulkner again and said, "My people are encoding the message as we speak and will send a broad-beam transmission directed at the *Pacifica*. Stay on this channel, and you will receive the message translation at the same time as we do. There will be no time for any tricks."

"Agreed," Faulkner said. He waited for the response he knew would come.

Meanwhile, in a quiet lab in the *Pacifica* that had been commandeered by Omega Section, Deneva linked with the devices he'd placed in the pod and constructed their response.

Te'eq came on a few seconds later and said, "The response is, 'Withdraw from the system. That is a direct order on my personal authority as a grand commander of the Alliance fleet. Denara enjoyed the sheed blossom. Take care of my fleet, Jeff.'"

Faulkner paused before responding, feigning anguish at having to obey the order. "I am satisfied that your troops are in possession of Commander North and that I am communicating with him. We will withdraw as ordered . . . but in a manner that satisfies both of our mutual suspicions."

Te'eq savored his victory. He'd staked his reputation on the fact that North would order them to leave, and he'd been right. Faulkner's last comment then registered with him, and he said, "What do you mean?"

"Our forces have a long history, Fleet Marshal. You don't trust us to keep our word any more than we trust you. If I withdraw my forces, I want guarantees that you won't change your minds and attack as soon as you have the commander."

"I can give you my personal guarantee."

"With respect, Fleet Marshal, I was thinking more in line with having my ships begin to withdraw to the starlane, *Pacifica* being last. Once my fleet is safe, your troops will be allowed to leave with the commander."

Te'eq thought about this for a moment. He didn't want to give up any tactical advantage to the humans, but Faulkner had a point about trust. If the generator didn't work, he'd intended to attack the human ships. Perhaps it would be better to allow them to leave in exchange for the chance to capture North without a fight. He knew enough about the human command structure to know that Faulkner would withdraw as ordered but would not do so foolishly. If he smelled a trap, he would attack. Te'eq didn't want to push his advantage too far.

"How would we do this, Admiral?"

Faulkner said, "Stand by."

North's voice came through the speaker in Faulkner's chair, and he said, "Don't be too much of a pushover, Jeff. Te'eq is smart. He won't buy it if you make it too easy."

"Agreed, sir. I think I have a good idea of what to say."

North said, "All right. Make it good."

Faulkner opened the channel again and said, "We'll permit an escort squadron of your fighters to approach *Pacifica* and stay within weapons range until your ships move away from the primary starlane portal. We will not fire on them unless fired upon. I know better than to ask you where your troops and their ship are. If I were you, I wouldn't reveal their location either. I assume they're within our shield perimeter in one of your stealth pods?"

Te'eq said, "Correct on both counts."

"Once my ships are close enough to start to enter the starlane, *Pacifica* will be the last to leave, keeping your squadron targeted. When *Pacifica* and the other ships are within range of the starlane, *Pacifica* will drop a portion of her shields to allow your pod to leave and rendezvous with your fighters. All of our ships will then leave, you'll have what you want, and my fleet will be safe."

Te'eq pondered Faulkner's plan and said, "Agreed. I assume you will be evacuating your subs as well?"

"Subs? What subs? If there were subs, they would naturally be evacuated as well and offer cover. By the way, if there were subs in this system, they'd also be armed with the new missiles."

"Perhaps," Te'eq answered, trying to sound much surer than he actually was.

Now came the act. "Fleet Marshal, make no mistake . . . I disagree with Commander North's decision, but I am duty-bound to obey. If I had my way, we'd be shooting at each other right now, but I follow orders. If we sense any deception at all, we will start shooting, and we will destroy the pod with Commander North ourselves. I'd rather see him dead than hand him over to you."

"I think we understand each other, Admiral."

"Very well then. Launch your fighters and have your ships give us access to the primary portal, and I will order the withdrawal."

"I need to brief my commanders. I will contact you shortly once orders have been given."

"Very well. Faulkner out." He then reactivated the secure command link between the carriers and the Cathedra.

"Good job, Jeff. Deneva has activated our present to the T'Kharr commander in the stealth pod and will be awaiting the order to launch," North said. "My display shows that Te'eq's ships are already moving away from the primary starlane portal, and a squadron of T'Kharr fighters are launching from the *Thola'aris*. I'm moving *Victory*, *Challenger*, and *Valor* toward the portal. *Pacifica* and *Endeavor* will withdraw slowly with *Kegar* on our flank. I want those specials ready to fire at a moment's notice."

Faulkner acknowledged and watched the drama unfold.

Ka'awon monitored the exchange and forced back the feeling that things were going too easily. Gra'akk's harsh voice interrupted his thoughts.

"Tar-Vel, the scientist has nearly finished assembling the protective shielding around the generator and says she will be ready to test it shortly. What are your instructions?"

"Stand by, Gra'akk," Ka'awon said as he switched channels. "Comm, get me Alta-Tar-Vel Te'eq."

Ka'awon explained to Te'eq that the test was nearly ready. Te'eq beamed with satisfaction. As smoothly as things seemed to be going, Te'eq couldn't resist rubbing it in the humans' faces.

"Move the *Ka'athiol* and her fleets to cover our flank, and transfer the generator and their scientist to the *Thola'aris*. We will hold off on the test until we have their commander. I want them to go back home knowing that we have both a working device and their commander. This will demoralize them for years to come."

"Are you certain you want to risk a transfer at this juncture, Tar-Vel? It might be dangerous."

Te'eq, misinterpreting Ka'awon's caution as selfish ambition, replied, "I know you want the glory of the test to be performed on your own ship, Ka'awon. You will be given due credit when the time comes. Carry out my orders."

"As you command, Alta-Tar-Vel," Ka'awon said, not wishing to antagonize his superior further.

Te'eq noticed his subordinate's lack of enthusiasm and said, "Why are you sullen, Ka'awon? We have scored a great victory."

"Something . . . does not feel right, Tar-Vel. I cannot put it into words."

"You worry too much, Ka'awon. If the burden of command is too much for you, I can find a replacement."

Ka'awon bristled at the rebuke but answered, "That will not be necessary, Tar-Vel."

"Good," Te'eq said. "Once the shuttle with the generator is transferred, move your ships to the secondary portal to cut that off as an escape route."

"As you command, Tar-Vel," Ka'awon said.

"One more thing, Ka'awon . . . as soon as we have both North and the generator on the *Thola'aris*, I will order an attack on the *Pacifica* and any ships still remaining. Not only will we take their commander, but will destroy his flagship as well."

SAS Pacifica

In the Cathedra, North watched both fleets dance and consolidate around each other, his fleets moving cautiously toward the first starlane portal and the enemy ships cautiously combining and cutting off any exit to the secondary and tertiary portals. North's five carriers and their escorts would take several moments to jump out of the system and were still within attack range of the T'Kharr ships if Te'eq reneged on his part of the deal. He saw the shuttle leave the *Ka'athiol* and head toward the *Thola'aris*, escorted by four destroyers. They were well out of range of their weapons. Nothing could be done.

Drake's calm voice chimed in. "Commander, Doctor Trent tells me that that shuttle has the energy wave of the generator. They are transferring it to the *Thola'aris*."

"Not surprising, Mat. Te'eq will want it as a prize. He won't allow a subordinate to steal his glory."

"What do you want to do?"

"Order targeting solutions on the *Thola'aris*. Follow the plan as we've laid it out. It doesn't matter which ship the generator is on just as long as we know where it is. They may not know we can track it. The only problem would be if it looked like they were heading to one of the starlane portals. We can't allow that. *Thola'aris* has moved far enough away that we could intercept them if they made a move to leave. If that looks like the case, I'll order the package to detonate."

"Aye aye, sir."

North saw that the bulk of the Alliance fleet had moved close enough to the portal that they could jump out fairly quickly. The squadron of T'Kharr fighters hovered off *Pacifica's* port quarter, looking menacing and deadly. *Pacifica* was in no danger so long as they kept their shields up, but point defenses had them targeted just in case. So far, so good.

Te'eq opened a channel to the *Endeavor*. "Admiral Faulkner, all ships are in position. Order *Pacifica* to drop her shields to allow the pod to pass through."

Faulkner drew a deep breath before responding over the open frequency, allowing Te'eq to monitor. "Stand by. Admiral Drake, lower a portion of your shields large enough to accommodate the pod."

Drake relayed the order, and on North's display, he saw a small gap appear in *Pacifica's* shields, just in front of the T'Kharr squadron. He could imagine how difficult it must be for those T'Kharr pilots to watch a gap open in an enemy ship's shields and be required to sit and watch without firing. He knew, however, that they would be disciplined enough to follow their orders. Te'eq was rumored to have many exotic and unpleasant methods of discipline and torture for those who disobeyed him.

North communicated with Deneva.

<Stand by, Major.>

<*Thola'aris* just sent a wide-beam transmission ordering the pod to launch.>

<Launch, Major.>

Deneva detached the pod from its hiding spot on *Pacifica's* hull and moved it toward the gap. The pod quickly shot through the opening and maneuvered toward the fighters. The T'Kharr ships gave no indication that they noticed the Alliance sub slip by them and into *Pacifica's* safety envelope. Once through, Drake ordered shields raised.

On the bridge of the *Thola'aris*, Zha'ar said, "Tar-Vel, a detector sweep confirms five T'Kharr life force signatures and one human on the pod. Also, the shuttle from the *Ka'athiol* has docked."

"Order recovery of the fighters and pod as quickly as possible, then tell the human commander they may begin their withdrawal," Te'eq said, relishing the coming meeting with Gra'akk and the scientist. "I am on my way to the landing bay to take a look at our new prize."

North began sending withdrawal instructions to the fleets. He watched as multiple flashes appeared on his display and felt his relief growing stronger with each flash. If he did have to order the package to be detonated, at least some of his ships would survive.

<Commander, this is Deneva. The sub is now armed with eight Mark 112 specials. Ready to launch on your command.>

<Very good, Major. Proceed.>

On the *Thola'aris* bridge, the detector subling saw a momentary dip in power of the *Pacifica's* dorsal shields. He thought about reporting it but figured the more inconspicuous he was, the better. Besides, it appeared to be a random power fluctuation.

North watched the sub leave *Pacifica's* shield perimeter and move toward the *Thola'aris*. North ordered *Pacifica* and *Kegar* to move closer to the *Thola'aris*, decreasing the range and exposing their port missile launchers to the ship. Once her shields dropped, North would fire so many missiles from *Pacifica* and *Kegar* that even if three quarters of them were destroyed before impact, the remainders would be more than enough to obliterate *Thola'aris* and the generator. *Pacifica* would undoubtedly be destroyed by the counter attack that would come shortly thereafter. They were too close to run.

Victory and her ships exited through the portal. The next part would be more difficult. Three fleets gone, two to go.

Te'eq walked into the landing bay just as Gra'akk, Julie, and the guards were leaving the shuttle, trailed by the anti-grav pallet containing the generator. The pictures Te'eq received from Ka'awon looked different from the device he saw before him until he realized that the protective alloy shielding had been assembled and now surrounded the generator.

He walked up to Julie Newman and towered over her. Gra'akk snapped to attention as Te'eq walked up along with the two guards. Julie felt malevolence emanating from this being. The sooner she was out of his presence, the better she would feel.

"Vett-Tar-Von Gra'akk, Alta-Tar-Vel," Gra'akk said. He hoped that Te'eq would remember his name when credit was doled out for this victory.

He looked at Gra'akk with little interest and said, "Is it ready?"

Gra'akk said, "It is ready to test on your command, Alta-Tar-Vel. This human scientist assures me it will perform as promised now that the shielding alloy is in place."

Te'eq turned toward her and noticed the translator clipped to her collar. He then spoke to her directly.

"Activate it."

Julie averted her gaze from his cold eyes and walked up to the device, retrieving the remote she'd taken from Jared. She touched several studs on the front of the remote and was rewarded with a low hum as the generator began to cycle up to full power. Once the energy buffer was primed, she could fully activate the generator and prove her worth. She walked over to the generator and touched a button on the surface of the cover that produced a small control panel and status screen. As the generator continued its power up, a message popped up on the screen demanding the activation code.

Te'eq grew impatient and demanded, "What is taking so long?"

Julie continued without looking at him and said, "I need to enter the activation code. We didn't just make this with a switch you flip to turn it on."

"Take care with your words, human. You may be of value to us now, but I will not tolerate insolence from an inferior species."

Julie continued working and replied, "No offense intended, Fleet Marshal. I am verifying the activation code and preparing to enter it now. It should only take a few moments . . ."

On the *Pacifica*, Jared Trent was studying his screen.

"Admiral Drake!" he shouted, drawing looks from all over the bridge.

Drake looked his way and said, "What is it, Doctor?"

"The signal from the generator . . . it's changing. They're channeling energy into the activation buffer. They're about to turn it on."

Drake's eyes went wide. "What will happen when they do?"

"We need to get out of here!"

"Doctor!" Drake demanded. "What will happen?"

Jared took a deep breath and forced himself to calmly explain, realizing that these men and women weren't scientists.

"If the alloy is installed, calibrated, and properly aligned, nothing will happen other than a change in the power readings on the screens. But I programmed a failsafe into the activation sequence. The unit will ask for an activation code, then after a little while, ask for a second code. Julie only knows about the first code."

Austin, who'd been standing in the background next to Jared, said, "So what happens when they can't input the second code? Will it blow up? That might actually be a good thing . . . solves our problem for us . . ."

"No, you don't understand," Jared said, forcing calm into his voice. "You can't install a self-destruct into this type of device. I programmed it so that if the second code isn't entered within sixty seconds, the unit will intentionally de-calibrate itself and activate."

Drake caught on first. "So you're saying that the generator will disconnect itself from the shielding that protects everything around it, then turn itself on?"

"That's exactly what I'm saying."

Drake lunged toward his chair and stabbed the direct voice link to the Cathedra.

"Commander! We need to get out of here now! Doctor Trent has rigged the generator to activate without a proper security code, and it looks as if the T'Kharr are trying to turn it on!"

The sub pilot sent, <On station, Commander. Ready to fire on your command.>

<Belay that. Break off and head toward the starlane. Jump as soon as you can.>

<Yes, sir.>

He switched to voice and said, "How long it will take the field from the *Thola'aris* to envelop our ships?"

Jared stepped closer to Drake's chair and said, "At this close proximity and being stationary, no more than five minutes from activation. Not much time."

North quickly sent orders to *Endeavor* to jump out and slaved *Pacifica's* ships to jump out on a single command from him. He knew this move was dangerous. He risked a collision in the starlane by jumping all the ships at once, but he had run out of time.

"This is Faulkner. We won't leave you, Commander."

"I have no intention of sacrificing the *Pacifica*, Admiral Faulkner. Jump now!"

"Yes, sir," Faulkner replied reluctantly, and he turned and issued the order.

By the time the other ships jumped, he would have just enough time to jump himself before the wave front struck. At least, that's what he hoped.

North realized at that moment there would be no chance of recovering Remy if the T'Kharr activated the generator. The realization felt like a knife through his heart. He saw the purple signature at a point near the Miratev star, in position to deploy when ordered. He opened a link to the young man.

<Remy, this is Commander North.>

<Yes, sir. I'm in position and ready to fire.>

<I know, Lieutenant. The T'Kharr are trying to activate the generator. Doctor Trent made sure that if they do, the result will be fatal.>

<That's good to hear, sir. I realize that leaves no time to recover me. I'm too far out.>

<Yes.>

<I was prepared for this when I volunteered, Commander. I'll wait until *Pacifica* is safe before activating the package.>

<That may not be necessary. If we escape, you wouldn't need to detonate the weapon. We could send a sub back to recover you.>

<You know as well as I do that the T'Kharr will still try and salvage the generator even if it kills a few of them. Besides, those other seven carriers will follow you and hit you as soon as they can. I can make sure that doesn't happen. Sir, please allow me to atone for my failure.>

<There was no failure, Lieutenant. You carried out your mission admirably, but if this is what you want, I'll respect your decision. Transmitting authentication authority and final activation codes now. You are a credit to Omega, Lieutenant. A credit to the code.>

<For the code, sir.>

<For the code. May the Creator bless you.>

North switched to his display and watched as the last of *Endeavor's* escorts blinked out. He then noticed something that he'd anticipated but hoped they could avoid. Three of the enemy carriers were moving toward his position and were flanking the *Pacifica*.

Now that they had everything they needed, there was no need to live up to their bargain. Not surprising, but he still had a trick or two up his sleeve. He figured that the pod, supposedly containing him, had just landed on the *Thola'aris*. Things were about to accelerate quickly. He wished he could be there to see their faces.

Imperial flagship Thola'aris

Te'eq turned to observe the pod containing North landing in the bay. He looked back at Julie and figured she could continue her work while he welcomed their newest guest in person. He walked over to the pod, flanked by a full attack squad, rifles at the ready.

"Open it!" he barked to the nearest trooper, who immediately slung his rifle and cycled the lock to the door.

The door hissed open, and Te'eq puffed up his chest in anticipation of this meeting. He waited for several moments, seeing nothing emerge from the pod. His senses screamed caution, so he ordered troopers into the pod. Four armed troopers dashed through the door and were inside for several moments before the lead trooper came out.

"The pod is empty, Tar-Vel."

Blind, hot fury enveloped Te'eq, and he pushed past the trooper to see for himself. As he reached the control center, he saw six small pulsing orbs that he immediately recognized as life sign simulators. His eyes dilated in anger. Then he saw the small squ-are box next to one of the orbs.

The lead trooper saw Te'eq focus on the box and interjected, "It appears to be a relay transmitter, Tar-Vel. It is tied in to the navigation console and pods transmitter, giving the illusion that the sender is communicating from inside of the ship."

Te'eq spun on the trooper and snarled, "I know what a trans-mitter relay is used for! Vile, dishonorable—"

A hologram sprang to life, and the image of Major Deneva appeared in the cabin in front of Te'eq and the others.

The hologram then spoke in perfect T'Kharr. "Greetings. This hologram has been programmed to recognize certain mem-bers of the T'Kharr hierarchy and address them personally. Ahh, Alta-Tar-Vel Te'eq. I see the shi'ia-khar wanted his personal lap-dog on this particular project. I do wish this was a personal meet-ing, but we can't get everything we want."

The image shimmered slightly, accessing the prerecorded message that would have played no matter who was present.

"Grand Commander North expresses his deepest regrets that he cannot attend this meeting. He currently has more pr-essing matters to attend to on the *Pacifica*, where he is safe, so-und, and still in command. We wanted to thank you for the intelligence your shock troops provided us. It allowed us to get a good look at your new stealth pods and learn how they work. This is only one of eight that survived, by the way. The other sev-en left with the ships that just jumped out. I pushed to have a bomb placed aboard this pod, but the commander wanted events to play out as they obviously have. Thank you for your coopera-tion."

The hologram morphed into a symbol that Te'eq didn't rec-ognize. The symbol floated in the air, spinning slowly.

Te'eq roared in fury and said, "I will reduce the *Pacifica* to cosmic dust!"

He walked directly through the slowly spinning symbol on his way to the door. Even if he'd had knowledge of human Greek letters, Te'eq wouldn't have understood the significance of the letter Ω floating in the air in front of him.

Te'eq burst out of the pod and stalked toward Gra'akk and Julie, who was still bent over the generator. He was just about to signal the bridge to attack when Julie spoke.

"Something is wrong . . . it's asking for a second activation code."

Te'eq looked at her and walked closer.

"What does that mean?" he demanded.

Julie shook her head, panic rising in her voice, and said, "I only know of one code that the science team had for this device."

"Well then, try entering it again!" Te'eq shouted.

Julie furiously entered the first code again, and a metallic voice said, "Incorrect. Sixty seconds to activation."

Julie's eyes grew wide as she watched the status screen change.

"It . . . it's decoupling from the shielding . . . all by itself."

The metallic voice intoned, "Forty-five . . . forty-four . . . forty-three . . . forty-two . . ."

"Stop it!" Gra'akk screamed.

"I can't! There are literally billions of possible combinations and codes!"

"Then destroy it!" Te'eq yelled as he grabbed a rifle from one of the guards and took aim. Julie got out of the way just before Te'eq opened up with the rifle and emptied a full magazine into the machine. The projectiles harmlessly bounced off the casing.

"Thirty-two . . . thirty-one . . . thirty . . . twenty-nine . . ."

Te'eq threw the rifle to the deck. Then he and Gra'akk turned and ran toward the lift that would take them to the escape pods.

Julie slowly sank down on the deck next to the device. "Jared . . ." she whispered. Despite herself, a smile crept across her face, and she shook her head slowly. "You sneaky bastard."

The guards who had been tasked with guarding Julie watched Te'eq and Gra'akk running as quickly as they could from the area of the generator. It didn't take them long to figure out what was happening and to run after their leaders.

Julie didn't even try to run, knowing that there was no safe place within an AU.

"Twelve . . . eleven . . . ten . . . nine . . ."

She felt the lump form in her throat as she thought of her family. How she'd disgraced them. She prayed they would be safe and would never learn the details of her involvement.

"Four . . . three . . ."

At least she would be free of the implant. And free from the pain.

"Two . . . one . . . activation matrix enabled . . ."

Te'eq had just reached the lift when the generator activated. Immediately, he felt the temperature drop sharply in the room and continue to go down.

When the lift doors opened, he pulled the two technicians out and leapt inside, followed by Gra'akk. As the doors closed, he could hear screams coming from the landing bay.

Then he saw a wave of T'Kharr running in his direction. He slammed his fist against the button that closed the doors and felt the lift come to life. As the lift doors closed, he saw the pleading eyes of a technician just approaching the door and felt an icy breeze from the corridor.

The lift accelerated upward, and the lights abruptly went dark. Both he and Gra'akk were lifted from the floor and slammed down hard as the lift screeched to a halt well short of where they should've been.

"What is happening?" Gra'akk said in the pitch black of the lift car.

Te'eq felt along the wall until he felt the panel he was looking for and smashed his fist into it. The chemical emergency lighting panel activated, illuminating their car in a greenish hue. Te'eq could see his breath in the air and realized that the temperature was still dropping rapidly.

He tried to activate his personal comm and said, "Bridge . . . bridge, this is Te'eq. Respond."

He examined the device and saw that the power cell was being drained as they spoke and was now below usable levels.

Gra'akk looked down and saw the kinetic energy wave coming up from the floor, which quickly enveloped his feet, freezing them to the deck plates. He screamed in agony as Te'eq jumped up onto the railing just in time to avoid the wave himself.

He looked up and tried to reach the access panel leading out onto the roof of the car, then chanced another look at Gra'akk. His face was twisted in pain as the wave crept up his body, then enveloped his head, his eyes freezing and turning milky white.

The wave next caught Te'eq, freezing him instantly to the railing and to the wall. He didn't even have time to scream as the wave overcame him and accelerated up and away from its origin.

A small shift in the car broke Te'eq free from his perch, and his frozen form tumbled down, striking Gra'akk, who was still standing upright, frozen in position. As Te'eq's body struck Gra'akk, the two bodies shattered into millions of small shards, all heat and energy sucked out of them.

SAS Pacifica

The bridge crew of the *Pacifica* watched a white wave begin to emanate from the area of one of the *Thola'aris's* flight decks. As the generator voraciously absorbed every bit of kinetic energy, every power source and every life it encountered went completely dark. The wave moved quickly toward the front and rear of the big ship.

"Their shields just dropped!" Ensign Craig shouted excitedly. "The carrier is completely unprotected!"

"Missiles are arming . . . tubes one through twenty and forty-one through sixty. Firing on command from the Cathedra. *Forty*, repeat, *forty* missiles are away!"

Generally, a missile launch couldn't be felt on a ship as large as the *Pacifica*, but forty simultaneous launches actually could affect the ship's course. The effect was felt on the bridge.

"The commander isn't taking any chances," Drake said as he jumped into his chair. He saw the tactical readout from his Cathedra interface and hit the button for fleetwide broadcast.

"All commands, prepare to jump."

"Incoming! Every T'Kharr ship in range just launched missiles at us! Impact of the first wave in ninety seconds!"

North saw his missiles streak toward the dying hulk of the *Thola'aris*. He noted over a hundred enemy missiles heading toward his one ship. They'd completely ignored the escorts and fired everything they had at him. This was obviously personal. He slowed his slaved ships to .0012 light speed and prepared to jump them into the starlane.

"Do not let them escape!" Ka'awon shouted as he commanded a course correction to intercept. He'd watched in fascination as the life signs on the *Thola'aris* blinked out one by one. The *Thola'aris*, the pride of the shi'ia-khar's fleet, was dead. As a final insult, *Pacifica* had launched an immense wave of missiles against the now unprotected carrier, not only trying to deny them the generator, but also deprive them of the shi'ia-khar's favorite ship.

He watched in satisfaction as *Thola'aris's* escorts, along with the other three carriers in range, had launched a massive wave of missiles at the *Pacifica* on his command. They wouldn't be able to jump before the first wave struck.

North realized that approximately twenty-five enemy missiles would reach them before they could make the jump. "Point defense batteries on automatic control. Let's hope we can thin out the wave before they can hit us."

Normally, the escort ships could intercept many of the missiles fired at the carrier, but they were locked on course and speed for the jump.

"Admiral, twenty of our missiles that were fired at the *Thola'aris* have changed course toward the closest wave of enemy missiles," Craig said. "The triggers have been switched to series proximity detonation. I think the commander is trying to blow them up at once and make a wall of fire and try to take out a few of them."

Drake smiled. It was a long shot, but they might be able to take out a few of them before they hit. It just might make the difference.

"Time to impact on the missiles fired at the *Thola'aris*."

"Admiral, the missiles . . . they're slowing down!" Craig yelled as they watched the screen. The missiles had met the expanding wave emanating from the *Thola'aris*.

Jared Trent looked at the screen and said, "The generator . . . it's drawing the kinetic energy from the missiles."

Drake and the bridge crew watched with frustration as the forty missiles fired from the *Pacifica* at the dying *Thola'aris* slowly stopped, frozen in position inside of the voracious energy wave well away from striking home on *Thola'aris*.

A cheer went up over the bridge of the *Ka'athiol* as the emperor's flagship was spared destruction.

Ka'awon shouted, "Status of our missiles fired at the *Pacifica*?"

A subling answered, "Most were caught in the energy field, as were the enemy missiles, but sixteen remain on target. Impact in twenty seconds."

Ka'awon commanded, "Move all ships away to a safe distance to avoid the energy field. Order *Bi'imsaar* to launch fighters and attack the *Pacifica*."

"Yes, sir," Zha'ar answered with glee.

"All hands, brace for impact!" Craig said as the sixteen missiles slammed into *Pacifica's* port shields. Everyone who had been on his or her feet was thrown to the floor, and sparks erupted from several panels.

Drake was smart enough to be sitting when the missiles hit. "Damage control, all stations!"

Captain Frost reported, "Damage to the main drives. As of right now, we are unable to maintain .0012 light speed and are falling behind the escorts. Shields are down to 10 percent and barely holding. If more had hit simultaneously, they might have taken down our shields completely. Shields are regenerating. Heavy casualties in all portside sections, and the air plant is out of commission. Damage control is moving to seal the hull breaches and bring the plant back online, but it's bad down there."

Without .0012 light speed, they would be unable to breach the portal . . . or jump.

Drake took in the report and nodded. "Start moving non-essential personnel to the rescue decks."

Frost looked alarmed, "Sir?"

"Do it!" Drake snapped. "While we still have time."

Frost nodded and said, "Yes, sir."

North felt the impact of the missiles and watched *Pacifica's* shields drop into the lower red status. They'd held and were re-generating, but the ship was now vulnerable to fighter attack.

Worse, the mains were damaged, and they were no longer able to jump. They were out of time. He knew what had to be done.

<Remy, this is North.>

<Go, Commander.>

<You are cleared to execute.>

<Yes, sir.>

"Let's see you try and outrun this," Remy said to himself. He pushed forward on the yoke used to fly the device and dove into the heart of the star.

Ka'awon watched the missiles impact *Pacifica* and felt frustration that the first wave hadn't taken down her shields completely. He noted with satisfaction that *Pacifica's* engines were damaged. They wouldn't make it to the starlane. There was no hope of surviving the approaching fighter onslaught.

"*Pacifica's* escorts have jumped, Tar-Vel, but the carrier remains."

"Order all wings from *Bi'imsaar* to attack," Ka'awon ordered with a smile.

Drake saw the command come from the Cathedra as soon as the escorts jumped and hit the klaxons.

"Launch everything we have! Abandon ship! I repeat, abandon ship! This is not a drill! All starlane-capable craft, jump out immediately! The commander has assumed ship control. All bridge crew, make your way to the rescue decks!"

Austin shouted from the upper deck of the bridge, "Admiral, what about the commander?"

A powerful explosion from somewhere deep in the ship nearly knocked them off their feet.

"He's ordered us to evacuate, General. There's no way we can get to him right now even if we wanted to. The Cathedra is inaccessible while engaged. We'll have to hope he can make it to his personal rescue pod in time."

Austin pounded the railing in frustration, and Drake said, "I don't like it either, General, but I've been ordered to personally evacuate you on the commander's corvette. Our fighters are launching and will cover while we escape. Follow me, sir. Please!"

Reluctantly, Austin followed Drake to the lift that would take them to the dorsal bay.

Pacifica's alert squadron was the first to scream out of the landing bays, scrambling to avoid the enemy fighters as soon as they cleared the ship.

"Alert Leader to Alert Squadron, the uglies are picking off rescue pods as they launch," Lt. Commander Jericho said. "Split up and cover the launches from the rescue decks. Try and give those people a shot at getting away."

As he turned to fly toward the starboard rescue deck, Jericho saw streams of ships leaving *Pacifica* from all three bays and rescue pods firing straight out of the side of the main carrier structure.

T'Kharr fighters were sweeping in unopposed and picking off the rescue craft, blowing up as many as they could. Other enemy fighters were pounding at *Pacifica's* weapons platforms, assuring they would pose no threat to them. A bright flare caught his attention as one of *Pacifica's* main antenna arrays exploded in a brilliant blue-white flash.

Drake and Austin made it to the dorsal bay and made sure to stay out of the flight line as tugs, bombers, and anything that could fly launched at a furious pace. The commander's corvette was already warmed up and ready to launch. Austin and Drake both shouted to anyone in proximity who wasn't boarding a ship to get aboard the corvette as quickly as possible. Several maintenance techs turned and ran to the ship, grateful to be one of the lucky few.

The pilot called back to Drake, "We're at emergency capacity, Admiral! We have to leave! The bay looks like it's about to buckle!"

Drake took one last look around and saw that everyone was heading to a ship. He slammed the hatch controls.

"Launch!" he yelled as the pilot punched the thrusters and shot toward the atmosphere shield. Just as they cleared the shield, a missile fired from a T'Kharr fighter slammed into the emitter and explosively depressurized the bay.

The corvette shuddered violently as it cleared the shockwave. Drake looked back and saw the air venting into space, carrying with it debris, bodies, and ships expelled into the cold void.

The corvette pilot said, "We're on course for the starlane, Admiral, but I'm picking up a new group of signals from ahead of us in the direction of our retreating ships. They . . . they look like Alliance fighters, sir."

Austin said, "Can't be ours. They're all back at *Pacifica*."

Drake went to the nearest scanner and pulled up the images. Three distinct waves of ships were coming toward them. Suddenly, a large flash from the starlane appeared in the center of his screen.

"Admiral!" the pilot shouted excitedly.

"I see her, Lieutenant," Drake said with a grin.

Twenty-three years late, SAS *Lysithea* had arrived to take care of unfinished business.

"Striker Leader to all wings, thin out those fighters attacking *Pacifica*. Her shields are down. Let's give her rescue ships the time they need to jump out."

Six full squadrons of Valkyrie fighters from *Lysithea* streaked past the corvette and toward the *Pacifica*, forming a protective bubble around the carrier. Even in outdated fighters, at three to one, the T'Kharr fighters were no match. The waves of Valkyries swept over the enemy fighters and thinned them out, keeping them from engaging any more rescue ships or fleeing craft.

"Start recovering as many of the non-starlane-capable escape pods as possible!" Admiral Thorne yelled to his bridge crew. "Flank weapons platforms open fire with everything you have!"

North opened a channel to Thorne. "Nice to see you again, Admiral, even if you are an insubordinate bugger."

Thorne's image coalesced on a holo screen in front of North. "We knew what we were getting into, sir. Everyone on this ship volunteered to come back and try and make a difference. We may have failed at Tig Ferendal, but not this time . . . not this time . . ."

"Save as many of my people as you can, Admiral. *Pacifica* is lost. I'm headed to my—" Suddenly, a violent explosion cut off their transmission.

"Commander?" Thorne yelled. "Commander North, come in, please!" He then turned toward the communications station when he heard Drake's voice come over the speaker.

"Thorne, this is Drake. Glad to see you, but you must stay ahead of that energy damping wave. It's from the kinetic generator and will kill anything it touches. I'm issuing recall orders to all of our fighters and ordering them to jump into the lane now. *Pacifica's* engines are down. Don't get caught, Admiral."

"Understood," Thorne said. "Recall all fighter wings. Order them to jump into the lane as soon as possible, and transmit a warning about that energy wave. Bring us in aspect to jump."

As *Lysithea's* fighters received their recall orders, one ship headed for the *Pacifica* slammed onto the deck in a combat landing and skidded to a halt in front of the crew members who were boarding the last shuttle. The pilot exited his ship and threw his helmet into the cockpit.

As his feet hit the deck, a crew chief yelled, "Are you crazy? This ship is—" then stopped mid-sentence.

"The bridge!" the pilot screamed. "Which lift goes to the bridge?"

The speechless crew chief pointed toward one of the lifts and watched as the pilot sprinted in that direction. The chief could only look after him, at a loss for words as the door to his ship slammed shut.

North arrived in his office just off the command deck and stumbled out of the cart that had brought him up from the Cathedra. His head exploded in pain as he tried to take several steps toward the door leading to the bridge.

The pinprick hemorrhages, nausea, and blazing headaches that were common after an extended Cathedra session were hitting him full force. Normally, a medical team would be on hand after he disengaged, but they'd all left. Hopefully, they were safely in the starlanes. An explosion rocked the ship, and he felt something strike him in the head.

He fell to the deck and put his hand to his head, seeing it come away covered with blood. He crawled to the door as a new wave of vertigo swept over him. As he hit the button to open the door, he looked up into the face of a man standing in the doorway. Blood ran into his vision, and his eyes refused to focus. At first, he thought it was an illusion until the man grabbed him and put an arm over his shoulder.

"Jason?" North said, struggling to focus his eyes on the man.

"Come on," Jason North said as he dragged his brother to the lift. "Time to go home . . . Commander."

Brandon faded in and out of consciousness and woke up seated in the rear seat of a fighter craft.

"Entry in three . . . two . . . one . . ." Jason said.

Brandon saw normal space disappear and felt the familiar shift into the starlane.

ICC Ka'athiol

Ka'awon slammed his fists into his chair in frustration as he watched the ships blink out. The appearance of the unidentified human carrier had taken them by surprise, but she'd only stayed long enough to recover escaping ships and hadn't stopped to engage them. Let them run. They still had their prize, even though they would have to figure out a way to recover it.

Also, the enemy had abandoned the *Pacifica*. Ka'awon reveled as he watched her burn in space. He wished they could capture what was left of her and bring her back home, but the kinetic wave would overwhelm her long before they could salvage her.

A subling spoke. "Tar-Vel, we are able to stay ahead of the kinetic wave, but it continues to expand."

Ka'awon turned to Zha'ar and said, "The data from the human scientist said the wave has a limited range. Eventually, it will stabilize and we can figure out how to salvage it."

"Very good, Tar-Vel," Zha'ar said with a smile. They would have plenty of time now that the enemy fleets were gone.

"Tar-Vel! Something is happening to the star! It is destabilizing!"

Ka'awon spun and said, "What do you mean destabilizing?"

"We just registered a quantum detonation at its core. The star is collapsing on itself and is about to go supernova!"

"Impossible!" Ka'awon said. "We would have had some type of warning. Stars don't just spontaneously explode!"

"How long?" Zha'ar demanded.

"The shockwave will reach us in just under one-third of a twelfth cycle."

Ka'awon spun and shouted to Zha'ar, "Order all ships to escape through the nearest starlane portal! Do it now!"

Every space-faring race knew the consequences of a supernova. Zha'ar didn't have to be told twice. He immediately ordered his fleet to head to the secondary starlane portal and told the survivors from the *Thola'aris* fleet to exit through the primary.

He knew those ships wouldn't make it. Those three carriers and their fleets were much closer to the star than they were. They were doomed. He wasn't completely certain they would make it themselves. He'd never jumped out of a system where the star had gone nova. He didn't know what it would do to the starlanes.

Zha'ar and the bridge crew all watched the feed from the starlane buoy next to the primary portal as the quickly expanding wave from the exploding star swept over the *Thola'aris* fleet—eighty in all—and swept them away like feathers scattered in a strong wind. Within seconds, the ships were gone, along with the prized kinetic generator.

"Tar-Vel, the wave is accelerating! It will reach us in moments!"

"Ready to jump," the navigator said.

"Jump!" Zha'ar yelled, and the *Ka'athiol* blinked out of normal space and into the compressed space of the starlane.

As they confirmed entry into the starlane, Ka'awon yelled, "Report! How many ships made it?"

The detector subling checked his readings several times before swallowing hard and reporting, "Tar-Vel . . . I am reading only the destroyers *Bi'istin* and *Ca'alodek*. I am not receiving transponder signals from any of our other ships. I fear they are lost."

Ka'awon nearly collapsed from the reality of that news. One hundred fifty-seven ships. Tens of thousands of crew, and they had left with nothing to show for it. They'd lost the technology, failed to capture North. North . . . He was responsible for the sabotage of the device and the star's destruction.

Ka'awon felt the blind, raw anger boiling up inside of him and swore on the blood of his own offspring that he and North would meet again someday, and the outcome would be very different. He would extract every bit of useful information from him, then torture him to within an inch of his life. Afterward, when he begged for death, he would oblige, then feast on his corpse. This was not over, not by a long shot.

Miratev starlane

"*Lysithea*, this is Striker Four. I require priority clearance to land. I have Commander North on board. Request a medical team stand by."

Suddenly, a different voice broke in and said, "Striker Four, you are ordered to change course and land immediately in *Endeavor's* dorsal bay. The commander requires special medical services only available here. Acknowledge."

"Acknowledged, *Endeavor*," he said. "I'm in the pattern." He approached the atmosphere shield and gently settled onto *Endeavor's* flight deck.

As the canopy rose, the pilot quickly jumped down and got out of the way while Brandon was gently lowered to a gurney that had been wheeled up next to the ship. He saw an admiral and a marine general with six stars on his collar approach the gurney and talk in hushed whispers to the medical team. The general patted Brandon on the shoulder and stood aside as they wheeled him away. The pilot removed his flight helmet as the admiral and general walked up to him.

He snapped to attention and fired off a crisp salute. Drake and Austin stopped in their tracks as they laid eyes on the young man, a carbon copy of Brandon North, minus twenty years.

"Lt. Jason North, sirs. Is the commander going to be all right?"

Drake returned the salute and said, "He'll be fine, Lieutenant, in no small part thanks to you."

"That's good to hear, sir," he said with a smile.

"At ease, Lieutenant," Austin said, and the man relaxed.

"Lieutenant, we were monitoring the traffic between the fighters and *Lysithea*," Drake said. "You were recalled but disobeyed orders and boarded the *Pacifica*. She was all but abandoned at that point. How did you know that the commander was still aboard, let alone where he was on the ship?"

Jason looked pensive for a moment and said, "Sir, I'm not sure. It was an overwhelming urge to go aboard and find him. I don't know what exactly happened, but I swear—and I know this sounds strange—but I swear I heard him call for help in my head. I was compelled to go to him regardless of orders." He then broke eye contact with Drake and said, "I realize that's no excuse for insubordination, sir, but—"

Austin said, "I think we can let this one slide, Lieutenant."

Jason met their gaze again and smiled. "Yes, sir."

Drake then said, "Now, why don't we see how your brother is doing?"

SAS Endeavor

"You okay, Brand?" a concerned Austin asked.

Drake looked at Austin and said, "This is common after an extended link with the Cathedra. It's not generally known, but the user suffers small pinprick brain hemorrhages after disengaging from the Cathedra after an extended session. Nothing our doctors can't repair. They've done it before. Headache, nausea, nosebleeds, those are common."

"Has this ever killed anyone?" he asked, the concern plain in his voice.

"Not yet, you old codger," Brandon said from his bed in *Endeavor's* medical bay, eyes still clamped shut, bloody bandage still on his wound. "Give me ten minutes in the medical reaction chamber, and I'll be good as new."

Drake smirked at Brandon and said, "That's not entirely true. The first enhanced Cathedra test subjects suffered severe brain damage. Some did die."

"That was before it was discovered that a user implanted with a telesponder could operate the device with minimal and repairable side effects," Brandon chimed in. "Only then did the technology become practical."

"Insanity. How is it that I never knew this? I've known about the Cathedra project from its inception."

"Did you know the technology was going to be abandoned until Omega grabbed it?" Brandon asked.

"You're kidding."

"They're everywhere, my friend. More entwined in events than anyone realizes. Always in the shadows. It must've killed Tyler, Deneva, and the lot to have to work so openly with the line soldiers and crew, but we couldn't have succeeded without them. I'll be sure to remind Terred about that."

Brandon looked concerned for a moment and said, "*Lysithea* . . . she's safe?"

"Tucked in behind us in the starlane."

"He saved us. Thorne, that insubordinate, heroic bastard . . . he saved *Pacifica's* crew. I'll make sure the insubordinate part doesn't appear on his record."

Austin nodded and said, "You might want to thank someone else too, Brand."

Just then, a young man in an old-style flight suit came up to the bedside. Austin and Drake moved out of his way and let them chat.

"I'll be damned . . ."

"Hey, Brand . . . Commander . . . sir . . . I'm not even sure what to call you."

"Jason . . . I'd hoped . . . they didn't know if . . ."

"I just happened to be among the last group of stasis tubes to be revived," he said with a smile as they grasped hands warmly. "I wish we could've met sooner, but that's not how it worked out."

"That's okay," Brandon said with a laugh. "I guess we have some catching up to do."

Brandon was suddenly overcome with a wave of nausea and lay back down on his pillow. Jason stepped back as the doctor placed a scanner on Brandon's forehead. He promptly applied an analgesic injection and applied a hyperfeuron patch onto his neck.

Austin leaned in close to Drake and said, "He knows about the implant, I assume?"

Drake answered, "He's been cleared to treat current and former Omega operatives and knows about the tech. He's the only member of the medical staff cleared to look at the commander after a session."

"Omega?" Jason asked.

Austin replied, "Later."

The doctor closed his scanner and said, "Fairly common symptoms after an extended session. We need to take you for a rest in the reaction chamber, Commander. No more than an hour this time. I promise."

"Doctors . . . all of them lie, you know that? I get to walk this time, though. No gurney."

Austin and Drake both smiled at that. North seemed fine, albeit a bit surly. Understandable.

The doctor smiled and said, "If you say so, sir."

North arose from the bed, the pain killer already taking effect, and walked toward the door, doctor in tow.

He looked back at Jason and said, "We'll talk later."

"You got it," Jason said, returning the smile.

CHAPTER TWENTY-FOUR

Earth

Symons had already heard the news, and it wasn't good. The whole thing was a gigantic failure. They'd failed to obtain the technology, both his operatives were presumed dead, and he'd heard through one of his contacts that North's fleet had even managed to decimate the T'Kharr ships sent to Miratev and locate his long-lost twin. How could things have gone so wrong? All the planning, all the money spent, and he felt the need to medicate himself just to avoid a stroke.

The worst part now was that his "associates" were looking for him in order to bring him back to T'Kharr space and answer for the failure. If not for the compliance implant they'd put into him, he'd already be off-world, plotting a new round of revenge against the Norths. The implant would kill him if he tried to leave Earth. He knew he had to disable the implant before they found him or he was dead for sure. There would be no talking his way out of this one.

The contact had put him in touch with another individual who'd sold him a procedure that would allegedly nullify the implant. When Symons had read the instructions, he wasn't sure if death by the implant would be any worse than the cure.

He sat in the tiny, anonymous motel room and pondered the mixture in the glass before him. There was enough Verterax-20 liquid nerve compound in the mixture to kill most people. Even if he survived, he would require a completely cloned lower intestine and repairs to his spinal column. He checked the status screen on the modified medbot/defibrillator machine that he'd obtained from the same source and made sure the settings were correct.

He took several deep breaths, closed his eyes, and downed the solution in several large gulps. He immediately wished that he'd opted for death as the poison and other ingredients attacked his digestive tract where the implant was lodged. When it hit his stomach and slid into his intestines, the real pain began.

Symons was no stranger to pain, but even he was overcome by the sheer agony he felt. The nerve agent had seized his vocal chords, only allowing the sound of air rushing out of his mouth as his body spasmed involuntarily and let out a silent scream.

After several agonizing moments, the pain shut down his nervous system, and he passed out, his heart stopping at the same time. The medbot immediately administered several shocks, restarting his heart. At the same moment, it called for emergency services to be sent to the motel, continuing to administer shocks as needed to keep his heart going until they could arrive.

The machine sent information ahead that the victim had suffered irreparable damage to his intestinal tract and minor reparable damage to his spinal cord. At the hospital, cloned parts were placed on standby and would be ready when the patient arrived.

Symons slowly became aware of his surroundings and realized he should be feeling more pain than he was. He glanced at the medbot and reveled in the feeling of the painkiller it had given him. He looked over at the table where the nullifier lay and saw the light blinking a fast amber, indicating that the implant had malfunctioned and was offline.

He glanced down at his stomach and saw that it was distended and covered with purple and black bruises. It looked just as the instructions had described if the procedure was successful. The concoction had neutralized the implant and converted the mutagenic enzyme inside of it to an inert state. His body would absorb and eventually pass what was left of the implant, and after several days in the hospital, he'd be all right.

The important thing was that he'd survived. He needed to get off-world as soon as he was able. Someplace remote where he could plan things out. Now he had another North to kill. No more games. No more attacks on targets intended to make North suffer. This time, when he finally met Brandon and Jason North in person, he would be there when the commander and his brother drew their last breaths.

SAS Endeavor

Brandon purposefully walked down the corridor leading to the forward missile batteries on the carrier *Endeavor*. Once in the starlane, they'd received news about the deaths of Lan and Denara. He'd ordered Faulkner not to tell Rando Falco about his parents. He felt that job was his. He owed it to Rando.

As he rounded the corner leading into the compartment, he saw Rando running checks on the weapons and barking orders to his section crew. Brandon couldn't help feeling proud of him. This news would devastate the boy.

One of the specialists caught sight of the grand commander and snapped to attention. The rest followed suit.

"As you were," Brandon said. "I need to speak to Ensign Falco alone."

All the crew members quickly left the compartment.

Rando smiled and said, "Good to see you, sir. That was a close one."

Brandon nodded his head but didn't return the smile. Rando sensed there was something wrong.

"What is it?"

North found he couldn't meet the boy's gaze and had to take a moment to compose himself.

"Rando . . . I have some bad news. It came with the batch updates from Earth when we hit the starlane. Your parents . . . they've been killed."

Rando's face fell, and he said, "Killed? How?"

Brandon struggled for words and said, "They were assassinated . . . by a man trying to make me suffer for a past mission I participated in. He couldn't go after any of my family, so he went after them. I'm so sorry, Rando."

Disbelief scrawled on his face, Rando stumbled backward against a storage locker behind him. Brandon stepped up and supported him by the arm. Rando looked down toward the floor and suddenly became overwhelmed with grief. Heavy sobs racked his body for several moments, and all Brandon could think to do was grasp him in a tight hug until he composed himself.

After several moments, Rando abruptly pushed Brandon away, anger filling his features.

"Who . . . who killed them? I want to know his name."

"Rando . . . I . . ." Brandon started.

"Tell me!" the boy shouted, unable to keep his emotions in check. "Tell me his name!"

Emotion overcame him, and he collapsed into North's arms. The commander guided Rando to a chair and held on to him.

"Rando, I'm sorry," Brandon offered. "I don't know what else to say. I'm so sorry."

Rando whispered, "Sorry . . ." then wiped his eyes and looked around the room. "Thank you, Commander . . . for telling me in person. Is there anything else? My crew needs to complete the diagnostic of this turret."

"Rando, I've arranged for a relief officer. She'll complete the diagnostic."

"Commander, I want to keep working—" he started to say.

Brandon replied, "I know, but I need you to come with me."

An officer quietly came into the room and said, "Reporting as ordered, sir. I'll take it from here."

"Thank you, Lieutenant," Brandon said. "Carry on." He guided Rando out of the room.

"Walters, Baron, Terrell, get back in here on the double!" the lieutenant shouted. "We have a diagnostic to finish. The commander is leaving."

As the crewmen filed back in, giving North a respectful distance, he led a shocked and emotionally spent Rando from the room, headed for his quarters.

SAS Endeavor, *several days later*

Jason North and several others crowded around the viewport that would give them the best view as they exited the starlane and entered the Sol system. From the perspective of the crew of the *Lysithea*, they'd only left a year ago, when in fact almost twenty-four years had passed. A cheer rose up around the room. They were finally home. They were still hours away from Earth but were relieved to be in their home system.

Jason noticed quite a bit of traffic around the starlane portals and had been told that several new portals had been mapped in the system since they'd left. As anxious as they were to get home, Fleet Command had ordered *Lysithea* and the remains of *Pacifica's* fleet to dock at the Titan Anchorage for debriefing. There were many questions to be answered. What would happen to them now? Would they all be retrained, reassigned, or retired?

"Lieutenant North?"

Jason turned around and saw the young yeoman standing before him holding a datapad.

"Yes?"

"This is for you, sir. I was instructed to deliver it personally."

"Thank you, yeoman," he said as he activated the pad. "Dismissed."

Orders to report to Grand Commander North's office immediately. *Official* orders.

He and Brandon had the opportunity to talk at length many times during their return trip. He was sad for Brandon when he received the news about his good friends, the Lareens. He hoped they found this Symons character soon.

When he entered his brother's temporary office, he saw a man in all black clothing whom he didn't recognize sitting in a chair in front of Brandon's desk. The man had a long scar on his face and looked very intimidating. Brandon smiled when he saw Jason.

"Have a seat, Lieutenant," Brandon said.

Jason took the seat next to the other man.

"Jason, this is General Tyler. He belongs to a special forces branch that was responsible for many of our victories at Miratev."

"Lieutenant, what are your plans exactly? Tyler asked.

"I wasn't quite sure yet, sir," he said, looking between Brandon and Tyler.

"I want you to consider a proposal I want to offer you. We need good officers in our branch. I'd like to offer you the opportunity to join us. If you're half the operative your brother was, we would be lucky to have you. I also hear you're a fine pilot."

Jason felt conflicting emotions rise up in him. The first thought was that Brandon had pulled strings for this. That wasn't something he wanted. He wanted to make his own way on his own merits, not on the influence of his relatives.

Brandon saw the look on his brother's face and correctly guessed what he was thinking.

"Before you jump to any conclusions," he said, "I had nothing to do with this. General Tyler informed me that upon review of their records, you were due to be approached by their group for recruitment about the same time I was. Your disappearance scuttled that at the time, but the invitation still stands."

Jason said, "So this had nothing to do with the commander?"

"Other than the fact that you possess the same genes, no," Tyler said. "Not everyone is cut out for this type of thing. People with certain genetic traits fare better than others with some of the technology we employ."

Jason pondered the comment for a moment and said, "What exactly would I be doing?"

"While I can't get into specifics, you will have access to weapons and technology that are ten years ahead of what the regular military has. You will fly ships that are a generation ahead of the fighters that are on the most state-of-the-art ships right now. I won't lie to you. It can be extremely dangerous, exciting, and amazing all at once. The best part is you'll be able to stick it to the enemy like you've never been able to before."

Brandon nodded at the last comment and added, "It's true. I don't regret any of it. Bear in mind, though, you can go back to your ship, become the best pilot around on a brand-new ship all on your own. You could also retire with all the back pay coming to you. No one would think less of you or any of your shipmates. You've been through a lot."

Jason thought long and hard about what was being offered, weighing the options in his head. Realistically, there was no need for contemplation. He knew what he would do.

"I'd like to accept, General."

Tyler looked pleased, and Brandon looked apprehensive but smiled anyway. He knew firsthand what Jason was volunteering for. He just hoped that he'd survive long enough for them to swap stories someday.

Tyler offered his hand and said, "Welcome to Omega Section, Lieutenant North."

Upon returning to the quarters that had been assigned to him on *Endeavor*, Jason North's head was still spinning. He'd accepted General Tyler's offer without getting any details. Despite accepting, Tyler had asked him to take a few days to consider everything and not to speak to anyone about it. He'd decided to follow through with his decision, no matter how it turned out. It was too exciting to turn down.

He keyed open his door and walked in to find a man sitting on a chair in his temporary quarters, searching the system web on his desktop computer.

"What the hell? Who the hell are you? How did you get in here?"

The man spun to face him and said, "Easy, Lieutenant. My name is Major Deneva. I've been asked to brief you on Omega. Please close the door and have a seat. Let's start with 'the code.'"

Earth, Del Mar Police Department

Yvonne Wilson limped over to her desk, eased herself into her chair, and activated her console. She was still somewhat stiff from her ordeal but had been given a clean bill of health. She could've had a few extra days to convalesce. Instead, she'd returned early to get back to finding Symons only to learn the military had taken over the investigation themselves and had decided not to share any more information with her.

Perkins had fared slightly worse than she, and although he would also recover fully, he'd opted for a couple more days at home, likely at his wife's insistence. Truth be told, she was a bit envious. Must be nice to have someone at home to care about you that much. Well, at least her golden retriever loved her.

As she intently read recent reports on her screen, she noticed that the normally boisterous squad room had suddenly fallen silent. Puzzled, she looked around and noticed the man walking up behind her, flanked by four of the biggest marines she had ever seen.

The man walked up to her and said, "Inspector Wilson?"

Wilson looked up from her seat, eyeing the five men and said, "Yes?"

The man smiled and offered his hand. "Brandon North. I'm glad to finally meet you. I hear you were looking for me."

Wilson's eyebrows shot up in surprise as she returned the handshake.

"Grand Commander North?" she said, nearly stumbling as she attempted to stand.

North held up his hand and said, "Please don't get up." He turned and grabbed an empty chair next to her desk and said, "May I?"

She cleared her throat and said, "Please."

North turned to the first marine and said, "That'll be all for now, Sergeant. You and your men can wait outside. I think I'm safe surrounded by all these police officers."

"Yes, sir," the big man said, who motioned for the others to follow him outside.

"Bodyguards?" she asked.

"My boss insisted," he said, watching them leave the room.

"Um, it's true, Commander, that we were looking for you in order to speak to you, but things went in a different direction. The military has taken over my investigation. They may have some questions for you. You seemed to have dropped off everyone's radar for a while. I don't suppose you can tell me where you were recently or what you were up to."

North smiled and said, "I'm afraid not, Inspector. Just rest assured that it was extremely important and was resolved in the Alliance's favor."

She nodded and said, "I didn't think so, but I figured I'd ask anyway. I'm sure by now you know all about Symons and his involvement in events."

North nodded and said, "I do now. I spoke to Colonel Malone at length."

"*Colonel* Malone. That figures. You keep interesting company, Commander."

"You could say that. As I understand it, Symons is responsible for the deaths of my wife and son, as well as my caretakers."

Wilson nodded and said, "That's correct. I'm so sorry about the Lareens."

North looked down and said, "Thank you." He paused for a moment and said, "Um, Inspector, the reason I came down here was to thank you and your partner, Detective Perkins, for all that you did. I was hoping that the two of you would accept my invitation to dinner tonight. I have some great stories about your chief."

Wilson looked disappointed and said, "Perkins is still off injured."

North nodded and said, "Well, if it's all right with you, the invitation is still open. Would you consider joining me for dinner? I've been thinking of my favorite Italian restaurant since I was deployed. The only problem is that those four marines eat a lot. I hope you're not easily offended."

Despite herself, Wilson laughed out loud. "Yeah, I think I would like that. Sounds good."

"Seven okay? I can pick you up at your house if you'd like."

She nodded and said, "Sounds good, Commander."

North smiled and said, "Brandon."

Wilson returned the smile and said, "Yvonne."

"See you at seven, Yvonne."

END OF BOOK ONE

Coming soon: Book Two

The Ghosts of Mandis

Alliance Officers:

Grand Commander Brandon North, stationed aboard carrier S.A.S. *Pacifica*, 17th fleet

Supreme Commander Dekker Terred, Alliance supreme military commander, stationed at Alliance High Command

Fleet Admiral Fidel Carlo, stationed at Alliance High Command diplomatic corps

Fleet Admiral Lucille Arlington, Fleet Security and Intelligence

Vice Admiral Jeffery Faulkner, commanding officer 2nd fleet, carrier S.A.S. *Endeavor*

Vice Admiral Nelson Price, commanding officer 28th fleet, carrier S.A.S. *Challenger*

Rear Admiral Mateo Drake, *Pacifica* commanding officer and North's executive officer

Rear Admiral Steven Thorne, commanding officer, S.A.S. *Lysithea*

Brigadier General Kyle Logan, commander marine detachment, *Pacifica*

Captain Michael Trent, (PAC-SGC) Space Group Commander, *Pacifica* flight wing

Captain Gerald Walker, aide to Fleet Admiral Carlo
Colonel Shaddra, *Pacifica* marine detachment
Colonel Fargo, *Pacifica* marine detachment
Colonel Garrett Malone, Alliance intelligence
Major Terrence Monsoor, science officer, S.A.S. *Lysithea*
Ensign Rando Falco, Lan and Denara's son
Gaspar, the special interrogator

Omega Section:

General Tyler
Major Deneva
Lieutenant Remy
Lieutenant Henna
Chief Petty Officer Angus
Sergeant Sulak
Sergeant Kenyon
Sergeant Kiproff
Petty Officer Eli
Petty Officer Keever

Civilians:

Lan and Denara Lareen, caretakers of the North home
Detective Billy Perkins, Del Mar Police Department
Chuck Ryther, gossip rag editor, "The Whole Truth"
Arvil Symons, terrorist
Kate Singer, office manager for Supreme Commander
    Terred
Inspector Yvonne Wilson, Del Mar Police Department

Miratev Research Facility:

Doctor Hugo Kloke, researcher

Doctor Julie Newman, researcher

Doctor Jared Trent, researcher, Michael Trent's brother

Dram Hunter, lab technician

Glend Olk, Jaaleadi researcher

Jeenan Tar, Jaaleadi researcher

The T'Kharr:

Shi'ia-khar (Emperor) Tri'in Du'uk Va'al Vod Ke'el, T'Kharr Emperor

Alta-Tar-Vel (Fleet Marshal) Da'akta Te'eq, supreme commander of T'Kharr space forces

Rinn-Tar-Vel (Full Admiral) Ve'erdren Ka'awon, commander T'Kharr 7th sector space forces

Dath-Tar-Vel (Rear Admiral) Zha'ar, commander of the carrier *Ka'athiol*, Ka'awon's flagship

Dath-Tar-Vel (Rear Admiral) Va'adja, commander of the carrier *Ba'akteer*

Vett-Tar-Von (Brigadier General) Gra'akk, commander of the T'Kharr invasion ground forces

Khetal (Captain) Thi'is Shi'il, captain of the destroyer *Ra'aktaka*

Rinn-Khetal (Commander) Ri'isha, second in command of the *Ra'aktaka*

Ever since I was a kid, as far back as I can remember, I've loved science fiction. My older brother Roger and I used to eat up anything to do with space, the space program, or any science fiction program, movie, or series. We watched them all—*U.F.O.*, *Space:1999*, *Thunderbirds*, *Land of the Giants*, and, of course, *Star Trek*. I remember when we got to see the original *Star Trek* series on our twenty-five-inch color console television and thought it was the most glorious thing to ever happen to our young lives.

Our disappointment at the cancellation of *Star Trek* in the late '60s was tempered with the Apollo missions and then the shuttle missions, which kept the dreams alive. Between us, I think we possessed models of most of the NASA launch vehicles, an "eagle" spaceship from *Space:1999*, the *Spindrift* from *Land of the Giants*, and, naturally, several versions of the *Enterprise*, Romulan ships, Klingon ships, and other alien vessels.

Then, as if by some miraculous gift from the gods, in the late 1970s, science fiction began a sort of renaissance. In the late '70s came *Star Wars*, *Battlestar Galactica*, *Buck Rogers in the 25th Century* (yes, we even watched that ridiculous show), and a whole slew of others. Later came the *Star Trek* movies (*Wrath of Khan* is still the best), the *Next Generation* series, more *Star Wars* movies, more *Star-Trek*-based series . . . the list continues.

And, of course, there were the novels, some based on those series and some original works by authors who were and are still considered some of the best sci-fi writers in the business.

During this time of my life, other life-changing events were taking place, such as college, marriage, kids, and, eventually, employment as a police officer in the San Francisco Bay Area where I grew up. While a police officer, I improved my writing skills due to report-writing requirements, and I began to sketch out a science-fiction story that I'd been mulling over in my imagination for quite a while.

I ended up writing out approximately 150 or so pages on my Tandy 1000 desktop computer and stored the pages on a 5¼-inch floppy disk. I wisely gave those first pages to Roger for his review and opinion. Life eventually went on, and I forgot about my aborted attempt at writing the great American science-fiction story.

Eventually, after many years of police work, including working as a police detective among other assignments, I found myself retired and starting a second career, working with youth programs in Utah. Ironically, although I attended school in Utah, it was a place that I swore I'd never move to. Now I can't imagine moving or living anywhere else. About eight years after the move from California, my younger brother Steve talked me into resurrecting and updating my old story.

Although my Tandy 1000 and 5¼-inch floppy disc were long gone, Roger still had my original pages, and I ended up completing and modernizing what I think is a pretty decent story. My police experiences helped my imagination in no small manner, particularly with regard to investigative techniques used by some characters in the book, and for one of the most satisfying interrogation sequences (highly illegal in this day and age) I could have come up with.

The list of people who helped in this endeavor is vast, but certain people definitely had a larger role. I'm very grateful to Jason

Aydelotte and my fellow Geckos at Grey Gecko Press for taking a chance on me and giving me the tools I needed to make this come about. Jason approached me with the idea of doing a crowd-funding campaign to bring the book to press sooner than later, and we were successful thanks to many generous donors.

So a big shout out to Alayne S., Anders Y., Antha A., Cliff M., Jeremy H., Judy N., Linda W., Lukas C., Matthew C., Roger N., Steve N., Scott N., Leslie E., Ronnell P., Steven L., Teresa Q., Tyler N., Cristina J., Cynthia K., Josh B., Jaclyn W., Janice N., Christian S., Jared M., Lindsay N., and a number of other generous backers who wished to remain anonymous. Thanks also to Charles Bernard for some awesome artwork, better than I had imagined.

In no particular order, I'd also like to thank the following additional people for their help and support: my brothers, Roger and Steve; my wife, Cheryl; my kids, Lindsay, Lauren, and Tyler; Mom and Dad, who read every revision and offered advice; Steve's friends in his book club; and anyone else who helped me in my quest.

Finally, I'd like to thank the following, even though I know I'm dating myself: the Tracy family and Thunderbirds 1 through 5, Commander Straker and the members of SHADO, Captain Steve Burton of the *Spindrift*, Commander Koenig of Moonbase Alpha, Captain Kirk, Commander Spock, Doctor McCoy, Captain Picard, Commander Riker, Commander Adama, Captain Apollo and Lt. Starbuck, Luke, Leia, Han, and Chewie, and heck, even evil old Emperor Palpatine.

Thanks for the dreams.

Brian Nicholson

ABOUT THE AUTHOR

As a boy growing up in Northern California, Brian Nicholson loved anything to do with science fiction, the space program, and watched or read everything to do with both of these things, including every televised space mission, starting with the Mercury and Gemini missions, Apollo and the Shuttles. Along the way there was *Star Trek*, *Land of the Giants*, *Space:1999*, *UFO* and, of course, *Star Wars*.

These stories inspired him and let his imagination run wild. Although it took 50 years, marriage, three kids and now grandchildren, he finally put some of those dreams down on paper and wrote the first book in the series *The Omega Chronicles*.

Today, after a career in law enforcement, he lives in southern Utah with his wife and within a couple of hours of his kids and grandkids. He finds the peaceful setting very conducive to writing and has plans to keep *The Omega Chronicles* going for as long as the ideas continue to come. When not writing, he loves to fish with his dad and work with troubled youth and the programs that help them.

CONNECT WITH BRIAN

EMAIL: brian.nicholson.writes@gmail.com

FACEBOOK: facebook.com/BrianNicholsonAuthor

books2read.com/
aristeia1

books2read.com/
aristeia2

books2read.com/
aristeia3

ARISTEIA

One small team, one giant tyranny. Can they hope save their people?

"...kept me turning pages as fast as I could. A must-read for any space opera fan."
—*Jason Kristopher, author of* The Dying of the Light

AMAZON/GOODREADS READER REVIEWS

"Great book... I wanted more!"
"...an exciting and adventurous story."
"Very good pace and characters."

A former naval starfighter pilot turned smuggler, his over-eager and rebellious little sister, and a ne'er-do-well thief... how can they hope to overthrow a tyrannical galactic government?

Read the complete Aristeia series now, filled with action, political intrigue, and more!